The Stonecutter's Daughter

By the same author

A Dorset Girl
Beyond the Plough
A Handful of Ashes

Born and brought up in Parkstone in Dorset, Janet Woods now lives in Perth, Western Australia, although she returns to her English roots on a regular basis to visit family and friends.

The Stonecutter's Daughter

Janet Woods

POCKET
BOOKS

LONDON · SYDNEY · NEW YORK · TOKYO · SINGAPORE · TORONTO

First published in Great Britain by Simon & Schuster, 2005
This edition first published by Pocket Books, 2005
An imprint of Simon & Schuster UK
A CBS COMPANY

Copyright © Janet Woods, 2005

This book is copyright under the Berne Convention
No reproduction without permission
® and © 1997 Simon & Schuster Inc. All rights reserved
Pocket Books & Design is a registered trademark of Simon & Schuster

The right of Janet Woods to be identified as author of this work has been
asserted by her in accordance with sections 77 and 78 of the Copyright,
Designs and Patents Act, 1988.

1 3 5 7 9 10 8 6 4 2

Simon & Schuster UK Ltd
1st Floor
222 Gray's Inn Road
London WC1X 8HB

www.simonandschuster.co.uk

Simon & Schuster Australia
Sydney

A CIP catalogue record for this book is available from
the British Library

ISBN 9781849833547

This book is a work of fiction. Names, characters, places and incidents are
either a product of the author's imagination or are used fictitiously.
Any resemblance to actual people living or dead, events or locales
is entirely coincidental.

Typeset by SX Composing DTP, Rayleigh, Essex
Printed and bound in Great Britain by
Cox & Wyman Ltd, Reading, Berkshire

To my agent, Bob Tanner,
who has done so much to help my career along.
Many thanks, Bob

*

The author is happy to receive feedback from readers.
She can be contacted via her website
http://members.iinet.net.au/~woods
or by post
PO Box 2099
Kardinya 6163
Western Australia

Acknowledgement

The poem attributed to the character Richard Lind
was published in the original poetry section of
Pawsey's Ladies' Fashionable Repository for 1873
'A Likeness
(To a Lady)'
was signed with the initials H.A.S.

1

Darkness was settling in early on the isle of Portland. Joseph Rushmore rose from his chair near the fire to tap the dottle from his pipe against the smoke-stained stone of the chimney-piece. 'I'm off out for a bit, Anna.'

'It's a good dark night for it.'

'Aye. As well as the French Brig a packet went down today, lost with all souls, I should imagine. The bay is full of wreckage and bodies.'

'Poor beggars, but I daresay there'll be pickings to be had.'

'Aye, she would have broken up about now. The seas have been treacherous. November of 1838 will go down in the record books as being a bad year for storms and wrecks alike.'

'The seas are always treacherous hereabouts. Portland soil is full of the drowned. 'Tis not long since the *Caroline* went down and we buried the Wesley missionary and his wife in Brackenbury churchyard. Sometimes I feel guilty robbin' the dead.'

'Don't be so daft, woman. If we don't, somebody else soon will.'

'Aye, I know.' Fashioning a pair of socks from wool teased and spun from her pair of domestic sheep, Anna gave a sigh as she laid her knitting aside. 'Most of us profit from the disasters one way or another, we always have. Doesn't make it right in the eyes of the Lord, though.'

Joseph grinned at that. 'You silly old puddin'. Indeed, 'tis a shame to let anything go to waste when the Lord rewards us for risking our own lives to save the lives of others. The beach is fairly littered with wrecks and cargo this month. Would you let it all be washed away and sink to the bottom, especially since the roof over your own head is supported from good oak taken from the wrecks. And a damned snug roof it makes, too.'

Indeed, the whole house was snug, for Joseph was a stonecutter and mason and had built the place with his own hands on the field Anna had inherited from her father. It stood in Fortuneswell, overlooking the bay and the expanse of pebble beach to the left. To the right was the towering Verne hill, over which the mist poured like a cataract of milk towards evening.

Like most homes on Portland, theirs was built to withstand the winter storms and the salt-laden spindrift carried from the sea in the wind. Joseph had fitted one block of the local freestone precisely into the next, edge-bedding the cornices and window sills. There was a porch with an arched door and he'd roofed it with slat limestone from Tout quarry. The house had been built with room enough to accommodate the family they'd never had.

Anna couldn't argue with Joseph's logic, so she

changed tack. 'What happened to those two young boys they pulled from the water today?'

'They have relatives,' Joseph said gently, for the disappointment in her face at their own inability to bear a living child was hard to take. Anna was past forty now and had slipped the last one just two days previously. This time the infant had survived to eight months inside her. A boy it had been, perfect in every way, except he hadn't drawn breath and his face had had the look of a moon-face about it. Not that Joseph had told Anna that. He'd sewn the boy in a linen shroud so Anna couldn't look on him and grieve. His body lay in the outhouse waiting for the storm to abate, so Joseph could arrange his burial. 'George Gray has given those youngsters to the rector's wife to care for until he can contact their kinfolk.'

Anna, tall, plump and round of face, her greying brown hair tied in an untidy bun at the nape of her neck, pulled a scarf from the hook as he donned his oilskins. 'Wear this under your collar, Joseph, it will stop your neck chaffing.'

Despite grumbling, Joseph did what he was told, for it was a howler of an evening and the wind was riding around the house, driving the rain this way and that. The storm couldn't last for ever though. 'It'll blow itself out in a day or so, be devilled if it doesn't.' He caressed Anna then, his callused fingers stroking gently against her cheek so she turned her lips into his palm to kiss him. 'You rest whilst I'm gone, my Anna. You should still be abed.'

'Keeping busy takes my mind off things.' She made an

annoyed noise in the back of her throat. 'And we've got enough troubles without your calling up the devil, Joseph Rushmore. Now, away with you, and don't you go dealing up the Lugger Inn tonight. You know what a pack of thieves those Barnes brothers are. They buys things cheap, but it costs people dear to buy those same things in the Weymouth marketplace. I might as well have a stall myself. And take that dog with you, the lazy lump is hogging so much of the fire I can smell his fleas roasting.'

Joseph grinned as he whistled to his dog. Rufus immediately leapt to his feet and stretched. Strong-shouldered and sturdy, he was a Portland Sea Dog, bred specially to bring ship's plunder or contraband ashore. Like most of the islanders, Joseph regarded smuggling as an industry rather than a crime. The cargo of goods washed ashore from wrecks was fair plunder. It was not as if the ships were deliberately lured on to the shoals or rocks. The waters around Portland were treacherous at the best of times, so even the most experienced of skippers could come to grief.

'And don't you come home drunk, else I'll fit the skillet around your backside,' she called out as the door closed behind him.

In the outhouse, Joseph took a long coiled rope from a hook, setting it around his shoulder and across his chest. For a moment, he gazed with a mixture of anger and regret at the still, shrouded form laid on the bench. Ten cheils, his woman had lost. What had they done to deserve this when his brother had three strong sons to help him in his fishing boats, and a bonny daughter or

4

two to help his wife around the house? He and Anna had loved each other as a man and wife should. They lived as good a life as most around these parts – better than some. They worked hard and always attended church on Sunday.

It was obvious the Lord didn't intend them to have infants of their own. ''Tis a cruel thing for a man and his wife to go through time after time, having their hopes built up then having them dashed down again,' he said directly to God. 'Anna has suffered over the years. If you intend to give us an infant to love, let it be soon before we grow too old. If you can't find it in your heart to do so, then allow Anna to remain barren from now on.'

He fondled the dog's ear. 'I'll be needed back home soon, Rufus, so don't you lead your master into drinking trouble.' Dog at his side, Joseph set off downhill – had Anna but known it, with the Barnes brothers and the climb up to the Lugger Inn at Weston the last thing on his mind.

The sou'westerly would be depositing its final bounty on shore before the gale blew itself out. The tide would be at full flow soon and most of the preventative men would be home having their dinners. But, anyway, more often than not they turned a blind eye, for too many were in on the game themselves.

It was the revenue men you had to look out for, for they were armed to the teeth with guns they didn't hesitate to use, and their cutters were fast. Not that they bothered him, for Joseph had been apprenticed to a quarrymaster, not become a fisherman like his father. Though he had seamanship and muscle enough to oar his elder brother's sturdy lerret on occasion.

During the day, from the clifftop at Fortuneswell there was a fine view of the shingle beach. Now, the length of it was dotted with flares, and fires were lit to guide survivors ashore and warm their rescuers. The scene was alive with scurrying figures. The sea roared in fury to the shore, to suck noisily at the shingle before spitting it back. The water boiled and foamed, crashing against the rocks behind him and throwing spray high into the air as he walked along its length.

It was too rough for the fishing lerrets to put to sea, even though they were regarded as being unsinkable. As Joseph approached the shore he turned his eyes away from several drowned corpses pulled above the high-tide mark and laid in a row. But one of them drew his glance back. It was a young woman, her clothes torn and sodden, her lips blue tinged and her hair spread like dark strands of seaweed. She looked vulnerable, with one of her breasts uncovered, pale, but swollen and blue veined, as if she'd been suckling a child. She wore no jewellery, but whoever had pulled her from the water would have taken it. He stooped to pull her cloak around her to give her some dignity.

Carts came and went, piled up with wooden planks, canvas, kegs of brandy, anything the scavengers could lay their hands on. The beach would be picked clean within a few days, as if ants had dismembered the corpse of a cockroach.

Joseph's brother, George, was with his boat, passing

kegs of brandy along a line of men, to be deposited on a cart. He nodded. 'Brother Joseph.'

'Brother George.'

George stopped to gaze through dark eyes at the water after the last keg was handed over. Glumly he said, 'She be having a fine old tantrum now, but she'll blow herself out before too long. I'm not risking the boat tonight. 'Sides, I've got to get this lot hidden away from the revenue men. I'll be down here at first light, though.' He passed over a bottle of French brandy, wiping the neck on his palm. 'Here, warm your cockles on this, Joseph. It'd be a shame to waste it, though there be plenty more littering the beach.'

'Anna will shrivel my ears if I get myself too spirited up. Last time I forgot to shut the front door and the wind blew the furniture straight out through the back door. It took me a week to find it and I had to swim all the way to the Channel Islands.'

George grinned at him and spat into the pebbles at his feet, his phlegm stained brown from the tobacco he chewed. 'You tell a bleddy good tale, our Joseph. The last one you told my youngsters kept them shivering in their beds every night for a month.'

Tipping up the bottle, Joseph took a swig and sighed as he felt the liquor gently warm him. 'It's a rare drop.'

'That it is.' George waved a hand at him when he tried to hand it back. 'There be plenty more where that came from. You keep it.'

As Joseph walked along the shingle, sipping at the brandy, he recovered several more bottles. He slid one into his trouser pocket before burying the rest in a hole above the high-tide mark. He also recovered a couple more bodies, dragging them up the beach to where they could be found, stripping them of their valuables, but leaving their identification intact.

It was a sad business to end up in the hands of strangers, who neither knowed nor cared. He thought of the young woman, who would be buried in the Kimberlin cemetery above Chiswell, along with the bottom folk and other strangers. 'Time to go home and get the cart before the ebb,' he said to Rufus. 'I wished I'd thought to bring it with me.'

The dog whined and pressed against him, his body quivering and his eyes and nose intent on the sea.

'What is it, boy, what do you see?' Joseph saw it himself then, a white bird floating on the water. ''Tis only a seagull.'

Rufus gave a sharp bark and Joseph looked again. Odd, the bird was, looking as if it was standing on something as it spun this way and that. It resembled a gleaming white figurehead on a small boat beneath it – and that boat was heading straight for the rocks beneath the cliff.

As a long wailing cry came to him on the wind, goosebumps trickled coldly down his spine. Joseph had never heard a gull cry like that before, as if a spirit had risen from the deep. And he remembered his father telling him a tale of a white gull that carried the souls of drowned seamen, but only if they'd lived good lives.

As the object rose to the crest of the next wave, the ragged clouds above him parted and the moon appeared. But only for a moment, long enough to give him a clearer glimpse of the boat, which was lashed between two wooden kegs tied together. 'It can't be a boat because it's too small, and it has a hood,' he whispered, denying his first impression. 'It must be a chest of some sort with the lid open.'

And a chest often contained valuables! Taking the rope from his shoulders Joseph tied it around the dog. 'Fetch it back to me, boy.'

Without hesitation, Rufus plunged into the maelstrom of water. Joseph could feel the undertow dragging against the rope, but Rufus was strong and was bred for such conditions. He dived through the waves rather than pit himself against them and, soon, his strong jaws took a firm grip on the rope lashing on the side of one of the kegs. With a raucous squawk, the seagull soared skywards, circling and sailing on the wind above them as Joseph hauled the dog and his plunder ashore.

God had answered his prayer, Joseph realized as he whispered, 'Be damned if it's not a cradle.' And what he'd thought was a lid was an oilskin buttoned and tied over what was left of some fancy frilled curtains – a hastily rigged sail.

The infant inside was saturated with water, which lapped over its stomach. Face red and screwed up from crying, its body was bound tightly to the cradle by a length of rope wound several times around its middle, and propped against a pillow so its head couldn't be immersed unless the sea broached the craft. Arms and legs punched at the storm.

Someone had done this out of desperation, knowing they were not going to survive but trying to give their infant a chance at life. It was only by good luck that the little craft hadn't overturned or completely filled with water.

Joseph stared down at the distressed baby for a second, then freed the infant from its restraints. 'By God, you're a skinny un,' he told it, 'and loud with it, too, though I daresay the paddy you're in has kept you from freezing. Best we get you back to my Anna as soon as we can.' Dipping his finger in brandy he placed it in the baby's mouth for a few moments, allowing it to suck at the warming liquid. Then, without bothering to undress it, he wrapped the child firmly in his scarf and placed the bundle in his sou'wester. 'Here,' he said, giving it to Rufus to carry. ''Tis precious, mind, so don't you go dropping it.' The kegs were half full, he realized as he cut them free. He'd pick them up later.

Grunting, he hefted the cradle in his arms. It was heavier than he'd thought it would be, fashioned as it was from solid wood, and a good deal more fancy than the cane basket prepared for his own infant, he thought, as he saw the carvings.

'It's heavy at the bottom,' Joseph muttered, his hands finding purchase under the rockers. 'The reason for the half empty kegs became clear then. The weight of the liquid would have remained in the bottom, acting as extra ballast and keeping the little craft stable.

Joseph set off back up the hill with long strides, all the time thinking that the Lord had answered his prayer, though his conscience would keep denying it. The infant protested all the way, the sound almost swallowed by the howling wind.

By the time he reached his house, the Lord had won the battle, as Joseph had counted on him doing. He couldn't stop grinning as he wondered what his Anna would say.

'Keep the girl as our own! Have you gone daft in the head, Joseph Rushmore?'

'Who's to know she ain't ours, since I told nobody about the one in the outhouse, and as far as folks know you still be waitin' to birth ours? He tenderly touched a roughened finger against a dark curl. 'Look how bonny she is. And she has the same coloured eyes as you.'

'Mine are a lighter blue,' Anna pointed out, her voice softening as she gazed at the child. 'What if her mother comes lookin' for her?'

'Her mother is lying on the beach, as cold as marble. I covered her up, for her breasts were all swollen with milk and it didn't seem decent to leave her exposed to the stares of men. Young, she was, and a beauty. I reckon it was her husband who tied the babe to the cradle, for it was seaman's knots he tied her with.' His voice dropped. 'Anna, God meant this child for us, but you'd have had to have been there to have knowed it for sure. He sent a seagull to guide her cradle ashore, and I believe that seagull was the soul of her father.'

They both shivered as they gazed at each other, their eyes conveying the same message of conspiracy. Sometimes, it was easier on the conscience to heed signs and instinct than use common sense and logic. Even the church believed in signs and matters of the spirit.

Almost convinced, Anna muttered, 'Poor lamb. Aye,

could be you're right, Joseph. Perhaps she was meant for us. We can certainly provide her with a good home.'

Anna had dried the infant, and had dressed her in the clothes she'd prepared for their own. Amongst the wet clothes she had found a brooch pinned to the infant's wrap, fashioned in the shape of a rose, picked out in sparkling red stones. She had hidden it safely away. Not because she wanted to deceive Joseph, but because he would sell it. It was a pretty piece for the girl to have when she was grown, and Anna wasn't about to deprive her new daughter of it.

With a child warm and snug in her arms, Anna felt the call of nature as the tiny mouth nudged against her bodice for sustenance. Her breasts throbbed with the need to satisfy the child, who made frustrated cries as her head turned blindly this way and that.

Could she feed the infant? Her teats were seeping milk after the stillbirth and were hard and sore. If she could feed the girl she would know for sure the Lord had meant it to be, she thought. Bringing the infant under her shawl she opened her bodice and placed the girl against her breast. Immediately, its mouth closed on to her and it began to suckle. Anna felt the pull of it reach to the very pit of her stomach.

Tears trickled down her face as she felt the fulfilment of being a mother after all this time of hope and disappointment. After a few moments, her other nipple began to secrete milk against her bodice. She closed her eyes and basked in the contentment this simple act of nature brought her. Any lingering doubts she'd harboured fell away from her. Joseph was right. It was meant to be. God had sent her this infant to care for. Oblivious to her husband's presence she began to rock back and forth in her chair, humming a lullaby.

In the chair opposite, Joseph smiled to himself as he rose to his feet. He had another task to perform. 'I'm taking the dog cart down to the beach. There's some fine liquor to be had and the ebb tide will leave behind what it doesn't want. And I'll make sure the woman doesn't go to her grave with her arms empty. I'll give her our son to hold.'

'Aye, it'll be nice for them to have each other. If you see George again, let it out that the babe has been safely born, like. I'm of a mind to call her Joanna after us. And I like the name Rose because it's pretty, like her.'

'Joanna Rose Rushmore,' Joseph said, tasting it on his tongue. ''Tis a name fit for fine folk, and here was me thinkin' that if I ever had a daughter I'd call her Hannah, after my late mother.'

'As if I'd call her after that bad-tempered besom. She'll have her own name. It will be Joanna Rose and no arguing,' Anna said firmly.

Joseph chuckled. 'No arguing? Can't say I ever met anybody called that before.'

'Oh, get away with you. Sometimes you're as daft as a trapped snalter. Though, come to think of it, those sweet little birds ain't fool enough to go running around in this weather, let alone get caught in the traps, for I hear tell they go to somewhere called Africa in the winter, where it's warm.'

Joseph's eyes twinkled with amusement now he'd got

a rise out of her. 'Have it your own way, woman. You always do.'

Dear Joseph, Anna thought as her husband left the room. But she had caught a glimpse of their son's face before Joseph had taken him away, and she was glad he'd not lived to face the sly taunts of the islanders.

Twisting a dark, wispy curl about her finger, she whispered to the infant. 'I've got it into my head that you should be called Rose. Perhaps that was your mother's name, for 'tis young you are to have a brooch of your own, and such a pretty and precious one it is. From now on you are to be called after Joseph and myself, because we've made you ours. 'Tis right and proper that you should have your dead mother's name, too, so her spirit can find you and guide you through life. So, should anyone ask you, Joanna Rose Rushmore is your name.'

Joanna Rose stopped suckling. She gazed towards the strange voice, her recent ordeal already forgotten now she was comfortable again. Her eyes were dark blue and remained fixed on the woman holding her, for she was able to focus for small amounts of time. Her mouth pulled down at the corners and she gave a soft cry of alarm. But instinctively she knew the smiling mouth and kind blue eyes didn't threaten, and the arms supporting her were soft and comfortable. She was tired, too, for the hunger had returned and she'd been forced to suckle harder at the alien teat to produce her supper.

The infant was smaller than the son she had recently given birth to, Anna thought, for his head had been large. Joanna couldn't be more than a month old.

Holding her baby protectively against her heart she began to sing her a lullaby.

After a moment, the child offered her a tremulous smile, then she turned her face to the lure of the teat and began to suckle again.

Tears filled Anna's eyes, for that moment of acceptance had been sweet. 'You're a survivor, Joanna Rose, and don't you forget it,' Anna whispered softly against the girl's ear.

2

Alexander Morcant smiled as he gazed out of the window of the London office of the Darsham and Morcant Shipping Company.

Even though he had only just turned ten, he appreciated the richly glowing wood-panelled walls, the buttoned leather chairs, the heavy brass-based lamps with their glass chimneys, and the lingering aroma of tobacco smoke.

The company was run by the capable twenty-two-year-old Tobias Darsham, who had reluctantly relinquished the more exciting life the sea had to offer to help run the London office after Alexander's grandfather, a man of fierce gaze, bristling eyebrows and boundless energy, had suffered a sudden and debilitating paralysis.

The company founder, John Darsham, whose portrait hung on the wall behind Tobias's desk, had been dead a year since. Tobias looked remarkably like his father, with his astute grey eyes. Of medium height, slim and wiry, he possessed a smile of great charm, which he used sparingly. Tobias Darsham had an air that commanded respect, and he dealt honestly with himself and others.

The flames leaping up the chimney from the open fireplace crackled and danced, sending light and shadows leaping about the walls, making it cosy despite the dreary weather outside the window.

'You did well in your exams, lad.'

Alexander turned to smile at Tobias. 'I'm lucky, scholarship comes easily to me. I'm not so good on the practical side, though.'

'Have you stood on the button yet?'

His uncle was referring to the terrifying punishment of making a cadet stand on the topmost point of the yardarm. At the thought of the ordeal, for the button wasn't much bigger than a dinner plate and hardly had room for the feet as it swayed in the wind. Alex's smile fled. 'I have.'

'And?'

'As you can see, I survived it. I was sick afterwards, though.'

'So was I when I was put through it. It's a test of a man's courage as well as a punishment, and you passed that with flying colours. A seaman who lacks the stomach to climb the rigging is a danger to himself and to the rest of the crew.

'I have no intention of following my father into the profession. I suffer too readily from seasickness.'

'Aye, I know. I've never thought a life at sea would suit you, young Alex. Neither did my father. Before he died he told your grandfather and father so in no uncertain terms, when you were first enrolled at the marine school.' Tobias grinned. '"Alexander goes green around the gills every time he looks at the ocean," he yelled at them. "He should be trained to manage the affairs of the company. Someone might take advantage of the fact that there isn't a Morcant sailing a desk to rob us blind, and it might be my son, Tobias Darsham, here."'

'What did my father say to that, sir?'

'Lucian just laughed and told him the training would not go amiss and you could make up your own mind when you were older. It seems as if you have.'

'Aye, I have. And yours was made up for you.'

'It was, but although I still get a hankering to go to sea, it's not part of my blood. A voyage round the coast now and again will replenish the salt in me, but your father and brother need to breathe it in constantly.' Tobias's eyes probed the depths of his. 'Something is bothering you, lad. D'you want to talk about it?'

Alexander hesitated, then told Tobias what troubled him. 'One of the cadets slipped and fell to his death from the button.'

'It happens.'

Turning to gaze out of the window again, Alexander muttered, 'How can you be so calm about it? It didn't *have* to happen. They knew he was terrified and didn't want to go up on the yardarm, but they made him. It was one of the boys from the workhouse. Nobody seemed to care that he died.'

'Aye, well. Life at sea is a dangerous profession. People die and you have to train yourself not to mourn.'

Alexander caught a reflection of Tobias in the

window. He liked him a lot. Tobias was always there for him when he had a problem, unlike his father or brother, who were almost strangers to him, for he only saw them on occasion.

'What if it had been me who died?'

'It wasn't you, Alex, and thank God for it. If it had been we would have had to accept that someone we love had left us and wouldn't be coming back. That wouldn't mean we didn't care. Would you like me to talk to your father about a change of school? Since you have no intention of going to sea, Rugby might suit you much better, hmm? The headmaster is Leonard Arnold, who insists his pupils receive a well-rounded education to develop intellectual ability, moral principle and gentle-manly conduct. The school has a good reputation.'

'Described like that it sounds just the place a boy wouldn't want to be.' Alexander's eyes began to shine. 'However, my friend and neighbour, Anthony Grantham, is being educated at Rugby School and he likes it fine. So I expect I would like it there, too. Thank you, Tobias. I'm sure my father will listen to you.'

Tobias didn't think he'd have any trouble persuading Lucian.

'Any sign of the *Cormorant* yet?' he asked the boy.

'No, sir, but I'm looking forward to meeting your wife and daughter.'

A wide smile spread across Tobias's face. So was he. It had been three months since he'd last set eyes on Honor. Over the past few months he'd moved into the house his father had left him, furnished it and had it decorated from top to bottom. Honor's portrait smiled down at him from the drawing-room wall. Her eyes reflected the vivid blue of cornflowers, her hair was a tumbling torrent of darkness. As for his daughter, he had not set eyes on her at all.

Tobias had met Honor Palmer in New York and she had swiftly become the love of his life. Barely eighteen, his bride had quickly become pregnant. But Honor had been ill right from the start, so when Tobias had been called home to attend his grandfather's funeral, he'd left her in the care of her parents until after the birth of their baby.

Tobias had visited her twice, sailing aboard the packet captained by Lucian Morcant, adding to his own seamanship skills and taking gifts for both his wife and his unborn child. He'd commissioned the portrait of her in the first month of their marriage, and was glad he had, for it had helped brightened the lonely days without her.

Finally, he'd received word that his daughter had been safely delivered, though she'd arrived early, needed constant care and was too small to travel. Now his love would shortly be in his arms, for the pair had taken a cabin on board the *Cormorant*.

Tobias was impatiently waiting for the ship to arrive. So was Alexander, for he was looking forward to seeing his father again. The man joined the boy at the window. On clear days there was a view of the Houses of Parliament, the clock they called Big Ben and the River Thames. Today, the landmarks were almost hidden by a grey sheet of icy rain, which lashed with whip-like fury against the building. Their combined breath steamed against the glass as Alex traced with his fingertip the raindrops chasing each other down the window pane.

'I don't like this weather, I don't like this at all,' Tobias muttered almost to himself. 'The sea is as greedy and capricious as a whore in weather like this. But your father's a good seaman and the *Cormorant* is a sound ship.'

Alex said idly, 'All the company ships are in good order. They've been surveyed and placed on the new Lloyds' register.'

'But that's nothing to do with the underwriter.'

'It proves the ships are sound, so they're more likely to attract underwriters.'

'You've got a good head on you for business, Alex, despite your age. You should study law later on, especially maritime law.'

'Aye, I probably will. Did you want to follow your father to sea?'

'I was his only son, so followed him as a matter of course. However, I've spent most of my time ashore since he died. Your brother Oliver is doing well sailing under Captain Scott. The captain is pleased with his progress.'

'Oliver loves the sea. May I ask what a whore is, sir?'

Tobias laughed as he turned away. 'You may, but don't tell your father who told you. It's a woman of loose morals who lifts her skirt to any man and promises him a good time. However, she exacts a price, and some-times he can pay dearly for his pleasure if he doesn't watch out. It's nothing you need worry about yet, though. Any sign of the *Cormorant*?'

'No, sir, though the rain seems to be clearing a little.'

Tapping the barometer on the wall, Tobias growled. 'Pressure is still low. I might go over to Lloyds.'

'May I come, too?'

'I don't see why not. I can take you home to your mother afterwards.'

Buffeted by the wind, they reached the Royal Exchange to find Lloyds crowded. It had been a bad month for wrecks, and the underwriters wore expressions of gloom on their faces.

'Any news of the *Cormorant*?' Tobias asked a fellow ship owner.

'Not so far. News came though that the *Flemish Star* is safe, though. She took on several last-minute passengers just before she sailed, and detoured to Liverpool.'

'That's good,' Tobias muttered, then turned to smile at Alex, trying to hide the worry he felt. 'Right, lad, let's take you home.'

'They will be all right, won't they, sir?'

'Of course. The eastward crossing from New York can take up to four weeks.'

But they both knew that Lucian Morcant usually managed the Atlantic crossing in three.

As they turned towards the door a hush came over the crowd. A chill ran through Tobias's bones as a man cleared his throat and stepped forward with a sheet of paper in his hands.

A week later, Tobias Darsham stood side by side with Alexander Morcant, his elder brother, Oliver, and their mother, Clara, whilst their respective loved ones were laid in the stony earth on a windswept Portland hill. The fine view it offered was wasted on its inhabitants.

At the age of thirty-eight, Clara Morcant was composed, elegant and upright, though her eyes showed the strain of several sleepless nights. Tobias had always found her to be rather cold on the surface. Though when he'd been sixteen he'd been forced to repel her drunken advances, and he now avoided her.

He had been lucky to find their loved ones' bodies and had been able to identify one or two crew members, as well. It had been a grisly task, but at least their kin would know where they were buried.

Lucian Morcant's chest had been crushed, probably by a falling mast. He would have died instantly.

Tobias was pleased he'd thought to bring Lucian's best uniform to bury him in when Alexander had asked to see his father's body. Both he and Oliver had gazed down at him for a long time before Tobias had asked the undertaker to nail down the lid of the coffin. Oliver was almost twenty and had accepted his father's death more easily than Alexander. The boy had been racked by heart-rending sobs.

'Do control yourself, Alexander. You're far too old for tears and are making a display of yourself.' Clara held a lavender-scented handkerchief to her nose as she took a quick look at the body of her late husband. 'Goodness, Lucian does appear to be an odd colour. Is that your wife and baby, Tobias? She looks to be so very young. How sad it is to be a widower when you've hardly been a husband and father. Luckily, you're young enough to meet someone else and marry again. We both are.'

Honor was pale, her lips blue and swollen. Her dark hair was laid in one long braid over her shoulder to reside against her breast. Someone had wrapped her decently in a linen shroud. She didn't look like the laughing girl he'd married such a short time ago, and although he felt sorrow he also felt curiously remote, as though he'd never known passion in her arms, had never laughed with her as they'd planned a future together.

It seemed odd that the baby in her arms was his daughter. He'd never seen his child, but she was not as he expected. She looked old and wizened, as if she'd aged a hundred years in the few precious weeks of her life. Her eyes were open slightly, giving her a sly look as if she was watching for his reaction. He could see no resemblance to either himself or Honor. In fact, her appearance repulsed him slightly.

Tobias felt his lips tighten as Clara walked away. How unfeeling she was. He doubted if he would ever marry again. 'Oliver, escort your mother on to the cemetery, if you would. I'll see to Alex and we'll accompany the coffins together.' He allowed the boy the comfort of crying himself out in private before handing him a handkerchief to blow his nose on.

'Thank you for letting me see him, Tobias. At least I was able to say goodbye. I'm sorry about Honor and your daughter.'

'That's nice of you, Alex, when you are grieving yourself. It's been a hard day for all of us. Best we get it over and done with now, for, much as we'd like to, we can't go with them.' Honor's wedding ring was missing from her finger. He slid his own ring on to her hand, forcing it because her fingers were bloated. With his fingertip he caressed the signature ring on his other hand, Honor's gift to him. He laid her hand back under the shroud, trying not to gag when the disturbance released a faint smell of corrupting flesh.

Tobias buried his wife and child in the plot next to Lucian. The appearance of the child still bothered him somewhat. It didn't look as if she had been immersed in water.

'Was this the only infant found?' he said to the reverend who was to conduct the burial service.

'Yes, sir. They were together. The child was tucked into her bodice and tied there with a strip of her skirt, as if she thought to keep it with her. A mother wouldn't want to part with the body of her child when there was no hope left in her.'

'Yes, I suppose most mothers would have wanted to keep their infants with them. My wife's wedding ring was missing. Have you seen it?'

The man shrugged. 'The islanders have no respect for property, they take everything.'

'Damn them for their dishonesty! A wedding ring signifies a sacred promise made before God by a man and wife.'

'Nevertheless, the islanders are courageous men who would have risked their own lives to save hers if they'd been called on to do so. They saved many souls during the storm.'

Nodding, for Tobias knew he couldn't dispute something the islanders were renowned for, he whispered,

'Find peace in heaven, my darling. There will never be another to take your place.'

Alexander slipped his hand into Tobias's in an effort to comfort him. He gave the lad's fingers a quick squeeze. After the graves were filled, Clara and Oliver moved off, but he and Alex stayed there a little while, watching the diggers fill in the graves, for he sensed the boy needed to talk about the father he'd loved, and Tobias was always ready to listen. By the time Alex had run out of things to say, and they were ready to leave, a mason was already chipping words on to the simple stone tablet, referring to the paper Tobias had given him.

In memory of Honor Jane Darsham (née Palmer) beloved wife of Tobias Darsham. January 12th 1819–November 29th 1838. In her arms, their infant, Rose Darsham, aged 6 weeks. Both drowned off Portland when the Cormorant *was wrecked.*

Honor had not lived to celebrate her twentieth birthday, Tobias thought, as they began the long walk downhill to the ferry at Smallmouth, where the ferryman would pull the boat across the gap to the mainland by the ropes attached to posts at either side.

As soon as he got back to London he'd have the unenviable task of calling the families of the crew to the office to hand over their loved ones' dues. God knew how they would manage without an income coming in. He shivered, feeling heavy hearted, for it was not a task he relished on top of his own loss.

At the cemetery the stonemason turned to one of the gravediggers, paper in hand. 'Wasn't that a boy you buried with the woman, Hiram?'

Hiram nodded. 'I helped my woman put the pair into the shroud. 'Twas one of them sly looking moonies and he fair gave me the creeps. The mother was young to have given birth to one of them. I hear tell they're usually born to women who've reached the age of spoilin', since it's caused by the womb decaying.'

'Nothin' decayed about that 'un. It be a damned waste of a good-lookin' woman, if you asks me. Rose?' he muttered, shaking his head. 'That be a girl's name, I reckon, though I never heard anyone called by it.'

'Joseph Rushmore, him who's head cutter up at the Broadcroft quarry, just called his newborn daughter Joanna Rose. Says his wife got it into her head to give her a fancy name.'

'About time that Anna of his had a cheil. They could've had a dozen by now if she'd been able to keep them after she caught them. I nearly courted her meself, but Joseph got her in the way and took her to the altar while I was still thinkin' about it.'

Taking the paper from his hand, Hiram squinted long and hard at it before handing it back. 'I met a Scotsman once, who went by the name of Ross. It could be that.'

'It do seem like a Ross now I look at it proper.' Picking up his pencil, the stonemason crossed out the E and deftly added a second S to the infant's name.

*

The sisters-in-law had never really got on, but they tolerated each other.

Fanny Rushmore, surrounded by her four children, sniffed as she gazed at Joanna, lying in her cradle. 'She be a good size cheil for one who came early. Don't look like a newborn, that's for sure.'

'What're you saying, Fanny Rushmore?'

'Are you deaf, or somethin'? I said, this cheil don't look like no newborn to me. Look at her face, all plump and rosy, and she smiled at me.'

'Don't be so stupid. Joanna grimaced more like, and who wouldn't at the sight of your sour face. As for her plumpness, I've got more milk than a goat and she drains me of every drop. If you're going to sit there and say nasty things about my daughter, Fanny Rushmore, you can go home to your husband, and you needn't bother coming back.'

'I didn't say nasty things. You're twisting my words like you always do. Joanna Rose is a bit unexpected, that's all. She's bonnier than I thought she'd be considering her mother is a tall lump of a thing. And I can't see anything of either you or Joseph in her, as if the stork was blown off course in the storm and dropped the infant down the wrong chimney.'

Fanny's attempt at humour touched on a raw nerve. 'It's not my fault you can't see past the end of your nose, is it? There's nothing to say a child has to look like its parents. You should be pleased I've safely delivered one, at last.'

So saying, Anna slapped a plate of buttered scones down on the table, slathering them with butter and gooseberry jam. 'Help yourself,' she said to the children, then pursed her lips as they all snatched at the biggest scone. It broke into little pieces, and sticky crumbs flew everywhere. She'd make sure Joanna Rose was brought up with better manners, she thought.

'Behave yourselves,' Fanny snarled, clouting the eldest one around the ear. 'Use the plates and help your brothers and sister.

Fanny wasn't a bit pleased about Anna's live birth. She'd always coveted this fine house her brother-in-law had built for his wife. If they didn't have children, her own would stand to inherit it. A good sized field it stood in, too, big enough to keep a couple of sheep, several hens and to grow vegetables all year round. Around it was a stone wall, high enough to break the path of the wind. Anna also owned two fields at Tophill, which were used mostly for growing grain. Her sister-in-law never had to go hungry, and she was careful, taking her wares to the market at Wareham, though she bartered some of it for fish from time to time.

Fanny's own cottage was small and dark and smelt of fish guts. The family crowded into three rooms. There was never enough money to spare, though always enough for drinking. She envied Anna her husband, too. Joseph Rushmore was nicer looking than George, and he didn't have such a vile temper, leastways, not that she could see. He always talked nice to Anna, too, teasing her and such, never so much as laying a finger on her in anger.

She'd always liked Joseph, but George had been the one who'd courted her, and in the time-honoured

Portland tradition of getting her with cheil first. The fact that she'd been an unwilling partner hadn't bothered George. He'd given her a thump that had nearly knocked her senseless, pushed her on her back, then had thrown her skirt over her head and simply had his way with her. As soon as he'd got her with cheil he'd taken her to the church and the words had been said over them.

It had been that way ever since. No tenderness or thought for her feelings; she was just someone there to make his meals, bear his children, keep his house and expend his lust on. No wonder she was sour.

'Aye, I'm pleased,' she lied, feeling like crying, for there was no denying that the infant was fair. She would be given all the things Fanny couldn't afford for her own children. Hating herself for her own envy, Fanny drew her daughter against her, her words lumping thick inside her throat so she could hardly utter them. 'Look at your pretty cousin, Tilda.'

Six-year-old Tilda, thin, lank haired and dark eyed, smiled. 'Can I hold the babby on my lap?'

Tilda's skin was grimy and her clothes dirty and ragged. George Rushmore didn't have much time for girls. 'They're good fer nothin' but to help around the house,' he always said. Both Tilda and Fanny were low on his list of priorities, though Mary, his daughter from his first marriage, fared better.

After a moment's hesitation, Anna reluctantly lifted Joanna from her cradle and, making sure the girl was seated well back in the rocking chair, placed the baby in her arms, hovering over her in case she handled her roughly.

But Tilda didn't. She beamed proudly around at everyone. Not that anyone was looking at her, they hardly ever did. Then Tilda and the baby made eye contact. For a breathless moment they stared at each other, then Joanna smiled.

Luckily, Fanny had been distracted by one of her boys, who were more interested in the food than in Joanna.

'I think she likes you, Tilda,' Anna whispered, noticing that the girl was clearly enchanted by Joanna, as she gently unfurled her tiny fingers to look at her palm. 'You'll have to come and play with her when she gets a bit bigger.'

'Play!' Fanny snorted. 'There'll be no time for playing in our house. Once that Mary ups and marries, though nobody has shown any interest in her yet, more's the pity, Tilda will have to help me look after the menfolk, great lazy lumps that they are.'

Feeling sorry for Tilda, Anna said impulsively, 'Let her help me after school during the week, Fanny. She can watch over the baby whilst I do things around the place.'

All at once, Fanny's eyes became calculating. 'And what's in it for Tilda?'

'Oh, I don't know. I'll make her a new dress when she needs one, and buy her a pair of boots from time to time. And she can have her dinner here, so you won't have to feed her. I'll teach her to sew later on, too, and cook.'

'Well, I can't say she wouldn't be better off out from underfoot sometimes, and the boys treat her rough, so the poor little tyke is always covered in bruises.' Fanny checked that the boys weren't listening and lowered her voice. 'You can pay her sixpence a week, as well.'

'Sixpence! She's only six years old.'

'Fourpence for her services and tuppence for her education. I want you to save the fourpences up for when she grows older. It ain't no fun being poor and married to someone like George. I want better for Tilda, and perhaps the money will give her the chance to get away from the place. She's much better at lessons than the boys, but George said he won't fork out the tuppence needed to pay the teacher to educate her. Perhaps she'll be taken on as a maid in one of those big houses on the mainland later, if she's given the chance.'

'I'll have to talk to Joseph about the money.'

'He gives you everything you want. He's a good man, is Joseph Rushmore. Everyone says so.'

Anna sighed, knowing she could afford the money, and didn't have to ask Joseph. She gazed at Tilda, absorbed in Joanna and oblivious to the bartering taking place over her future. She was a dear little girl who deserved more from life.

'I can't afford sixpence. Tuppence for the teacher and tuppence saved, that's all I'll pay. That's one shilling and fourpence a month it will cost me, Fanny. Plus the food and clothing.'

Fanny nodded, satisfied that she'd done the best she could for her daughter, but not foolish enough to concede completely. 'I'll be agreeable to that, for now. Perhaps she can earn more in a year or two, when she's older and is more use to you.'

'Perhaps.'

'And I want the money kept a secret from George, else he'll have it off her later.'

Anna nodded.

'Good, then it's settled,' Fanny said. 'Hand that babby over and go and make us some tea, Tilda.'

'Leave her, she might scald herself. I'll do it myself.'

You've got yourself a soft job here and no mistake, Tilda Rushmore, Fanny thought, smiling in satisfaction as Anna walked off towards the kitchen.

3

By the time Joanna was six, Tilda had finished her education and had moved into Anna and Joseph's house permanently.

'Mary won't have her in her room any more,' Fanny whined to Anna. 'She said she intends to marry one of the soldiers. When she does, he'll have to move into her room, since she can't live with him in a tent with his companions. I don't see why not, though, since she hasn't settled for one, yet, as far as I can see. I think she entertains them when George and the boys are fishing, and I'm out doing my cleaning job. Her belly will swell up one of these days, and she'll have a hard time telling who fathered it, I reckon.'

'Those soldiers are causing us a lot of trouble. They're always staggerin' around drunk, accosting women, pissin' like dogs against the walls, and fighting with the locals. Everyone's fed up with them. Joseph said there's going to be trouble one of these days. He tells me to keep the doors locked at night. And he makes sure Tilda doesn't go home alone.' Head to one side Anna gazed at the bruised face of her sister-in-law and felt sorry for her. 'Perhaps it *would* be better if Tilda slept here permanently, since she often stays overnight.'

Fanny heaved a sigh of relief. 'I can't put her in with her brothers. They be men now and young Brian has been showin' an interest in her, of late. 'Tis only to be expected, men being what they are.'

Shocked, Anna stared at her. 'He hasn't . . .?'

'No, but I caught him holding her down on the bed with his hand up her skirt, so it'll only be a matter of time.'

'But Tilda is his sister and she's only twelve. Did you tell George?'

'A lot he cared. Brian said he was just ticklin' Tilda. George laughed and said that it was all females were good for, that Tilda took after me for looks and should be lucky any man paid her attention. Well, that's what he thinks. He might have a shock comin' to him one of these days.'

'What's that supposed to mean?'

'Never you mind,' Fanny said evasively, then demanded her daughter's savings, saying defiantly when Anna protested, 'I'm her mother. I can look after it now.'

Lips pursed, Anna handed over the four pounds reluctantly, for she knew Tilda wouldn't see a penny of it.

'Don't look at me like that, Anna Rushmore. 'Twas George's idea for Tilda to move in here. He's already asked Joseph, who's agreeable to take her in.'

'Does he know about her savings that you've just had off me?'

'No, and neither will he find out, if you knows what's good for you.'

'What's that supposed to mean?'

Fanny nodded towards Joanna. 'There's some who say you found that cheil. What if the magistrate found out?'

Anna paled. 'That's a wicked thing to say.'

'She bears no likeness to either of you, and where did that fancy cradle she used come from?'

'From the wrecks. Joseph found it washed up on the beach.'

'Very convenient,' Fanny sneered. 'How come he kept that fancy piece of goods when he sells everything else that comes from the wrecks, same as all of us.'

Heart thumping, Anna folded her arms over her chest and tried to stare Fanny down. Her own eyes flickered away first as she grumbled. 'You've got a nasty mind on you, Fanny Rushmore. If my Joseph hears you say such things he'll tell George and you'll get a good clout.'

'It were told to me by George hisself. He said he was on the beach the night Joseph got that cradle. He saw the dog bring it in and heard a baby crying.'

'The pair of you are mad. Knowing your George, he probably had a skinful. 'Sides, Joseph told me there was a seagull on the cradle when it came ashore, crying all pitiful, like. It fair gave him the shivers. It were that George heard.'

'That's not what he told me. Who's to say he's wrong and you be right?'

'I do. I should know what came out of me and who put it in there, shouldn't I? Now, look here, Fanny. Any

36

more talk about me stealing babies from their mothers and you can get out and stay out. Tilda is welcome to stay, but if that Brian of yours comes lookin' fer her I'll set the dog on him and chase him back down to where he belongs.'

'You do that. And from now on, Tilda gets sixpence a week, because that's what she'd earn if she went to work as a maid for one of the quarry owners. George has agreed that amount with Joseph. He says I'm to come and collect the two shillin' on the last Friday of every month, so no use you trying to change the arrangement.'

'Tilda would have to work much harder for her wage with a quarry owner, scrubbing on her knees from morning until night, most likely,' Anna pointed out.

'Now don't you go making this into a haggling matter, Anna Rushmore. Tilda's strong enough to do the work, and I happen to know that scholarly feller, Richard Lind, needs someone.'

'It's said that Mr Lind is mazed in the head, and sometimes he cries and carries on. That's why nobody will work for him.'

'Dr Scutts said he's harmless. What's more, Mr Lind is willin' to pay more on account of his rantings. I'll have your answer about Tilda, since I'm going straight to Richard Lind's house if you don't want her.' Hands fisted on to her hips, Fanny stared at her sister-in-law, waiting for her answer.

And since Tilda was an agreeable girl and Anna had made sure she was clean in her habits and well mannered, she nodded her agreement. She'd work for

Richard Lind herself if there was a profit in it, that she would.

'Joseph,' she said worriedly when her husband came home. 'Fanny suspects about Joanna.'

Joseph lowered himself wearily into the armchair. 'Ah, take no notice of her, my love. She's just fishin'.'

'She said there are rumours, that George saw you, and she might tell the magistrate what she suspects.'

'If George had seen me I'd know about it by now. There are always rumours, and nothing can be proved. Fact is, today I heard a rumour that Fanny is planning to leave her husband and run off with a Weymouth fish carter.'

Anna began to laugh at the thought of something like that happening, though, God knew, George deserved it.

Joseph grinned. 'I thought that would tickle your funny-bone. Rumours be rumours. You don't mind about Tilda moving in, do you love? She's a right pleasant little lass. She's not like her mother, that's fer sure.'

'Of course I don't. Tilda has grown to be like our own, and she's good with Joanna. Though I thought sixpence a bit steep, considering we've practically brought the girl up. I can't start treatin' her like a servant now, can I. They should be payin' us.'

'Ah, we can afford the sixpence. George doesn't make that much.'

'That's because he drinks it down instead of looking after his family. He always has. And his sons be takin after him. But, anyway, I've taken that job that was going with Richard Lind. He's paying me well, mind. And his ranting won't bother me none. Now don't give me that look of yours, and don't try and tell me I can't do it. I can and I will.'

'Hush, Anna, love. I've never known you to be a scold and would be obliged if you didn't start now. I've had a tiring day and my back's aching. If you want to earn a few extra shillings to put aside, I'll not be preventing you. Doubt if I could, anyway, for you're as stubborn as a mule when you puts your mind to it.'

Ruffling his hair, Anna smiled. 'Put your feet up then while I go and fetch your supper. The girls are helping me.'

Joanna peered around the door at the sound of her father's voice. Her eyes lit up. Dark hair swinging, her white starched smock covered in flour, she yelled, 'Pa!' and came running to climb up on his lap and give him a hug. 'Me and Tilda are making dumplings to go into the stew.'

'Are you, now?'

'An' Tilda is going to sleep here always.'

'I know, luvvy. That'll be nice for us.'

'Is Tilda my sister now?'

Joseph's glance went to Tilda, who gazed anxiously at him through dark eyes from the doorway. The contrast between the two girls was marked. Joanna was everything Tilda wasn't. Beautiful, vibrant and as clever as a monkey, she made people smile just by being alive.

Tilda looked a lot like her mother. Her face was angular and her eyes heavy-lidded, giving her a closed in, secretive look. But she had fine skin and pretty brown hair, which curled just enough. She was shy and sometimes stuttered when attention was on her, but she was a loyal girl who would do anything for them, and she never gave them any trouble.

Nobody could mistake the two girls for sisters. But, then, Joanna didn't look anything like Anna or himself, either, and usually nobody questioned that, 'cepting him being teased about it by the navvies, who reckoned some handsome soldier had crept into his bed in the dark and Anna hadn't noticed the difference. The teasing was kindly meant, though, and he didn't take offence.

'Tilda can't be your sister, because she's your cousin. That's just as good, for it's nice for a girl to have close female kin, and for them to love one another, like the good Lord says.'

'I do love Tilda, and she loves me. But she only says so when we're alone, because she's shy.'

He smiled when Tilda's face turned red. 'Then there's nothing more to be said, because me and your ma, we love Tilda too, just as if she was our own precious girl.'

Tilda's smile crept over her face like a mouse, lingered for a while, then disappeared. She edged into the room as if she wanted to hug everyone but didn't know if she dare. Sensing her hesitation, Anne put an arm around her shoulders and cuddled her against her side.

Watching the dog slink towards the kitchen, Joseph warned them all, 'You'd better get back to those dumplin's before the dog has them out of the pot.'

He laughed as there was a flurry of flapped aprons and agitation towards the door. Shortly, the dog skittered back out, his tail between his legs, to subside to the floor with a rumbling sound, his dignity in tatters. Flour decorated his head, as if he'd been swiped with a dirty dishrag.

Joseph filled the bowl of his pipe, rotating it on a small heap of tobacco in his palm to pack it tight. The tobacco glowed as he put a lit taper to it and inhaled. He sighed in satisfaction as a cloud of smoke drifted up to the ceiling, before saying to Rufus, 'Serves you right for trying to steal what doesn't belong to you.'

His glance fell on Joanna's cradle then, kept with the spinning wheel and used now for Anna's wools and needlework.

Someone had taken time to carve it. At the head and foot there was a ship in full sail, with dolphins at her prow and seagulls flying overhead. Soldiers marched all the way along the sides, beating drums and playing pipes. Beneath, horses snorted and pranced and dogs, cats and mice played chase. A single rose was carved inside, just above where the infant would lay its head. How odd, when Anna had chosen Rose as a second name for the child, and before she'd seen the carving.

It was as if the cradle had been carved by a man with a son in mind, for the rose seemed like a last-minute addition. The cradle was a work of love, and, although tempted, because it would be worth a pretty penny, for that reason, and for the fact that Anna wouldn't hear of it, Joseph would never sell it.

'It's a family heirloom, and when Joanna grows up and weds, it will serve her own cheils,' Anna had said.

Not for the first time since that fateful night, Joseph wondered what sort of life Joanna would be living now if he hadn't kept her for himself. She might have brothers and sisters, aunts and uncles . . . grandparents, perhaps. Suddenly, he felt a strong surge of guilt.

After dinner he shrugged into his coat and went to the inn. It had been a long time since he'd got himself a skinful and the urge was on him.

He staggered a bit on the way home and, tripping over, hit his head on a stone, knocking himself senseless for a few moments.

He woke with Rufus licking his face. 'Gerroff! I'm not a dog's dinner yet,' he said, pushing the animal away. He stood up and staggered, feeling dizzy, but his condition improved when he vomited into the gutter. 'By heck,' he said afterwards. 'That was a strong brew.'

Anna gave him a reproachful look when he let himself in. He grinned at her, even though it hurt. Best to keep on her right side since she had a tongue on her like a cat-o'-nine-tails when the devil drove her.

'Bedtime, you two,' she said to the girls, planting her hands on her hips, so Joseph knew he was in for a tongue lashing when she got the opportunity.

'I want my pa to tell me a story,' Joanna said.

'Bedtime! You might have to wait until morning for your story, for your pa's come home with his tongue all tied in knots from the drink.'

Reluctantly, Joanna followed Tilda to the stairs.

'A fool, you are,' she scolded, fetching a bowl and a washcloth. 'Look at this head of yours. Not that it's much to look at since it's got clay for a brain. There's a lump as big as a spoil heap on it, and you're bleedin' all over your good coat. Get it off so I can clean the stain before it sets.'

'I tripped over my feet.' The blow had left him with a dull, throbbing headache and he winced as she washed the blood from the wound, feeling a bit sorry for himself now.

'Ah, don't be such a big babby,' she said, bringing the candle closer. 'The wound isn't much and will soon mend. I'll bind it to stop you bleeding all over the pillow tonight.'

Joanna had sneaked back down the stairs. She smiled when she caught his eye. 'Are you going to tell me a story, Pa?'

'Off to bed with you,' Anna scolded. 'Can't you see he's had an accident?'

Ignoring Anna, Joanna came to look at the blood, then scrambled into his lap and hugged him tight. 'Poor Pa.'

'Leave her be,' he said when Anna opened her mouth. 'It won't take me long to tell her a story while you fetch me a cup of tea.'

'Tell me our secret story about the cradle,' she whispered, when Anna went off in a huff to the kitchen.

'Ah,' he said, lowering his voice to suitably mysterious levels. ''Twas like this, Joanna Rose. On a dark and stormy night when the waves were higher 'n the houses and the wind was howling around the house like a ghoul lookin' for a way to get inside and eat my Anna . . .' A snort came from the kitchen '. . . Rufus and me was down on the pebble beach, when we spied a tiny ship

43

with a seagull standing on the prow. All shining and white, it was, and luminous, as if God had sent an angel gull from heaven to light its way ashore.'

Joanna's eyes widened and she laid her head against his chest. 'Then what happened?'

'The wind and thunder and lightning was roaring overhead when Rufus went into the stormy sea to bring the little ship safely to shore. Tossed and turned about he was, but he bravely dived through the waves to reach the little craft. Guess what we found?'

Joanna's lips turned up in a smile. 'That it wasn't a ship, at all, but a cradle with a baby princess inside.'

Joseph nodded. 'And that baby princess was crying fit to burst because she was cold and hungry and just wanted someone to love her.'

Joanna's eyes closed as she murmured, 'That baby princess was me, and you put me in your hat and Rufus carried me home to my ma.' Her eyes fluttered open and closed again. 'What's a princess?'

'A very precious girl who needs to sleep so she can grow up to be beautiful and good.' He kissed her gently on the cheek and, rising to his feet, took her up the stairs to tuck her into her bed. 'Goodnight, Princess. Sweet dreams.'

'Goodnight, Pa.'

Anna was waiting for him downstairs, her eyes something fierce. 'She might grow up believing that tale you tell her.'

'Listening through the keyhole, was you?'

'Didn't have to, since I've heard it all before.'

'It's true enough, though, isn't it?' Joseph gazed at

44

her, his face troubled. 'Did we do the right thing in keeping her, Anna? She might have relatives.'

'Aye, and she might not, and then what? She'd have been thrown on the parish, most likely, and would've ended up in a workhouse. It's too late for regrets, Joseph Rushmore. Joanna is our daughter and I won't have anyone telling her different, not even you.'

She began to tear strips from an old linen sheet with an energetic ripping sound. 'Put your daft head to the side so I can bind that cut.'

'Don't be angry with me, love. My head aches something fierce.'

'It serves you right,' she said, but her voice had softened. 'By God, you men are fools sometimes.'

Even though it was painful, Joseph had to laugh at that.

Her words entered his mind again the next day, just for a fleeting instant.

It was May, and as fair a day as one could wish to see, with a faint luminescence hanging over the quarry as the humidity captured the finer particles of stone dust and the sun made them shine. The quarrymen had just successfully levered out a ten-ton block. It was as good a block of freestone as Joseph had ever seen.

Loosened from the Whit bed, the clay carefully picked out from around it, it was even textured and the grain was as smooth and as fine as the shell of an egg. All hands had lent themselves to levering it up, grunting as they applied their weight on metal bars longer than themselves by half a man.

They'd split the block using the plug and feather method, chiselling a line of holes, plugging them with iron wedges supported by metal strips and hammering at the plugs until the stone split along its length. Now they had to move each piece to the stone cart.

The horses between the shafts stood patiently, taking their rest while they could, for the beasts were worked to the capacity of their muscle power, and often beyond. Horses and flatbed would haul the load down a gentle incline to Castletown, where the beasts would be unhitched. When enough trucks were assembled they would be lowered by rail track and chain, the weight of the full trucks hauling the empty ones back up.

'*Round boys. Round . . .*' The words came as if from one throat, drowning out the sound of the screeching cogs of the jacks as the quarrymen's muscular arms turned the handles in unison. It was a routine manoeuvre the team had used hundreds of times.

Joseph's headache had grown worse as the day had progressed. Now and again a slight dizziness had disorientated him and made him feel sick. The glare reflecting off the white stone caused him to squint his eyes against it today. He put it down to the amount of drink he'd had the night before, and gritted his teeth. His team was a man short, and he didn't want them to get behind on the job.

A thin liquid seeped persistently from the wound on his head, soaking the crude dressing Anna had put there. It attracted insects, even though he kept his cap down over it, and he had it in his mind to ask the doctor to take a look at it on the way home. As the truck was backed under the stone block and it was being lowered gently on to the flat-bed cart, a wasp flew around his head. Automatically, he waved it away. He swore as the pain of a sting shot through his hand and sharply turned his head. The movement made him dizzy. His ankle turned on a loose stone, he stumbled then and, landing on his knees, fell forward.

'*Round boys . . .*'

Without his input the block landed on the cart awkwardly and the cart couldn't take the strain. There was a sharp snap as it tipped sideways. The horses gave loud, squealing whinnies as they tried to adjust to the sudden redistribution of weight. Men shouted.

One careless moment! Joseph didn't have time to roll free.

'*God, men are fools sometimes.*'

Aye, you're right, Anna love, was his last thought as darkness crushed in on him.

In contemplative silence, Tobias Darsham sat opposite Captain Thaddeus Scott, recently returned from a round voyage to the Australian continent. Both nursed a brandy.

At the age of forty-eight, Thaddeus was the company's senior captain. He commanded the *Nightingale*, which sailed to the southern reaches of the world, taking passengers and manufactured goods on the outward run, and usually returning with the same number of passengers and a cargo of wool and gold.

The *Nightingale* was being refitted at the moment, and Thaddeus was fretting impatiently to take command of her again, since he only felt really at home now on the ocean.

In front of them on the table was the fully rigged model of a ship of exquisite lines. 'Well, what do you think of her?' Tobias said after a little while.

'The clipper? She's heavy on the canvas and low in the water, but she's a beauty. Very nice indeed, though she looks as though she might ship water.'

'No more than any other ship. She's built for speed, Thaddeus. The smallest ones are longer than the packets. They can do twenty knots in the right conditions, and they carry fifteen hundred tons, at least.'

Thaddeus sucked a breath in through his teeth, clearly impressed.

'I've got two on order. There's a waiting list, but we take possession of the first one in a couple of years. She's being built in Boston.'

'At the McKay shipyard? He knows his way around a ship, does Donald McKay.' A pair of hooded brown eyes contemplated him. 'Have you told old man Morcant?'

'Not yet. I don't intend to, unless I have to. I don't want to be responsible for sending him to his grave.'

Thaddeus chuckled. 'His temper hasn't improved any, then?'

'If anything, he's getting worse. He wanders around the house at night, I believe. Clara's thinking of putting him in an asylum. She's become friendly with the American banker Samuel Nash, and having Grandfather Morcant around embarrasses her.'

'Last I heard, they lived in the old man's house. How can she put him out?'

'She can't. Oliver and Alexander will inherit it when their grandfather dies, and neither of them would contemplate turning him out.'

Thaddeus nodded. 'I doubt if Oliver will ever live in it, though. You should give him the clipper when she arrives. He's ready for his own command.'

'As senior captain I'm offering it to you. Oliver can captain the *Nightingale*. He can cut his teeth on a ship he knows and I'll consider him for the second clipper after he's proved himself.'

'That will work out well. He's served his time as first mate and is a good seaman and navigator. The crew respect him. In the meantime I'll start giving him more responsibility.' Getting to his feet, Thaddeus picked up the model, casting a more proprietorial eye over it now he knew it was his. 'You know, Tobias, you could have been at the helm of this beauty yourself. You had a real itch for the sea and you showed just as much promise as Oliver.'

'I take my yacht *Linnet* out on occasion; that scratches it. Someone's got to run the company.'

Thaddeus nodded. 'Aye, well you do that well, too. You're young yet. You should marry again, produce some children to pass the company on to.'

Tobias's smile faded. 'I've made Alex my heir. The Morcant brothers will eventually own all of the business, with Alex holding a controlling interest, since he's the more businesslike of the two. It'll be in good hands.'

Thaddeus's eyes came up to his. 'You still mourn the girl and the babe, don't you?'

'Not a day passes when I don't think of them.'

'It's been six years now. You should marry again.'

'I've never met anyone else I've wanted to spend my life with. Perhaps I never will. Leave it be, Thaddeus. I'm quite content at the moment.'

'It doesn't do for a man to dwell too much on what might have been. He should put sadness behind him and get on with the business of living. Have you had a woman lately, my friend?'

Tobias nearly choked on his brandy. There were always avenues to ease his baser needs, when necessary. 'I'm not exactly a monk yet.'

'I never thought you were. I just wondered if you knew of someone who'd provide a little companionship for a poor lonely old salt.'

'There are a couple of sisters I know of. They entertain discreetly at home on occasion. Black tie, intimate dinner parties. It can be interesting. I found myself seated next to a countess once.'

Thaddeus grinned at him. 'The more intimate the better. I've been at sea for four months.'

'I'll see if there are any gaps in their guest list. By the way, Thaddeus, my mother wants you to join us for dinner tonight. It's her birthday.'

'I know it's her birthday, for it's engraved on my heart.' Thaddeus took a wrapped package from his pocket 'I bet Charlotte doesn't look a day older than the last of her birthdays I was in port for.'

'Don't remind her of how long ago that was, if you intend to compliment her. What's in the package?'

'Scrimshaw. We put ashore to make repairs and found the carcass of a landed whale. It stunk a bit but that didn't put the crew off, they soon had the teeth out of its mouth. I carved it myself on the journey home. Funny looking native animals they have there. The one called a kangaroo looks like a huge rabbit with an enormous tail for balance. I've never seen such a lolloping great thing. They leap across the ground on their hind legs at a rate of knots. I would have brought Charlotte one if we could've caught one. They made me laugh.'

'The Australian continent sounds like an interesting place.'

'You'd like it there, Tobias. It's large and mostly unexplored. There's hardship, but the people have a pioneering spirit and a sense of working together. I reckon a man could make a future there on the strength of his arm and the sweat of his brow. I'd settle there myself if I was younger and not so set in my ways. The need for manufactured goods of any type will be urgent for years to come. A man could make a good living working as a storekeeper.'

'Perhaps we'll open a shop between us, put a manager in. It will be something for you to retire to. You surprise me, Thaddeus. I never picked you for hankering after a merchant's life.'

'I was given the chance to became a seaman when I was young, and I wasn't in a position to pick and choose. When you don't know where your next meal's coming from you tend to agree to any occupation that will keep your belly full. However, I'm happy with my lot and not looking to become a landlubber just yet. Probably I never will unless your mother changes her mind about splicing the knot with me. She's kept me on a string for the past few years, so I ain't holding out any hopes at the moment.' He placed the model down on the table. 'What will you name her?'

'*Charlotte May* after my mother.'

'Pretty . . . very pretty. Charlotte will like that.'

Tobias nodded. 'It was Alexander's idea, and his first management decision. He's not keen on calling the new clippers after birds. He'll be up for the dinner, by the way. He practically lives with me when he's home.'

'Clara doesn't mind that?'

'Clara doesn't mind at all. She's never been motherly. Having a son Oliver's age makes her feel old. And Alex, coming as he did ten years later, has always been regarded as a nuisance by her.'

'Did you know that Lucian had his doubts about Alexander's paternity?'

Shocked, Tobias stared at him. 'That's not true, surely.'

'Lucian heard whispers that Clara had been seeing other men in his absence, that she had taken lovers into her bed. She denied it, of course.'

'And?'

'They had a terrible row. The following month she became *loving* towards him, he said. She told him she wanted another child. Alex was born seven months later.'

'Infants do arrive early,' Tobias said, remembering the drowned daughter he'd never known.

'Aye, they do. But Lucian hadn't had much to do with Clara in between voyages. He said she always managed to be indisposed. He told me he thought she was having an affair and he didn't really care, as long as she kept it private. But he wondered about Alex's paternity.'

'Who was the man? Did Lucian suspect anyone in particular?'

'If he did, he never said anything to me. Clara was very discreet and the affair was still going on when Lucian died.'

'Does anyone else know about this?'

'Not to my knowledge, and it won't go any further, Tobias. I don't even know why I told you.'

Tobias gazed directly at Thaddeus. 'You know . . . I wouldn't like Alex to be hurt. He absolutely worshipped Lucian.'

'Lucian knew that, which is why he never left Clara. He just accepted the boy as his own, as well he might have been, and made the best of the situation. Lucian was a good man.'

'Yes, he was.' Tobias rose to his feet and reached for his hat. 'Let's be off then, Thaddeus. I've got to pick up my mother's birthday present.'

'Which is?'

'It has four legs and yaps a lot, so no prizes for guessing what it is.'

4

Fanny Rushmore had collected the first month of her daughter's wages. She slipped it into her pocket.

Anna was a fool to part with her cash, especially now she had no man to support her, Fanny thought, as she gazed at her daughter. Tilda would never be handsome, but she had a nice figure and Fanny wondered if anyone was courting her. But no, Anna had a canny head on her, and would guard the girl from being caught too early. Tilda had a good home with Anna, better than her father would ever provide for her. In fact, George didn't want Tilda back.

Anna would have to watch out for Joanna, though. With her fine skin, bright eyes, wide smile and friendly manner, she'd attract both men and boys alike, from an early age.

'Well then,' she said, sighing, for the house was full of silences, with its atmosphere of mourning. The three females who inhabited it wore deep circles under their eyes along with an air of support for each other. They were dressed in linen aprons and bonnets, as if they were about to go out and work the field. The dog stared at her, unblinking, a soft growl rattling in its throat. Fanny felt like an outsider. 'I'll be leaving then.'

'Aye,' said Anna. 'You do that.'

On the doorstep, Tilda recoiled as Fanny went to kiss her cheek. 'What's the matter?' Fanny snarled. 'Has living in Fortuneswell made you too good for your own mother now?'

Tilda stared at her, as impassive as a cow. She'd like to know what went on in Tilda's head sometimes. Nothing, she suspected. But as soon as the thought was loosened from her mind, Tilda gave a faint, twisted smile, which made Fanny itch to slap her face. Joanna came to stand by Tilda, slipping her hand into hers. The pair exchanged a smile that excluded her.

'Goodbye, Ma,' Tilda said and closed the door on her.

Not that it mattered, Fanny fumed to herself as she set off down the hill to her own mean cottage. She wouldn't be here much longer.

When Fanny reached Chiswell the men were loading their nets into the lerrets. George was beginning to lose his hair, but he was muscular of body still, and mean with it. She'd have to be careful.

Her sons looked just like him, rat faced. Leonard, the better looking of the three, was silent natured, his expression closed. Being the eldest he'd always born the brunt of his father's anger. Unlike Brian and Peter, she never knew what was going on in his mind.

Fanny didn't really love any of her children, for they'd been forced on her. She hated George. She wished it had been him who'd been crushed under the block of stone instead of Joseph. Becoming a widow would be sweet. She wouldn't mope, like Anna. She'd put ribbons in her hair, drink some gin and dance in the street, and to hell what anyone thought of her.

Mary was leaning on the window-sill, looking sullen. Despite her efforts to better herself by marrying a soldier, she wasn't having any luck.

'Just wait,' Fanny whispered to herself. 'Your father will find a use for you after I've gone.'

George sent her a hard-eyed look. 'Where've you been, woman? The house is a pigsty.'

'I went up to see how Anna was getting on.'

'She'll be getting along fine. She's a sensible woman who was a good wife to my brother. A pity there aren't more like her around.'

'And it's a pity you aren't more like your brother,' she muttered under her breath as she disappeared into the dark interior of the cottage. She nearly gagged on the smell after the fresh air. 'Mary,' she shouted. 'Get down here and help me clean this place up.'

After a little while her stepdaughter sauntered downstairs. She was wearing a new bodice of green watered taffeta cut low at the front, and a straw hat with ribbons. She was a fancy piece of goods. 'And where are you going dressed like a trollop?'

Mary tossed her head. 'I'm meeting someone, if it's any of your business.'

'Does your father know you're sellin' your wares to the soldiers?'

'I'm not selling anything. Can I help it if they want to give me gifts? Money is money and I'm not about to refuse. One of these days I'm going to leave this place, you'll see. I'm saving up for the future – it's got to be better than this.'

Fanny's eyes sharpened as she watched the girl walk away, her hips twitching from side to side. When she'd gone she turned her eyes towards the sea. The water was calm and the lerrets were being rowed towards the fishing ground. She could see George standing in the stern, the tiller in his hand. He seemed to be looking at her – as if he knew.

But nobody knew about Ben Rowbothan. She had met him on the quay round Castletown way, where he'd been buying fish. Soft he was, big bellied and with ginger hair. He wasn't very attractive, but then neither was she. He was kind and had listened to her troubles. He'd said he needed a housekeeper, but Fanny had understood he needed more than that.

Turning her back on George she went inside and up to Mary's room. Now, where would the girl have hidden her money? Careful to return everything to its place, Fanny smiled as she squeezed the toe of an old pair of boots. Her eyes widened as she tipped several pounds into her palm. The girl had been industrious, indeed. She replaced the stash with the same weight in pebbles, then added the cash to the money she'd received from Anna for Tilda's wages over the last month.

With a change of clothes hidden in her basket under her shawl she headed for the bridge at Smallmouth.

'It's not often you cross to the mainland. Where are you off to this fine morning?' The tollkeeper asked her, holding out his hand for her halfpenny.

'The market at Weymouth, if it be any of your business,' she snapped, though she was really heading for Poole. On the other side she was lucky in finding herself a seat on an overcrowded coach, and clung precariously to the rail as it made a headlong dash through countryside so astonishingly green her eyes ached from the sight of it.

But when she reached the bustling harbour town, her new man wasn't there waiting for her, as agreed. She waited at the designated meeting place until nightfall, marvelling at the sight and sounds of the people coming and going. It was nearly dusk when she was about to go to enquire in a fishmonger's establishment. Before she could, a shadow moved towards her.

'Ben?' she whispered.

'Ben won't be coming. He's had a nasty accident.'

Fear leapt into Fanny's throat and her heart set up a painful clamour as George's hand closed around her hair when she turned to run. She could smell the drink on his breath. When a fist slammed into her midriff she doubled over.

George roughly felt for her purse, ripping it from where it was pinned under her skirt. Then he set about her.

When she woke the sun was beating warmly down on Fanny.

She didn't know how long she'd been lying there. The last thing she could remember was the motion of the lerret in the water, and the laughter of George's crew when she was sick from it.

She hurt all over, as if every bone in her body was broken, and she whimpered when she tried to move. Her tongue was dry and she needed a drink. Pebbles pressed into her cheeks. She opened her eyes, squinting against the glare of the day. A little way away she could see the fishermen repairing their nets.

Nobody looked at her. It was as if she didn't exist. The day pressed on, her skin began to burn. Mary came to look at her and, although shock came into her eyes, she tittered. 'You thievin' cow, did you think he didn't know?'

'To hell with him! I hope he dies.'

'More'n likely you will. You're in a state, right enough.'

'Come away from her, Mary. Get inside and cook the dinner.'

'Why should I? I'm not your bleddy wife.'

'But you're my daughter, and while you live in my house you'll do as you're told.' The sound of a slap was followed by a cry. Holding her face, Mary went running indoors.

Darkness eventually fell, bringing Fanny relief. The cottage windows reflected light, the doors were closed. A foot nudged her in the ribs, sending pain tearing through her. George said, 'You've got no home with me now, woman. You're nothin' but rubbish.'

Fanny slept for a short while, drifting in and out of pain, listening to the sound of the sea sucking at the shingles. It would never grind the shore of this stone island into sand. She could taste blood in her mouth and her face felt like pulp. If she could have moved, Fanny would have crawled across the shingle and into the bay, for death seemed to be the only way out. Groaning, she shouted out, 'Will nobody help me?' The effort of it caused her bladder to empty.

The cottage lights went out one by one and there was silence, except for the odd cough as somebody cleared their throat in the night, or the cry of a babby wanting its mother's teat.

Her body throbbed with hurt and her throat was as dry as if she'd inhaled chalk dust.

It was said that midnight brought the spirits of the drowned souls forth from the bay to wander the shore and cry out for their loved ones. She'd dismissed it as fisherman's folklore, but now she heard the shingles move under the surreptitious tread of feet. She whimpered in fear.

It was Mary. 'He's fallen into a drunken stupor. I'll fetch help.'

Soon, some soldiers arrived and Fanny was lifted on to a cart.

'Take her to my aunt in Fortuneswell, for he'll not have her back and neither will he soften towards her,' Mary told the men. 'I'll have to go back in. He'll thrash me if he finds out I've helped her. I'll meet you on the hill tomorrow, when he's gone to fish.'

The movement of the horse making its way up the hill was agony, since the cart wheels seemed to bump through every pothole. Fanny groaned with the pain of each movement, and perspiration soaked through her clothes.

Anna finally opened the door to their repeated

knocks, the two girls pressing against her sides. When she saw the red uniforms she turned up the oil lamp and said nervously, 'If it's my man you want, he's upstairs. I'll fetch him down for you.'

'Your man's dead, missus, and we're sorry to bother you in your time of grieving. We mean you no harm. Mary asked us to bring this woman here. Someone has given her a beating.'

''Tis my ma they have,' Tilda said, with a gasp.

Anna gave a small scream when she saw the bloodied bundle they carried between them. 'What has George done to her? Bring her inside and put her on the settle.'

'The woman has broken bones, I think,' one of the soldiers told her, as they set Fanny down as gently as they could. The pair looked on awkwardly when Fanny began to cry. 'Is there anything else we can do to help?'

And these were the same soldiers she and Fanny had grumbled about earlier. 'Thank you, but no, unless you'd call in on Dr Scutts and ask him to visit as soon as possible? It will save me going out.'

The pair nodded and edged towards the door when Rufus lifted his head to growl menacingly at them. 'I'll tell him it's urgent,' the taller one said.

There was a flurry of activity after the soldiers left.

'Tilda, take a poker to the fire, though the kettle should be hot enough to fill the washbowl by now. Use it, then put another kettle on to boil.' Anna lit a candle and handed the candlestick to Joanna. 'First, you can fetch the soap and a clean washcloth from the cupboard. Afterwards, you can bring a towel to dry Fanny on, and a clean nightgown from my dresser, the one that buttons

61

up all the way down the front. Can you remember all that?'

'Yes, Ma.'

'Good girl. Off you go now, and be careful of the candle.'

She turned to Fanny. 'I'll see if we can make her comfortable before the doctor comes. What did you do to make George do this to you?'

She whispered, 'I ran away from him and he came after me.'

'With your fancy man, I suppose.'

'You knew about him?'

'Everyone knew, but I didn't believe it. I thought it was just a rumour.'

'George must have frightened Ben off, the cowardly bastard.'

The conversation between the two women ceased when the girls came back. 'Set the bowl on the table next to me, Tilda, there's a good girl. And when the kettle boils you can make us a nice cup of tea. Joanna, you can go back to bed now.'

Joanna gave a big sigh. 'I want to watch.'

'Well, you can't. You're too young. Now, give me a kiss and go back to bed.'

'I want my pa to read me a story.'

'Your pa's not here any more,' Anna said with a catch in her voice. 'He's gone to heaven to be with the angels.'

'Peggy Marshall said my pa was squashed flat and they had to scrape him off the ground.' Tears came into her eyes. 'It's not fair. I miss him and I want him back.'

'Peggy Marshall's a liar,' Tilda told her. 'Your pa is

watching over you from heaven, right now. The next time the night is clear I'll show you the star God gave him to live on.'

'Is it the biggest star?'

'No, but it's the one that twinkles the brightest. Come on, up the stairs. I'll tell you a story while the kettle is boiling, if you like.'

'About my cradle?'

Tilda nodded. 'It's the only story I know.' She turned and caught Anna's eye, then jerked her head towards her mother. 'You should ask the doctor to give her a bed in the infirmary.'

'Hush, Tilda. She's your ma, and you should be more charitable towards her.'

'Hah! What kind of mother would steal from her own daughter's wages. And when did she ever come here to visit me, 'cepting when she wanted something from you? You'll live to regret takin' her in, just you wait and see.'

The girl has good reason to dislike her ma, Anna thought. Even so, the outburst from Tilda was uncharacteristic of her.

Whimpering with pain, Fanny couldn't believe what she was hearing from the mouth of her own daughter. It was all Anna's fault. The woman had poisoned Tilda's mind against her. Well, if Tilda thought she was going to get rid of her she could think again! This was a good house with room for all of them. Here she intended to stay, and that feisty little madam Tilda could look after her, like a good daughter should.

*

63

Adam Scutts was sour tempered at being hauled out of bed to deal with a woman who'd been beaten by her husband, though her injuries made his eyes widen. By God, she'd taken a thumping. No doubt she'd deserved it, he thought, though perhaps not quite as severe as this beating had been.

'Your bruises will fade in time, but I'm not sure if you'll regain the sight of that eye. I can't do anything about the broken nose. No doubt it will heal crooked. I can splint your arm and bind your cracked ribs. Both will mend in a few weeks.'

'What about her legs, Doctor?' Anna asked.

'The bones in one of her feet are crushed. I doubt if that foot will ever take her weight again, but when she's recovered she might be able to hobble with crutches.' He gazed down at Fanny. 'What did you do to deserve this?'

'I left my husband,' Fanny said sullenly, her pain dulled by a dose of laudanum.

'Well, I hope you've learnt a lesson from it.' He hesitated for a moment, then said more sympathetically, 'It looks like you'll be permanently crippled, Mrs Rushmore. You could report your husband to the magistrate. He'd probably be fined, or get a prison sentence.'

'And suffer another beating when he came out. It's not as if I can go anywhere to escape him now.' She shuddered. 'He won't have me back, and thank God for it, for he's a hard bastard who beat me in front of my own sons, and they not daring to lift a finger to stop him, strapping lads though they be.'

'If you can't go home where will you stay? I can probably find you a bed in the infirmary, and perhaps I could speak to your husband on your behalf.'

'There's no need to make such arrangements, Doctor. I wouldn't go back to George if he got on his knees and begged me. I'll stay right here with my sister-in-law and she and my daughter can look after me. There's plenty of room here for me, isn't there, Anna? After all, you've only got the one daughter. A dear little thing, too, though where she gets her looks from puzzles me. It's as if she was brought in on the tide.'

Anna paled at the threat. 'I don't know if I've got the room.'

'I can sleep in the back parlour, can't I? It's not as if you use it, and I won't get in anyone's way there.'

After a moment's hesitation, Anna whispered in a defeated voice, 'Yes, I suppose you can sleep there.'

Joanna Rose had just turned sixteen when Anna took to her bed.

Joanna was worried sick, because her ma was rarely ill. But a few weeks previously Anna had caught a cold that had gone to her chest. It was a lot better, though, and she hardly coughed at all, but she hadn't been her usual energetic self since then. Noting her flushed cheeks, Joanna asked her, 'What's wrong, Ma? Shall I fetch the doctor?'

'What, and waste good money payin' his fee? I'm feelin' a bit tired, my love, that's all. I'm doing too much, I reckon, what with working for Richard Lind and trying to keep the fields going, even with Tilda's help.

It's not as if I'm a young woman any more, and I seem to run out of breath at the slightest thing. Sometimes I can't get up the hill without stopping every five minutes.'

'You should sell the fields.'

'And what would we do without the income the produce brings in? I shall have to give up the job, though. It's a big house to keep clean.'

'The job brings in a steady wage we can rely on. I'll do Richard Lind's cleaning. It's not as if he doesn't know me, since I've helped you out before. And if you don't want to sell the fields, rent them out. The field the house is standing on produces enough to feed us. Tilda and I can work that at the weekends, and in the evening in the summer.'

'And who's going to look after Fanny?'

Sitting on the side of the bed, Joanna took her mother's hands in hers and lowered her voice. 'Fanny isn't as helpless as she makes out. She likes to see you running back and forth after her, that's all. Tilda doesn't take any of her nonsense, and neither do I. I've been told she comes upstairs when we're out, and looks through our things.'

'She never does,' Anna said with a gasp.

'Mrs Whiffin from across the road told me she's seen her through the upstairs window a couple of times.'

'Aye, Mrs Whiffin has always pried into other folk's doings, so she'd recognize another busybody when she saw one, wouldn't she?' Anna said.

Joanna chuckled. 'Be that as it may, I've hidden that brooch you gave me in case Fanny takes a fancy to it. Her sons visit her, too, when we're out. Sometimes,

Brian and Peter take her out in the wheelbarrow to visit people, and she's been seen up the Lugger's Inn talking with the Barnes brothers, by all accounts. Has anything gone missing?'

'Some tools that belonged to Joseph disappeared from the shed a couple of weeks back. And I thought some money I had put aside went missing. But then I figured I must have put it somewhere else, then forgotten where.'

'Not you, Ma. You're too careful with money to forget where you put it. We'll have to get one of those boxes you can lock with a key. Fanny is on the gin, I've heard. She's got to get money from somewhere to pay for it.'

'I wonder if George Rushmore knows that the boys be seeing her.'

'They're grown men, not boys, and since they're too old to be flogged I don't suppose they care what their father says. They're an unpleasant pair of louts, too. Leonard is the best of the three. He's a bit quiet, but he has his own cottage and his own boat now, and he treats his wife and youngsters well. He doesn't have much to do with the others if he can help it.'

'Well, make sure you stay well away from all of them. You're attracting the attention of men now, and you're too pretty to be wasted on the likes of George Rushmore's get. I want something better than that for you. Tell Tilda to stay out of their way, too, even though they be her own brothers. Look what the pair of them did to Mary. Held her down and planted an infant in her. She was lucky it died. Now she's gone, and the last I heard of her she'd become a lightskirt in Poole.'

'What's a lightskirt?'

'A woman who charges for her favours. Some would call her a slut.'

'Surely 'tis better than giving her favours away. How else can she earn money to keep herself?'

'She should have married an islander early on instead of trying to catch a soldier for herself. Mainland ways are different to ours. You want to be married, don't you? The island way is to find yourself a nice lad and get yourself with cheil first. Then you both know you're fertile. But if you lies down with the soldiers they'll all have you, then treat you like dirt.'

'But sometimes the island lads aren't so nice, and they want to kiss and touch you when you tell them no. Tilda said it might have been the soldiers who did that to Mary, since they asked if they could do it to her when Mary left, and she ran away.'

'Ah, poor Tilda. She hasn't attracted a man yet and I think she never will. She should stay away from the regiment, though. They don't understand our courtin' ways but take advantage of the way we go about it. There's going to be trouble between them and the islanders soon, you mark my words.'

Joanna kissed her mother's flushed cheek. 'If I get married it won't be until I'm much older, so it's no good encouraging the men. I've a mind to see the world after lookin' at that big globe at Richard Lind's house.'

'And you could do, if that's what you want. You should ask Richard Lind to tell you about things. He's a nice man to talk to, despite his fits. And he's clever with it, using long words I don't understand and never will in a month of Sundays now. But you could learn all of them from him just by listening and looking them up in that big book he has.' She allowed Joanna to plump up her pillow. 'Now, don't you tell Fanny I'm going to rest today, otherwise she'll have me running up and down all day.'

Joanna's eyes softened. 'Don't you go worrying about her, Ma. You stay in bed this morning. I'll bring you some breakfast, then I'll go and see to Richard Lind's house. I'll be back by lunch-time to help Tilda in the field, and I'll see Mrs Hawthorne and ask her if she wants to rent the top fields, shall I? She's looking for more land to plant grain on.'

'You do that,' Anna said tiredly. 'And I don't want any breakfast, love. Just fetch me up a cup of tea and I'll sleep till lunch-time.'

Joanna stoked up the fire before she left, placing the metal guard around it to stop sparks flying from the grate on to the rug. She closed the door gently behind her, so there was no draught to send smoke billowing into the room.

Richard Lind lived in a large house next to that of the Reverend Prosper Quinby and his family. It was only a short walk from the Fortuneswell church and the cemetery where her father was buried.

Drawing her shawl around her head and shoulders, for the weather had just tipped over into spring and the wind off the water was still bitter and laden with salty spray, she set out up the hill. The island had changed little, as far as she could remember. Tilda had told her there used to be a boat ferry where the bridge stretched across the gap at Smallmouth. Joanna couldn't remember it, since she'd been too small.

As far back as she could remember, she had never crossed the bridge leading to the mainland, either. The people who lived in Weymouth were not liked by the islanders. Sometimes gangs of them came across to gather in the inns and drink and cause strife.

Her mother had told her they were a bad lot. But surely they can't all be bad, she thought now, and her interest was suddenly aroused as to what lay over the water, and beyond. Her heart began to pound at the thought of crossing the bridge.

In the Fortuneswell cemetery Joseph Rushmore's headstone had weathered over the past ten years. Still standing firm against the wind it had faded to match the other memorials to the dead. Blooms of rust-coloured lichen decorated it.

Joanna remembered her father clearly as she stopped to pull some long grass from the grave. His pipe was still on the dresser at home, though the house no longer smelled of tobacco. Sometimes, if she closed her eyes and gently sucked air through the stem, the taste of it made her remember the fragrance of her pa's breath when he'd kissed her goodnight.

His oilskin and hat still hung on the hook behind the door of the shed. She smiled as she recalled the tale he'd told her, of Rufus carrying the lost princess home from the storm in his oilskin hat. It was only a silly story. But, still, there were toothmarks each side of the brim of the hat. Rufus had been buried in the corner of the field behind the house six years since.

Joanna liked to think he and Pa were together in heaven.

'There, Pa, that looks much tidier,' she said, brushing her hands free of dirt on her skirt as she stood up. 'Ma hasn't been well lately, but you needn't fret. I'm looking after her and we're managing all right.'

'Oh,' she said, turning as a chuckle came from behind her.

It was Richard Lind, getting on a bit and as thin as a sparrow, his fat old dog waddling at his heels. He gazed at her over his spectacles. 'I'm sorry, I didn't mean to startle you.'

'I didn't know you were behind me, that's all,' she said.

'That's because your head was full of thoughts. That's all the company you need, sometimes, especially if they're happy thoughts. The other type are demons who can bedevil you if you let them.'

She thought she knew what he meant. 'I don't think I've lived long enough yet for demons to live in my head.'

'Perhaps they'll never live there, so the wonder I see in your eyes is never lost.'

'My ma is poorly and can't come, so you have me instead,' she told him as they fell in step together, the dog waddling after.

'It's an honour, for you bring beauty into my life, Joanna Rose. I do hope your mother improves. She's not been her usual energetic self lately.'

'I'll make her stay in bed until she's better.' A smile touched her lips. 'Except for my ma, you're the only person who calls me by both names.'

'It's a pretty name, which suits you. Do you always talk to the dead?'

'Sometimes I talk to my pa.' She grinned at him. 'I daresay you think it's daft, you being a scholar and all. But I imagine he can hear me and that gives me comfort.'

'Not at all. There's great comfort in talking to the dead, since they can't disagree with you. I talk to the voices in my head all the time. People think I'm insane and am talking to myself. Little do they know that sometimes there are so many voices arguing inside me that they take over my head.'

'Is that when you fall on the ground and jerk about? What do your voices say to you, sir?'

His eyes came her way, haunted by sadness. 'They destroy the beauty I feel inside me, by telling me the world is not as I see it, that it's inferior.'

'How do you see the world then?'

'Much as you see it, I expect.' He drew her to a halt. 'Close your eyes, Joanna Rose. What do you feel?'

'I feel the wind against my face.'

'From where does that wind come?'

'Off the sea.'

'And what does it smell of?'

'Salt and seaweed.' She smiled to herself, not needing any more prompts. 'I can hear the gulls shriek as they glide upon the draught and the washing flapping on the line. The wind makes a soft sighing noise as it comes up over the hill, but sometimes it roars. Sometimes it finds its way under the crack of the door and draws smoke down the chimney and sends dust flying about.'

'Is that all?' he said when she hesitated.

'No. The grass rustles as it bends before it, and when it hits the stones in the wall it bruises itself, leaving behind particles of dust, sand and seeds from the mainland.' A raindrop touched her face, as soft as a teardrop. 'The rain makes the seeds grow so the church wall has little flowers growing between the stones come spring. That be a pretty sight to gladden the heart.' She opened her eyes, laughing, somewhat self-consciously. 'That's how I see the wind when my eyes are shut, Mr Lind, as if I was part of its breath.'

He smiled as they resumed their walk. 'It's a good way to see things. You have a touch of the poet about you, Joanna Rose. That's something I should like to encourage, if you'll allow me to.'

His words made her glow with happiness.

5

Anna died two weeks later, taken gently in her sleep by the congestion in her lungs. Joanna made the discovery not long after she came home from work. She called a boy in from the street and gave him a farthing to fetch the doctor.

The tea she'd taken up to her ma that morning was still on the bedside table. Joanna took Anna's cold hand in hers, patting it as she begged, 'Wake up, Ma. Please wake up!'

She noticed that the thin gold band Anna usually wore on her finger was missing, leaving a circle of pale indented skin in a hand work-roughened and callused. Her ma looked peaceful and rested. Joanna picked up a brush and began to pull it through the woman's hair, sniffling as she tried to stem her tears. Anna's hair gleamed like strands of silver thread spread around her on the pillow.

Tilda came home about the same time as the doctor arrived to examine Anna. She took Joanna in her arms as Dr Scutts pulled back the gaudy patchwork quilt the three of them had stitched between them on the cold winter nights. His pronouncement was as expected, despite Joanna's denials to herself. 'She's been dead for several hours, I should imagine.'

'She can't be dead,' Joanna sobbed. 'All she had was a little cough.'

'That little cough became pneumonia. You should have called me in earlier,' Scutts said almost angrily. 'I might have been able to do something to save her.'

Broken hearted, Joanna rounded on him, her eyes brimming with tears. 'My ma wouldn't let me. She said she was getting old and was just tired. 'Sides, we have Fanny Rushmore to feed, too, and we couldn't afford your fee. Tilda and I didn't know ma was dying.'

'Can you afford the funeral?' he asked, his voice softening, for he knew from Richard Lind how hard this girl worked to help look after her family.

'Aye, Ma saved for her funeral and she'll want to be buried with my father.' She fetched the savings tin from under the clothes in Anna's trunk. But before she even took the key from its hiding place to open it, she knew the box was empty. She gazed across at Tilda, horror in her eyes. Both of them knew where the money had gone.

Almost hurling herself downstairs Joanna threw open the door to Fanny's room and shouted, 'You've been up there, haven't you? You've been through her things and have taken her ring and her money. How could you rob a woman who took you in and cared for you, you damned ghoul?'

'I don't know what you mean,' Fanny said, her voice slurred. She managed to put a pathetic whine in it when she saw the doctor. 'You cruel girl. You know very well I can hardly see or walk, let alone get up those stairs.'

'Yes you can, Fanny Rushmore. Mrs Whiffen has seen you up there at the window plenty of times. Nosing around, she said you were.'

'That old crow can hardly see past the end of her nose. She's making mischief, that's what she's doing. She'll be saying I killed Anna next.'

Placing her hand on her hips, Tilda said quietly, 'How did you know Anna was dead, then?'

Fanny gazed round at them all, her eyes shifty. 'I heard you talking.' But Joanna knew she hadn't, for the walls and doors of the cottage were thick and voices didn't penetrate unless they were raised in anger.

Tilda pounced on a gin bottle. 'Where did you get the money to buy this from, then? You haven't got any of your own.'

'Brian brought me that the last time he visited. He's a thoughtful boy, is my Brian – both my younger boys are. A pity my only daughter wasn't more like them.'

Tilda turned to the doctor, her agitation clear to see. 'She stole it, I know she did. She's stolen money before from Anna, only we couldn't prove it.'

Adam Scutts stared from one to the other, reluctant to become involved in a family argument, though he believed the girls were right. 'I could fetch a constable to search Fanny Rushmore's room.'

'Search it yourself, if you like.' Picking up her crutches, Fanny swung to her feet and leaned on them with a martyred sigh. 'Go on then, search it. Don't let a poor, half-blind old cripple stop you.'

Adam shrugged. 'If she did take it, it's long gone now and there's no way of proving it. The parish won't bury Anna, because there's property to sell, which will pay for a funeral.' He looked about him at the comfortable room with its old but solid furniture. The doctor knew that the islanders often had bits and pieces they'd plundered from wrecks, hidden away to tide them over the hard times. 'No doubt you'll find something to cover costs.'

Joanna only had one thing of value to sell, something her ma had given her and that she was loath to part with: the rose brooch with the little red stones in. But she had no choice, so she nodded and went to fetch it from its hiding place in a knot-hole in the rafter, a place where Fanny couldn't reach. 'Will this cover the cost?'

'Well, you're a sly one,' Fanny said, her mouth pursed in annoyance, her eyes avid with greed. 'That looks like real gold. I never knew you had that.'

'Only because I hid it from you well.'

'There's no need to be like that, Joanna Rose. Where did you get the brooch from?

'My ma gave it to me.'

'And you dare to accuse me of stealin'. Most likely her Joseph took it off a corpse on the beach. Probably the same corpse he got you from, for you were no get of theirs by the looks of you.'

'Shut your wicked mouth, Ma,' Tilda said with an outraged gasp.

Adam Scutts tutted. 'Enough of this squabbling, all of you. There's a woman lying dead upstairs. Have you got no respect? I'll sign the death certificate and send the undertaker over. Good day to you.'

When the man had gone Fanny held out her hand. 'Give that brooch to me, Joanna Rose.'

'I will not. It's mine, and I'm going to make sure my ma gets a decent burial, like she wanted.'

Swinging her wooden crutch around, Fanny dealt Joanna a blow that knocked her flat. 'You'll do what you're told, miss. I'm in charge of this household now.'

Tilda twisted the crutch aside and pushed her mother on to a chair whilst Joanna scrambled to her feet. 'No you're not, you thieving crow. Go on, Joanna. Go and sell the brooch.'

'I don't know where to go.'

'Try Richard Lind. He might buy it if you explain what's happened.'

So a few minutes later Joanna found herself crying on Richard Lind's shoulder. Awkwardly, he patted her back, then pushed her gently to arms' length and handed her his handkerchief. 'My condolences, Joanna Rose. Your mother was a nice woman.' He turned the brooch this way and that, watching the tiny stones glow in the firelight. 'You know, these stones appear to be rubies. This brooch is probably worth quite a bit of money.'

'I just need enough to give my ma a decent funeral, but don't know where to sell it except to the Barnes brothers up at the Lugger's Inn. And Ma always said they were cheats.'

'Anna will have decent funeral, because I'll lend you the money. You keep the brooch, my dear, for I've got no use for it, and it will be something to remember Anna by in the years to come.'

'I daren't take it home. Fanny Rushmore will have it off me.' She fingered the bruised flesh on her arm, wondering if her pa *had* taken it from a drowned corpse. A shudder rippled through her.

'Then leave it with me for safe keeping. I'll put it in an envelope with your name on it and keep it in my desk drawer. You can collect it any time you want it.'

'I don't know when I'll be able to pay back the loan.'

'I was considering giving you a pay rise, since you do so much more for me than you need. I could put the extra towards the debt if you like. How would that suit you, Joanna Rose?'

Overwhelmed, she threw her arms around him and hugged him tight. 'I enjoy doing extra for you because you take the trouble to talk to me about things. Even if people think you're . . . strange, I know it's caused by your illness and I'm a better person for knowing you. You're a kind man, Mr Lind. Thank you.'

Richard's eyes filled with tears then, for he'd led a lonely life, having banished himself to this cold and stony isle because his affliction had embarrassed his family. Long ago the place had been known as the Isle of the Dead, and inhabited by those considered to be insane. That was why he'd chosen it. Here he wanted for nothing except companionship. He filled his days with long walks over the rugged hills, and gazed longingly at the mainland, wishing he was walking gentler, greener hills. On colder days he sat by the fire and read his books or wrote his poetry.

There was the occasional visit from Adam Scutts or the Reverend Quinby for a game of chess, and he coached one or two children who showed promise as well as ambition. But they were few and far between. Apart from his occasional seizures, Richard kept remarkably well. His condition repelled people, though, especially the superstitious, who thought it stemmed from communication with the devil. So generally he was left alone.

Sometimes, his brother visited, bringing with him his second son, who was Richard's godson and heir. Their visits were less frequent now, because David was studying at Cambridge university.

Richard would have liked to have lived a normal life with a wife and family, but he'd been frightened of passing his falling sickness on. The company of this lovely girl meant more to him than she'd ever know, for she was the daughter he'd never had. He did his best to unobtrusively mentor her, for he found her naivety stemmed from lack of knowledge rather than lack of intelligence. He hoped her future would hold more than the lot of most of the local women. For the most part they were traditional folk who led uncomplicated lives, with no wish to experience anything else.

'Go on home now,' he said gruffly. 'Tell the undertaker to send his bill to me.'

'Thank you, sir,' she said, her eyes shining with the relief she felt.

He watched her go, then looked down at the brooch. Not come by honestly, he'd be bound. It had probably come from a corpse, he thought, then grinned, for when all was said and done, the corpse wouldn't have missed it.

*

Anna's funeral took place three days later. Several of the villagers attended, including George Rushmore and his three sons, who'd walked up the hill from Chiswell. George had a heavy grey beard now, and stooped a little, but his arms were corded with muscle. His eyes were hard and mean, and buried in a mesh of wrinkles acquired from a lifetime of squinting against the light. The Rushmores hadn't bothered to change their clothes and they stank of fish.

Richard Lind and the doctor were there. The reverend said some beautiful words over Anna's coffin, calling her a fine, upstanding woman and a good mother.

A man who'd worked with Joseph had carved her headstone free of charge. It was propped up against the wall, waiting for the grave to be filled in. *Anna Rushmore, aged 56, taken by the Lord. Beloved wife of Joseph, beloved mother of Joanna Rose. Rest in peace.*

Tilda and Joanna had laid out some food for the occasion. Both of them were unused to hosting such an event, and hung about awkwardly as the people crowded into the cottage. The taciturn Leonard Rushmore gave her a nod, then went to stand in a corner. Half a head taller than anyone else, he seemed to be keeping watch over proceedings. The mourners talked solemnly. They ate the food and washed it down with cups of thick tea. One by one they left. Leonard Rushmore left with them and strode off down towards his own cottage.

There were commiserations, too.

'She thought the world of you, my dear.'

'Anna will be watching over you from heaven.'

'You're not alone. You have your aunt and uncle to care for you now.'

Fanny, who'd been hobbling around on her crutches, sniffing and weeping all afternoon, blew her nose as the last three women were departing and said loudly, 'Aye, there was none better than Anna. My sister-in-law took me in and looked after me when I was needy. The only thing I can do for her in return is to care for her youngster.'

Wishing the Rushmore family would depart too, Joanna took Fanny to one side and said quietly, 'I don't need you to care for me. Tilda and I both have jobs as maids, and there's rent coming in from the top fields. We can work the home field between us and you can give a hand around the house from now on.'

Fanny's eyes hardened. 'Can I now, you uppity little madam. I'm crippled, or hadn't you noticed.'

'You've never let me forget it. You're lazy, too. I'm not asking you to do anything heavy, and you're not so lame that you can't sew and mend, or cook a stew from time to time.'

Giving her a hard look, Fanny shoved her aside, then went to join her son Brian. For a moment the pair whispered together, then Brian sidled over to his father and said something in his ear. Fanny and Peter were beckoned over then. Fanny smirked and fawned like the underdog she was, now George had seen fit to notice her. After a while, George glanced over to where Joanna stood with Tilda. Then he elbowed his son in the ribs and laughed.

Goosebumps crept up Joanna's back. She turned and began to clear the plates away. Tilda followed suit.

'Leave that till later,' George said. 'I've got something to say to you both.

As they turned to stare at him, Joanna slid her hand into Tilda's, for she sensed the Rushmores were up to something that would bode them no good.

'As head of the family I've made certain arrangements, Joanna. It's time you got yerself a husband, and Brian here has shown an interest in you. So from now on, he'll be courtin' you.'

'No,' Tilda shouted out. 'Joanna's only sixteen. You've got no right to marry her off to that pig. She isn't your daughter.'

'She wasn't Joseph's daughter, either. He plucked her off the beach. So if she wants to keep a roof over her head, she'll do what she's bleddy told.'

'That's a lie,' Tilda said. 'I know what you're up to you low pack of curs.'

George dealt Tilda a bruising blow across the face, causing her to stagger into a wall. 'I was with Joseph when he found her, so don't you call your own father a liar. The girl's a Kimberlin, someone bred outside the island and not of our blood. I'll swear that on the Bible in front of a magistrate, if need be. She's entitled to nothing that belonged to my brother, and that includes this cottage. As for you, Tilda, 'tis too much to say for yerself, you've got. You'll be coming home with me to look after the cottage.'

'I will not. I'm staying here with Joanna.'

'You're my daughter and you'll do what you're told. Now, go and fetch your clothes.'

'*Daughter!* When were you ever a father to me? In all these years you've never paid a farthing towards my upkeep, and neither has she.' Tilda threw a scornful glance at the smirking Fanny. 'She stole money from Anna, who meant more to me than my own folk.'

'Be that as it may, you're coming home with me. I need someone to housekeep. The place is a pigsty.'

Joanna gasped when Tilda shouted out, 'That's because pigs live there. I hate you all.'

Peter and Brian looked at each other, laughed and made oinking noises.

'As for you two,' Tilda said fiercely, 'if you lay one finger on me again, you'll wake up with an axe through your skulls. Just see if you don't.'

The argument was lost when George gave her a hard, flat stare. 'Get your things, or you'll come without them.'

Nearly in tears, Tilda quavered, 'What about my job? I'm earning good money for myself.'

'Bugger your job. It's given you ideas above your station, if you ask me. You're a fisherman's daughter, not one of the gentry. Nobody will ever wed you, you're too bleddy ugly, and you've got too much lip. Someone needs to beat it out of you.'

Clearly aggrieved, Fanny said, 'This was my idea. I should be gettin' something out of it.'

'You've got a roof over your head, haven't you, and by all accounts you've dipped your fingers into Anna's savings. It ain't the first time you've thieved from your own kin, either, you gin-soaked rat. You're nothing as far as I'm concerned, and the less I see of you the better. If you don't keep your mouth shut you'll be out of here and in the workhouse. Brian might take it into his head to throw you out when he weds the girl and moves in.'

'I might, at that,' Brian said with a high-pitched laugh. 'Joanna's going to be enough woman for one man to handle, I reckon.'

The colour drained from Joanna's face at the thought of marrying Brian Rushmore, who was gazing at her now with a new awareness in his eyes. Drawing her shawl tightly around her shoulders, she shuddered when a pink tongue circled his lips suggestively.

After that, it seemed as if Brian was always at the house in the evening, trying to touch her body or kiss her. He was well built, and she thought him repulsive with his thick lips.

Joanna was working without rest except for a few hours at night, housekeeping for Richard Lind during the day, for she needed to repay him for her ma's funeral. Fanny demanded every penny she earned, now. Once, when she refused, Brian slapped her around the head and ordered her to empty her pockets.

After work she had to clean the cottage, wash and iron the clothes and cook the meals. At the weekends she slaved in the garden, preparing the plots for vegetables and keeping the beds free of weeds. The sheep were slaughtered by Brian, the mutton sold in the pubs.

Tilda's company was sorely missed, though Joanna managed to get a note through to her and they arranged to meet now and again in the Chiswell cemetery. Tilda appeared worn out and ill used. Her face and arms were covered in bruises, her eyes dull.

Crouching behind the wall where they couldn't be seen, they hugged each other for comfort as Tilda said, 'Pa said he'll kill me if he finds out we've met. I hate him so much, Joanna. He said you're a Kimberlin, and if you keep refusing Brian he'll throw you out on the street.'

Joanna pushed Tilda's unkempt hair gently out of her eyes. 'I'd rather jump off the rocks into the race and drown myself than marry Brian.' She didn't pay much mind to what George Rushmore had said about her not being one of them. He and Fanny were trying to unsettle her, scheming to get the cottage for Brian. She would bide her time, and when she came of age she intended to ask Richard Lind to advise her.

But that was precipitated by Brian Rushmore's attack on her.

'I'll have you one of these days, and when you least expect it,' he growled, when she slapped his face, one day. 'I haven't got much patience, so you might as well give in now.'

Fanny laughed when she complained to her. She was drunk on gin most of the time now, and was selling everything she could lay her hands on to pay for it. 'If I know my boy he'll take you by force before too long. That's what his father did to me. Wait till he moves into the cottage next week.'

'He's moving in?' Joanna said in alarm.

'Didn't he tell you? He must've been planning a nice little surprise for you. If you don't like what's goin' on, you can piss off and sleep in the fields.'

She gave Fanny a glare. 'I intend to.'

'Please yerself, miss, you'll soon come creepin' back. If you don't, my Brian will find you, because you can't leave the island without somebody seeing you. And don't take nothin' with you, for everything in this cottage belongs to the Rushmores.'

Joanna's glance lit on the cradle in the corner. 'No it doesn't. That's my cradle.'

'That big old thing.' Fanny laughed. 'Take it if you think you can carry it, but it's too heavy by far. I'll have my boy chop it into pieces and it'll be fuelin' the fire by nightfall.'

She was not going to leave the cradle behind. It was part of her childhood. Her father had woven tales about it for her. *He'd said she was a princess who'd been washed ashore in it!* Anna had told her it was a daft story he'd made up. But there was the brooch, the same rose that was carved inside the cradle. Where had her ma got the brooch from? She'd always been thrifty in her ways, and wouldn't have wasted money on buying such an expensive piece of jewellery.

Taking the stairs two at a time, Joanna went into her room and bundled her clothes into a pillowcase. It took all of her strength to heft the cradle up in her arms. She staggered out of the house with it, putting it down only long enough to pick up Joseph's oilskin hat from the shed, for the two were linked in her mind.

For a moment she hesitated, wondering where to go. April had brought showers, and the rain beat softly against her head. Apart from Tilda, who had her own troubles, there was only one person she knew of who might help her.

Her arms already beginning to ache from the burden she carried, with Fanny's harsh laughter echoing in her ears, she began her trek to the house of Richard Lind, stopping every now and then to rest her aching arms.

Hands behind his head, Alexander Morcant leaned comfortably back in his chair with his feet up on his grandfather's desk.

Tobias smiled broadly at him. 'Well, Alex, does the chair pamper your arse as well as the salesman said it would?'

'It moulds it as comfortably as a whore's palms, but causes me considerably less excitement. You couldn't have chosen a better gift for my birthday.'

Tobias laughed, because the young man had reacted as predictably as he'd thought he would. 'You've educated yourself long enough and have earned it. I'm proud of you, Alex, and so would your father be if he was here to see it.'

Alex's smile faded and the light fled from his eyes. Robbed of their lustre the black orbs became flat and impenetrable. 'My grandfather didn't show much interest when I told him.'

'You'll have to allow him some slack, Alex. He's in his mid-eighties now, though God knows how he's managed to last this long after his illness.'

'Sheer cussedness, I expect.'

Tobias chuckled. 'You could be right, but allowing a young lion to step into his den is not the easiest of things for the leader of the pack. You have to remember, Elijah Morcant is the surviving company founder.'

'I had the feeling it was more than that.' Alex stood and crossed to the window, staring down over the familiar view. The river was a metallic ribbon filled with swaying masts. 'Grandfather gave me the deeds to a house on Vauxhall Road this morning. He told me to get myself a woman and raise a houseful of kids. He said that family and blood ties mean everything, that it gives a man reason to live.'

Tobias nodded. 'A generous gift, indeed. And sound advice.'

'Yes.' Alex turned, his face puzzled. 'I'm wondering if I should accept the house. My brother Oliver has never received anything so expensive, and I don't want it to appear as though I'm taking advantage of an old man's generosity. I feel uneasy about it.'

So did Tobias. Elijah Morcant was well known for the tight grip he kept on his wallet. He shrugged the feeling away. 'If I were you I'd take advantage of his departure from his miserly ways. I'll be taking a glass of sherry with him later on this afternoon and, of course, I'll be at the dinner tonight. It's lucky your mother and her girls are visiting at this time. The *Clara Jane* has docked, too, so Oliver will be able to join us. It's been a long time since we were all together.'

'Will you tell my grandfather about the new clipper on order?'

'Oh, aye. After the tongue lashing I got over the *Charlotte May* and the *Clara Jane* I daren't keep it to myself. He'll have to admit, though, those ships have paid for themselves over and over again.'

'Can I see the designer's blueprint?'

'It's in the cupboard.'

Alex unrolled the plan out on the desk, securing the corners with books to keep it flat. His smile became all admiration as he studied it. 'If it's possible to fall in love with a ship, I just have, even though I think steam is the way of the future. Jesus, look at her lines. Now, that's what I call a ship. Two hundred and eighty feet long, three masted and with six sails to a mast. She'll fly over the water like a gull on the wind. What shall we name her?'

Tobias hesitated. He'd almost decided to call her Honor Rose, after his dead wife and daughter, for the other two had been named after his own mother and Alexander and Oliver's mother, and the family was short on females.

But to name this fine ship after those who'd lost their lives in a company ship seemed to be tempting fate. He rarely thought of his late wife and infant now. Sometimes he felt guilty for forgetting them and vowed to visit their graves. Alex went to Portland every once in a while to pay his respects to his father, but Tobias had never gone back.

Now Alex was a grown man who'd excelled at his studies. His future was assured with the company. He was a personable young man with healthy appetites, who might marry young. If that happened during the next year or so, the new clipper could be named after his wife.

Tobias had increasingly felt the urge for female companionship himself. Not the well-handled flesh of some slut, but a decent woman, one to warm his bed and bear him a child or two. He was only thirty-eight, after all, and had a large house that was practically unoccupied, excepting when his mother, Charlotte, was in town. Although energetic and upright, Charlotte was nearing fifty-eight now and usually lived in her own house in Poole, where the company had been formed and where Tobias had grown up.

'The shipyard hasn't even laid her keel down yet, so I'd like to leave the naming of her until nearer her launch time, if you wouldn't mind. In the meantime, you can train the new lad in the use of the telegraph. Hopefully, he can spell. And, by the way, the engineers are coming to install a flushing sanitary closet in the basement. Keep an eye on them.'

'I don't know anything about flushing sanitary closets.'

'You have engineering qualifications, don't you? Pick the brain of the sanitation engineer. Someone will need to learn the concept of how the valves of the Bramha work, especially since I'm having a couple of them installed in my home. I'll be able to call you out to repair it, free of charge, then.' Strolling through to his own office, Tobias plucked his hat from the stand, placed it on his head and smiled expansively at Alex, who'd followed after him, saying suspiciously, 'Where are you off to?'

'To enjoy a well-earned rest. The running of the company is entirely in your hands, Mr Morcant.'

'You bastard, Tobias. You're dropping me in the deep end?'

'Of course I am. If you think you're going to spend the day with your arse in the chair and your feet on the desk, you can think again. If you need me, I'll be lunching with Oliver on board the *Clara Jane*, and will be with your grandfather later in the afternoon.'

Alex had a big grin on his face now. 'Bugger off then, Tobias. I guess I don't need you breathing down my neck, after all.'

It will be nice to have a couple of weeks off, Tobias thought, whistling happily to himself as he strolled through the outer office.

His head clerk waved a sheaf of papers at him. 'Mr Darsham! You need to check and sign this cargo manifest before the *Nightingale* can sail.'

Tobias speeded up his pace. 'I'm afraid I haven't got time, Henry. Mr Morcant is in his office, though, and I think he's had enough education to be able to pen his name. Give him his schedule for the day, too, I forgot to tell him he had to actually work.'

Henry chuckled as the door closed gently behind him.

Oliver Morcant was a personable and dependable young man with a calm manner, who favoured his deceased father. He and Tobias had a pleasant lunch, then discussed voyages and the foibles of the *Clara Jane*.

Oliver said, 'I swear she could go into Boston Harbour with nobody at the helm. Sometimes I'm tempted to try it.'

Tobias raised an eyebrow. 'I had no idea you had

such frivolous notions inside you. I'd be most obliged if you didn't let the underwriters hear that, Oliver. By the way, Alex started work in the office today, so you'll have him to answer to now, as well as me.'

Oliver grinned. 'One of these days I might arrange things so he can gain some practical experience of what the company is all about. He needs to get some sea time in.'

'Not until I've enjoyed a couple of weeks' rest, you won't.'

Later in the day, Tobias found Grandfather Morcant in the drawing room. He was seated in the wing chair looking out over the garden, a blanket wrapped around his knees.

The butler poured them a sherry each as Tobias spread the parting in his coat and seated himself opposite the old man. Elijah Morcant's watery eyes were sunk into loose sockets and the flesh of his purple-veined face appeared to be melting over his skull. His nose was a sharp curve in the middle of it. Sparse tufts of grey hair stuck out like feathers from behind his ears. In fact, he looked like the battle-scarred old eagle that he was.

'How are you, Elijah?'

'I should be dead,' the old man said, his slur pronounced today. 'My legs are too weak to hold me up, I piss in my pants and I dribble down my front like an infant. If I had the strength to kill myself, I would.'

'Ah, I see you're in a good mood. Alex started work at the office today.'

'Aye, he told me. It's about time that lad did

something to earn his keep. He *can* earn his keep, can't he?'

'He's an extremely competent young man.'

'Good, then make sure his salary is commensurate with his skills, for we'll not want to lose him.' The old man sighed heavily. 'It's Alex I wanted to talk to you about.'

Tobias was puzzled. 'You don't have to worry about him. He's a fine young man who will do the Morcant family and the company proud. Since he's family, there's no reason why he should go elsewhere.'

'That's the whole trouble, Tobias. Alexander is *not* a Morcant.'

Blood rushed to Tobias's face. 'I'd heard whispers to that effect over the years, but surely they're not true.'

'I've suspected it for a long time and I charged Clara with it today. She laughed in my face and said it was perfectly true. She mocked me. She said she'd had an affair on and off over several years with a Frenchman she'd met at a ball, and at the same time was bedding the son of an aristocrat.'

Shocked, Tobias stared at him. 'And she doesn't care?'

'Why should she? She got what she wanted. Her banker husband has died and she's worth a fortune now. She doesn't need our money any more and, in fact, could buy us out several times over.'

The old man took a sip from his sherry, his hands trembling. 'I went through it with my attorney this morning. You do realize what this means, don't you?'

Tobias was very much afraid that he did. No wonder

94

grandfather Morcant had given Alexander such a generous gift. The young man had been cut from his will.

He tried. 'Lucian knew about this, I understand. It made no difference to him. He still wanted his share of the company to be divided between Oliver and Alexander.'

'Lucian had no share to divide whilst I was still alive. You inherited your father's share outright, and have the controlling interest in the company.'

'I've always been fair and honest in my dealings with the Morcants.'

'I know you have, Tobias, and, although we've had arguments, the company has gone from strength to strength. That's why I'm informing you of what to expect when I die. Don't think my heart isn't heavy over this, for I love the boy, I always have. But blood is blood, and Oliver is entitled to inherit his Morcant birthright intact. That means this house and his proper share of the company. I want you to tell Alex that. You've been a good friend to him over the years and he holds a great deal of respect for you.'

It was with a heavy heart that Tobias prepared to depart two hours later. Clara was in the hall and she came to lay a hand on his arm after he'd donned his topcoat. 'The old man's told you, hasn't he?'

'Yes.' He gazed down at her hand, at the fingers richly adorned with glittering rings. It was a hand that had never felt hard work. Her gown was a flounce of blue taffeta with a pretty lace overskirt. In her early fifties, her face was almost unlined. Clara had been sixteen when she'd married Lucian. 'Why did you tell him, Clara?'

'He already knew.'

'He only guessed. If you'd denied it he would have believed you, for he thinks the world of Alex.'

She shrugged. 'You know what the old man's like. He goaded me into it and called me a bloodsucking leech.' *A good name for her.* 'What's he going to do about it?'

'He's already done it. Alex has been cut from his will.'

'Oh God!' She drew in a deep breath. 'Oliver stands to inherit it all, then. Does Alex know yet?'

'Unfortunately, it's my unsavoury task to tell him.'

'Poor Tobias, everything always falls to you. You'll manage perfectly well, no doubt. What would we do without you?'

'Will you give me the name of his father, in case he asks?'

'Dear me, no.' Her eyes shifted away from his and her voice became vague. 'The man was a diplomat, and he's dead and gone.'

Tobias had the feeling she was unsure about who had fathered Alex. 'Did Lucian know about this?'

'It was such a nuisance having to resume a relationship with Lucian, for he was never entirely comfortable in the role of husband and considered his relationship with me his duty. But I had to account for the arrival of Alex somehow. Lucian may have suspected, but he never mentioned it to me and he accepted Alex as his own, since it reinforced his manliness. He and Alex got on extremely well when he was home. But, then, Lucian always did show affection towards good-looking boys.'

'Shut your filthy mouth, Clara. That's just not true.'

'He never showed that side of himself to you?' She shrugged and gave a slightly unbelieving smile. 'I'm surprised. I always thought that you and he were . . . well, *close*. You certainly preferred him to me, unusual in a male of the age you were then, I thought, since they usually can't wait to experience life.'

Affronted, he glared hard at her, hating her sneering mouth. 'You do realize you've withdrawn every expectation Alex ever had. Isn't that enough? Do you also have to smear the reputation of someone he always looked up to and loved?'

She reached up to pat his cheek, saying lightly, 'Not everything, Tobias. Alex still has you. I'm just surprised that Lucian didn't. I won't tell Alex if you don't.'

Jerking his head to one side, Tobias stormed from the house before he lost his reason and thumped her.

6

It was the measure of the man that Alex took the news so calmly, Tobias thought, though his face was stricken.

'I'm so sorry, Alex. I had no idea this was about to happen.'

'Damn them all, why wasn't I told sooner? And why didn't the old man tell me himself?'

'Elijah has only just discovered the truth, and the stuffing has been knocked out of him.'

'And he took my mother's word for it. That's what hurts me the most, Tobias. I've often wondered at my lack of resemblance to the Morcant side of the family. But nothing can rob me of the years of respect and affection I hold for the man I regarded as my father.'

Clara probably could if she applied herself to it, but Tobias wasn't about to add that vicious snippet to the pot.

'I'm grateful you're taking it so well, Alexander. This task is not to my liking.'

'Why did my mother do this to me . . . to us?'

'Mischief, I believe. She and Grandfather Morcant have never liked each other. Elijah charged her with a suspicion he'd always held. Clara blurted it out in the heat of the moment to get back at him and without giving a thought to how it might affect your future. All she needed to have done was deny it. That would have satisfied Elijah, for he wanted to believe it was lies. Whatever else is happening the old man has always thought highly of you. I believe he'll continue to do so.'

'Under the circumstances that's cold comfort. My mother must have entertained the man under his roof when my father was at sea.'

An observation that had already occured to Tobias. 'Surely not. People are usually more discreet in such liaisons.'

'When I was small I remember a particular man she used to entertain at the house. Did she say who fathered me?'

Such a seemingly casual question under the circumstances, but Tobias wasn't about to be fooled by it. 'She didn't name anyone.'

Alexander gave a slightly derisive smile as his glance came up to join with that of Tobias. 'Of course she didn't, but I'd wager it was that French diplomat, Louis Bernier.'

Startled, Tobias blurted out, 'You remember him?'

'Distinctly, for he had an odd accent and used to bring me gifts and sit me on his knee. One day he simply stopped coming. Has Oliver been told?'

'If he has, he didn't mention it when I saw him earlier.'

Alexander reached for his coat. 'I'd like to tell him

myself. You won't mind if I take the rest of the afternoon off? Not a good start to my career, I know.' He stared at Tobias, struck by a sudden thought. 'Now there's something. What am I to this company now? Certainly not the heir apparent.'

'Will the title of assistant managing director, suit you?'

'I'll be proud to work under you, Tobias.'

'As far as I'm concerned, we'll be on an equal footing. Don't do anything silly, will you, Alex? I need you.'

'Like place a pistol to my temple and blow my brains out? My life is worth more than that to me. I'm sorry you had to be the one to tell me this. It can't have been an easy task.'

'It wasn't. God, Alex,' Tobias said, his gruff voice hiding the deep affection he held for him, 'I wish I'd been the one to father you. I'd love to have a son like you.'

'That means you would have been about twelve years old at the time of my conception. Besides which, you've never been comfortable with my mother, nor she with you. You see right through her and she knows it. As for her, she has as much warmth as a two-day-old corpse,' he said bitterly. He headed for the door. 'I'll see you at my birthday dinner.'

'You're still going?'

'Of course. I'm a mature and civilized man, and since everyone will want to know how I reacted to the news, I don't want to disappoint them. The head of the household will expect my humble thanks for his generous gesture as he cuts the umbilical cord.' He gave a mirthless grin. 'And I'll enjoy seeing my mother squirm a little while the great man taunts her.'

Tobias suddenly grinned. 'Aye, It'll be quite a show, I expect, and I'll be proud to sit right next to you whilst you tell them exactly how grateful you are.'

'Thanks, Tobias. I know I can count on your support in everything I do.' For a moment Alex looked troubled, then he said, 'If it's any consolation, I wish you'd fathered me, too.'

Tears pricked Tobias's eyes as the door swung shut behind Alex. He'd never been more proud of him than he was at that moment.

'One thing that needs to be settled,' Alexander said to Elijah Morcant at the table that night. 'Am I entitled to use the Morcant name, or would you prefer I didn't?'

Napkin tucked under chin, Elijah gazed hard at him. 'Have I suggested otherwise, boy? This is to be kept within the family unless we want a scandal. That's if your mother can keep her mouth shut longer than her legs.'

His mother's mouth tightened into a thin line as her eyes skewered into Elijah, but she said nothing. He'd have to do better than this. 'But it's not up to you, is it, sir? You see, having suddenly been told I'm no longer a Morcant, and disinherited as a result, I rather feel that I have the freedom to choose my own name.' He slid a glance towards his mother. 'Perhaps I should use the name of my father. What was it, Mother? Bernier?'

Clara uttered a tiny gasp. 'You're making a fool of yourself, Alexander.'

'A bigger one than you've already made of me? I think not.' He smiled at his twelve-year-old twin half-sisters,

Lydia and Irene Nash, wondering if they should be listening to this. They were pretty creatures with pretty manners. Ringleted and dressed in silk and lace, they were spoiled by their nurserymaid, who danced to their every whim. Running true to form, Clara took very little notice of them, unless it was to chide. He was surprised Clara had risked bringing them to England at all, considering that London was in the middle of a cholera outbreak.

'Alex, I don't think this occasion is the right time to bring this up, since we're supposed to be celebrating your birthday.' Oliver's glance circled apologetically around the table. 'My pardon, I allowed him to have too much to drink.'

'*Allowed me?* Oliver, may I remind you that I'm old enough to make my own decisions. Actually, I've just had liquor enough to soften the edge of our mother's betrayal of me. Since we all know what has gone on, I see no reason to sweep it under the table.'

'I've had enough!' Elijah shouted, spittle spraying from his mouth. 'Do what you like about your damned name, boy. Call yourself Alexander Horseshit for all I care. I've given you a house to live in and a position in the company, be grateful for that, or go to hell!'

Alexander's chair tipped over with a crash as he dislodged himself from the table and strode to where Elijah sat. Drawing the house deeds from his pocket he dropped them in the old man's soup. 'This is what I think of your house. As for the position in the company, as far as I'm concerned I work for Tobias Darsham, not for you.' He strode off, banging the door behind him.

'Oh dear.' Charlotte Darsham gazed anxiously at Tobias. 'Shouldn't someone go after him?'

Tobias smiled reassuringly at her. 'Like Alex said, Mother, he's old enough to look after himself. We all know he's not as stupid as he just looked and sounded. Personally, I'm as proud as hell of what he's done. He has the right to have his say.'

Elijah cackled. 'So am I. I wish he *was* a Morcant, since the young cub is the only one of you – excepting for Tobias Darsham there, who happens to be a chip off his father's block – who has ever stood up to me, and he's as stroppy as a viper on occasion.'

Tobias raised his glass to him. 'Happy birthday to Alex then. I think it's one that he'll never forget.'

Elijah raised his glass, but his hand began to shake and he dropped it into his lap. Tobias leaped from his chair and crossed swiftly to where the old man sat. Elijah's eyes were bulging and he was perspiring heavily and clutching at his chest. Lips blue tinged, his breath came in gasps as he tried to suck in air.

'Go and fetch his doctor,' Tobias shouted at the hovering servant, bending his ear to the old man's mouth to try and catch what he was saying.

'Tell Alex . . .' He didn't finish, and there was a sudden and terrible silence as Elijah's head lolled sideways.

The doctor arrived too late, for Elijah was past saving now.

Dawn was breaking when Alexander was nudged awake. Cramped and creased from a night spent in the office chair, his head aching from the drink he'd consumed, he stretched, groaned, then offered Tobias a wryly apologetic glance.

The cup of thick coffee Tobias offered him was nectar from the gods. As he gulped it down, Tobias informed him of the demise of Elijah Morcant.

Stricken, Alex gazed at him. 'This was all my fault.'

'You mustn't blame yourself. He was an old man with a bad heart. There's a barber just around the corner. Get yourself a shave then go home, change into suitable dress and come back before the staff arrive. We are now a company in mourning for one of its founders.'

He dropped the deeds to the Vauxhall Road house on to the desk and set a bunch of keys on top of it. 'I've had your clothes sent around to your house, and one of my servants will be waiting there for you.'

Alex stared at the soup-stained paper and said sullenly, 'This is conscience money. I don't want anything from him.'

'Elijah Morcant didn't have a conscience. Before he died he told me to tell you that he's always loved you, and is expecting great things from you.'

'Like hell, he did! You're lying, Tobias.'

'Stop sulking! Take the deed before I cram it into your mouth and make you eat the damned thing. And take this to go with it.' Tobias drew back his fist and punched him in the midriff.

Alexander doubled over, retching for air. 'What the hell was that for?' he gasped as his muscles slowly relaxed.

'First for calling me a liar, second for indulging in self-pity and third for being such a sodding nuisance. You're a director of this company. As such, you need to present yourself with some dignity. What's more, Alex, you answer to me. Either you can accept that, or you can't. If you can't, leave the deeds on the desk, then get out and don't come back.'

'You'd throw me out after all that time you've spent training me for the position?'

Tobias nodded. 'Just you try me.'

They locked eyes, Alexander's dark and passionate against the cold, flinty surface of Tobias's.

It dawned on Alexander that he was being stupid. A Morcant by blood he wasn't, but nobody was about to eject him from the family. The man he'd always thought of as his grandfather had compensated him for his disappointment in the best way he knew how: with property.

His brother Oliver, who, as Alexander had suddenly discovered, could drink him under the table if need be, had told him that blood didn't matter a damn to him and he was proud to be his brother. Oliver measured a man by his qualities, he'd said.

Tobias, always his friend and mentor, had put the situation before him reluctantly, but in straightforward manner. He'd expect him to take it on the chin.

The steam suddenly went out of him. 'Hell! I believe you damned well would, too! You must be insane. You couldn't find anyone better qualified than I am.' Pocketing the deeds, Alexander picked up the keys and slouched off towards the door.

Tobias grinned as the door swung gently shut behind him. 'That's more like it.'

*

In the eighteen months she'd lived in Richard Lind's house, Joanna had been contented with her lot.

The only problems she had were Tilda's plight and the unwanted attention of Brian and Peter Rushmore, both of whom would lie in wait for her as she went about her business, with taunts of Kimberlin and princess. She avoided the pair as much as possible, never placing herself in the position of being alone with either, or both, of them.

She was aided in this by Richard Lind, who found a telescope in one of his trunks, which he set up in the attic room. It offered a fine view of the harbour and the bridge traffic. 'Now you'll know when the lerrets put to sea,' he said with a smile. 'And you can watch the fine folk from Weymouth come and go. The island is changing, Joanna Rose.'

'The change can't come quickly enough for me.'

'You don't have to stay on the island for the rest of your life, you know. There's a big wide world out there.'

'I'm scared of going, for they'd find some way of bringing me back. I might not be able to earn enough to eat. 'Sides, I wouldn't go anywhere without Tilda.'

'Ah yes, poor Tilda.'

Being able to spy on the lerrets through the telescope eased her tension slightly, but her worry about Tilda continued. Her friend was too thin, her bones pushed against her skin like sticks and her eyes were devoid of hope. Hair matted and lank, Tilda displayed signs of abuse, too. There were bruises on her arms and face.

'Oh, Tilda,' Joanna murmured, weeping as she held

her friend tight one day. 'What are they doing to you?'

'I'm too shamed to say. I swear, one of these days I'll run away. I had to warn you, though, I think my pa knows we're meeting. He locked me in my room this morning. I had to climb on the lean-to to get out. I only hope I can get back in again. Some of the fishermen's wives were outside the inn mending nets, including my brother Leonard's wife, so someone's bound to tell him.'

Joanna took some bread and cheese from her pocket. They sat behind the low stone wall of the cemetery out of the October wind, to eat and talk as the seagulls wheeled overhead. 'I've been thinking,' Joanna said, watching Tilda wolf hers down. 'Perhaps we should leave the island and get ourselves a job on the mainland.'

Hope sparked in Tilda's eyes, then they dulled again. 'You're only seventeen. Pa would send the boys after us.'

'I'm eighteen next month and old enough to be married to his son in his eyes, so I'm certainly old enough to fend for myself. After all, I'm doing so now.'

'I wish someone nice would offer to wed me, but I'm too ugly.'

'Oh, Tilda, some of those fine folk are worse looking than you. 'Tis because you're dressed in dirt and rags. You looked better when you lived with my ma. That Sammy Boulter took a fancy to you when you were eighteen, remember? He had a nice house and a steady business as an undertaker.'

'A randy old sod, he was, and twenty years older than me. He wed Hannah Rogers in the end, and her only sixteen at the time. He's given her three cheils already and she has another one in the pod.'

'Better to marry someone with a bit of cash behind them, even if they're older. I'd marry Richard Lind if he'd ask me.'

'Joanna, you wouldn't. What about his turns?'

'What about them? All that happens is that he falls over and jerks about, like this.' Lying on her back, Joanna stiffened her body and began to jerk, sending saliva bubbling from the corner of her mouth.'

Tilda began to laugh.

Joanna grinned as she opened her eyes and wiped her mouth on her apron. 'Sometimes he shouts and moans, as well, then he sleeps for a bit before he wakes up, perfectly normal again. Dr Scutts says that all I have to do is move things out of his way and make sure he doesn't hurt himself. I can always call on the reverend or himself if need be. Mr Lind is a kind man, almost like a father to me. He doesn't give my wages to George Rushmore now, even though your pa came up and demanded them once. And he teaches me all sorts of things. If I married him, at least I'd always have food in my belly and a roof over my head. I might suggest it to him.'

'Perhaps I'll ask him to marry me as well then, I could do with a good feed,' Tilda said, and though they both laughed at the thought there was no merriment in it.

Joanna handed Tilda her bread and cheese. 'Can you eat this or shall I feed it to the gulls? I'm not really hungry, I had something before I came out.'

Even knowing Joanna had lied to her, Tilda ate the extra food, for she didn't know when her next meal would be. She wasn't allowed to eat until her father and brothers had taken their portion, and usually that portion was her share as well.

After she finished, she bobbed her head up over the wall to look at the sea, squinting her eyes against the glare, for it shone like polished pewter in the sunlight. 'Damn, they're coming back early. I'll have to be quick.' Tilda scrambled to her feet, alarm evident in her eyes, then was gone, over the wall and down the hill. 'See you next week, Joanna,' she shouted out as she stopped to wave.

But Tilda wasn't there next week, nor for the two weeks after that.

Almost frantic with worry, Joanna asked Adam Scutts, 'Have you seen Tilda? Is she well?'

'Aye, I've seen her. She's had a fall and has broken a couple of ribs, though what she was doing climbing into her bedroom from the lean-to is beyond my reasoning. She was lucky she didn't break her neck. She'll be all right in a week or two.'

'I expect her pa had locked her in.'

The doctor nodded and said nothing more, for the young woman had been covered in welts, and the bruising on her body indicated she'd been subject to sexual abuse, too. But unless a formal complaint was made he could do nothing, and crimes of this nature were rarely reported. Tilda Rushmore had burst into tears and had refused to testify against her family. She'd made him promise not to tell Joanna.

Although Joanna went to the cemetery week after week, Tilda still didn't appear. The year had been a wet one, and November was no exception.

A couple of days after Joanna's eighteenth birthday the weather cleared. Through the telescope she watched the lerrets set out for the fishing grounds, then she headed for the cemetery, as usual. It was a cold, grey day, the wind was a persistent, icy breath. Mainland visitors and islanders alike were scarce as they stayed snugged down by their firesides. Today there was only one solitary man trudging up the hill from the harbour, huddled into his coat collar.

Joanna didn't recognize him as anyone she knew. Hugging herself into her shawl, she jammed her pa's old oilskin hat on her head, to keep her ears warm.

It came as a shock to find their usual meeting place behind the cemetery wall occupied.

'Waiting for Tilda, are you?' Brian Rushmore sneered. 'Well, she ain't coming.' His hand shot out to prevent her sudden departure, closing around her upper arm with bruising force. 'I'm glad you came, Joanna Rose, very glad. You and I need to have a little talk.'

He jerked her forward as she tried to struggle free. 'Oh no you don't. My pa thinks it's about time you and I settled things. So I brought you a little present.'

Joanna gazed wildly about her, hearing only the hiss of the wind as it flattened the ankle-high grass before it. The grass was tough, it would spring back easily. She was just as resilient, she told herself. Whatever Brian Rushmore did to her, she'd come back stronger. She wouldn't marry him under any circumstances. She'd see him in hell first!

'I don't want your present,' she threw at him. 'Let me go, else I'll scream.'

'And who d'ya think is goin' to hear you? Folks are in front of their fires, cosy and warm. By Christ, 'tis a cold day, though I'll soon get us warmed up.'

Despite her struggles she was pulled on to his lap and his mouth closed over hers. She bit his foul-smelling tongue and tasted blood.

'You bitch!' Blood dripping from his chin he slapped her viciously back and forth across her face.

As she screamed, he pulled his boning knife from his belt, pressed the point against her throat and yelled, 'Shut the hell up, else I'll slit your damned throat open like the belly of a fish.'

Her scream strangled in her throat. The knife moved down her bodice, its finely honed blade cutting through the cotton attaching the buttons to the material. Her breasts sprang free, goose-pimpling in the cold. 'Now there's a lovely pair of tits,' he muttered, roughly handling them. 'Better by far than skinny old Tilda's.'

'Let me go,' she whimpered.

'Aye, in just a little while, girl, for your strugglin' has got me all roused up and I've gotta get rid of the load.' He threw the knife to one side and loosened his trousers. 'Lift your skirt and open your legs.'

She brought her knee up, but he was ready for it. 'I was hoping you'd come easier than this, Joanna Rose. Still, a little bit of force always adds spice to the ways of courtin'.' Keeping a hand against her chest he dragged her skirt up over her hips and fumbled between her legs. 'Lovely, that little pie is, and I'm the first,' he gloated, 'though I might let Peter have a taste once you be broken in. Look at me, now, I'm as big as a post and you be nice and juicy. I'll slide in real neat, you'll see.' She began to struggle and scream, trying to squeeze her thighs together as he relentlessly pushed them apart with his knee, grunting like a pig all the time.

'No,' she screamed, 'I hate you.' As he tried to jerk the oilskin hat down over her face to muffle her voice, her flailing hand encountered metal and closed around it. *The boning knife!* Grabbing it up she was about to plunge it into him when it was wrested from her fingers. At the same time an arm snaked around Brian's neck and jerked him backwards. There came the sound of a fist landing, the crack of a bone and an agonized scream.

Scrambling backwards Joanna clutched her bodice together with one hand and pulled her skirt down. She slid her hat up far enough to see from under the brim that Brian's nose was streaming blood. He was cursing fit to bust as he gazed up at her rescuer.

'I'll get you for this,' he snarled.

'You can try.' The man kicked Brian in the rear as he turned to go, sending him stumbling. He watched him leave, then turned and gazed at her through eyes as grey as the sea. 'I'm Tobias Darsham.'

Remembering her manners, Joanna held out a hand to him, careful to keep her shawl pulled tightly around her nakedness, for she didn't want to inflame the passion of her rescuer, as well. 'I'm Joanna Rushmore. Thank you for helping me.'

'Who was the man attacking you?'

'My cousin, Brian Rushmore. He wants me to become his wife, but I won't. He thought that if he used force . . .' Joanna felt her face heat up. 'I won't marry him, whatever he does. I'd rather kill him first, for to marry a Rushmore will mean a life of hell.'

There was a movement and Brian's knife appeared in her rescuer's hand. 'You *would* have killed him if I hadn't stopped you.'

'It's his knife. He held it against my throat to stop me yelling.' Reaction set in then. Her face draining of colour, she began to tremble all over. She turned away from him, retching into the grass. Waiting until she'd finished, he handed her his handkerchief, then removed his coat and set it about her shoulders. 'Where do you live? I'll escort you home.'

Remembering Tilda, Joanna began to cry, her shoulders heaving. Her legs hardly had the strength to place one foot in front of the other as they made their way to the house of Richard Lind.

'What's happened?' Richard cried out as he opened the door and ushered them inside.

'The girl was attacked by her cousin. I think she's just shaken up. Are you her father?'

'Dear me, no. I'm Richard Lind, her employer.' He poured a small glass of brandy and held it to her lips. 'Drink this down, Joanna, my dear. It will do you good.'

''Tis usually me who looks after you.' She began to cough and splutter as she swallowed it, but the warmth spread down her body into her toes.

The two men smiled as she sucked in a deep, gasping breath. Richard held out his hand to Tobias. 'May I ask who you are, sir?'

'Tobias Darsham of the Darsham and Morcant Shipping Company.'

'What an odd coincidence. My second cousin Charlotte married a John Darsham, who was a master mariner with his own ship. Unfortunately, I couldn't go to the wedding, and I haven't seen Charlotte since I was a child. I rarely leave the island.'

'That would be my mother and father, sir. My mother lives in Poole and has been widowed for many years. So, it seems as though we are related somewhere along the way.'

'Excuse me,' Joanna said, feeling quite light-headed from the brandy and unable to stop smiling. 'I must go and tidy myself up.'

'Perhaps Mr Darsham would care to stay and have refreshment with us. I'm sure you would like to thank him properly, and what better a way than that delicious looking cake you left to cool when you went out,' suggested Richard.

She beamed a smile at them both from under the brim of her hat. 'Please do, Mr Darsham. Mr Lind enjoys having visitors. Call me if you need me, Mr Lind.'

Going to her room she pinned her bodice together with her rose brooch, then pulled a clean apron on. The bib hid the rents where the buttons had been. She would repair the bodice later, when she had more time. Brushing her hair, she grimaced at the fine, curling tendrils that instantly coiled from it, then fashioned its length into a braid and tied a piece of plaited wool around the bottom.

She gazed dreamily at herself in the rust-spotted mirror. Tobias Darsham seemed to be a gentleman, and handsome for his age. It had been brave of him to rescue her from her cousin. She hoped he would come again now he knew he was related to Richard Lind.

'Your maid seems to be a nice girl,' Tobias was saying to Richard.

'I don't look upon Joanna as my servant. She's intelligent, has an enquiring mind and a quick wit, which is disconcerting sometimes. I like the girl. She deserves better than what life has dealt her.'

'Her folks don't mind her living here with you?'

'Her parents were good people but they are dead now. Her extended family are a liability, though.'

'If the man who attacked her is an example, I know exactly what you mean. Why was Joanna in the cemetery?'

'There's a female cousin she's very attached to, for they grew up together. Joanna secretly meets her there sometimes. The girl is worried about her at the moment. There's been no sight of Tilda for several weeks, and her kin are a bad lot. And you, why were you in the graveyard?'

'My wife and infant are buried there. They were drowned in the storms of 1838.'

'I'm sorry. That must have been hard.'

'It was a long time ago. I've never remarried, but I must confess I've been thinking about it recently. I have a large house and sometimes I'm lonely.'

'Ah, I know the feeling only too well.'

Tobias brought the conversation back to Joanna. 'Your young . . . *companion* seems to have good reason to be worried about her female cousin, since the secret meeting place is no longer a secret. Why doesn't the girl just knock on the door and ask for this Tilda?'

'You only met one of the Rushmores. There are others like him. And in case you think there is anything untoward about my relationship with Joanna, our companionship is of a completely innocent nature. She housekeeps for me. In return, I pay her a wage and educate her, for she has a thirsty mind. That in itself gives me pleasure.'

Tobias didn't bother to deny he'd been wondering. They both turned their heads as Joanna came through the door carrying a tray, which she placed on the buffet.

Puzzled, Tobias stared at her. Without the oilskin hat hiding her face she was exquisite to look at. An oval face supported high cheekbones, and was framed by dark hair. Her pale translucent skin was as flawless as porcelain and her eyes were the colour of hyacinths.

Tobias realized he'd stared too long when she coloured. 'My pardon, Miss Rushmore,' he stammered. 'I have the feeling we've met each other before. Have you been to London recently?'

'I've never been to London at all. Lordy, no, for I've heard 'tis a wicked place.' She gazed at Richard Lind and grinned. 'Mr Lind has been making me practise my manners in case Her Majesty Queen Victoria ever invites me to take tea with her, though.'

Richard laughed. 'Joanna has never even been across the bridge to Weymouth, but she could probably tell you quite a lot about London.'

As the afternoon progressed Tobias grew more and more attracted to the young girl, and Richard Lind seemed to encourage it. It was late when Joanna went to bed.

'She's an entirely delightful creature,' Tobias said, as he and Richard settled down in front of the fire with a bottle of brandy between them.

Soon, there were no secrets between them, as confidences were exchanged.

'You know,' Richard said thoughtfully, 'if you're really thinking of taking a wife, you should marry Joanna Rushmore. She's a bit rough around the edges, but she's young enough for it to be educated out of her.'

'Since your illness doesn't bother her, why don't you marry her yourself, Richard?'

Richard gazed into his glass. 'Because, my dear friend, I'm unable to function as a husband now, and, even if I could, I wouldn't risk passing on my illness to any offspring I might have. Take her away from here, Tobias. Give the girl a better life, I can see you're attracted to her.'

Giving in to impulse, Tobias said, 'Who wouldn't be? Do you think she'd have someone of my age?'

'Joanna likes you, and she has a sensible head on her shoulders. She will not be looking for love, but will marry to better herself if she thinks her husband will be kind to her. She's young, too, so will probably provide you with half a dozen healthy children to replace the one you lost.'

A rather attractive proposition that lent credence to his impulse to wed.

'I'll write her a note before I leave. Perhaps you'd give it to her, and talk to her. I'll be back with a licence and, if she's agreeable, we can wed.'

'Do it quickly then, Tobias, whilst you still can, for the predators are becoming bolder and are closing in for the kill. Unfortunately, I haven't got the strength to hold them off.'

7

Tobias Rushmore had returned to Portland within a week, bringing with him a special marriage licence issued by a bishop, and a large box, which he handed to Joanna.

Inside was a skirt and matching jacket of dark blue velvet to wear over a cream blouse with little pearl buttons and a lace collar. There was a velvet bonnet, too, trimmed prettily with flowers.

She stroked her fingers over the velvet. 'This is so pretty, Mr Darsham. Thank you. I've never owned anything so nice.'

'It's very plain, but it was the best I could buy at short notice, and at least you will be warm. He took her hands in his. 'If we are to be married, Joanna, you must call me Tobias.'

Head slanted to one side, she gazed at him, filled with alarm, for, being young, she'd planned her whole future around him in the days they'd been apart. 'If? Do you wish to change your mind?'

He smiled. 'Have I given you cause to imagine so?'

'You've been most kind.'

'Actually, you haven't answered my proposal of marriage yet. Do you want to be wed to me, Joanna? If not, you must say so.'

For a moment she gazed at him without saying anything. Before her, she saw a man of about forty years, a man of upright bearing with only a few threads of grey in his hair. His eyes were a clear grey, and although they contained a core of hardness they had an honesty to them. Instinctively, she knew she could trust Tobias Darsham. And she liked him more than she'd ever liked any man, except for her pa and Richard Lind.

'I don't think I could find anyone better, Mr, uh . . . Tobias. There is one thing I'd like to ask of you, though. But it's not really an ask, more of a condition. Oh, I know I'm not in the position to ask anything of you, but—'

'Out with it, girl, before it sticks in your craw.'

'I don't want to abandon my cousin, Tilda. Can we take her with us when we leave? She has nothing to her name, but she is like a sister to me and I love her dearly. I value her friendship and companionship and cannot abandon her.'

He stared at her for a moment, then nodded. 'I don't see why not. We'll collect her on the way to the boat. Has the lad been with his dog cart for your luggage? He said he'd stow it aboard my yacht, so it'll be waiting for you.'

'That was very kind of you, Tobias. Yes, there wasn't much, but it was heavy, even though I haven't got many clothes.'

His eyes softened. 'Aye, well, we can solve that

particular problem later.' He brushed his mouth against her forehead. 'Here's Mrs Quinby, who will help you to get ready. I'll be waiting at the church for you, Joanna.'

Half an hour later, her scuffed boots hidden by her velvet skirt, she became Joanna Rose Darsham in the eyes of God and the couple of people who had stood as witnesses. A quick glass of sherry at Richard Lind's house was followed by a tearful farewell, then she and her new husband set off down the hill.

When they reached the cemetery at Chiswell, Tobias brought her to a halt. 'I'd just like to say goodbye to my wife and child, for I doubt if I'll be back this way again.'

'Honor knows about the marriage,' Joanna said timidly. 'I told her when I cleared the weeds from her grave yesterday, so she'd understand that you're not pushing her memory to one side. I think she was content.'

He smiled at that. 'Then Honor will not mind if you come with me.'

'It must be hard to lose a son,' Joanna said as they gazed upon the grave.

'My infant was a daughter, and I'd never met her.' He squatted on his haunches and traced around the name. 'Someone made a mistake. Her name was Rose.'

'The same as my second name?'

'Aye.'

'A stonemason is working over there. Perhaps he'll change it if you ask him.'

The old man straightened up when they approached him. He broke into a smile when he saw her. 'Why, it be Joanna Rose. You look as pretty a piece as I've ever seen, damn me if you don't.'

'This is Mr Tobias Darsham, whose wife and infant lie over yonder.'

'I do remember her, and thee, too, sir. Drowned in the storm of 1838, she was, off the *Cormorant*. It was a bad year for storms. Your woman was a young un, not much older than Joanna Rose, there. Her son was tied to her bodice, as if she didn't want to be parted from him, that it was.'

'The infant was a female. Her name was Rose.'

'Pardon me, sir, but something ain't quite right, indeed it isn't. Silas's missus got her ready for the coffin. A boy, they said. I remember it special because we talked about the name. Auld Silas said it couldn't be Rose, that being a girl's name, and all, when the babe had definitely been a boy.'

'Then it couldn't have been my infant.'

'No, sir. Your'n must have been washed out to sea and the other two must've got tangled up together somehow. Women have soft ways. She probably picked him up because he was crying and needed comfort and she didn't want him to go to a watery grave alone. Or perhaps she thought it were her own, since she wouldn't have had time to check his little arse for a pecker, beggin' your pardon, Joanna Rose.' He wiped a tear from his eye. 'What would you have me do then, sir?'

Trying to hide a smile, Tobias slipped him a coin. 'Change the name to Rose if you would. Since we don't know what the other child was named, I believe my late wife would have preferred it that way.'

The stonemason touched his cap. 'I'll do that when I've finished this one. 'Tis for Abel Brown, who got the typhoid fever from drinking dirty water. Dangerous stuff, water. He should've stuck to ale, that he should.'

Most of the lerrets were still out fishing, thank goodness, Joanna thought as they neared the Rushmores' cottage. But Leonard Rushmore's crew had just pulled his boat up on the shingle and they were heading for the inn as Tobias pounded on the door.

Leonard didn't recognize her in her finery and jerked his thumb towards the horizon. 'My pa and brother are on their way in.'

Joanna gazed fearfully at Tobias, then said to Leonard, 'We're looking for Tilda.'

'Are you now?' He looked at them directly then, and a shock of recognition came into his eyes. 'I haven't seen Tilda for several weeks. She had an accident and I thought they'd taken her back to her ma to be looked after. Not that ma's much good for anything. The gin's soaked into her now.'

Joanna laid a hand on his arm. 'Leonard. I'm married and I'm leaving the island. I want to take Tilda with me.'

'I don't know about that, Joanna. You'd have to ask pa.'

'Tilda is twenty-four. She can legally decide that for herself, you know she can.'

Leonard shrugged. 'I've had a bellyful of Rushmore problems. I don't bother myself with my father and brothers' business unless I have to.'

Tobias said shortly, 'There will be more trouble if we can't find the girl. I'll fetch the constables and your father can answer to them.'

'It would serve them right.'

Standing back, Joanna shouted out, 'Tilda, are you in there?'

A woman came out from the next cottage, her arms folded over her chest. 'Last time I saw Tilda she could hardly stand up from the beating your father had given her, Leonard Rushmore.'

'Shut your mouth and stop meddlin' in other folks' affairs, Betty.'

'I won't shut up just because the likes of you thinks I ought to. Tilda's up in that back bedroom. I heard her moaning, not an hour ago.'

'Will I go for the constables, Tobias?' Joanna said. 'We'll need them if my uncle and cousins come back.'

'Like as not they'll kill you, but Mary's fate is a naggin' at me.' Leonard's eyes filled with resolve. 'There be no need for constables. If Tilda's in there I'll fetch her down.' Feeling along the ledge above the door, Leonard brought down a key. 'You'd best come with me.'

Joanna nearly gagged at the stink as they went inside. The door to the room Tilda was in was locked. Joanna rattled the handle. 'Are you in there, Tilda? Answer me!'

There was a groan.

'Stand back,' Tobias said, and heeled the door with enough force to smash it back against the wall. 'Jesus,' he whispered as Joanna followed him inside. 'Is that her?'

Tilda, almost skeletal and with her wrists bound, was tied to the bed. Dressed in rags, her knees drawn almost up to her chin, she shivered with the cold.

Bursting into tears, Joanna threw her arms around

her friend. 'Oh, Tilda. I'm leaving this place for good, and you're coming with me.' Joanna gazed at the neighbour, who had followed them in, her eyes avid with curiosity. As Joanna unwrapped the bundle of work clothes she'd been carrying, she said to her, 'Quick, help me get her into these. I want her out of here before her father comes home.'

Tilda opened her eyes when they'd finished dressing her. She plucked weakly at Joanna's arm. 'Brian saw the yacht coming. He guessed you'd try to leave with me, and he said he owed the owner a beatin'. They'll be waiting for us at Castletown quay.'

'Are they, then,' Tobias said from the doorway, his mouth pulling into a grim, determined line. 'Don't you fret about anything, girl. Can you walk downstairs if the women support you?'

'I never knew,' Leonard whispered when they were out of the stinking cottage and drawing strength from the freshness of the sea air.

'You knew, all right. You closed your eyes to what was going on. What kind of man are you?' Brian's boning knife appeared in Tobias's hand. As he threw it, it sliced past Leonard's ear in a blur of steel and buried itself in the door of the cottage.

'Listen to me,' he said, looking around at the people who were huddled together in groups, watching them. They were decent fisher folk, most of them. 'That knife belongs to the people who live in this cottage. One of them used it to threaten a defenceless woman as he tried to bend her to his will, and you can see how they treat their own kin.'

'He's a hard man, is George Rushmore. I remember him beating his own wife and leavin' her in the gutter to rot. If her sister-in-law hadn't taken her in, Fanny would be dead now.'

'And Fanny took advantage of my ma any way she could, then they stole what was mine,' Joanna said bitterly as she grabbed up a piece of driftwood. 'I'm not letting the Rushmores prevent me from leaving with Tilda. I'll brain the whole lot of them first.'

Tobias wasn't about to listen to the experiences of the fishermen and their wives, or the empty threats of Joanna, for even with the driftwood the girl hadn't the strength to fight off a man. He had more pressing problems of his own. 'It seems that the Rushmore family are waiting for me. If I don't sail with the tide I'll be beached. I'd appreciate any help you can give me to get these women safely aboard my yacht.'

'Why should we help a Kimberlin?'

'Tilda and I are not strangers. We were born and bred here,' Joanna pleaded.

Someone laughed. 'No doubt about Tilda, but there be some doubt about you, girl, don't you know?'

An old woman stepped forward, leaning on a stout stick. 'Shut your mouth, John Rattan. Joseph and Anna Rushmore were right proud of their girl, and so they should be. I'll give you a hand, mister. I'll crack George Rushmore round his thick head when he's not lookin' for you, 'cause they won't fight fair.'

Tobias smiled at her. 'Thank you for the offer, Mother, but I don't want to see you hurt.'

There was grumble of dissent as Tobias picked up Tilda.

'What about you, Leonard Rushmore? 'Tis your father and brothers who cause all the trouble around these parts. If they ain't careful, the Rushmores will find themselves without crew to work their boats. Then where will you be?'

Leonard sighed. 'My crew is treated well and have no reason to go elsewhere. 'Sides, I was just about to offer. Where's your yacht tied up, Mr . . .?'

'Darsham. The *Linnet* is at Castletown quay.'

' 'Tis a fair step. Here, give our Tilda to me to carry,' Leonard said reluctantly. 'I'll stand up with you against my father and brothers, else they'll have you gutted before you know what's happened. It's about time somebody did.'

His crew joined them, silent, but grinning at each other in anticipation of the showdown. Egged on by the old women, the fishermen's families chased after them, like seagulls after crabs on a receding tide.

It didn't take long to encounter George Rushmore, who, with his two younger sons and their boat crews, blocked their way to the *Linnet*.

His arms burdened by Tilda, who began to tremble with fear, Leonard stared hard at his father. 'Stand aside, Pa. This man has the right of way.'

'Not with our Tilda and Joanna, he hasn't.'

Tilda whimpered, 'Don't let them take me back. I'd rather die.'

'You can't have either of them,' Tobias stated with determination. 'Joanna is now my wife, so her place is

127

with me. The marriage is duly licensed and was solemnized in front of witnesses by the Reverend Quinby. Tilda is old enough to choose, I understand, and she has chosen to leave the island and sail with us. Stand aside.'

Brian and Peter, their courage shored up by the presence of their brother, who always caved in at the first sight of trouble, swaggered forward. Brian poked Tobias in the stomach. 'Make us.'

The next minute he was sprawling on his back, holding his jaw and spitting out a couple of teeth. Peter followed him down, hugging his stomach with both hands.

Placing Tilda in the care of one of his crew, Leonard said from the corner of his mouth, 'Get the women aboard, trim the sloop's sail and be ready to cast off as soon as the mainlander is on board.'

He quickly disarmed his father, sending him stumbling into the arms of one of his crew. 'You're too old to hit anyone but defenceless women, Pa, and you've done that once too often as far as I'm concerned. Bugger off home, now, for your cowardly ways have shamed me enough for one day.'

His brothers were on their feet now and, surrounded by their crews, they threw taunts at him. Leonard left Brian to the mainlander, who seemed to know what he was about, whilst he floored Peter with one blow, then pushed him into the water with a boot applied to his arse.

It erupted into a free-for-all between the crews as Leonard tried to guard the back of the the mainlander.

Tobias Darsham was not a man to fight by the rules when the odds were stacked against him, Leonard noted. He weighed in with both fists, and he wouldn't give any quarter. Darsham used no weapons apart from his hands, and a grudging admiration for him lodged in Leonard's soul.

Finally, the mainlander began to breathe more harshly. Blood ran from his nose and a cut over his eyebrow, and one of his eyes was almost closed.

The fight began to move towards the beach, though several people had ended up in the water and were floundering towards the shore, Leonard's brothers among them.

One of his father's crew picked up a loose stone, fisted it and tapped Tobias on the shoulder. Clenching his fists together, Leonard hit him from behind. The man dropped without a sound, and the stone rolled from his hand.

'Thanks,' Tobias grunted. 'You're a dark horse, Leonard Rushmore. If you ever need a job . . . let me know . . . Darsham and Morcant Shipping . . . London. Mention my name.'

Leonard thought that he might need a job at that, for he didn't know what the reaction to him taking the side of the mainlander would be. His father and brothers would no longer fish with him, that was for sure.

In the respite he held out his hand in friendship and Tobias took it. 'For the moment I'm content amongst my own. You look after Tilda, d'you hear? I don't want her becoming a lightskirt like her sister, Mary. You've taken enough punishment. Now get in the boat and get out of here while you have the chance, for the buggers have got their second wind.' Leonard gave him a hard shove.

'The constables are coming along the beach,' someone shouted out.

As Tobias tumbled into the yacht a crewman jumped ashore, cast him off and pushed the boat away from the quay. The sail filled with wind, then flapped back and forth as if seeking direction. Scrambling to the stern, the mainlander grabbed the tiller and pulled the boat expertly round, setting her on course.

Neat – very neat, Leonard thought, as he went down under a mass of struggling bodies. Tobias, who hated to fight and run, grinned as a shot rang out. Two constables were running along the beach. The heap of struggling fishermen stopped what they were doing and began to depart. Leaving the quay and scuttling in all directions, they dragged the wounded between them. Within the space of a few minutes there was no sight of any of them.

The constables stopped and gazed towards the boat, hands shading their eyes.

When Tobias waved they both waved back, then they turned and began to trudge back from whence they'd come.

Joanna came up from the cabin to join him, concern in her eyes as she gazed at his battered face. 'Are you hurt?'

He grinned. 'A bloodied nose and black eye, that's all.' He bade her sit down beside him and placed the tiller in her hand. 'See that buoy over there? Keep her pointed toward it whilst I wash my face.'

He dipped a handkerchief in the sea and began to slop the blood from his face. The surface of the sea was like moving glass. The mass of liquid shushed beneath them as the bow sliced through it, leaving white bubbles churning in their wake.

'Where are we going?' she asked him when he finished his makeshift ablutions.

'To Poole.' He left her in charge of the tiller, watching her as she tried to keep the boat lined up with the buoy. 'You're drifting sideways, pull a little to the right. Don't hold her so tightly, adjust with the movement of the boat. You'll soon get used to it.'

Her eyes seemed to pick up the essence of the ocean, turning a deep blue-green. She turned to smile at him when a seagull wheeled around them to perch on the mast. 'My pa used to say that seagulls are the souls of drowned sailors, and will guide a ship to safe harbour.'

Tobias nodded. 'He could be right.' He hoped so, the sea was rougher now they'd left the shelter of the harbour. The isle of Portland had receded to become a smudge behind them.

A haze was closing down on it and there was a bank of sea mist along the horizon. He took the tiller back from her. They were moving at a fast clip, but would be becalmed if the mist caught up with them. 'It's cold. You should stay in the cabin and look after Tilda now.'

'She's asleep, poor soul. I'll get your oilskin from the cabin else you'll be soaked through if that fog bank catches up with us.'

He'd thought she hadn't noticed it. 'Be careful, then. The sea's choppy and I don't want you falling overboard.'

They reached the safety of Poole harbour with hardly enough wind in the sails to get them to the quayside. The fog clung to them as they tied up, muffling all sound, so all Tobias could hear was his own heartbeat.

' 'Tis eerie, as if a thousand ghosts have risen from their graves to form a clammy blanket,' Joanna said with a shudder.

Tobias chuckled. 'We'll soon be out of it. Wait here with Tilda while I go and see if there's a carriage for hire, and don't go wandering off else you might fall into the quay. I won't be long.'

There was a vehicle available. 'You were just in the nick of time, sir, since I was about to go home to my fireside,' the driver said as Tobias lifted the linen-wrapped cradle into the carriage with the women. 'You were lucky to make it to the quay in this.'

'We had a seagull to guide us in,' Tobias said, sending Joanna a grin.

'Yes, sir,' the coachman said, grunting as he climbed up on to his seat.

Soon they were clip-clopping slowly up a long hill. The sea mist trails spun around them so they seemed to be going through a white tunnel. Tilda was barely awake and leaned against Joanna in the corner of the cabin, her gaze vacant, her mouth slack. Tobias could smell her from where he sat. Joanna didn't seem to notice the stench as she peered out of the window, but she'd been in the cabin with Tilda during their passage along the coast, so was more used to it than himself.

'I'm afraid you won't be able to see much until the fog clears,' he said as they turned into a carriageway and drew up to the front of a house.

Alerted by the sound of his key in the door, his mother came from the drawing room to greet them, a wide smile on her face. 'Tobias, how wonderful, I wasn't expecting you. Goodness, you look quite battered. Have you met with an accident?'

'More of a general fracas, I'm afraid. The damage was inflicted on me on purpose, but the other fellows came off much worse.'

'Aren't you getting a little old to indulge in fisticuffs?' she said gently.

As he stooped to kiss her cheek, her glance wandered curiously to the two women, still standing in shadow.

'Mother, there's someone I'd like you to meet,' and he held out his hand and drew Joanna forward into the light. 'After all your nagging, you'll be pleased to hear that I have married, at last. I'd like to present Joanna Rose, my wife. The lady with her is her friend, Tilda Rushmore, and she's in dire need of attention. Joanna, this is my mother, Charlotte Darsham.'

Charlotte was already staring at Joanna, bewilderment in her eyes. They widened when Joanna smiled at her. '*My God, it is her!*' She gave a small scream, then clapped her hand over her mouth and backed away.

'Mother, what the devil is it? You knew I was thinking of marrying again. Surely the event has not upset you to such an extent?'

He got no answer. Charlotte collapsed to the floor as her knees buckled under her.

A strange reaction to the news, Joanna thought, but Tobias swiftly sorted everything out. Soon, Charlotte Darsham was lying on the sofa with smelling salts under her nose.

She recovered quickly from her faint and apologized profusely. 'So silly of me, my dear. Let me look at your friend. How ill she looks.' Her nose wrinkled. 'And she has a rather peculiar aroma, as if she's fallen into something nasty.'

'Tilda's bound to stink like a goat, since she wouldn't have had a wash in months, I reckon,' Joanna offered

Tobias quickly explained the situation when Charlotte looked askance at her unasked for guest.

'She has been through much if her appearance is anything to go by. We must call in a doctor to examine her. One lives just two houses away. Tobias, perhaps you'd go and explain the situation to him. In the meantime we'll bathe the poor girl, which will make her feel much better. Then, when Tilda is in bed, we shall see if she can swallow some beef broth.'

With two female servants rushing hither and thither, Tilda was conveyed to a pleasant upstairs room, where a fire had been lit in the grate. A tub was brought in and filled to hip height. The unprotesting Tilda was lowered in. The maids washed Tilda's hair, using the carbolic soap provided by Charlotte. The water was grey when they finished rinsing it.

'Even the lice scorned that head,' one of them muttered, as Joanna applied a soapy flannel to her friend's body. 'I've never seen anyone so filthy.'

Joanna gave her a dark look. 'You'd be filthy if you were tied up, abused and half starved for weeks on end. Look at the bruises on her and be thankful it ain't you who was on the bleddy receiving end of it. Go and fetch some fresh water, please. I can't wash her in this.'

'Sorry, miss—' The other maid elbowed her in the ribs and she became flustered. '*Mrs Darsham* . . . I didn't mean no disrespect. I've never seen the like afore, that's all. The poor thing's so thin, like a starved dog.'

Charlotte came bustling in with a clean nightgown over her arm. 'Then we must feed her up. Off you go, you two. We need clean water to rinse off our unfortunate patient. While you're in the kitchen warm some broth.' She turned to Tilda, blanching at the sight of her many bruises. 'And you'd better bring me the arnica. There, there, my dear, we'll soon have you feeling more comfortable.'

A tear tracked down Tilda's face at being spoken to so kindly as the maids scurried off, and her nose began to run as well. When Joanna lifted her skirt and wiped it for her on the hem of her petticoat, Charlotte looked askance at her and said faintly, 'I'll find a handkerchief for her.'

Finally, Tilda was settled, but she ate only a spoonful or two of the broth. The doctor prescribed a tonic and Tilda fell asleep from sheer exhaustion, brought about by the exertions of her bath, no doubt.

Later, Joanna sat with Tobias at a long, polished table with a lace tablecloth and a lamp with a pretty coloured glass shade and dangling beads. The light shone on sparkling glass and silver cutlery, and there were white napkins to catch any drips. She tucked it into the neck of her bodice and picked up a spoon. It was a simple meal of broth, cold ham, cheese, bread and pickles. The broth was delicious and she scooped it into her mouth as fast as she could. Joanna ate everything put in front of her, for she was excessively hungry.

Tobias grinned at her afterwards. 'You were hungry, I take it?'

'I haven't eaten since breakfast. I was too excited.'

'There's some fruit on the sideboard.'

'I'll take an apple for later.'

'Then I'll ask Stevens to show you to your room, for you must be tired and I want to talk privately with my mother.'

About herself, she supposed. She doubted if his ma approved of his hasty marriage, but she liked the fact that Tobias had not consulted Charlotte Darsham about it in the first place.

She unpacked her change of clothes from the cradle and hung them inside a large empty cupboard. With a brush Richard Lind had bought her for her birthday, she teased the tangles from her hair. Only too aware it was her wedding night and wondering what lay in store for her, Joanna had a sponge bathe herself. Then she waited with some trepidation in the large, comfortable bed for her husband to arrive.

She was in a pleasant room, the walls covered in pink and white wallpaper. Although she felt safe for the first time in months, she also felt sad and, despite trying to stop them by squeezing her eyelids together, tears escaped to run down her cheeks.

'None of that, Joanna,' she said, wiping them away. 'You've got yourself a good man there even if he is older than you. Just be grateful Brian Rushmore didn't get you in the way.'

Shadows danced across the wall as the fire crackled and flared in the grate, making her feel warm and comforted. Her eyelids drooped, drifted shut, snapped open once or twice, then stayed shut.

Downstairs, Tobias was trying to deny what his mother was telling him.

'I swear, Tobias. I thought it was Honor come back from the grave. She looks the image of that portrait you have hanging on your drawing-room wall in London. And she's so young and uncultured. What were you thinking of? If you take her to London, people will mock her.'

'I thought to leave her here so she could be improved. I've never heard anyone slurp soup from the spoon quite so loudly. But Joanna is curious, and a fast study. Her voice is pleasing, too, for it displays no shrillness. Richard Lind has educated her and she knows a surprising amount for someone who had never left Portland before now.'

'That's a splendid idea, Tobias. I like what I've seen of the girl, despite her tendency to be outspoken. I'd be pleased to teach her some graces, but that's something she will unconsciously pick up over time, anyway. It's her resemblance to Honor that bothers me, though. It's uncanny. You must look into her background before . . .'

Tobias spared his mother the embarrassment of

spelling it out for him, for he'd not felt the urge to become a husband to her, as yet. 'I will, I promise, if only to put your mind at rest. People often bear resemblance to others. I have not noticed it myself. I feel comfortable with her, Mother, and you're making too much of it, I think. As soon as I set eyes on her I had the oddest feeling, as if we belonged together. I was compelled to go back for her, and thank God I did, for I think she would have suffered the same fate as poor Tilda.'

'Richard Lind was looking after her, you said? I've not seen him since we were children together. He was always gentle and pleasant, and he made up wonderful stories. I'd very much like to see him again.'

'He rarely leaves the island for he has seizures, and his relatives are ashamed of him, he says. He'll miss Joanna Rose, for he thought highly of her.'

'Perhaps I shall invite him to come and stay with me for a while.'

'I doubt if he'll come. He's a solitary man.'

'I shall invite him anyway. At least he'll know somebody thinks of him occasionally.'

After his mother went to bed Tobias poured himself a brandy and sipped it, feeling the warmth of contentment growing inside him. The clock struck midnight before he stirred. Joanna would be asleep by now so would harbour no expectations on their wedding night.

He didn't need to hurry back to London. Alex could run the company competently without him. He had to be back to name the new clipper though. *Joanna Rose*, she would be named. He'd telegraph the name through to Alex in the morning, without telling him why he'd chosen it.

His mother's initial reaction to Joanna still bothered him. He took up a lamp and entered the bedchamber Joanna had been given, which was connected to his through a small sitting room. He gazed down at her. How sweet and flushed she looked in sleep. When he bent to kiss her cheek she muttered something and turned her face away from the light.

As he turned away to go through to his own room he stubbed his foot on a piece of furniture. It was the object she'd refused to leave behind. He saw it was a cradle. His smile suddenly fled. This was not just *any* cradle – this was the cradle he'd made himself, carving each piece with love. Inside was the rose he had hastily carved when he'd learned Honor had given him a daughter who had been named after the flower.

His fingers ran lightly over it. Lucian had taken this same cradle to America for Honor to lay their child in. It had been his labour of love and would have been on the *Cormorant* when it had gone down.

Perhaps the cradle *had* carried his daughter safely home! Perhaps her parents had found Joanna washed up on the beach, thought her an orphan and had given her a home.

'*Oh God!*' Tobias discarded the idea as soon as it formed in his head. It was too hard a concept to grapple with, despite the evidence before him. The cradle was a coincidence, that was all.

He spent a restless night, tossing and turning, dawn finding him hollow-eyed.

Tobias knew he couldn't take a risk by ignoring this, for if his mother's suspicion was correct and word got out, it would ruin the company as well as his own reputation!

8

A rooster woke her. Disorientated by her surroundings, Joanna gazed around her in surprise. What a pretty room she was in. The white wallpaper was dotted in pink rosebuds, the curtains were delicate and lacy and the bedcovers a deep rose.

Then she remembered she was no longer on the island but in Poole. And she was no longer Joanna Rose Rushmore, but Mrs Tobias Darsham. How grand it sounded.

A smile spreading across her face, she swung her legs over the side of the bed and rushed to the window. Below her was a small field, picked free of stones and covered in grass, which looked as though it had been shaved, so neat was it. Shapes were cut into it, filled with crumbly dark earth that held small shrubs and flowers. Larger shrubs lined the boundary of the field the house was built on. To one side, a grey-limbed tree stood, deprived of leaves for winter. Ivy rambled at will over a dividing wall. Set in the wall was an iron gate through which she spied a vegetable garden and, beyond that, the gnarled and mossy limbs of some fruit trees.

There was no sign of any livestock, but she could hear the cluck of chickens and had heard a rooster crow. Ah, at least Mrs Darsham didn't waste all of her field on grass. Perhaps her sheep were kept beyond the wall, too, though how she stopped them from eating the vegetables was a mystery.

She turned when a knock came at the door. It was the maid with a jug of hot water; she filled the basin on the dresser.

'What's that for?' Joanna asked her.

The maid looked askance at her. 'To wash yourself with.'

'But I washed myself last night.'

'Yes, Mrs Darsham. But you'll be wanting another one before I help you dress.' The maid went to the cupboard and threw the doors open. 'I'm sorry, ma'am. That Mavis has forgotten to unpack your luggage. I'll do that first. She picked up a skirt and blouse and threw them on the floor. 'I don't know where those dirty old rags came from. I'll get rid of them.'

'They're not dirty rags,' Joanna said with some indignation as she picked them up. 'They're my clothes. I washed and repaired them just two days ago.'

'And are these your boots?'

'Yes.'

'Lordy me.' The girl's eyes widened.

'What's wrong with them?'

The maid came to stand in front of her, sighing when she saw her repaired nightgown. 'The mistress will have a fit when she sees what you're wearing. She's most particular about her dress.'

142

Joanna sat on the edge of the bed, twisting the golden wedding ring Tobias had slid on to her finger. Suddenly she didn't feel married, but as if she was still the poor island girl she'd been the day before. 'I can wear the velvet skirt and jacket my husband bought me.'

'They're for travelling in.' The maid sighed. 'I'd better go and see the mistress, tell her you've got nothing to wear. I'll polish your boots when I come back.'

Joanna's chin tilted. She didn't need this girl running around after her, making her feel inferior. 'You needn't tittle-tattle to your mistress. I'll polish the boots myself, and I'll wear what I have, the skirt you call a rag, and my new cream blouse and my shawl.' She rose to her feet, dying to have pee. 'Where's the chamber pot kept?'

'Chamber pot? Lordy, the master has had a sanitary room installed with the latest closet and bath. He likes modern things, does Mr Darsham. It saves the servants a lot of running around, I can tell you, because cold water can be pumped up through a pipe. The closet is through that door in what used to be the dressing room. If you can't work the valves, I'll show you how.'

Half an hour later, Joanna presented herself in the dining room, a clean apron protecting her blouse, though it was creased a little. She'd cleaned the outside of her boots in her washing water and polished them with soap

'Good morning, Joanna. I hope you slept well,' Charlotte said, a slight frown creasing her brow.

'The bed was so comfortable it was like sleeping on a cloud. Indeed, I thought I was going to float away on it.'

Tobias grinned. 'And when did you last sleep on a cloud?'

She offered him a smile and turned to Charlotte. 'I'm sorry if my dress offends you, Mrs Darsham. The maid told me that my clothes were rags, but they're all I have so they will have to do. At least they're clean.'

Charlotte eyed her up and down. 'They do not offend me, and the maid shouldn't have offered an opinion. If she does so again, take her to task.'

'She was only trying to be helpful, I reckon.'

Charlotte suddenly smiled. 'Of course she was. We shall soon have you suitably gowned, Joanna, and I shall enjoy the process enormously.'

Tobias caught Joanna's gaze and smiled too. His bruised eye was very noticeable this morning.

'You look like a pirate with an eye patch,' she said. 'Does it hurt?'

He chuckled. 'It's sore, but the bruise will soon fade.' There was an awkwardness about him and Joanna wondered if he was regretting the hasty marriage he'd made. Every now and again she caught him observing her, but he quickly looked away when she returned the scrutiny.

Eventually, he put his napkin down. 'I'd like to talk to you after breakfast, Joanna. We'll use the private sitting room that separates our sleeping chambers.'

'About what?'

'Your background. I know so little about you.'

'And I you, except for the fact that you're a widower, have a little boat called *Linnet*, and you like modern sanitary closets.'

Charlotte gasped. 'Such a subject is not fit for the dining table.'

'To which subject are you referring, Mrs Darsham?'

'To the sanitary closets, of course.' Charlotte's face took on an expression of annoyance. 'There, now you've made me say it.'

'They're only words, but if they offend you I'll not say them again. A pity, since I thought it a most wonderful contraption. I suppose you save the contents all winter to tip on the garden in spring, like we do on the island. 'Tis a great help to the crops, for the soil is very poor there.'

Tobias laughed out loud when his mother looked scandalized. Then she exchanged a wry glance with him, relaxed and laughed too. 'Well, you did warn me that I'd have a job on my hands, Tobias. I'd better start now. Joanna, from now on you will not mention sanitary arrangements or crop fertilization, especially when you're in company. It's just not polite. Do you understand?'

Crestfallen, Joanna gazed down at her hands. 'I'm sorry. I'm not used to acting the lady.' Her spread hands encompassed everything – the food, the room and Charlotte Darsham's splendid gown with its sweeping skirt, which would have curtained her former bedroom with fabric to spare. 'It's rather overwhelming. I don't even know which fork or spoon to use.' Sliding Tobias a glance, she giggled. 'I saw you make a disapproving face when I ate my soup last night. I was so hungry you were lucky I didn't eat it straight from the pot, like a horse in a nosebag.'

A spontaneous laugh choked from Tobias. 'You made as much noise as a horse in a nosebag. I was wondering how the guests would react if we were invited to a dinner party.'

She gazed at her lap as her face heated with embarrassment. 'I'll try to learn better manners.'

'Tobias wasn't chastising you, dear.' Charlotte said softly. 'You have a lot to learn about how to behave, but it's early days yet. We'll work on it together. Now, get on with your breakfast before it gets cold. Help yourself from the dishes on the sideboard.'

'Yes, Mrs Darsham.' Being careful not to overfill her plate, Joanna nevertheless attacked the coddled eggs, bacon and toast with gusto, frightened it would be removed by the fancy maid who whipped dirty plates from under everyone's noses to replace them with spotless ones – and that before they had time to wipe them clean with their bread. Suddenly, she remembered her cousin. Placing her knife and fork down she laid her hand on Tobias's sleeve. 'Can I go and give Tilda half of my breakfast?'

'There is no need for you to worry about Tilda. She has her own breakfast and is being looked after,' he said gently. He laid down his napkin, pushed his chair back from the table and nodded to the servant. 'Have some coffee sent up to my sitting room. Joanna, finish your breakfast and I'll see you there in ten minutes.'

Picking up her knife and fork Joanna gazed at Charlotte after he'd left. 'Are you sure Tilda has got some breakfast?'

'I'm quite certain, my dear. You may visit her after Tobias has talked to you and see for yourself,' Charlotte said, tears gathering in her eyes.

Joanna stared at her, trying not to reveal the alarm she felt at the sight of her tears. 'You must tell me the

146

truth, Mrs Darsham. Tilda will recover, won't she? I couldn't bear it if she died, especially since Tobias risked his life to rescue her. He was very brave and fierce, like Saint George slaying the dragon, even though he is not a young man. Not that he's elderly, of course,' she said hastily. 'My ma would have described him as a prime bit of mutton.'

Pressing a lace-edged handkerchief to her damp eyes, Mrs Darsham giggled loudly, though Joanna couldn't imagine why. Her eyes brimming with laughter now, she choked out, 'Eat up, my dear. Tobias is elderly enough to dislike being kept waiting. Besides, we have a full day ahead.'

Joanna found the small sitting room without difficulty. It was cosily furnished with brocade-covered chairs in dark blue. Small tables were placed here and there, a writing desk stood against the wall. A model of a ship stood on a shelf. On the wall the pendulum of a clock swung back and forth with a stately tock . . . tock . . . tock. There was a glass-fronted cabinet filled with books. She gave them an interested glance before seating herself opposite Tobias.

The fire burning cheerily in the grate caused her to remark, 'There's a lot of fuel burned in this house. 'Tis a waste of money to have a fire in every room.'

His eyebrow lifted. 'Since this is my mother's house, you needn't concern yourself with such things, Joanna.'

The rebuke made her flush slightly. 'Sorry,' she mumbled and scrambled for something better to say. 'This is a nice room, Tobias.'

'It's rarely used and may be a bit dull for a woman's

taste. You may decorate it to your own liking, if you wish.'

'Oh no. I like it exactly as it is, since it's yours. Have you read all of those books?'

'I doubt if there is much to interest you there. Most of them are about ships, with some engineering and history mixed in. There might be something by William Shakespeare, since I vaguely remember my tutor trying to force some literature into me.'

'He was born in Stratford-upon-Avon in 1564 and was fifty-two years old when he died.'

'Who, my tutor?' But she could tell he was teasing for his eyes were crinkled at the corners and he had a grin on his face. 'You're not about to quote me from Hamlet, are you?'

She returned his grin. 'There are more things in heaven and earth, *Tobias*, than are dreamed of in your philosophy.'

'Ouch,' he said. 'Kindly behave yourself and help yourself to coffee.'

The silver coffee pot had a matching jug filled with cream, and a sugar basin. The cup and saucer were fancy, white with a dark red band decorated with golden swirls. The handle of the coffee pot was hot to the touch so she used the skirt of her apron to prevent her fingers from burning.

'You should use the napkin provided, and I'm sure my mother would prefer it if you didn't wear that apron.'

Her cheeks heated. 'Would you prefer it, Tobias?'

'Yes, for it makes you look like one of the maids.'

Quickly she untied the garment, to stuff it behind her cushion. Silence stretched between them. Desperately searching for something to say she burst out with, 'I have a book of Richard Lind's poetry he gave me for my birthday. He has signed it. *To Joanna Rose Rushmore, with my best wishes for your future. Your good friend, Richard Lind.*'

'A gift you should treasure.'

'I shall that. Imagine writing a whole book.'

'We wouldn't have anything to read if people didn't.'

'But when you read you can't imagine somebody sitting there writing down all those words to go in it. Books just *are*.' She shrugged, unable to explain herself any further.

'I know what you mean. The author is remote from the reader.'

'Not quite that.' She screwed her face up in concentration. 'It's more that the story belongs to the person who reads it rather than to the person who wrote it. It's as if it escaped from the author and lives a life of its own.'

He gazed thoughtfully at her, then a smile touched his lips. 'You have surprising depths to you, Joanna Rose.'

She didn't know whether that was a good thing or a bad one. She leaned forward. 'What did you want to know about me, Tobias?'

'Tell me about the cradle you brought with you.'

'Ah that.' She smiled. 'I've had that since I was first born. I believe my pa made it, because he was a stone-mason and clever with his hands, but he wouldn't admit to it. He was a great storyteller, too, and he spun a story about it. Would you like to hear it?'

'I'd be very interested to.'

Searching her mind Joanna evoked a scene from her childhood, of herself seated on a stool at her pa's feet. If she closed her eyes she could smell his tobacco in the air and hear the sound of rain splattering against the window-pane and the fire crackling in the grate. Her pa's voice inside her head was soft and low as she retold one of his many versions of how the cradle was come by.

'A long time ago there was a great storm. My pa was walking his dog Rufus along the beach when lightning split the sky in two and the sea began to boil around him. Suddenly, there came the cry of a gull, and Rufus began to sound off fit to bust a gut. There, on the terrifying sea, he saw a small boat was adrift. On the prow a seagull perched, one who'd swallowed the soul of a drowned sailor. It had been sent by the Lord to navigate the little craft safely into port. Old Rufus, not fearing for his own safety, dived into the waves with a rope tied to his body, and took the little boat in his jaws. But it turned out to be a cradle lashed to brandy kegs to keep her stable. A sail had been rigged, too, to send her safely on her journey to the shore.'

Goosebumps prickled up Tobias's spine.

'Inside the cradle was a beautiful infant girl, with a face as long as an eel. Complainin' fiercely, she was, because she was a real princess, who was cold and wet, and most likely had swallowed half the storm, as well. She thought she had the right to complain, Pa reckoned. He cut her free with his knife, for she was lashed to the cradle with her head out of the water it shipped, to stop her from drowning in her bed.'

Her eyes had a faraway look to them. 'He wrapped the infant in his scarf and put her into his sou'wester. Rufus carried her home to my ma, who was in sore need of a cheil of her own, on account of her breasts were bursting with milk for the boy they'd just lost.'

Joanna thought Tobias was smiling when she finished her tale-telling, but her eyes were blurred with tears when she looked up at him. 'My pa told me that the princess was me. He told wonderful tales, but my ma said it was all made-up nonsense, and he sometimes said daft things that didn't make sense when he'd got a brandy or two inside him.'

But it made sense to Tobias. Lucian, even knowing the *Cormorant* was doomed, would have tried to save Tobias's wife and child. But had he succeeded in part? Was this girl his daughter Rose, or was it just a coincidence? He knew he must make further enquiries before he could even contemplate becoming her husband in the true sense.

'Do you think there's any truth in the tale, Joanna?'

She looked troubled. 'I'd be lying if I said I've never wondered, and there are teeth marks each side of the sou'wester, as if a dog had carried something heavy in it. Though just as likely my pa would have put them there in case I looked.

'There are those who say it's true, that I'm a Kimberlin, for the word of the tale has been spread, and by its spreading it took on the ring of truth. The Rushmores took possession of the cottage after my ma died. George Rushmore said that since it was his brother's property in the first place, and Anna had brought the fields into her marriage to him, I didn't have a claim to it. Of course, I could've had the cottage back had I married Brian. But the price was too high to pay.'

'We could challenge that in a court of law if you wanted.'

'Richard Lind looked into things for me. He said there was no record of my birth at the parish church, and nobody attended Anna at the birthing. And George Rushmore said he'd swear on the bible that he was with my pa when he found me. So will Fanny Rushmore and her two youngest sons.'

'Aye, well, the odds are certainly stacked against you.'

Gazing down at her hands she twisted the ring around her finger. She was nervous for she sensed a withdrawal in him. As a result, she was talking too much, but not saying what was really on her mind. 'You're not going to send me back, are you? I'm afeared of the Rushmores.'

Tobias wanted to take her in his arms then, hold her tight and reassure her. 'I'll never send you back, Joanna. That's a promise.' He rose then and walked to the window to stare out at the grey day. He didn't know what to do next. Go back to Portland and ask around, perhaps? But no, they were a tight-lipped community who were wary of strangers. He'd been lucky that Leonard Rushmore had come down on his side yesterday, but he didn't think he'd escape so lightly a second time. A strange one, was Leonard Rushmore. Hard to read.

London, he thought. He could take a look at the

passenger lists to see how many infants were travelling at that time. He turned. 'I'll be going back to London tomorrow. I'll leave you some money of your own to spend, for I daresay you could use some. My mother will take you in hand and I'll expect you to treat her with the respect due to her.'

'Of course, Tobias.'

'Good, then I'll be off. I have some things to do about town.' He hesitated for a moment, then pressed a perfunctory kiss against her forehead. 'I'll see you at dinner tonight, most likely.'

He chuckled when she said gravely, 'I'll try not to slurp my soup.'

After Tobias had left, Joanna went through to her room and gazed at the cradle. It had been moved away from the door to a corner of the room. It seemed odd that Tobias was so interested in it. It didn't seem an unusual item to her. But that was because it was familiar to her, part of her life. She could see clearly the love and craftsmanship that had gone into it. She didn't like to think that her pa had found it on the beach – had found *her* – for she'd always loved and trusted her parents. One day her own child would sleep in it, and she felt a small thrill of anticipation run through her.

She followed a maid to where Tilda lay, to find Charlotte Darsham already in attendance. Tilda was propped up on the pillows, her hair loose around her shoulders. Fully awake after a good night's sleep, Tilda's eyes appeared large and dull in the gauntness of her face. She managed a small smile for Joanna and made a tiny mewing noise in her throat.

'Ah good, I'm pleased you're here,' Charlotte said. 'I can't get a word out of this young lady, and the maid said she refuses to eat.'

'I'm not hungry,' Tilda whispered.

'Don't be so bleddy daft, Tilda Rushmore, of course you are.' Joanna took her in a gentle hug, appalled at the way Tilda's bones pushed against the sparse covering of flesh. After she released her, she scolded, 'A crow wouldn't find enough flesh on your bones to pick off for breakfast.' Trying not to burst into tears at her friend's plight, Joanna picked up the napkin from the tray and tucked it under Tilda's chin, saying sternly, 'Now, I'm going to spoon some of this gruel into your mouth. If you don't swallow it I'll hold your nose until you do.'

Gradually, she spooned the gruel into Tilda's mouth, managing to get half of it into her cousin before she balked. Clearly exhausted afterwards, Tilda's eyes closed and tears began to squeeze from under her lids to trickle down her cheeks.

'As soon as you're ready, join me downstairs,' Charlotte said with a watery smile and left her to it.

'Now listen, Tilda. Don't you go worrying about any-thing,' Joanna told her. 'I'm going to look after you. I daresay I'll boss you around while I'm doing it, because if you want to get better you've got to eat something and you've got to take this medicine.' She uncorked the bottle, recoiling as she took a sniff before pouring the foul liquid into the spoon. 'This stuff stinks so bad that I wouldn't feed it to a dog. Unfortunately, you're not a dog. Open up your mouth, now. Wider, else the spoon won't fit in . . . Good, in it goes now. Don't leave it hanging around in there else it'll rot your teeth. Swallow.'

Tilda grimaced and shuddered, but she swallowed it.

'What about the egg and milk, miss?' the maid ventured. 'The doctor said—'

'Never mind what the doctor said. Give the gruel time to settle in first, else it'll all be coming back up again. And you should give her the milk in sips, not expect her to gulp it straight down.' Dabbing Tilda's lips with the napkin, Joanna kissed her on the cheek. 'If the medicine tastes that awful it must be good for you. Promise me you'll drink the milk in a little while, when the maid gives it to you.'

Tilda nodded.

'Good. I'll be up myself later in the day, to feed you some broth. We'll soon have you on your feet again. I'd better go and see what Mrs Darsham wants me for, since I promised Tobias I'd do what I was told, and his mother has plans of turning me into a lady.'

Tilda plucked at her hand. 'Who are these people, why are they lookin' after us?'

'Why, 'tis guests in the home of my husband and his mother, we are.' She held out her hand, showing Tilda the golden band on her finger. 'This says I'm Mrs Tobias Darsham, and a right brave gentleman my husband is, too. He took the Rushmore family on single-handed, though he got a black eye for his trouble. 'Twas quite an adventure we had to get off the island with you. And who'd have thought it? Your Leonard threw his lot in with us.'

Charlotte Darsham was in the drawing room surrounded by garments of every type and colour when Joanna knocked and entered.

'We'll take half a dozen of the frilled longcloth nightgowns plus nightcaps. A dozen pairs of plain flannel drawers, a dozen petticoats, six of flannel, two of book muslin, two cambric and two quilted. I suppose we should take a crinoline hoop, though personally I find them an abomination and prefer petticoats. The hosiery and gloves I've set aside. Two dozen handkerchiefs, lace edged.' She looked up and smiled. 'Good, you've arrived. Come here, my dear, so Mrs Tate can measure you.'

Mrs Tate's assistant, who'd been busy unpacking boxes, took over the notepad and pencil, while Mrs Tate busied herself with the tape measure. Joanna turned this way and that, while every part of her was measured and written down.

'Now, we need some day gowns for immediate use. Tell me, Joanna, what do you think of the cut of these two gowns?'

One was dark blue, the other grey. Both had matching bodices, decorated with a touch of lace and pearl buttons. Long sleeves had a puff of detachable lace-edged cambric at the cuff, and they came with extra ones. So the cuffs could be washed on a daily basis, Joanna supposed.

Joanna had never seen the like of such gowns except

on the mainland women who had occasionally crossed the bridge to gawk at the quarries and to picnic on the beach, and she didn't quite know how to answer. Something in Charlotte Darsham's face stopped her from saying what was in her heart, that the garments were too fine for the daughter of a Portland stonecutter. With relief, she remembered a phrase Richard Lind had used when he'd bought a new suit a few months previously.

'The fabric is serviceable and the colours sensible, I think.'

Charlotte's smile widened into one of approval. 'Exactly my thoughts on the matter, my dear. We shall purchase them, Mrs Tate, but Mrs Darsham the younger will require many more gowns, so we'll go through the pattern book, then come into your establishment later in the day to choose the materials.'

Mrs Darsham the younger? Joanna nearly laughed out loud. Why couldn't she just be called Joanna? What odd ways of referring to people these mainlanders had. She supposed she'd have to get used to it, though, since she was one of them now.

''Tis a right carry-on being a lady,' she said after they'd spent an exhausting hour scrutinizing every detail on several gowns, and the dressmaker had left. 'I've never worn drawers before.'

'And will not mention such items again.' Charlotte rang for a maid and instructed, 'Take these garments upstairs and help Mrs Darsham to change. Can you dress hair, Stevens?'

'Yes, ma'am, I've been taking instruction on my day off, for 'tis my aim to better myself.'

'Good, then as well as your other duties you're temporarily appointed as Mrs Darsham's personal maid. We'll see what you make of the job.'

Stevens beamed a smile at her and bobbed a curtsy. 'Thank you, Mrs Darsham, 'twill be a pleasure and I'll do my very best to please.'

'Of course you will. Get on with it then, Stevens. Mrs Darsham will join you shortly.'

Picking up the garments and barely able to see over the top, the girl scurried away.

'Joanna,' Charlotte said as she was about to follow after her, 'you will say excuse me when you intend to leave a room. And once you don your new gown you will no longer say 'tis or 'twas, for it sounds dreadfully common. Understood?'

'Yes, Mrs Darsham.'

Her new mother-in-law smiled. 'There, that's enough etiquette for today, I think. You may call me Charlotte when we're not in company.'

'Thank you, Mrs, uh . . . Charlotte. May I ask you something?'

'What is it, my dear?'

'Why did you faint when you first saw me?'

Charlotte's eyes slid away. 'You reminded me of someone . . . someone who's been dead for a long time.'

'Tobias's first wife, Honor? She's buried on the island. That's where I met Tobias. He saved me from . . . from someone who was attacking me.'

'So Tobias informed me. Actually, I never got the chance to meet Honor. She and her infant were drowned before I could.' Charlotte's eyes engaged hers for a couple of seconds. 'It was a long time ago. How odd. Honor wasn't much older than you when she drowned, and her infant would have been about your age now.'

Joanna placed her hand on her arm. 'You think I'm not good enough for Tobias . . . ?'

'Whether I think you're good enough is immaterial, Joanna. You're a lovely girl who has a good heart and who just needs to learn a few graces. I'm so happy you're here, with me. With us.' Emotion almost choking her, Charlotte took Joanna in a brief but heartfelt hug.

After Joanna was released, Charlotte bustled around, straightening the cushions in an abrupt, angry sort of way. Then she sighed and bent to pick up a glove from the floor. 'Look, Stevens has already dropped a glove. Go and get ready now, dear, for we have much more to do today. Boots and shoes, dress fabrics. I'm having the carriage brought around in half an hour. Try not to keep me waiting.'

'Excuse me then, Charlotte,' she said and hurried off, acutely aware her question had been left unanswered.

Tobias had been scrutinizing the passenger lists held by one of the Poole shipping agents. As far as they went, he couldn't find any records of any infants being passengers on board the other doomed ships in the disastrous 1838 storm, let alone a boy.

Except for Rose Darsham, of course. That didn't necessarily mean there had been no other infants aboard. The one buried with his late wife might well have been born on board the *Cormorant*. The log would have gone down with the ship, so if Lucian had recorded the birth of an infant, nobody would ever know it now. Sometimes people were taken on board at the last minute by the captain if there was room for them, so didn't make it on to the lists.

He shook his head. Nothing he'd learned was conclusive, and his suspicion was simply based on his mother's recollection of a portrait of Honor on his wall in London – one that was so familiar to his own eyes that seeing it there barely registered with him now.

But then there was the cradle. And also the tale Joanna had told him. Perhaps it was a clever hoax by the Rushmore family to marry Joanna off to money. He dismissed the thought instantly. From what he'd seen, her kin wouldn't have the intelligence to concoct such a ruse – though Joanna did, which in itself was odd. Was she the cuckoo in the Rushmore nest? He needed to see Honor's portrait again, judge for himself.

His mother and Joanna had not yet returned from town, the maid told him. Going into the upstairs sitting room he had the urge to inspect the cradle again. A glint of gold on the dressing-table caught his attention and his face paled when he saw a brooch lying there. He ran the ball of his thumb over the tiny rubies. He'd designed it himself as a gift for Honor and had taken it across the Atlantic to give it personally to her. The brooch had suggested the name for their child to her.

He felt the small scar on his finger, then returning to the cradle turned it over, grunting with the heaviness of it. He was looking for the groove he'd made in the wood where his knife had slipped and the point had stabbed into his finger. Somebody had filled it in. In fact, the bottom section between the rockers had been boxed in and the seams caulked.

Prising the caulking from the seams, he then removed a layer of wood from the bottom and uncovered something wrapped in oilskin. Unwrapping it, he stared in astonishment at a bar of gold secured to the centre. No wonder the cradle was heavy. Another oilskin pouch contained Honor's jewellery, and a wad of yellowed paper.

Tobias felt his hands trembling as he opened it, extracting, his marriage certificate and his infant's birth certificate. There was a note, written in Lucian's hand.

The ship has broken her back and is drifting in heavy seas off the isle of Portland. To whoever finds this cradle, the infant's name is Rose Darsham. Deliver the cradle and the precious contents to Tobias Darsham of the Darsham and Morcant Shipping Company. If the infant perishes, please inform him of the same.

Tobias, if you read this, I did my best. Tell my two sons they mean the world to me, and I love them dearly.

Lucian Morcant, captain of the Cormorant

Giving a groan of anguish Tobias fell to his knees, gazing at the brooch in his hand. He was sure now that what his mother had suspected was true. There was too much evidence to support her theory. So if Joanna was his daughter it was impossible for her to remain his wife. But what the hell was he to do about it?

Scrambling upright, he cleared away the evidence of

his investigation and placed the brooch back on Joanna's dressing-table. He had to think, but he couldn't do it here.

He would sleep on the *Linnet* tonight and head back to London in the morning. He shrugged, thinking dolefully that if he were to disappear at sea the problem would be solved.

9

The harbour town of Poole proved to be a delight to Joanna. So busy, it was, with people, horses and carts going in all directions. The harbour jostled with boats, their masts spiking into the sky and swaying to and fro, so it was a wonder they didn't get tangled and tied up together like a bunch of bean poles. Although she looked, Joanna couldn't see Tobias's little craft, but no doubt the *Linnet* would be hidden amongst her taller cousins.

Poole smelled of the sea, and of the backwater mud flats they'd passed, where people dug for cockles and whelks. It was a place Joanna thought she might investigate once Tilda was well, for there was nothing as tasty as shellfish dug fresh from their beds. Seagulls wheeled and shrieked as they dived to snatch up a titbit from the reeking flats, but the birds were part of her life, so she was used to them.

Not long after their carriage emerged from a pleasant park, Charlotte indicated a mysterious looking and thickly treed stretch of land across the water with a wave of her hand. 'That place is called Brownsea Island.'

'Two hundred years ago they used to mine copperas there,' said Joanna, eager to make a good impression on her. 'I read all about it in one of Mr Lind's books.'

'What is copperas, exactly?'

'Exactly? I couldn't really say, for 'tis . . . it's science and I had hardly turned my mind to the whys and wherefores of it when Mr Lind had one of his turns, so I had to put the book aside. I believe it was washed from the rocks by the rain. It's boiled in big pans so it looks like green candy. They used it for dyeing and tanning leather and such.'

'Boiled rocks? How ridiculous. Your brain has been filled with nonsense.'

'Yes, Mrs Darsham,' she said, figuring it was best not to argue with her over it.

So many shops lined the streets that it was a bewilderment to Joanna. They sold everything anybody could ever need – and it seemed to her that her mother-in-law thought she needed everything. Her own opinion was sought, but constantly overruled.

'No, my dear. That colour, though pretty, will clash horribly with the bodice. Those boots are a little heavy for elegance. See, here are some nicer ones with pretty heels, and these silk ones with side lacing are suitable for grander occasions.'

The richness and price of the goods scared Joanna witless. She decided that her husband must either be very generous or very wealthy. Charlotte didn't pay for anything, just told the shopkeepers to charge it to the Darsham account.

'That's very expensive. Won't Tobias mind?' she

constantly asked, to which question Charlotte usually gave a light laugh and said, 'You mustn't worry about such things. We've not yet reached the limit Tobias set upon your wardrobe.'

They arrived home just as dusk was falling. Joanna's heart sank into her boots, for it was a blow to discover Tobias had departed without a word of farewell to her, especially since she'd been bubbling over with excitement over her purchases, and wanted to thank him for his generosity. He'd left a note for his mother, however.

The ache that settled around her heart was inexplicable to her, since she wasn't in love with Tobias. At least, not in the way she'd expected love to feel. Relieved he hadn't touched her in the way a husband was supposed to, her feelings towards him were affectionate and warm nevertheless, and she felt hurt and abandoned, as though she was lacking in his eyes.

But perhaps she *was* lacking with her island ways, for even the servants seem to speak nicer than she did. But if she worked hard she was sure she could overcome her defects and turn herself into something much more acceptable. Then Tobias might take her to see London.

'Did Tobias say when he'd be coming back?' she asked Charlotte.

Charlotte looked up from her embroidery to gaze out of the window at the bleak rainy day. 'Tobias comes and goes when he pleases. He has a great deal of responsibility on his shoulders and visits whenever he can find time.' Joanna's feet came under Charlotte's scrutiny. 'Try to remember not to cross your ankles, Joanna, dear. It looks untidy and prevents the proper circulation of the blood.'

Hastily uncrossing her legs, Joanna sighed, wondering how she'd ever remember all the things she was supposed to do, let alone all the things she was *not* supposed to do.

Placing her sewing aside Charlotte gazed at her. 'You seem restless.'

'My life seems to be one of idleness at the moment.'

'Then we must find you something to do. Some sewing, perhaps. You could learn to embroider your initials on your handkerchiefs.'

'I can already sew. I can patch and darn, turn up hems and sew seams. Why do I need to embroider my initials on handkerchiefs?'

'Why?' Charlotte spluttered, and a frown creased her brow. 'That's what young ladies do. They also learn to play an instrument or sing, concern themselves with the intricacies of the latest dance steps and the art of painting with watercolours. Once your wardrobe is complete and your manners are more refined, we will go visiting. I daresay you'll enjoy getting to know a few people.'

'Couldn't I do some gardening? We could be growing produce to eat, and sell anything we don't need to the neighbours. There is too much grass, and a man being paid to cut it short and to keep it looking fancy. It's a waste of money. A pair of sheep would do the same job as well as providing . . . well, never mind that process, seeing as I can no longer mention it for fear of offending. If we buy a spinning wheel, I could spin the wool to fashion into shawls, and I could knit Tobias some warm socks, too, for my ma showed me how.'

'I'm sure your mother was a good woman, Joanna. But what you are describing is in your past. I'm certainly not about to turn my home into a farm. My gardener has a family to support, too, so would miss the income his job provides him with. He also does other work, such as cleaning the windows and general repairs. As for shawls and socks.' Her nose wrinkled slightly. 'The shawl you wear about the house smells rather peculiar to me, especially when you stand near the fire.'

' 'Tis . . . sorry, *it is* the sheep's wool. Full of grease, it is. It keeps the rain out, though, and the warmth in.'

'I daresay the garment does, it's designed to keep sheep dry. I've seen the peasants in the fields wearing them.' Charlotte's tone of voice alerted Joanna that she would prefer her not to wear the shawl again. Well, she thought, waste not, want not. Tilda would need a warm shawl to go out in when she was better, so she'd give it to her. And she'd bought her cousin a warm flannel petticoat, skirt and bodice with the money Tobias had left her for her own personal use, though the clothes would hang on Tilda like a sack at the moment. But Charlotte was asking her a question. 'What do you like doing besides gardening and farming?'

'I like to read and I also like to walk. In Portland there were many hills to climb, with fine views from the top. Sometimes, when the day was clear, you could see the Channel Islands on the horizon. And I used to look at the mainland and wonder what it was like here. But now I am here folk are not so bad as I thought they'd be, though their ways are strange to me, and I don't understand them.'

'They're only strange because you've been brought up using different ways, and the way we do things is simply unfamiliar to you. Has it occurred to you that the island way of doing things might be strange to us?'

Joanna shook her head, slightly chastened by the thought. 'That could be true, I suppose.'

'It is true. The sooner you learn our ways the easier it will be for you to settle.' Charlotte took hold of her hands. 'I'm pleased you like to read, for that will serve two purposes. My eyesight is becoming poor, so perhaps you could read to me for an hour a day, and I'll assist you with pronunciation at the same time. And there is no reason why we should not go into the countryside when the weather improves, although I cannot walk as far as you. If we purchase a tablet of paper and some pencils, you could try and sketch what you see.'

Joanna grinned, remembering her pa helping her draw pictures when she was small, and the way he'd chuckled at her efforts. 'I would look forward to seeing the countryside. We could take Tilda when she's better.'

'When she's stronger an outing would do her good, I'm sure. Now, my dear, if you fetch me a piece of paper and a pencil, we'll design your initials for your handkerchiefs. Then the servants will know to whom they belong. I'll find you some silks and show you how to embroider them in satin stitch. You need not do them all at once, of course, just when you have some spare time on your hands.'

And that, Joanna thought with a slight grimace, was

nearly all the time, and the task would be about as much of a pleasure as observing Charlotte's gentle manipulation of her. She wondered: if Charlotte had to fend for herself without servants running around after her, how on earth would she cope?

Tobias sailed the *Linnet* up the Thames to Southwark. It was late in the evening. He was tired after battling a choppy sea against headwinds for the past sixteen hours and having been forced to tack back and forth for most of the way. Securing the yacht to the jetty, he strolled up the path to his house, letting himself in through the front door.

The grandfather clock in the hall was striking eleven when he handed his oilskins to his housekeeper, who was in the process of lowering the lamps and locking the doors.

'Were there any messages in my absence, Mrs Bates?'

'Mr Morcant dropped by to deliver the painting you commissioned of the *Joanna Rose*. I've propped it against the sofa. Can I get you anything, sir? A brandy perhaps?'

'I'll help myself to brandy. I'd like some hot food if there is some.'

'Cook left a pot of beef and vegetable broth keeping warm over the fire for you, just in case you arrived home late.'

'Thank you. I'll have it on a tray with some bread. And some coffee. Is the fire in the drawing room lit?'

'Yes, sir. I'll go and stoke it up a bit.'

'I'll do that. Just bring me the broth. I can fend for myself, after that.'

He took the lamp into the drawing room, turning up the flame so he could examine the portrait of Honor, hanging over the fireplace.

Smoke had darkened it over the years, he realized. Her cornflower eyes were now navy blue, the dark torrent of her hair dull. The soft curve of her mouth still enticed, but her once porcelain white skin was now yellow. Honor would be nothing but bones now, he thought, surprised by the detachment he felt. Yet it could have been Joanna Rose gazing back at him from the frame, except Honor's mouth was smaller. He groaned, his worst fear now confirmed. Why the hell hadn't he seen the resemblance before he'd married her? Or had he simply married Joanna because she reminded him of Honor?

After Bates had served him his broth and retired for the night, Tobias said out loud, 'Our daughter is alive, Honor, and she looks to be the very image of you. I suspect she has my disposition, though, for there is an independent air about her. Her name is Joanna Rose, so she still has the name you called her.'

Honor gazed serenely down at him from her painted eyes as he hungrily consumed the beef and vegetable broth, then set the plate aside. Aloud, he said to her, 'I'm in a terrible dilemma now, for I was attracted to the girl and her plight touched my heart. I wed her before I investigated her background and knew the truth of it.'

Sparks flew up the chimney as he attacked the smoking coals with the poker. 'Only my mother suspects our relationship is father and daughter, and she's the only one who's aware of this unnatural marriage. If this gets out, my reputation, Joanna's and that of the company will be in ruins. It will never recover, because people love a scandal and will want to believe the worst. Then the predators will move in. So, I'm taking the only option available that makes any sense to me at the moment. And that means you must be banished.'

Standing on a chair he removed Honor's portrait, replacing it with the painting of the *Joanna Rose* in full sail on a glassy green, foam-flecked sea. Thaddeus would complain, but what the hell.

'Out of sight, out of mind,' he said, heading for the attic. But he'd been free of Honor's memory for many years, he thought, as he stowed the painting in the darkest corner. It was the sight of others he feared now, in case somebody else noticed the resemblance.

The next morning Tobias went to the office, as usual, greeting Alexander Morcant with a broad smile.

'I dropped in on you a day or two ago. You were out,' Alex said.

'Checking up on me, young Alex? Thanks for dropping the painting off. I'm keeping it.'

Alex grinned from ear to ear. 'Stop calling me young Alex. I'm twenty-eight years old, and it's bad for my image.'

'I stayed longer with my mother than expected. Did you get my telegraph?'

'Of course. *Joanna Rose*, it is. Who is she, Tobias?'

His eyes slid away from Alex, then came back. 'I went to Portland on the anniversary, to visit my wife's grave, and—'

'You named the ship after your infant daughter.'

'That's right,' Tobias said, seizing on the assumption with a wry smile, for he was reluctant to reveal the presence of Joanna until he'd worked out how he could resolve the problem with the least damage to all concerned. He changed the subject. 'Has the new crew been signed on yet?'

Joanna Rose was to set sail on her maiden voyage in two weeks. Thaddeus Scott would have command of her as she transported passengers south to the Australian continent.

'The day after tomorrow. No doubt Captain Scott would prefer your input into the matter to mine. He doesn't think much of desk sailors. His officers are to be dispersed for various reasons. John Manders is retiring, Edward Staines is assuming command of the *Nightingale* and Bishop and Hayes have elected to join my brother on the *Clara Jane* and the shorter American run. Oliver has met a woman he likes in America and is thinking of proposing marriage, by the way.'

'Is he, by God! Well, I suppose it's about time. We need some fresh blood in the family for the future of the company. It'll be your turn next.'

When Alexander shrugged, Tobias suddenly remembered he was not a Morcant by blood. 'Sorry, Alex, that was insensitive of me. Actually, I never think of you as anything else but a Morcant. If you'd rather be a Darsham, I could arrange to adopt you. I'm sure my mother wouldn't mind having a grandson. It would take the heat off me, too. I'm in my forties and sometimes she treats me as if I was still in knee britches. She sends you her love, by the way.'

Punching him on the shoulder, Alexander grinned. 'If you want a son I suggest you find yourself a wife and produce one of your own. Now, sod off, some of us have work to get on with. Go and have a look at the *Joanna Rose*, you haven't seen her yet.'

Tobias nodded. 'I'm visiting Thaddeus later. No doubt he'll take me over her. Then it's over to Lloyds to see who's willing to insure *Joanna Rose* on her maiden voyage to Australia.'

Alexander's face assumed a pained expression. 'I'm not just a pretty face; the insurance is already taken care of. I escorted the underwriters on board for a tour of the ship. Captain Scott put on his best uniform and fed them navy rum. After that, they literally fell over themselves to insure us.'

'Is there *anything* at all you need me to do?'

'Come and have dinner with me on Saturday, Tobias. We can take in the theatre afterwards, and there's a couple of dancers in the cast I've struck up an acquaintanceship with.'

Tobias chuckled as he headed for the door, feeling slightly superfluous. Alexander was terrifyingly efficient and the company was in excellent hands. 'What's wrong with you, Alex, can't you handle the pair of them by yourself?'

Laughter in his voice, Alex hurled after him, 'Sure, I can, Papa, but one of the dancers prefers older men.'

'Ouch,' he said as the office door closed behind him.

*

Joanna Rose looked like the aristocrat she was, with her long, low hull and her tall masts. Thaddeus, his hair greying now, but his body still upright, watched as Tobias craned his neck to see the top of the mast. His lips pursed into a long, low whistle and he said, 'That's a long way up. Permission to come aboard, Captain Scott.'

His old friend smiled when he stepped aboard. 'I was expecting you to be on the quay when we tied up.'

'You arrived earlier than I expected.'

'Ah, the ship's a dream to sail . . . a dream I tell you. She couldn't wait to spread her wings. If you fancy going aloft, be my guest.'

'I'm too old and out of practice to go swinging amongst the spars like a monkey. Am I to take it that you like her, Thaddeus?'

'I'd throttle anyone who tried to relieve me of her command. She loves the ocean and cuts through the water at a rate of twenty knots if need be.'

The enthusiasm in the master mariner's voice made Tobias smile. 'A fast lady, then.'

'Last year, Captain Forbes did the Liverpool to Melbourne and return voyage in five months and nine days on the *Lightning*,' he said with some pride. '*Joanna Rose* could probably equal it given the same conditions.'

'Forbes pushes his crew and ship to the limit, and to my mind he takes risks with both his vessel, his crew and the passengers,' Tobias said sternly. 'Besides, the weather would have been in his favour.'

'Could be, but I heard that he ran into a squall on the way back and lost some canvas. He's an excellent seaman and navigator, though. Come below and look at the accommodations.'

There was ample height between decks to stand upright. The officers' quarters bordered on sumptuous. 'See these,' Thaddeus said, pounding his fist on a padded seat. 'Life preservers. So are the mattresses. They can be clipped together to form a raft. Ninety passengers can be carried aboard this ship, and almost every available berth is booked.'

'You don't have to sell her to me, Thaddeus. I've been living and breathing her for the past two years.'

'So you have.' Pulling out a bottle and two glasses, Thaddeus poured them a generous tot apiece and seated himself in the master's chair. 'Let's be having it, then.'

'Having what?'

'You tell me. I've known you since you were a midshipman, Tobias, and I'm well aware of when something is on your mind. Woman trouble, is it?'

Taking a sip of rum, Tobias grimaced. 'This still looks and tastes like varnish to me.'

'It's the best grog you can get, Royal Navy issue. Someone in the know supplies me with the occasional cask or two.' Draining his glass, Thaddeus set it down with a bang and stared hard at his employer. 'Spit it out, mister. I haven't got all day.'

'I married a wonderful woman a few days ago.'

A smile split the captain's face in two. 'Well damn me, Tobias, you're a dark horse. That's something to celebrate. Where is she? I'll want to look her over before I leave port.'

'She's in Poole with my mother.' He swallowed the rest of his drink for the courage it would afford him and felt his nostrils narrow as he deeply inhaled. 'I haven't finished. It's me who's damned, and the company as well if this gets out. The girl is only eighteen, and although I didn't realize it at the time, I believe she is my own daughter, Rose, who was reported lost from the *Cormorant* all those years ago.'

Tobias managed to raise a wry smile at the stunned expression on Thaddeus Scott's face. 'Luckily, she's remained my wife only in name.'

Thaddeus found his voice, though it sounded cracked. 'That's a blessing. Can't the pair of you simply get the marriage annulled?'

'I've thought of that. Something as unusual as this would be discussed and debated amongst the bishops. The secret would get out. If the papers got hold of it, the speculation would be vicious and damaging to all concerned. Think what it would do to me, to my family and to the company. Besides which, Joanna Rose doesn't know she's my daughter.'

Thaddeus nodded as the origin of his ship's name was revealed. 'Does Charlotte know?'

'It was my mother who first brought up the likeness Joanna had to the portrait of Honor. She fainted when she first set eyes on her. There are other clues, too. Joanna was in possession of the cradle I carved for Rose all those years ago, and she has a brooch I gave to Honor. Her *father*, so called, told her some tale about her being carried ashore in the cradle, with a seagull navigating from the prow. He told her God had given the gull the soul of a drowned seaman.'

Seriously, Thaddeus said, 'It would have been Lucian's soul, I reckon. How else would the cradle with its precious cargo have survived the treacherous seas around Portland that year?' He rubbed the edge of his thumbnail gently along the grain of the table, smiling as the full significance of the clipper's name clicked into place. *Joanna Rose* would be a lucky ship. His gaze came up to meet that of Tobias. 'What do you intend to do about this situation, then?'

'I'm going to die.'

Leaning across the table Thaddeus grabbed him by the lapels, shook him hard and threw him a ferocious glare. 'Like hell you are!'

'Put me down, would you. I didn't mean literally. But I have no choice but to disappear, and I want you to help me, for there's nobody else I can trust my plan to except you and James Stark.' He subsided back into his chair when Thaddeus let him go. 'Remember when we talked about opening a shop in Melbourne . . . ?'

'Ah, I was just joshing.'

'I know, but it gave me the idea.'

Thaddeus grinned as Tobias began to outline his plan. 'I can give you a new identity if you like. I had a younger brother called Gabriel who never made it out of childhood. Had he lived, he would have been about your age now.'

'Gabriel Scott. Hmmm . . . I like it.'

'Gabriel Tremayne. My mother had married a Cornishman by then.'

'When will we do it?'

'You'll want to say your farewells first. What about cash? If you suddenly empty your bank account it will look suspicious, and you'll only be able to take what you stand up in.'

'I have some gold nobody knows about.'

'You can do nothing to draw attention to yourself. Give the gold to me as soon as you can. As you know there are gold rushes going on all around the Melbourne area. Some of the gold remains unaccounted for. I have contacts in England. I can exchange it for cash, and at competitive rates.'

Tobias raised an eyebrow. 'Have you been using company vessels to run a business on the side, Thaddeus?'

Thaddeus gave him a steady look as he growled, 'If I had, would I be telling you about it? Come to that, would you mind informing me where *your* gold has come from?'

'Would you believe that, not a week ago, Lucian donated it to secure a future for my daughter? It was used as ballast to keep the cradle steady.'

'Aye, I'd believe that of Lucian, but not that *he's* still alive. He'd never have denied Alex as his son.'

'He left a message for both his sons. It was concealed in the cradle Joanna came ashore in, along with my wife's jewellery.' Taking Lucian's note from his pocket, Tobias slid it across the table for Thaddeus to read. 'Unfortunately, under the circumstances I can't pass it on to them.'

Thaddeus shrugged as he handed the note back. 'Are you sure you want to do this, Tobias? Your mother will grieve. And what about Alex? You told me you'd made him your heir. As your widow, Joanna Rose will have claim to your estate, now.'

'Something she's entitled to have as my daughter. However, as to all intents and purposes she is my wife, I shall have to provide for her in a different manner.' The enormity of what he was about to do flooded through Tobias. The most bitter price he'd have to pay for knowing his daughter had survived would be to be denied the joy of getting to know her, or ever seeing her again. Already grief was settling around his heart at the realization.

'I've thought about Alex, too. I want Joanna Rose to be cared for, so I'm going to change my will. She'll inherit everything.'

'And Alex?'

He watched Thaddeus's eyes widen as he told him of what he'd come up with.

'You're taking one hell of a chance,' said the shocked sea captain.

'If I know Alex, he'll do what's best for the company, and for himself.'

But it was something Alex wouldn't like one little bit, for it would test his pride to the limit.

Tilda was looking much better. Tucked up on the couch in Joanna's sitting room with a rug over her lap, she was embroidering initials on to one of Joanna's handkerchiefs. Still thin and gaunt, her hair and eyes had a faint sheen to them now and her sickly pallor had been replaced by a tint of colour.

Tilda looked up from her task, and smiled. 'You look like a real lady in that gown.'

'And you'll look like a lady in yours, once Mrs Darsham allows you to get dressed.'

'I'll never be pretty like you. Look at your hair, all smooth and shiny and pulled back into that curve at the back. It looks so pretty.'

'The style is called a chignon. I'll ask Stevens to do yours like this when you're allowed out of bed. But there's more to being a lady than looks, Tilda. You have to walk and talk properly. And when you eat dinner you have to know which piece of cutlery to use for what, instead of a spoon and your fingers. Mrs Darsham is a stickler for these things. And all the servants have to be called by their last name.'

'I daresay you'd please yourself, if you wanted to. You always have before.'

'But I'm married now, so I'm trying hard to learn to do what's expected of me. I attend dancing school, which is good fun and warms me up on cold mornings. Most of the girls there are very young, about twelve, and they giggle a lot. And I have a voice teacher of my very own.'

'"We'll soon take the rough edges off young Mrs Darsham's voice,"' she said. 'Now repeat after me.' Standing, Joanna placed her palms against her middle and sucked in a deep breath, allowing it to escape in a slow, steady stream. 'Aaya – Eeya – Iya – Owa – Yohwa.'

'Owa deaya,' said Tilda, giving a snort. 'And here was me thinking it was a poor old dog howlin' at the window to be let in.' She sighed. 'Will Mrs Darsham mind me being in here? I'm not supposed to be out of bed.'

'She's gone out to play cards. Anyway, it's my own private sitting room, where I can entertain my friends. And since you're my friend, you can be my guest any time I wish it. Of course, the room belongs to my husband as well, in case we want to discuss private things.' She shrugged. 'Not that he's here to discuss anything with, privately or not, and his mother said he comes and goes as he pleases, and with no warning.' She brightened then. 'Not that I'm in any hurry to become a wife to him, either, though I daresay it would be nice to have a baby of my own, one day.'

The small shudder Tilda gave developed into a bigger shudder, and an expression of abject misery settled upon her face. Instantly, Joanna was by her side, holding her close, guessing what was behind it. 'You mustn't allow your brothers to ruin your life like they did Mary's. They're just pigs who will come to no good in the end. Try and put it behind you.'

'There's something I haven't told you, Joanna.'

'Then spit it out, so it's gone.'

'I think one of my brothers has planted a child inside me.'

The breath whooshed from Joanna's body in a rush, to be slowly regained as she gazed at Tilda's shamed face. 'Oh, Tilda.' Caressing her cheek, Joanna felt the dampness of her cousin's tears and gently dabbed them away with her handkerchief. 'With the state you were in when we found you, surely an infant wouldn't have survived inside you.'

'I'm scared that there is one. I'm that worried, since I've missed my courses for three months.' Tilda clutched her sleeve. 'Joanna, what if there is an infant? I couldn't bear it. I'd kill myself.'

Joanna rocked Tilda back and forth, scolding. 'Hush, Tilda. You'll not do such a wicked thing to yourself. I won't allow it.'

'But Mrs Darsham will throw me out on the street when she finds out. Where will I go, what will I do?'

Holding Tilda even tighter, Joanna vowed, 'If she does throw you out, I'll go with you, I swear.'

'You're wed now. You'll have to do as your husband tells you.'

'Will I, indeed? If he thinks that's going to happen, to hell with him as well. I'm young and strong and I'm learning things all the time. I'll find a job and support us both if need be. In the meantime, we'd better keep quiet about your suspicions, just in case. Anyway, it might not even be true.'

And Joanna hoped it would prove to be a false alarm, because Tilda had been through too much in her life already, and she didn't need any more bad things happening to her.

10

A week later, Joanna was gazing out of the window at the gathering dusk when she saw Tobias turn into the gate. He was dressed warmly in a seaman's dark jumper, trousers and cap. The collar of a short jacket was pulled up around his ears as, head lowered, he butted into the fresh breeze.

'Tobias has arrived,' she said, straightening her skirts as she turned.

She'd regained her seat by the time he came into the drawing room. His wintry glance swept over her, then he smiled – a wonderful smile that was so irresistible it brought one just as wide from her. It was all too brief, however.

'You look beautiful, Joanna my dear,' he said.

'Thank you,' she said simply, feeling her face heat at the compliment and looking towards Charlotte, who had smiled too, and was gazing from one to the other, as if comparing them.

Charlotte gave a self-satisfied nod, then she turned her face up to be kissed by her son. 'You look cold, Tobias. Come over by the fire and warm yourself.'

There was a tense, strained look to him, Joanna thought as she sat watching him talk with his mother that evening. When the clock chimed ten, Charlotte announced her intention to retire.

Tobias gave his mother a prolonged hug. 'Don't be surprised if I'm gone when you wake up. There's some urgent business I have to attend to, and I'll be leaving early.'

'Not in the *Linnet* again, surely? You don't usually sail her in the winter. The wind is strong and you've only just got here.'

'I need to get back. *Linnet* is perfectly seaworthy and the wind will blow itself out. The water isn't as rough as you might think; I've sailed in worse conditions in the summer.'

Charlotte hesitated, as if she sensed something untoward. 'Is there some trouble concerning the company, Tobias?'

'With Alex doing most of the work, the company is in better hands than it's ever been.' He kissed her again. 'Stop worrying about me, I'm a big boy now. Goodnight, Mother.'

Left alone with Tobias, Joanna could only gaze silently at him. She was somewhat in awe of him, for he wore an air of unconscious authority it felt natural to defer to. The bruise around his eye had dispersed, but he needed a shave, for his whiskers were a dark shadow against his face. She grinned, for he looked rather disreputable with a beard, and said, 'How tired you look,' when he raised a questioning eyebrow.

'I haven't been sleeping well lately. How is your

cousin Tilda getting along?' he asked, and the interest in his grey eyes warmed her.

'Her health is improving now she's eating properly. I have you to thank for that, for if you hadn't risked your life to rescue her she'd likely be dead by now. You're tough when put to the test.'

Her praise seemed to embarrass him, for he shifted from one foot to the other. 'I'm pleased she's beginning to recover. Good friends are hard to come by and we should look after them. And you, Joanna, are you happy here? How are you getting on with my mother?'

'Charlotte is very kind to me, even though I vex her sometimes. She's teaching me all the things I'll need to know when you take me to live in London. I don't want you to be ashamed of me.'

For a moment he looked startled. 'Good Lord, is that what you think? I'll never be ashamed of you, Joanna. What my mother teaches you is for your own sake.' From his pocket he took a velvet bag and placed it in her lap. 'This jewellery used to belong to my wife, Honor. I'd like you to have it.'

Loosening the strings, Joanna gazed at the selection of glittering stones and gold. 'I've never had anything so precious before, except for a brooch that my mother gave me,' she breathed in wonder.

Tobias picked out a ring set with a heart-shaped blue stone, sliding it on to her finger. 'I gave Honor this when we first met. Her eyes were a lighter blue than yours. I was going to buy you one of your own, but the sapphire picks up the colour of your eyes perfectly, and I doubted they could be matched so well.'

She gazed up at him, seeing beyond the strong, stern face to the kindness of the man inside. 'This must hold strong sentiment for you, Tobias. I'll look after it carefully, and I'll think of Honor and all she meant to you when I wear it.'

'Honor would like that, and I think she would have approved of me giving you the ring. You resemble her in many ways.'

Retying the ribbons, Joanna set the bag aside, pleased he hadn't married his first wife for position. 'Did you love her very much?'

'Aye, girl, and I still do, for in my heart she'll always be the young girl I first fell in love with and wed. But a man cannot mourn for ever, and her living presence faded long ago. I can think and talk of her easily and with fondness, but without pain now.'

Sensing the need in him, she said, 'Tell me about her then, Tobias.'

'There was a merriment and mischief about her, she smiled easily. And she spoke differently to English folk, for she was born and brought up in America.' His eyes took on a distant expression. 'Honor was vivacious, quick witted and how she used to tease me. Once, I remember when she . . .'

By the time Tobias finished talking, Joanna knew just about everything there was to know about Honor Darsham, and she liked the woman Tobias had presented her with.

'I will try to live up to her memory,' she said uncertainly, wondering if she could ever be as admirable or beloved.

Taking her hands in his, Tobias pulled her from her seat. The ring he usually wore on his little finger was missing, leaving a white shadow against his skin. He smiled as his eyes thoroughly scrutinized her face, as if he wanted to imprint it on his memory. 'My intention was not to encourage you to compare yourself to her. You're a lovely woman in your own right, Joanna Rose. I feel privileged to have found you, and I'll never regard you as anything other than the person you are. I think our meeting was meant to be, you know.'

'Like destiny?' Shyness filled her then. 'Perhaps you're right, for you were certainly there when I needed you. I'll try to be a good wife to you, Tobias. I promise.'

He kissed her forehead, then pulled her into his arms and hugged her tight. He smelled of the sea air. She felt warm and protected being held by him, her ear against his beating heart. But it was a reassuring warmth rather than a passionate sort of warmth. She remembered her ma hugging her in such a comforting manner, and knew she loved Tobias in the same way as she'd loved her ma and pa.

'I know we've only been acquainted a little while, but in my own way I do love you, Joanna Rose,' he whispered against her hair. 'Whatever happens, I want you to remember that, always.'

His words sounded sincere, but her mother had said men often duped women with words of love, when all they really wanted was to lay with them and slake their lusts. Then she thought, Tobias is an honourable man, for he married me, and for whatever the reason, he has the right to me.

She told him, but hesitantly, because she didn't know what her response to such an avowal of love should be, 'I like you a great deal, Tobias. I feel I've known you all my life, and I know I'll learn to love you in time. Meanwhile, I'm grateful for the affection and care you offer me.'

'Go to bed,' he said, his voice gruff as he released her. 'Don't stay awake on my account for I'll be off in a couple of hours.'

The relief she experienced was overwhelming as she picked up the jewellery. When she reached the door she turned to gaze at him. He had a smile on his face and tears in his eyes. And there was such a naked longing in his expression that she felt the urge to comfort him. But all she could say was, 'Take care of yourself, Tobias, dear.'

His expression was quickly masked. 'Go now, I need to be alone,' he said softly, and she went.

But Joanna couldn't sleep, and the downstairs clock gave four chimes before she heard the front door click shut and the sound of his boots crunching on the gravel path. The sound became softer and softer, then it ceased.

She thought of his brave little boat, *Linnet*, so small a craft on such a big sea, and so willing and responsive to his touch. 'May the wind carry you safely to your destination, Tobias,' she whispered before sleep claimed her.

Linnet was found adrift on her side two days later, carried along by the tide and currents several miles from where she'd been abandoned. She was towed into Southampton by the son of the fisherman who'd found her.

On being questioned, the man told the port authorities, 'The jib were still rigged, but the mainsail was draggin' in the water so we had to cut it free before we could get her upright and bale her enough to tow. We reckon her skipper got knocked overboard when the halyard broke. We searched the area, but we found nothing. If there'd been a body we would have dragged it up in the nets. Judging by the tide and currents we think he must've gone overboard over Portland way.'

Enquiries were telegraphed to harbours along the coast to keep a watch for a body. *Linnet*'s owner was quickly identified as Tobias Darsham in Poole, where the sloop was registered.

Mr Darsham is part owner of the Darsham and Morcant Shipping Company, which is jointly managed by Mr Alexander Morcant, the Poole harbour master telegraphed back.

A sloop had been reported to be in trouble the previous day. The crew of a fishing lerret from Portland has sworn a statement that they saw a man knocked overboard. Although they searched the area and dragged it with their nets, they couldn't recover his body. In each statement, and on being separately questioned, the description of events and the man who was lost overboard, coincided. The water was choppy, the tide on the ebb and running fast. I alerted the coast-guard, who were of the opinion that if the fishermen couldn't rescue the man, nobody could. One of their cutters was sent out. Although they found a life preserver, they were unable to find the sloop. We concluded it had sunk and the skipper drowned.

That same afternoon, Alex was at his desk when the sudden silence from the outer office alerted him to the fact that the telegraph was spelling out something he might not like.

With growing unease he waited for the head clerk to knock at the door and, curbing his impatience, crossed to the window to train the telescope on to the *Joanna Rose*. She was loading stores, the new crew going about their business under the watchful eyes of the officers. The passengers would be going on board the following morning and she would sail on the tide.

The day was bleak, flurries of snow melted on the wind, descending as icy slush. He hoped the weather didn't hold the ship up, since she'd taken a big slice of the company's capital to build and she needed to start paying her way as soon as possible. At least she had a full passenger list, and there had been some last-minute cargo.

Thaddeus Scott would be sailing with a full complement of crew and officers, some experienced and some fully certificated, who would gain experience under his tutelage. *Joanna Rose*, commanded by the company's most experienced and senior master, would carry a good payload on her maiden voyage to Australia.

'Come in,' he said when the expected rap at the door sounded. His dark eyes searched the ashen contours of Henry Wetherall's face. 'What is it man? One of our ships?' *Not the* Clara Jane. *Surely, not his brother, Oliver!* 'Which one? Cough it out?'

'It's not one of the company's ships. It's Mr Darsham.'

After an initial reaction of relief, shock thudded into Alexander's midriff like a stone fist. 'Tobias? What's happened to him?'

Wetherall cleared his throat. 'His yacht *Linnet* was found drifting with its mainsail dragging in the water and its decks awash. There's no sign of Mr Darsham, either on board or in the immediate area. They think the halyard broke. It appears he was knocked overboard and drowned the day previously, for the crew of a Portland fishing boat witnessed him falling overboard. The authorities want to know if they should inform Mrs Charlotte Darsham direct.'

Alexander stared at him. 'Tobias could swim. He might have made it to shore.'

'The boat was several miles out, there was a heavy swell and the water was cold.'

Alexander sat heavily in his chair. *Tobias gone? Oh God!* He made a conscious effort to banish any sign of distress, knowing he'd be howling like a baby if he was alone.

'Can I get you anything, sir?'

'A brandy, if you would, Mr Wetherall. Have one yourself.'

'Thank you, sir.' Wetherall headed for the decanter, coming back with a snifter apiece. Alexander downed his in two swallows, grateful for the strength it immediately gave him. He was tempted to have another, but was aware of the heavy responsibility that now lay on his shoulders. He had to draw on his own strength, not find it in the bottom of a bottle.

He rose to his feet. 'Telegraph them back and tell the

harbour master I'll go to Poole and inform Mrs Darsham personally. Can you handle the company for a while, Henry? I'll need to tell Captain Scott before he sails, then I'll have to see Mr Darsham's household and his lawyer. After that, I'll have to travel down to Poole. It might be two or three days, but I'll get back as soon as I can.'

'Yes, sir.'

'Try to remain calm, and reassure anyone who enquires. Our customers must be given no cause for alarm. The company will continue to accept cargo and passenger bookings, and will carry on conducting business as usual. You understand?'

'Yes, Mr Morcant.'

'Good.' Feeling strangely detached, Alexander snatched his coat from the rack and made his way to the outer office, with Henry Wetherall trailing after him. He gazed around at the employees, some of whom had been with the company for several years. They looked as stunned as he felt, and all of them were looking at him, expecting him to say something. He drew in a shuddering breath. 'You have heard the sad news. We will all miss Mr Darsham, who has been my friend and mentor since I was a child.' Feeling his voice begin to break, Alexander finished hurriedly, 'Tobias Darsham would have counted on your support in a crisis, and I hope . . . indeed, *know* I can do the same. Thank you all.'

There was a murmur of voices as he walked away from them, into the light of a cold and uncaring day. He was glad of the rain that beat against his face, for it blended with his tears and hid them from the world.

Nobody would know that this figure in his dark coat, who lowered his head into the wind-driven rain, felt entirely alone in his grief.

By the time he reached the *Joanna Rose*, Alexander had composed himself. He found Captain Scott in his cabin and came straight to the point, convinced his pain lay naked on his face for everyone to see. 'Tobias has disappeared from his yacht. He is believed drowned. I wanted you to know before you sailed, Captain Scott, for I don't know what you'll be returning to.'

Gravely, Thaddeus gazed at him, the expression in his eyes impenetrable. 'Tobias set great store by your skills, Alex. He told me you could run the company better than he ever could, and I know for a fact that it's true. Wherever he is, I reckon Tobias Darsham knows you won't let him or the company down.' Thaddeus held out his hand. 'Let's shake on that before we both go about our business. And if at any time you have doubts to air, you know where I'm likely to be. Give Charlotte Darsham my regards. Tell her I'll personally present my condolences, upon my return.'

'I will. God speed, then, Captain Scott.'

'I'll trust better to my own skills to navigate the oceans with,' Thaddeus said with a slight grin as he took Alex's proffered hand in a strong grip. 'I understand ships, and sailing the *Joanna Rose* will be as smooth as silk. She'll carry me to the far reaches of the earth. A pity you won't be aboard to see her canvas fill with wind as she begins to fly. You'll have to sail with Oliver to America one day. It wouldn't take long to find your sea legs.'

'I feel ill enough just standing on deck.'

'It's all in your mind, Alex lad. You could do it if the incentive was strong enough. I haven't given up on you yet.' The pair went up on deck together, where the ship's crew bustled about, heaving stores and luggage aboard with a chaotic abandonment, curses, whistles and shouts. Both officers and crew moved respectfully out of Captain Scott's way, touching fingers to their caps.

'Should I tell them?' Alex said, suddenly unsure.

'Nay, for seamen are a superstitious lot, and to hear of a death before a maiden voyage might be a bad omen for some of them, and there'll likely be desertions. I'll tell them when we've safely returned and are back in port. Good luck, Alex. I'm sure you'll manage.'

Alexander didn't linger. He didn't have the time, not even to ponder why Thaddeus hadn't seemed to be quite so upset by the news as he'd expected him to be.

Alexander and the lawyer, James Stark, who wasn't much older than Tobias, and had nondescript dark eyes and hair to match, travelled down to Poole together.

They took the train from London to Southampton where, after a tedious wait, they boarded another train to Dorchester. Alighting at Poole junction, which was the nearest they could get to the bustling port, they hired a carriage to take them the rest of the way, because it was a long walk.

Alexander had been pleased to have the lawyer's company. James had an astute mind, but an annoying habit of ignoring any questions he thought were none of Alexander's business. The man had been as close as an oyster regarding Tobias's estate, except to hum in his throat and tell him that Tobias had recently updated his will, and there were two main beneficiaries.

To be fair, it was not surprising that James was tight-lipped, for he'd attended school with Tobias. Not only had Tobias been godfather to James's eldest son, the two belonged to the same clubs and were firm friends. James would be feeling his loss keenly.

Alexander had reason to believe he was one of those beneficiaries, since Tobias had hinted strongly as much on at least a couple of occasions. Whom Tobias had willed his share of the company to was of the utmost importance, since business could become quickly destabilized under circumstances such as this. It was unrealistic to suppose that Charlotte Darsham would have inherited the company.

Because it was late, they spent the night at a boarding house. Alexander's numbness was gradually being replaced by feelings of anger and sadness at the loss of so fine a friend, so he tossed and turned for most of the night. When he woke he still felt tired; nevertheless, he rose to wash and shave, then dressed in the sober suit he'd thought to put on before he left. His face in the mirror looked taut, his eyes hollow and ringed by darkness.

'If you'd like to break the news privately to Mrs Darsham first, I'll follow you in half an hour,' James said over breakfast.

Alexander nodded, not looking forward to such a task.

*

Charlotte herself opened the door to his knock, a smile instantly appearing on her face when she saw him. 'Alex! How wonderful. I haven't seen you for several months.' Her smile faded. 'My dear, you look quite dreadful. Is Tobias with you?'

As he gazed at her, almost mute from his own grief, her face suddenly drained of all colour. 'Something has happened to him, hasn't it?'

He stepped inside the hall when she stood aside, closed the door behind him and took her in his arms. 'Charlotte, I'm so sorry. They found his yacht disabled and drifting two days ago. James Stark will be here to see you shortly.'

A sob wrenched from her. 'It's been three days since Tobias left here. Is there no chance that he made it to shore?'

Slowly, Alexander shook his head. 'There's been no sign of him.'

Hearing a sound on the stair he looked over Charlotte's head to see a young woman of exquisite beauty. Dressed in a blue gown, her dark hair smoothly styled into a chignon from a centre parting, she was poised on the landing, her mouth forming a soft exclamation. 'Oh!'

Eyes the colour of hyacinths gazed into his, widened and stayed there for a few seconds, then they shifted to Charlotte and alarm filled them. Rapidly, she descended the stairs.

'Who are you?' she asked, and, without waiting for an answer, 'Is something wrong with Mrs Darsham? What has happened?'

Charlotte abandoned his arms to take the girl into hers. 'Joanna, my dear, something entirely dreadful has occurred, and we must be strong.' Charlotte seemed to pull herself together, though her face retained a gaunt tenseness as the skin was pinched into creases, emphasizing her cheekbones. In front of Alexander's eyes she seemed to have aged ten years in as many seconds. However, she remained calm and broke the news forthrightly. 'Tobias is dead, my dear. Let us go into the drawing room. I'll order some refreshment when the lawyer arrives.'

Arms about each other's waists the pair preceded him into the drawing room. Tears trickled down the girl's cheeks as she took a seat beside Charlotte on the sofa, looking stunned. The two women joined hands, clinging together for comfort in their shared tragedy.

Who was she? Alexander wondered. Her face was familiar to him, but he also knew he'd never met her before. Joanna, Charlotte had called her. His heart thumped against his ribs. *Joanna Rose?*

Clearing his throat, he leaned forward, saying to her, 'I'm Alexander Morcant.' When she gave him a blank stare he experienced a twinge of pique. Surely someone in the house had mentioned him to her. After all, it was not as if he lacked importance in the affairs of the Darsham family.

Charlotte started. 'I'm so sorry, Alex, I should have introduced you. This is Joanna Rose Darsham. Alex manages the company, Joanna.'

'Company? Ah yes, where Tobias works . . . worked.' She seemed singularly ill informed. A poor cousin perhaps, brought in to act as companion to Charlotte? Though he couldn't recall Tobias ever mentioning any Darsham cousins.

As if she'd read his mind, Charlotte added, 'Joanna is Tobias's wife.'

'*Wife?*' Bewildered, he stared at her. 'Tobias had a wife? He didn't tell me.'

'They were wed only two weeks ago.'

His shock was absolute, and he didn't realize he was staring at the young woman until colour tinged her cheeks.

'Do you always stare so, Mr Morcant?'

'I'm sorry . . . I didn't know . . . You're so young. Forgive me.' Awkwardly, he stared down at his hands, which were dangling uselessly between his knees. His mind was in a whirl as anger and hurt jostled together inside him. Why hadn't Tobias told him about this Joanna? Good God! She must have meant much to Tobias, since he'd named the company's newest ship after her. Was she some little trollop who'd managed to sink her talons into him?'

'Where did you meet Tobias?' he heard himself ask.

'In Portland. He was visiting Honor, his first wife's grave. Somebody . . . a man attacked me. Tobias intervened.'

Tobias had talked to her about Honor? 'What were you doing in Portland at the time?'

'I lived there.'

She was an islander, and he'd heard of the free and easy island way of courting. He couldn't stop his lip from curling slightly. 'Who was the man, and why did he *attack* you?'

Her chin lifted as she held his gaze. 'I find your tone to be quite hostile, Mr Morcant. Why do you imagine it's any your business?'

Charlotte squeezed her hand. 'Joanna, my dear, Alex is almost one of the family; he doesn't mean to be rude.'

Her gaze didn't waver from his. 'That I would hear from his own lips. Did you mean to be so rude, Mr Morcant?'

This was a feisty piece of goods Tobias had married! Alexander could see why his mentor would have been attracted to her, for she'd be more than a match for any man, and he imagined her looks would have attracted quite a few. He was saved from the distasteful task of apologizing again by a rap at the door. A few moments later, James Stark was ushered in.

Charlotte dismissed the maid after the refreshments arrived. 'I'll see to it myself, Stevens. We don't wish to be disturbed and I'll come and talk to the staff later.'

Once the inevitable condolences had been gone through and the tea had been served, James sighed as he opened his satchel, as if he wasn't looking forward to revealing the contents.

'Tobias changed his will about a week ago. At the same time he appointed me executor of his estate in the event of his sudden death.'

He gazed round at the three of them. 'Tobias has left all his worldly goods to Joanna Rose Darsham. The estate consists of his property in London, his business interests and his share of the Darsham and Morcant Shipping Company.'

Charlotte gave a faint smile and inclined her head as Joanna looked at her, uncomprehendingly.

'No,' Alexander whispered. 'He indicated I was to be his heir. Tobias wouldn't do such a terrible thing to me. How can a girl such as she own a shipping company? She must have used her wiles to rob Tobias of his senses.'

A tiny hiss of annoyance reached his ears.

'Please let me finish, Alexander. Tobias wants you to remain as head of Darsham and Morcant.' James hesitated a little. 'We discussed this at length, Alex, because there's no doubt Tobias wanted you to have control of the company. But nothing I could say would shift him from what he had in mind, and the condition is absolutely irrevocable.'

'What is it?' Alex said harshly.

'There's no easy way of saying this.' James drew in a ragged breath. 'Tobias stipulated that after a suitable time has elapsed, you marry Joanna Rose Darsham. In his words. "Thus, all I hold dear will pass into Alexander Morcant's capable hands, a man I love as if he was my own son."'

Alexander sat back, half stunned, heedless of what he was saying. 'Marry her? My God, she's from Portland. She's probably savage, dim-witted and has loose morals as well as being . . . *inbred*.'

There was silence after his insult. He looked around him. Both James and Charlotte wore disapproving expressions while Joanna Darsham's eyes were wide with shock and wounded feelings as she contemplated him. Teardrops quivered on her dark eyelashes.

'You'll apologize, Alexander,' Charlotte said quietly.

The breath went out of him. 'I'm sorry, that was unforgivable of me.' He appealed to Joanna. 'You do see, don't you, Mrs Darsham? You must know you would make an entirely unsuitable wife for me.'

She rose, straightening her skirts. 'The only thing I see is a man who is rude and boorish in the extreme. I'm afraid, Mr Morcant, that you would make me an unsuitable husband. I would not wed you under any circumstances.'

He hadn't expected that and muttered, 'The hell you wouldn't!'

'Tobias seems to have thought highly of you and I'm loath to question his judgement, for he was a man of good sense and sensitivity whom I admired greatly. Because of that I'd be grateful if you'd continue to manage the company, whatever that company is. If, however, you find the price you have to pay – namely the existence of myself – too onerous, please convey your pleasure to Mr James Stark. I'm sure he can find someone else just as skilled, but less judgemental and self-opinionated, to manage it. I wish you a good day, gentlemen. Charlotte, you'll excuse me under the circumstances, I think.' She left the room, closing the door behind her.

'Well, what have you done now, Alex?' Charlotte said. 'Tobias has offered you everything he owns, as he has always done. He wouldn't have expected you to throw it in his face in a fit of pique.'

Feeling trounced by the ear blistering he'd received, and totally ashamed of himself, for the ramifications of what Tobias had arranged were just sinking in, he said, 'Considering the circumstances of my visit, I've behaved with neither thought nor dignity. I hope you'll accept my apology. I'll leave a note for Mrs Joanna Darsham, in the hope she will read it and forgive me. Tobias would have expected me to consider the matter of marriage to her carefully, and I will.'

'But will Joanna Rose allow you to reconsider when you have wounded her feelings so deeply?'

James shrugged. 'Mrs Darsham strikes me as a sensible young lady. She will get over her megrims in time and Alex will have time in which to get on a better footing with her. The affair has yet to go through the coroner's court, and that can take some time, years perhaps. I have favours to call in, however, which might expedite matters. And it will help if his body is found. An alert has been put out and a search is being made along the coast. But if there are storms he could end up anywhere, and might never be found.'

'It all sounds so callous. I don't like to imagine Tobias floating across vast expanses of oceans for ever,' Charlotte said, the tremor in her voice pronounced.

'I expect he would sink eventually,' James said in a misguided attempt to comfort her.

'It's going to be a sad Christmas.' Charlotte suddenly began to cry and the two men gazed awkwardly at each other. Alex gave her his shoulder to cry on and finally she was composed again.

She said, 'I must go and tell the staff, then I must comfort Joanna. She is too young to experience grief by herself.'

After they left, Alexander gazed back at the house, to find Joanna watching them from the window on the landing. She didn't bother to hide herself, and her body had a dejected droop to it, which made him feel instantly guilty.

He gave her a small bow, which was all he could do. As she turned her back and moved away without acknowledgement of it, Alexander followed after James Stark, his face burning as he damned Tobias for placing him in such a predicament.

11

Alexander had never known such anger, for his sense of betrayal by Tobias was so very strong, and his loss had come as a bitter blow to him. In vain did James Stark seek to counsel him.

'If you think Tobias placed this responsibility on your shoulders out of betrayal, Alex, think again. He has offered you everything he holds dear.'

'Including his woman.'

'His widow, Alex. I know for a fact that she has no idea of the extent of Tobias's holdings. If I were you, I'd grab the fair Joanna with both hands before she discovers what she stands to lose.'

'She's an ignorant island girl.'

'An ignorant, *wealthy* island girl. You might have to bury your pride on this one. When word gets out and the fortune hunters set eyes on her, somebody might beat you to it.'

'Let them have it. I haven't even decided whether or not I intend to stay on as head of the company yet.'

James Stark's eyes hardened. 'In case you decide to allow your arrogance to overcome your good sense, just remember that your contract is a four year one. It still has a year to run and it stipulates that three months' notice in writing is required.'

'The hell it does.'

'Don't think I won't hold you to it, either. If you decide your future is no longer with the company I'll need time to interview and appoint your successor. But I'd advise you not to act hastily in this matter unless you intend to deliberately ruin the company.' James packed his papers away and held out a hand. 'Think about it carefully, Alex. Talk the matter over with your brother when next he's in port, for your decision will affect him, too. Oliver might decide to try and run the company himself.'

A snort of laughter told James what Alexander thought of his advice. 'What Oliver knows about running a company could be written on the head of a nail.'

'Exactly. But he's level-headed and you couldn't ask for a better adviser. Now, I must go. I don't want to miss the train. I'll start the ball rolling with the legalities when I get back to London.'

'Perhaps you'd get a message to Henry Wetherall for me. Tell him I'll be staying a day or two and will be back in the office on Thursday.'

As soon as James had departed, Alexander slumped into an armchair in the corner of his room. His long legs spread out in front of him, he kept his glance fixed on a water stain on the ceiling. After a while, the brown edges took on the shape of a steamship with smoke billowing from her funnel. He smiled, for despite his spirited arguments with Tobias over the merits of sail versus steam, Alexander was still convinced that steam was the way of the future.

Although he'd fallen in love with the company's new clipper, *Joanna Rose,* he considered her to have been a waste of money. When steam became common, as it would when the fueling stops were sorted out, sailing ships would become a liability to the company rather than an asset. If Alexander had his way the company would be training key staff as engineers for the future.

Now Tobias was gone he *could* have his way. In fact, he could own the company jointly with his brother. All he had to do was marry that wretched island girl!

Joanna Rose Darsham. She came instantly into his mind when he closed his eyes. He let out a slow breath when he recalled those intense blue eyes of hers and the tears trembling on her dark lashes. He'd never seen eyes quite as beautiful as hers before. She was altogether too exquisite a female. No wonder Tobias had been smitten at first sight.

He sighed, his conscience troubling him, for he'd spoken harshly to her without cause. His words had been unforgivable and he must recant them before he left.

He presented himself at the house again later in the day. The door was decorated with a holly wreath tied with a dark green bow. Charlotte would resist making a public show of mourning, he knew. Like Tobias, she didn't indulge in self-pity.

When he was announced, he stood awkwardly in the doorway, hat in hand, noting that the two women wore black armlets. Self-conscious with two pairs of eyes upon him, he crossed to where Charlotte sat and kissed her cheek. 'I didn't want to leave without seeing if I could be of further service to you.' The required apology stuck in his throat as he turned his eyes to the girl.

'Excuse me, Charlotte. Mr Morcant.' Rising from her chair, Joanna left the room without giving him another glance.

Alexander watched her depart, her trim figure graceful as she walked. 'I also came to apologize to . . . Mrs Darsham.'

'Joanna will have gone to her own sitting room.' Charlotte's eyes approved his course of action as her glance went past him to the maid. 'Stevens, take Mr Morcant's card and ask Mrs Darsham if she'd be good enough to receive him in her private sitting room.'

At least the demeaning act would be carried out in private. The maid was taking a long time to come back with an answer, during which time he spoke with Charlotte.

'Tobias and I talked about dying once, and he indicated he'd like to be buried at sea,' she told him. 'It seems as though his wish has been granted. I've decided to wait a little while to see if his body is found. If it is, he'll have the funeral he wanted. If not, we shall have a remembrance service on one of the company ships on the first anniversary of his disappearance.'

'I'd be honoured if you'd allow me to read the eulogy.'

'Of course you shall, Alex. You know how much you meant to him.'

Alexander had thought he did, but the fact that

Tobias hadn't confided in him about his hasty marriage had come as a complete shock. Perhaps he'd expected too much from Tobias, taking him for granted, as he'd taken the Morcant family too much for granted when he'd thought he was related by blood.

He frowned as he looked at the clock, drumming his fingers on his knee. What the devil was the girl doing, taking a bath?

'Would you like me to find out what the delay is?'

He spoke without thinking. 'Am I that obvious? I know what the delay is. She's all woman, that one. No doubt she's exacting every ounce of punishment she can from the situation before she makes me grovel at her feet.'

Charlotte smothered a weary laugh. 'You could be right, my dear. You deserve it, though. You were completely obnoxious to Joanna. She was not responsible for the way Tobias worded his will, after all. I thought he arranged things in the best way he could for all concerned.'

'Still, I cannot understand why Tobias didn't tell me about his marriage when he was in London.'

'Perhaps he thought it was nobody's business but ours, Mr Morcant,' Joanna said from the doorway, distancing him from the man he'd always looked up to. 'I'm sorry to keep you waiting. I was in the middle of reading to Tilda, and she looks forward to it so.'

She was obviously going out, for she wore a loose-sleeved cloak and matching bonnet, and carried a wicker basket over her arm.

'Tilda?'

'Tilda is my cousin, who at this time is upstairs recovering from an illness.'

So, she'd brought some family baggage along for Tobias to support, and an invalid at that. He nodded. 'I'd like to talk to you in private for a moment or two, Mrs Darsham.'

Her voice was as soft as a feather floating on the evening air. 'There's really no need, for I can guess what you wish to say to me. I'll save you the indignity of being obliged to formally apologize. I understand your disappointment, for Charlotte has told me of the special relationship that always existed between yourself and Tobias. It's hard when your expectations are stolen, I know, for it's happened to me in the past, too.'

Alexander felt as though he was being taken to task rather than being forgiven. 'I'm grateful for your forbearance, Mrs Darsham. However, I'd rather frame my apology in my own way.'

Her eyebrow lifted the merest of fraction. 'Then I mustn't disappoint your need to punish yourself. Unless you wish to wait for me to come back, you may apologize while you accompany me into town. Unless we are accosted by passers-by, that should provide you with the privacy you require.' She smiled at Charlotte. 'I have your list, and I'll not be too long.'

'I do wish you'd go in the carriage, dear. It's cold outside.'

'I need the exercise, and I don't mind the cold.'

As they set off together down the hill Joanna turned to Alexander Morcant, her eyes troubled. 'Now we're on

209

speaking terms, perhaps you would tell me about Tobias.'

'You married him. You tell me.'

Damn him, he was as tetchy as a wasp, she thought. She slid him a glance, her eyes coming up against his and surprising a moment of hurt and sorrow in their dark depths. It was swiftly masked. Her heart softened, for his pride had been wounded badly.

'I'm sorry,' she said.

'For what? Marrying Tobias?'

'Certainly not. Tobias was a wonderful man and I feel privileged to have known him, even for such a short time. I'm sorry you're so set against me, Mr Morcant. Since we had just met it was unfair of you to act as my judge and jury.'

His mouth tightened a fraction. 'I apologize.'

'Because you want to, or because you feel it's expected of you?'

'Because—' He gazed at her, a wry twist to his mouth, then shrugged. 'Mrs Darsham, you are making me feel even more the churlish fool than I am.'

'I beg to differ, since a *fool* you obviously are not. And although your disposition warrants improvement at the moment, I'd imagine it has more good days than bad ones.'

'Not if you keep goading me,' he warned

She smiled at him. 'Then I shall stop. Your apology is accepted without reservation.'

'I wasn't aware I had made one, yet.'

'You certainly did. You distinctly said, "I apologize". It was shortly after I compared you to a wasp in my mind.'

With a hand on her arm he brought them to a halt in front of a high brick wall overhung with evergreen shrubs. Turning to face her, he said incredulously, 'You compared me to a wasp?'

'It was the best description my mind could come up with at the time, though I was referring to your disposition, I'm sure. I shouldn't imagine your belly is striped in yellow and brown – or is the mention of that too indelicate for your ears?'

The spontaneous chuckle of laughter he gave was entirely delightful.

'No wonder Tobias married you, you're so alike,' he said, and gently ran a finger along her lower lip. 'I don't know exactly what it is about you, for the likeness is fleeting. Your smile reminds me of his, I think.'

Joanna softly quoted one of Richard Lind's poems.

> *Ye are alike, and yet 'twere vain*
> *To say what likeness I discover,*
> *For that which seems to me so plain*
> *Was never seen by any other.*
>
> *'Tis not in figure, voice, or face,*
> *In no one feature can I place it,*
> *It dwells in no particular grace,*
> *And yet how plainly I can trace it.*
>
> *I trace it in the transient smile,*
> *The ever-varying quick expression;*
> *Yet as I look, 'tis gone the while,*
> *And I alone retain the impression.*

'Ah yes,' Alexander said, looking surprised. 'It's exactly like that. How very apt. I've never heard that poem before; who wrote it?'

'Richard Lind.' She took a step back from his caress, her lip quivering from his touch, and said as they resumed their walk towards the distant town. 'Did you know Tobias all your life?'

'Ever since I can remember. My father and elder brother Oliver were always at sea. My father lost his life when I was ten. Tobias stepped into his shoes as mentor and friend.'

'Your father was Lucian Morcant, master of the *Cormorant*, was he not?'

There was a moment of hesitation. 'You knew him?'

'Of course not. Lucian Morcant drowned in the year I was born. But he's buried in Chiswell cemetery near Honor Darsham and her infant. I've seen his grave often, and wondered what sort of man he was.'

'A good, loving father to me . . . when he was home.'

'You must have missed him when he died. A boy of ten would need a father to advise him.' Smiling, she lapsed into the island way of speaking for a few moments, and there was something restful and comforting about it. ' 'Tis a good place for Lucian Morcant's body to rest, for the grass of his bed is nourished by the spindrift coming from the waves and he can watch the seagulls soar on the wind. 'Tis said the gulls take the souls of drowned sailors into them, so they can navigate the oceans of the world. If your pa was a good man, he'll be flying with them.'

Alexander closed his eyes for a moment, imagining

the scene and indulging in a sudden urge to tell her about himself. 'Lucian wasn't my real father, but I didn't know that until recently. My Morcant grandfather disinherited me when he found out. Tobias was handed the task of telling me. He didn't like doing it. Now he's gone I feel so . . . *alone.*'

'It's a great responsibility to be alone and answerable only to yourself.'

He opened his eyes and gazed at her. A faint smile had touched her mouth and her eyes were intensely blue. How fine and translucent her skin was, and how dark and glossy her hair. Alexander was also feeling unusually raw and vulnerable. She'd drawn him out of himself, like a sea siren who lured the unwary to a watery grave with her song. But he wasn't some superstitious sailor to believe in such folklore, however prettily presented, he was a man of logic. So why did he now feel his father's grave tugging at him?

'Now you know all about me and I've learned absolutely nothing about you,' he said, for revealing his inner feelings had left him with a slight sense of shame, as if he'd diminished himself in her eyes.

A smile briefly curved the width of her mouth. 'I think there's a lot more to you than you've told me, or even care to reveal. What did you want to know about me?'

Everything, Alexander thought to his surprise. 'Who are your parents?'

Her eyes flickered slightly, but she held his gaze. 'Joseph and Anna Rushmore from the isle of Portland. Joseph was a stonecutter and a mason. He died when I was six, and my mother died two years ago, when I was sixteen.'

'And you never considered . . . *marriage* to an islander.'

Her eyes widened, then she blushed, as if she knew exactly what he was asking her. She answered in a slightly curt manner, which made him think he was lucky not to have had his face slapped.

'My relatives wanted me to marry one of my cousins. I went to work for the scholar Richard Lind instead, who, although I didn't know it at the time, was a relative of Charlotte's.'

When they came to a crossroads she stumbled on a stone and he took her arm to steady her. There was a lingering smell of roses about her as she looked up at him. Her mouth was ripe and luscious. She was all woman and he suddenly wanted to crush her mouth with his and taste its sweetness. His groin tightened. He knew he wanted more than that as he murmured almost to himself, 'Perhaps I'll marry you, after all.'

She had read what had been in his eyes. As she tried to jerk her arm away she said angrily, 'Have you no decency? My husband has just died.'

'It's what Tobias wanted, isn't it? For you to love, honour and obey him.'

'We were almost strangers. He never told me what he wanted from me.'

His eyes sharpened. 'And he didn't love you either, did he? Why did he wed you then?'

'I don't know. Because he felt sorry for me, I suppose. I liked him, he was easy to talk to . . . and he said I reminded him of his first wife, Honor.' Nervously, she held out her hand so he could see the gold ring with a heart-shaped blue stone on her finger. 'See, he gave me her jewellery the last time I saw him.'

'Ah, yes . . . that must be it.' Alexander could see it now, that resemblance. 'Tobias adored Honor. I doubt if you'd ever have measured up to her for him, though. He would have realized that, of course, that's why he didn't tell me of what he'd done. He married you for the wrong reason, and would have been ashamed by his action.'

'Right now, I do believe it would be *you* whom Tobias would be ashamed of. When are you going to stop sulking and grow up, Mr Morcant?' His luck *did* run out at that moment, for this time she managed to free her arm, and she used it to vent her anger. Her palm flattened against his cheek with a stinging crack that made him stagger backwards.

Her eyes glittering, she turned away from him and began to move rapidly away, as if she'd expected him to retaliate with similar violence. He'd never hit a woman, and had no intention of starting to now, though the indignity of being treated thus had brought instant fury bubbling to the surface.

God knew, he'd deserved the slap, he thought, but much worse for him was what she'd said. He cringed inside at the thought of being regarded as a sulky child, especially since she'd gone out of her way to be nice to him in the first place.

Alexander was of a mind to catch her up, but she was justifiably angry and he'd only collect another tongue-lashing. Besides, she'd already looked over her shoulder twice and would probably start to run if he went after her. Then she might trip in one of the potholes on the road, which – though it would please him personally if she fell flat on her face in a puddle – would attract attention from the riders going by, or the drivers of the occasional horse and cart. He didn't want to add injury to insult and be charged with accosting her. Right at the moment, though, he'd enjoy throttling her!

Something about that ring she was wearing had bothered him, too, but he was too angry to figure out what it was. It would come to him, he was sure.

'Damn it, Tobias, why did you dump your problem on my shoulders?' he grumbled.

Barely two weeks after she had left port, *Joanna Rose* was sailing off the coast of Spain. The wind was strong and the sea surged with a rolling foam-flecked swell.

It was dusk of the fourteenth day at sea when Tobias pulled on a warm jacket and was able to leave his cramped cabin to go up on deck and take some much needed air. One of the lascars in the crew would place clean linen on his bunk and would clean the place before he returned. The cabin would smell all the sweeter for it.

He caught a whiff of foul-smelling smoke from Thaddeus's tobacco before he spied the captain in the shadows, puffing contentedly on his pipe. Tobias tapped him on the shoulder.

'Good evening, Thaddeus.'

Turning his head, Thaddeus grinned. 'Ah . . . you've surfaced at last, Mr Tremayne.'

'I've been hanging over a bucket since we left harbour.'

'Aye, I know. You're not the only one, but the passengers will find their sea legs and begin to emerge soon. That set of whiskers looks good, I wouldn't have recognized you.'

By Christ! The air was cold up here after the confines of his stuffy cabin, Tobias thought, hauling the fresh air into his lungs to chase away the stale, lingering fumes on his breath that his recent affliction had left there. He stroked his grey-flecked beard and smiled, mostly because he felt liberated from his unexpected and prolonged bout of seasickness.

'How's the ship handling?'

'Like most virgins she needed coaxing a little at first, but now I've spread her skirts to show her how, she responds eagerly enough.'

'I doubt if you know what a virgin looks like after all these years.'

Joanna Rose intruded into his mind then. He shuddered as he thought what might have happened between them had his mother not recognized Joanna's resemblance to Honor. But he must put all he knew and those he loved behind him now so he could concentrate on the future, for he doubted if he'd see any of them again.

It was good to be at sea again. The *Joanna Rose* seemed to be alive, her decks quivering beneath his feet as she gave flirtatious little dips and bobs. She spoke to him. The slapping ropes, the hiss of the wind in the sails and the prow slicing into the curling water had a music all of their own. Had he pursued his seafaring career he might now be her master. But although the sea still tugged at him, his early seamanship skills and instincts had not been developed, and were now inadequate to sail a ship of any size larger than his sloop, the *Linnet*. He felt guilty about abandoning her to her fate.

Tobias couldn't help wondering what effect his faked death had had on those he loved. It would be a long time before he got word from James, and he was also feeling guilty about his mother, who would be beside herself with grief, although she would hold it all in. However, she had gained a granddaughter to compensate her. Joanna wouldn't mourn, of course, for they'd hardly known each other, something he regretted.

'I'm beginning to wonder if I took the wisest course,' he murmured.

'What's done is done. Worrying about it won't change anything, so let matters lie.'

'Lie being the operative word. What if someone finds out?'

Thaddeus grinned. 'Then we'll all be in big trouble, I reckon. Do you feel up to some dinner?' he asked.

'I'm ravenous.'

'Good. Then join me in my cabin. We'll eat together in private tonight. We probably won't get the chance again.'

'What if someone recognizes me?'

'With those whiskers, not a hope. But if you skulk around in the dark trying to avoid everyone you'll draw attention to yourself.'

'Aye, I suppose I will. Won't your officers wonder why we're dining together?'

'You won't see me that often, besides which I often

invite guests from amongst the passengers to dine, usually about five at a time once they're feeling more human. It helps people to socialize and makes them feel the company is looking after them. We also have card evenings in the salon most nights, and occasionally a dance social. There's a fiddler and a piper amongst the crew, and one of the ladies is bound to be able to play the piano.'

'There's a piano on board?'

'Bolted to the bulkhead and deck, so she doesn't go careering all over the place. You signed the requisition yourself.'

'Did I, by God? I think I should like to see you dance, Thaddeus.'

An eyebrow was raised slightly. 'I'm the ship's master, I'm too dignified to dance, though I daresay my grace would surprise you. We also have a parson on board, so there will be a service in the salon every Sunday morning. I'll expect to see you there, praying on your knees with the rest of us sinners.' Thaddeus grinned, then tapped the dottle from his pipe on the hatch cover and stood up. 'There's one thing I'd like you to get into your head. While you're a passenger aboard my ship it would be better if our relationship remained on a formal basis. Address me as Captain Scott from now on, if you would, Mr Tremayne.'

About to remind the captain that he was part owner of the shipping company Thaddeus worked for, Tobias bit down on his lip as it suddenly hit him. Tobias Darsham no longer owned anything, for he didn't exist. He bowed slightly. 'Certainly, Captain Scott.'

Thaddeus nodded. 'I'll leave you to get some air then, Mr Tremayne. We dine at twenty hundred hours and I don't like to be kept waiting.'

'I understand, Captain.' Feeling nettled as Thaddeus turned away, he added, 'May I remind you of something?'

A pair of amused brown eyes settled on his face. 'What is it, Mr Tremayne?'

'I'm no longer your damned midshipman. I'm a passenger.'

Thaddeus chuckled as he walked away. 'And a prickly one at that, brother.'

'What do you make of Alexander Morcant?' Charlotte asked Joanna a week before Christmas.

Spots of colour appeared on the girl's cheeks. 'He's the most infuriating man I've ever met.'

'He's handsome, though, do you not think so?'

'I cannot say I've noticed his looks in particular.' She glanced up from her embroidery, her eyes sparkling with indignation. 'He told me he doesn't know who fathered him. It was probably the devil with his dark eyes and hair and his sour disposition. He breathes fire with every word. Also, his nose is too straight, his mouth too firm and his voice cracks like a whip when he's angry, which seems to be a permanent state for him.'

Tilda laughed. 'I thought you said you hadn't noticed him.'

'I haven't.' She smiled at Tilda. 'Are you warm enough? I can fetch you a blanket if you like.'

'I'm already roastin' like a pig on a spit.'

'Except you haven't got any cracklin' on you yet to roast.'

'Crack*ling*,' Charlotte said with an exasperated sigh. 'You must not allow your speech to become lazy. That includes you, Tilda. Pronounce the end of the word as ing, not in.'

'Yes ma'am. I be roast*ing*.'

'Not I be, I am,' said Joanna, mimicking Charlotte's voice perfectly, and Tilda grinned at her.

Charlotte smiled too. She enjoyed the company of the two younger women, even though they lapsed into youthful silliness at times. Tilda was looking much better now, she thought. By spring she would have gained a little weight. Then Charlotte knew she must find something to occupy the girl. Perhaps she could teach her some skills, so she could be gainfully employed. But what? Who knew what untapped skills the girl had inside her? Housekeeping was the most obvious, of course. Tilda was neat at stitching, though. A dressmaker might employ her when she was stronger.

Under the circumstances, they were spending a quiet Christmas. But there would be presents for both girls, and Charlotte had another surprise for Joanna.

Joanna knew somebody was coming, for the fire had been lit in Tobias's room and the bed made up.

Charlotte smiled when she enquired about it, for the girl's curiosity was refreshing. 'I have a guest coming for Christmas. I hope you don't mind me putting him in that room, Joanna. It's much more convenient for the maids.'

Joanna just hoped it wasn't Alexander.

*

The guest arrived two days before Christmas in a hired carriage. The knock on the door was answered by the maid and Joanna heard the rumble of male voices, one of them familiar to her.

'Richard Lind,' she breathed, a smile lighting her face. Jumping to her feet she ran down the stairs, standing stock still and grinning at him when she reached the bottom. 'I'm so glad you've come. You look exhausted,' she scolded. 'Are you looking after yourself properly?'

He managed a faint smile. 'It was a tiring journey, Joanna Rose. How lovely to see you again. You look wonderful. I was so sorry to hear about the disappearance of your husband. I liked him enormously.'

The man behind him coughed. 'I don't believe we've been introduced, Uncle.'

'Ah yes. Joanna Rose, this is my nephew, David Lind. You've heard me talk of him. David, this is Mrs Tobias Darsham.'

David Lind was tall and slim, with brown hair, kind brown eyes and a more than passing resemblance to his uncle.

'You were studying at Cambridge, I believe,' she said.

'I've recently gained my doctorate in theological studies.'

'Goodness, how wonderful,' she exclaimed, not having the faintest idea what he was talking about. 'Have you met Mrs Darsham? I was so surprised to learn you were related.'

Just then the study door opened and Charlotte

appeared. 'You mustn't keep Richard all to yourself, Joanna.' Her smile came as she swept forward. 'Dear Richard, how lovely to see you after all these years. You haven't changed a bit. I've been so looking forward to your visit.'

After further introductions and some small talk, David Lind declined refreshments and excused himself. 'I must go, my mother will be expecting me home.'

'I'll show you where your room is, Mr Lind,' Joanna said, as she hefted Richard's bag up. 'Follow me.'

Richard gave a sigh as she began to unpack his things and place them neatly in the chest of drawers. 'I hope this trip isn't going to be too much trouble for everyone.'

'It won't be. You'll feel better after a rest. You've got the look on your face, so get yourself under the quilt before you have one of those turns of yours. I'll bring you up some refreshment later.'

She'd just got him tucked in when he began to jerk. She gazed down at him, so helpless at these times, and felt sorry for him as she wondered how long a body could accommodate such a strange affliction.

12

The old year ticked quietly over into 1857. The four people living in the Poole house were companionable and content with each other's company.

Tilda's fears had proved to be unfounded, for she came to Joanna's room one day smiling with relief, to whisper, 'My monthly bleeding has come.'

Drawing Tilda into her arms Joanna hugged her tight, for Tilda had been through enough as far as she was concerned.

'I do wish you wouldn't go,' Joanna said to Richard one day when he announced his intention to depart. 'I've missed you. I don't like the idea of you going back to Portland with nobody there to help you.'

Richard rewarded her with a smile of pure pleasure. 'Alas, I've outstayed my welcome already, Joanna Rose.'

'You most certainly have not,' Charlotte said immediately. 'Why don't you consider staying in Poole permanently? '

'I'm afraid my affliction embarrasses my brother and their friends, and his wife refuses to have me under her roof.'

'I'm talking about your staying here, with us. We enjoy your company. Since Joanna and Tilda spend most of their time with me, you can use the little sitting room adjoining your room for your work, and for times when you want to get away from female prattle.'

'Then where will Tilda create her artistic work?'

All eyes turned to Tilda, who blushed under the sudden interest in her. 'It's nothing, Mr Lind. I didn't know you'd seen it, that I didn't.' Her hands covered her heated cheeks. 'I'm mortified.'

'You have nothing to be mortified about, Tilda dear. You seem to have a rare talent. But you'll have to find a better hiding place than the writing bureau if you want to conceal it.'

Since Joanna had given Tilda a box of paints, some pencils and a tablet of paper as a Christmas gift, she was naturally interested in the outcome. She rose to her feet. 'I shall go upstairs immediately and see for myself.'

Tilda put a hand on her arm to stop her, imploring, 'Please don't, Joanna. I'm just learning and it's not very good. You'll laugh at me.'

'I won't look if you're embarrassed, but I daresay I shall sneak a peek at it when you're not looking.'

Charlotte said, 'I should be interested in seeing it, too, Tilda. Come, don't be shy. You're amongst friends, and if Joanna dares to laugh she'll be denied supper and I shall lock her in the cellar with the mice for the night.'

So a reluctant Tilda went upstairs and came down with three pieces of paper to hand to Charlotte, who exclaimed with surprise. 'This is excellent work. You have a good eye and have caught the likenesses beautifully. Here, Joanna, take a look.'

In one drawing, Joanna gazed out of the window, a small smile on her face, her eyes dreaming into the distance. Then there was Charlotte, her head bent over her stitching, and Richard, pen in hand, with a pair of spectacles perched on the end of his nose.

Surprised, Joanna gazed at her. 'You've amazed me, Tilda. They're wonderful.'

A smile trembled on the older girl's lips. 'You truly like them?'

'Of course I do. I'm seething with envy and will probably strangle you in your sleep as a result. Mr Tibbets, who instructs me in the arts, says painting lessons are wasted on me and I should concentrate on writing stories. Not that he can draw with any great display of talent himself, but he explains it so well, so he's a good teacher.' She gazed at Charlotte with something like a plea in her eyes. 'Perhaps Tilda should have the lessons instead of me.'

'And perhaps she should not, because how will you learn anything if you don't apply yourself to it. However, it would be a very good idea if Tilda accompanies you, for her talent needs encouraging.' She bestowed a fond smile on Tilda. 'I was wondering what you would prove to be good at. Now I know.'

Tilda looked at her lap. 'I'm already living on your charity, I can't afford tuition.'

The other three looked at each other in consternation, for they'd forgotten about Tilda's circumstances.

'But once you've learned how, you'll be able to tell

other people how to do it, so you can earn money from teaching the craft of painting. I'm sure you'd be able to paint designs like those pretty greeting cards. There, I shall commission you to paint me a set to send to people I know next Christmas.'

'But you only know us, Joanna.'

'Then I'll order three . . . four with David Lind, and I'd better send Mr Morcant one. Put some holly on his since he has a prickly nature. And I'll have a spare one in case I think of someone else. So that makes six.'

'I know several people and will commission a dozen also,' Charlotte told her. 'I shouldn't be at all surprised if you couldn't sell your work to a Christmas greeting card company if you approached them. I believe cards are becoming increasingly popular.'

Richard added a practical suggestion of his own. 'And if I'm to stay here permanently, I shall employ you to watch over me, so you can buy your materials. What's more, I shall sponsor you by paying for your tuition.'

'You mustn't. It's too much,' Tilda protested.

'Of course I must. All great artists have sponsors, and when you become famous I shall lay claim to nurturing your talent. We shall share the sitting room between us, for you're always as quiet as a mouse and will then be on hand if I need you.'

'There then, everything is settled to our satisfaction,' said Charlotte, exchanging a smile with Richard.

And it seemed that it was, because Tilda gave a tremulous smile, then stuttered, ''Tis wonderful to have such good friends . . . indeed it is. I don't know how to thank you.' Bowing her head she began to weep into the handkerchief she was embroidering.

Alexander had been working non stop. News of the disappearance of Tobias had unsettled the company's regular customers and many of them had to be persuaded, with lower rates applied to their shipping services to woo them back. Insurance fees went up. He hoped *Joanna Rose* arrived in Australia before news of Tobias's disappearance did, and the Melbourne agent had secured cargo to fill her holds for the return voyage. One of these days he intended to appoint an agent exclusive to Darsham and Morcant.

Like the smaller clippers, as elegant as she was, *Joanna Rose* was a working ship and she had to pay her way. There had already been some passenger cancellations for the next voyage, from people who were afraid their fares would not be honoured.

'I think I can contain the downward trend overall as long as the cash flow isn't impeded by too many cancellations,' he said to Oliver when the *Clara Jane* docked and he went on board to tell his brother the sad news about Tobias.

'I can always sell the Morcant family home,' Oliver told him, clearly shocked by the event. 'I'm hardly ever in it and Susannah wants us to live in America.' An awkward note came into his brother's voice. 'Though, to be quite honest, I had been toying with the idea of offering Tobias my share of the company as well.'

Horrified by the turn of events, Alexander stared at his brother. At the age of thirty-eight, Oliver's face was seamed and slightly weathered from a life spent mostly at sea. If anything, it gave him a raffish air, reminding Alexander of Lucian, the man Alexander had thought of as his father.

'You intend to leave the company?'

'And life at sea. Susannah wants me to stay home when we're married, and the sea has taken enough of us as far as I'm concerned. I always thought the sea was in my blood and did what was expected of me, but now I've found a woman and a home that's going to be more to my liking. My future father-in-law has offered me a partnership in a wine importation business. If I'm living there, it stands to reason I should work there, too, especially since any children from my marriage will be American. I don't want to sell my shares outside the family unless I must, though. How are you situated?'

Alexander couldn't imagine Oliver working ashore. 'I can mortgage my house, too, if I must, but that would hardly be enough.' He couldn't keep the coldness from his voice. 'I'm only too aware that the house was a conscience gift from Elijah Morcant, but under the circumstances I don't feel entitled to keep it, since I'm not a partner in the company.'

Oliver punched him lightly on the shoulder. 'You and your damned pride. Keep your house. You're entitled to it. We would have been none the wiser if our mother had kept her counsel. But I understood Tobias was going to name you as his heir. Surely he hasn't left the company to Charlotte?'

Alexander gave a thin smile. 'He has named me as his heir in a way, but you haven't heard all of it yet. There is a condition attached.' He lowered his voice as a knock sounded on the door. 'Look, we must talk this over where we can't be overheard. Come up to the house tonight, where we can talk privately. I'll invite James Stark along and we'll explain everything then.' Alarm coursed through him. 'Have you told anyone else of your plans?'

'Our mother knows, and Susannah and my future in-laws. But I fully intended to talk it over with you and Tobias before doing anything rash.'

'Then for God's sake, Oliver, I beg you, don't tell anyone else you're thinking of selling out. The company is in enough trouble as it is and your share won't be worth a salted herring if news of this gets out on top of Tobias's disappearance.'

Alexander managed a smile for the incoming first mate as he departed, even though he felt the weight of the company sitting like a sack of stones on his shoulders. The employees would lose their livelihoods, for a start. And he'd have to battle James Stark every step of the way for money until Tobias was officially declared dead. That might take years, despite the favours James was owed.

It's not your responsibility, you're only an employee yourself, he told himself. But as angry as he was, Alexander knew he couldn't easily walk away from his past. It was a matter of pride, of loyalty and of feeling good about himself. Tobias would have known that, but it was pushing a friendship too far to add the extra shackle of marriage to the equation, especially from beyond the grave. Savagely, he pulled the collar of his coat snugly up around his neck and headed back to the office feeling like a trapped tiger.

Later that night it was with relief that he and Oliver came to an arrangement. Alexander would be given time to stabilize the company before a buyer for the Morcant house and Oliver's company share was sought. Otherwise, they'd end up with nothing to sell. And, although he didn't say so to Oliver, Alexander intended to try and raise the cash himself to buy his brother out.

March blustered into April, and the lawns at Charlotte's house were covered in daffodils. David Lind and his father had been frequent visitors over the winter, and David accompanied them into the countryside for a picnic one fine day.

Tilda was soon busy with her pencil, exclaiming over every bird that flew by, every flower that bloomed and every field they had passed on the way. Although she seemed unaware of it, she was beginning to look quite handsome now she was filling out, Charlotte thought. And her shy and quiet ways were appealing. Both girls were polite, though Joanna didn't have Tilda's patience, and her outspokenness was a little disconcerting sometimes. But their way of speaking had improved.

'I do think David is showing an interest in Tilda,' Richard said. 'He will be taking up a post in London soon.'

'He's a nice young man, who resembles you rather than your brother, who has a disapproving look to him. He should take a lesson from you and smile a little more.'

Gazing at her, Richard laughed. 'I shall take that as a compliment, Charlotte.'

'Please do, because it was one.' She watched as Joanna looked around her then slipped her shoes off. 'Did you know Joanna's parents?'

'I knew her mother quite well. Anna used to house-keep for me. Joanna Rose took over when Anna became ill and took to her bed. She was sixteen when her mother died and her father's family took the cottage she stood to inherit.'

'Couldn't she have taken them to court?'

'I offered to help her, but there were rumours that she wasn't a Rushmore – that her father found her on the beach and she'd come from one of the wrecks. She dismissed it as malicious gossip, but all the same, I believe that Joanna was worried that if she pursued the inheritance she might lose her identity. She had a very secure upbringing and loved and respected her parents.'

Charlotte's heart thumped enviously at the thought of Joanna harbouring fond memories of people who might have stolen her from the Darsham family. 'Was there any truth in the rumour, d'you think?'

'It's possible. There was no parish record of her birth, I believe, and she looks nothing like the Rushmores. Generally, the islanders keep their counsel about such matters, but the cottage was well built and the Rushmore kin were not typical of Portland fisher folk. A court case might have been very unpleasant. Joanna wouldn't have wanted to dishonour her parents' memory. Joseph Rushmore, Joanna's father, was a stonecutter and mason. He was a man of simple tastes, decent, and a good husband and father by all accounts.'

Richard's eyes flickered slightly when Charlotte cried out with some passion, 'Decent people do not steal children away from their families.'

'You have no proof they did that, Charlotte, my dear. Anna Rushmore brought Joanna up decently in the traditional island way, which is one of self-sufficency. But all the same, she has a mind of her own and she's intelligent and eager to learn, too.'

Picking up a stick, Charlotte drew a circle through the grass. 'Can I confide something to you in complete confidence, Richard?'

'Yes, of course. For some time now I've suspected you had something on your mind.'

'Promise you won't laugh.' She gazed up at him. 'I believe Joanna to be my lost granddaughter.'

He smiled. 'You suspect Tobias is her father? Isn't that a little far-fetched? After all, he married her, and he wouldn't have done that if he thought he was her father.'

'But Tobias didn't suspect anything until I pointed out Joanna's resemblance to his first wife, Honor.'

'Come, Charlotte. Surely not. People often bear a slight resemblance to other people. What you're suggesting would be too much of a coincidence.'

'Was it a coincidence that Tobias disappeared shortly after I told him my thoughts on the matter?'

Richard looked troubled, but said nothing.

'Tobias put his life and soul into the shipping company and he knew what was likely to happen if such a marriage became public knowledge. His body has never been found. If he was dead I'd feel it in my bones, and I don't.'

'Have you told Joanna of your suspicions?'

'How can I without proof? She'd be horrified.'

'Initially, yes, but she's grown up knowing that the islanders thought she was an outsider. She has clung to the thought that the Rushmores were her parents, because she was happy with them, and needed to belong to someone. If she was presented with an alternative I'm certain she would think things over rationally.' He patted her hand. 'By the way, David has found a tenant for my house in Portland and I'll be going back there to collect my books and clothing before too long. Are you quite sure you want me to live here? Island folklore depicts me as a man suffering from insanity.'

'Point made, Richard.' Head to one side, she laughed. 'There's no doubt in my mind whatsoever. I enjoy your company enormously and I hope you enjoy mine.'

'Despite my affliction?'

'I'm sorry you have to put up with it, Richard dear, but it doesn't bother me in the slightest. We will cope with it together, and someone will always be here to watch over you.'

He raised her hand to his lips, kissed it, then said softly, 'You're a rare woman, Charlotte.' Much to her annoyance, it made her blush.

The body was that of Paul Gasper Colbert, a French fisherman who'd drunk too much brandy and had fallen from a boat off the coast of Cherbourg just after

Christmas. His equally drunken companions had slept through his struggles.

His body had drifted for a while, then sunk. An easy meal for crabs, it had been dragged along the bottom for three weeks before it began to float slowly to the surface. It then drifted, face down and arms outstretched, gracefully breasting the waves as it decomposed. For a while it was battered back and forth on a rocky shoreline under an overhanging cliff on the Hampshire coast before being deposited on a narrow strip of sand.

Crabs and gulls came and went before a surging spring tide lifted the bloated carcass from the beach and bore it out to sea again and gently along the coast. Floating just under the surface it attracted a following of birds and small fish.

It was late in April when the commotion caught the attention of a lone angler on a beach. With each roll of a wave he saw the dark, swollen shape come nearer. Carefully casting his line over the water he hooked his catch and drew it closer. The smell coming from it was vile. Turning away, he vomited into the sand.

When the angler finished gagging, he secured the line around a rock, then headed off towards the nearest town to report his catch, vowing never to eat fish again.

'A body has been found.'

'Where?' Alexander asked James.

'Just along the coast from where *Linnet* was adrift.'

'You think it's Tobias?'

James shrugged, then crossed to look out of the

window. 'I hope so. It will make my job much easier. It's badly decomposed, I believe.'

'If it's Tobias it will put an end to the damaging speculation. Which of us is going down to identify it?'

'It would be better if both of us identified it. We'll go down to Southampton tomorrow. Then you can go on and break the news to the two Mrs Darshams. Have you thought any more about that other business?'

'Marriage?' Alexander gave a bark of laughter. 'I have. There's no doubt that Joanna Rose would be a warm armful for a man to have, but I doubt if she'd accept me after the way I've treated her.'

James laughed at that. 'You underestimate yourself, Alex. I'm sure you could win her round if you were persistent and turned on the charm. Take her a present. A kitten perhaps, women can't resist them. And if all else fails you could do things the island way. I believe Portland women respect a man who puts them in the family way, since it proves that the couple is fertile and suited for marriage.'

Alexander's smile faded. 'This is Tobias's wife we're talking about. As such, she should be respected.'

'Tobias's widow, Alex. She'll be fair game if she comes to London.'

'Why should she come to London?'

'To see what Tobias left her. She'll be curious, and I'll have to go through the estate with her sooner or later, since the papers are lodged, and a death certificate will finalize matters and make probate easy.'

'She'll have nowhere to stay. You've let Tobias's house servants go, except for the caretaker couple, and

I'm not offering her a bed in case she jumps to the wrong conclusion.'

'Mrs Darsham is the type who can manage without servants, since she grew up to shift for herself. Get some sense into you, Alex. Tobias has handed you everything on a platter. If you wed her you'll get her half of the company, plus enough cash from some of the investments he made to buy your brother out. It's not a bad deal.'

It most certainly wasn't, Alexander thought, as Joanna's blue eyes came into his mind. In fact, it was a damned good deal. He just wasn't easy about taking such a step.

The next day the two men travelled to Southampton by train.

The body was lying on a table in an underground cellar. The stench was awful and both men held their handkerchiefs to their noses as the morgue attendant pulled back the sheet for them to view the corpse.

With hardly any face left, the corpse could have been anyone. The hair was the same dark colour as Tobias's. He fitted the height and the build, though the flesh was pale, flaccid and waterlogged.

'Was there any identification on him?' James asked the attendant.

'A small wad of paper, sir, but the ink had washed out of it and it fell to pieces.'

The two men gazed at each other across the stinking corpse. 'What do you think, Alex?'

Alexander felt his gorge rise as he saw that the flesh had rotted from the blackened finger ends to expose the bones. 'It could be Tobias.' He was forced to tear his eyes away from the horrible sight when he started to gag. 'Mr Darsham was reported by his wife to be wearing navy trousers and jumper with a reefer jacket that last time she saw him.'

'His clothes fit the description, though they're a bit ragged. They're in the locker if you wish to see them.'

'There's no need.' Alexander just wanted to get it over with now. It would end some of the speculation. 'Yes, James, I'm almost sure it's Tobias.' He gagged, and holding his handkerchief against his mouth rushed rapidly towards the exit.

The attendant grinned slightly. 'It affects some people like that.'

'Yes, it would,' said James, his sharp eyes darting over the corpse and narrowing in on some faint blue marks that disappeared under the sheet. He waited until the sheet was pulled up over the corpse and gazed towards the door to make sure Alex wasn't coming back. 'As I recall, Mr Darsham had a tattoo on his stomach. I never saw it, of course, but I believe he said it was a fish of some sort.'

'He had one right enough, sir, but it's a mermaid.'

'Ah, yes, that's right. He got it done when he was a midshipman, I believe.'

'Mermaids are popular with the lads. It looks like you've found your man, then. Perhaps you'd come up to the office and do the paperwork, so I can release the corpse.'

'Mr Darsham expressed a wish to be buried at sea, but that's hardly practicable now, since the body is in such a state. It would be better for him to be buried immediately.'

'He can be buried in the seaman's cemetery at the church, sir. We would have had to bury him soon anyway, since we can't keep corpses for long. They stink the place out, see.'

James did see.

'The padre from the mission to seamen will conduct a service over him. We can go through the arrangements in the office. The doctor will sign the death certificate as soon as I have the details.'

So the body of the French fisherman was buried later that same day, the death certificate signed and a memorial for his grave ordered, one of fine black marble etched in gold lettering. James thought it was the least he could do for the man.

In life the crewman, Paul Gaspar Colbert, had been the illegitimate son of a French whore and father to five sons. Hated by his wife, whom he beat regularly, he was interred in death as Captain Tobias Darsham. Colbert couldn't have cared less.

Charlotte had given Joanna a small patch of garden to call her own. The earth was dark and crumbly here with hardly any stones to pick out. It was a joy to work.

The air smelled sweetly of the turned earth, made damp by the soft April showers, and the air hummed with bees. On the other side of her patch, a blackbird investigated for worms. It stopped for a moment to open its throat in song and she stopped to listen and smile. On her back the sun laid a sheet of spring warmth to make the sap rise in her veins, and she was filled with contentment.

The blackbird flew off to take up position on the branch of a tree. Taking a leaf from its book Joanna began to sing softly to herself as she thinned a row of carrot seedlings. It was Tilda's twenty-fifth birthday today, something to celebrate, since Joanna had wondered if Tilda would live to see it after she'd been rescued from her family.

Charlotte had taken Tilda out to buy her a new dress as a gift for the occasion whilst Joanna had overseen the laying of the table in the dining room for the feast of celebration.

Accompanied by his nephew, Richard had left for Portland two days before to collect his worldly goods. As it was getting late in the afternoon, Joanna hoped they'd be back in time for the celebration. David Lind was leaving for London the following month and they were going to miss him.

Joanna felt supremely happy living in this house with the people she loved and respected the most. Charlotte had almost become a mother to her.

She tugged at a weed. It wouldn't budge. Grasping it with both hands, she spread her legs apart, dug her heels in and pulled harder. The stem suddenly parted from its roots. She staggered backwards and sprawled on her back, to find herself staring up at a blue sky decorated with white puffy clouds and darting swifts.

'Damned weed,' she grumbled, but she knew she would have missed the delightful scene going on above her if the weed had been more cooperative, so she grinned as she spotted a dozen or so large birds flying in a straight line.

Somebody gave a soft chuckle and a head inserted itself between her and the sky. Scrambling to her feet she pushed the mess of hair back from her face to find Alexander Morcant smiling at her. She hid her grimy hands behind her back as she said unnecessarily, 'Oh, it's you, Alex.'

'Yes, I do believe it is me.'

'Charlotte is out.'

'The maid told me. I've ordered some lemonade to be sent out for us. I hope you don't mind.'

'I've got to thin the carrot seedlings out first.'

'Why?'

'If I don't the carrots won't grow to a decent size.'

'Don't you like small carrots?'

Exasperated, she gazed at him, then, noticing the amusement in his eyes, she laughed. 'It's too nice a day to allow your teasing to annoy me.'

'It is, isn't it? Here comes the maid, so your carrots will have to wait.' There was a basket on the garden table. A scrabbling noise came from inside it. 'I've brought you a gift.'

'Have you? Why? It's not my birthday, it's Tilda's.'

Flipping open the lid he lifted out a kitten and offered it to her. 'I'm sure you won't have to look far to find a credible reason for the gift,' he said drily, when she exclaimed with delight.

His peace offering drew blood from his hand as he handed it over. She laughed as she cuddled the purring tabby against her chest, gazing at him from under her lashes, even while knowing she was being provocative. Joanna didn't care. Alexander Morcant struck sparks from her and she enjoyed the cut and thrust of his personality.

'She's so pretty and sweet.'

'She's a male.'

'Ah, in that case he's a handsome rogue.'

'That might be misconstrued as gender bias, Mrs Darsham. Males can be sweet when the occasion warrants it.'

'So I have noticed. I have to say that you're trying very hard to be sweet at the moment, though you draw blood just as easily.' She placed the kitten back in the basket, where it immediately tried to claw its way out again. 'I must go and wash the dirt from my hands. Do you intend to stay for dinner? If so, I'll ask the cook to cater for an extra guest.'

His eyes were dark against hers, a breeze ruffled the dark curls of his hair. Softly, he said, 'Are you inviting me, Joanna Rose?'

'Yes, Mr Morcant. I'm inviting you. We're celebrating Tilda's birthday. In confidence, it's a very special occasion for me, for Tilda was badly treated by her family. Tobias rescued her just in time, but I thought she wouldn't survive. If he were here today, he'd be pleased to know his brave effort wasn't in vain, since he took on a dozen fishermen on our behalf.'

His eyes flickered away from her, then back again. They'd dulled slightly, as if her mention of Tobias had pained him. 'Yes, he would be pleased. On his behalf, I'll stay, for I've yet to meet your cousin. By the way, do you think you could bring yourself to call me Alex, like you did when you first saw me today?'

'Was that slip too forward of me? I'm never sure whether I'm saying the right thing at the right time.'

Her candour brought her a smile of great charm. 'There's a limit to standing on ceremony, I say. For the sake of the shipping company, we're obliged to deal with each other into the future. I'd prefer our relationship to be an amicable one.'

'Then you've decided to stay on and manage it. Thank you.' She eyed him, knowing he hadn't come all this way to bring her a kitten, and wondering what was the real reason for his visit.

Alexander waited until the celebration was over and Richard Lind and Tilda had retired to their respective rooms.

'I'd like to talk to you both before I leave,' he said, as he waited for Joanna to settle next to Charlotte on the sofa. 'I have some news which might distress you.'

'Tobias's body has been found?' Charlotte said immediately.

'You knew?'

'My dear Alex, I know when a man has some unpleasant task to perform, for he cannot act naturally until he has dispensed with it.'

'We buried his remains in Southampton, despite your request for a sea burial. We thought it was for the best, since under the circumstances . . .' He shrugged. 'It was for the best, Charlotte, really.'

'Yes, Tobias would have been in the water for some time. Who identified him?'

'Myself and James Stark. The body was wearing the clothes Joanna described. I'll arrange a memorial service for when Oliver returns from his current voyage next month.'

'Ah . . . yes. Identification must have been an unpleasant task.'

How unpleasant she'd never know, Alex thought, as Charlotte rose to her feet, perfectly composed. 'Could the body have belonged to someone else?'

He hesitated a moment too long, said too emphatically, 'I had no doubts. Neither did James.'

She gave a faint smile. 'Thank you, Alex. I'll retire to my room now. Perhaps you'd like to stay a little longer and talk to Joanna.

'Charlotte took it calmly,' he said when the door closed behind her.

'She doesn't really believe he's dead, that's why. I overheard her telling Richard Lind so.'

'That's a ridiculous notion.'

'Charlotte brought Tobias up and loved him all her life. She knows him better than anyone.'

'And what do you believe?'

'I don't know what to believe. My marriage to him made sense at the time, now it doesn't. It's hard to explain. Tobias has no substance for me, as if I married the shadow of a man I once knew. He was a good man in life who deserves to be mourned. But my heart cannot grieve for a shadow and I despise myself for it. I would have liked to have known him better.'

She was near to tears. Taking her face between his hands Alexander kissed her forehead, then without thought he tilted her face up and sought the yielding sweetness of her mouth.

There was a moment when the liberty he'd taken was accepted, when she clung to him in a moment of longing and realized the power of what had been ignited between them. But then she backed away, her hand over her mouth, her blue eyes wide and wild, denying it to herself. 'No . . . it's too soon . . . it cannot be.'

'It can. It will be. It's what he wanted.' Turning on his heel, Alexander left her, his heart pounding, hardly able to bring himself to believe what had happened.

This isn't love, he cautioned himself. Joanna was an island girl, beneath him in every way. The lust he was infused with was something he'd experienced with other women. It was something easily and enjoyably expended with a willing partner. How willing would Joanna Rose prove to be?

Alexander intended to find that out – and as soon as he possibly could.

13

Alexander didn't know what prompted him to visit Portland before he went back to London.

He found that Lucian Morcant's grave had weathered over time, that the man he'd regarded as his father was now remote from him, as if the steady corruption of flesh from bone had left no essence. Lucian's bones would eventually become part of the white stone, as were the creatures absorbed by the sediments that had formed the island in the first place.

Nearby was the grave of Honor Darsham and her baby. How scattered the families all were. Tobias should be here with them, not buried in Southampton, he thought, trying to dispel the last image he'd had of his mentor lying naked on a table.

Something about Honor's grave caught his eye, a fresh mark, as if a piece had been chipped off. He moved closer. The last letter on the child's name had been altered. The curve of what has once been an S had been straightened out to become an upright, and a stroke applied to turn it into an E. It was an expert job. Under his fingertip the curve of the old letter could hardly be felt where it had been filled in with crushed rock. A fairly recent alteration, it was already weathering and would eventually blend into the memorial.

An old man was piling stones into a barrow and using them to repair the wall. He walked slowly and was at one with his age and environment. 'Blessed things,' he said, stopping to wipe the sweat from his brow and exchange the time of day. 'The rain unearths them, I reckon.'

Alexander didn't feel much like talking. 'Aye, it would.'

The man tried again. ''Tis a nice day, sir, that it is, and a lovely view from here Honor Darsham has, she does at that.'

His way of answering his own question made Alexander smile. He imagined the old man talked to himself out of necessity, since the dead couldn't converse with him. It would be churlish not to accommodate the old fellow.

A faint haze lifted from the water, which was a shimmer of pale blue. It merged with a sky that graduated from a pearly white horizon to an intense blue overhead, a colour that reminded him of Joanna's eyes. The sun was high, the breeze a mere whisper. It was more like summer than spring.

It seemed as though he'd never seen the sky before. Certainly, his mind had never presented it to him in such a way, so vivid and poignant that a lump had risen to his throat and he felt the need to weep over its beauty. He gave a faintly abashed smile. Joanna seemed to have turned him into a poet.

'It's a wonderful view. Mrs Darsham would have appreciated it.'

'So her husband said, him who married young Joanna Rushmore. A grand girl was Joanna. Good to her mother, she was, and with a sensible head on her shoulders. Tobias Darsham could have done worse for himself, yes indeed.'

'You saw Mr Darsham recently?'

'Afore Christmas, it be. The day they married in the church up the hill. He tells me to change the child's name. Said it were a girl infant his wife had birthed, not the boy buried with her. He had me change Ross to Rose, said his wife wouldn't give no mind to whose infant was buried with her, on account of her loving all infants, but she'd want her own to be named.'

'He died not long ago.'

'Aye, Leonard Rushmore's crew saw him go overboard, but couldn't save him. They reported it, but no trace of him was found by the revenue men, and those boys have got eyes like soddin' hawks, that they have.'

Alexander's eyes narrowed. 'Where can I find this Leonard Rushmore?'

'He will be up Easton way in the Lugger's Inn, I reckon. He had a fallin' out with his brothers and woke one mornin' to find his boat had been turned over and someone had set a fire under it. Burned the bottom out and his crew were taken on by others. Now he's got no livin', that he hasn't. And him with a wife and a pair of young 'uns to feed.'

'Thank you. I wouldn't mind talking to him.'

'That Leonard is as close-lipped as a mussel, lessen he

thinks there be somethin' in it for hisself. It's a fair walk, too.' A pair of washed-out blue eyes regarded him in a shrewd sort of way. 'I could be takin' you up in my donkey cart, introduce you, like. I could that. It's nearly time for a bite to eat, and the landlord's missus makes solid mutton pies if you've got teeth to chew on the gristle. They go down a treat with a pint of ale to help them on their way, I'll be buggered if they don't.'

'Perhaps you'd care to join me, Mr . . .?'

'Hiram is my name . . . I'm fair obliged to thee, sir.' The old man held out a callused hand. 'And you be whom?'

'Alexander Morcant.'

'Son of Lucian Morcant, captain of the *Cormorant*. I guessed who you were as soon as I set eyes on you coming up the hill. Lucian,' I says to him, 'here comes that youngster of yours to visit. See how he's grown . . .'

Leonard Rushmore hardly flickered an eyelid when Hiram introduced Alexander.

There had been a temporary lull in the conversation at the sight of a stranger, but it soon reverted to a buzz again, interspersed with loud bursts of laughter.

The windows allowed through only a diffused light. The ceilings were darkened with smoke, the furniture was solid and stained by countless spilled liquids. The inn had an air of secrecy about it, as if the walls had retained the conversations of plotters and smugglers over the years.

Alexander waited until Hiram had retired to a corner with his pie and the tankard of ale he'd provided. He ordered two more ales and slid one over to Leonard Rushmore. The man's hand closed around the handle and he grunted in acknowledgement.

'I'd like to hear your account of what happened to Tobias Darsham.'

A pair of muddy eyes slid his way. 'What's it to you?'

'I knew Tobias Darsham well. He was no fool where the sea is concerned.'

'Aye, that he wasn't. He was a brave and honest man. But the sea ain't picky, mister. It takes who it pleases and when it pleases. I helped him out once, and lost my livelihood as a result.'

'What happened to him?'

''Zactly what I told the lawyer fellow. He fell overboard when the sail came down on him, though we wouldn't have known it was Mr Darsham, since he were too far away, 'cepting we'd seen his boat afore. The swell was getting up and the water was choppy. If she'd been broached she might have gone over on her side. By the time me and the crew had hauled in the nets and got there, he was gone. We couldn't see the sloop, but we didn't look for long.'

'It was found on its side a few days later. Could Mr Darsham have swum to your fishing lerret?'

'It wasn't impossible, lessen he was kept under water by the weight of the sail. The sloop would have floated for a while unless it was holed, so I reckoned he would have clung to that. There was another boat closer to him, though, on the other side. It suddenly hoisted a sail and headed off fast. I thought it must have picked him up since it was so close, but I reported the incident anyway. I should've searched longer but it was gettin' dark. The water was cold so he'd have sunk pretty quick.'

'Mr Darsham's body turned up a few days ago near Southampton where the boat was found.'

Leonard's head jerked. 'Could be he was held fast by a rock. A shame, for he was a good man who possessed the courage to take on my brothers for the sake of my sister and cousin.'

'Is that why they burned your boat, because of Joanna and Tilda?'

'I reckon. Now they be pickin' on my wife and young 'uns.' He turned towards him. 'How are the girls?'

'They're well, and Tilda has fully recovered. I saw them yesterday.'

Leonard gave a bit of a grin. 'It was worth gettin' a bit of a thumpin' then.'

'If there's anything I can do to help, let me know.'

'Tobias Darsham said he'd give me a job if need be, and I have kids to support. But now he's gone, I'd be obliged if you knew of honest employment anywhere. I don't care what. Not that I fancy London much, but a beggar can't be a chooser.'

'I know someone in Poole who's looking for deck crew to man a new paddle steamer going into service in a month or so. Coastal trade.' He took out his card and scribbled a note on the back. 'Present yourself to Stannards boatyard and I'll put a word in for you.'

An expression of relief chased over Leonard's face. 'Thank you, sir. I'll go right away. Once I get settled I can find a place for my wife and kids. They're staying with her parents at the moment, where they'll be safer.'

The pair left the inn together, Leonard shrugging into a coat. 'I'm obliged to you, sir. Give my regards to Tilda and tell Joanna I'm sorry she lost her man. She'll have a hard time replacing one such as him.'

'I'm catching the ferry back to Poole. I'll stake you to a ticket if you meet me there.'

'It'll save me walking, right enough. I've my savin's to fall back on when I need them, but they don't amount to much, and I ain't got nothin' left to sell. The Barnes brothers have just had my fisherman's knives off'n me. I'll go and tell my missus what's goin' on and see you before too long.'

On the way down the hill, Alexander stopped at the church where Joanna and Tobias had married. The place was deserted, the door standing open. Something was not sitting easy in his mind, and he was on a mission.

He found the parish registers in a cupboard in the back room and flipped them open. Charlotte had been right. There was no record of Joanna's birth, or of any birth attributed to the Rushmores at the time. He drew a blank with the marriage register, too. There was nothing recorded after August of 1856. Where were the licences kept? He found what he was looking for in a bottom drawer, bundled and tied with string.

Whoever ran this church had no method to them, he thought, shuffling through the bundle and extracting the piece of paper with Tobias's name on. So, there was a licence, but the marriage was not recorded in the register. When he inspected the register again he saw traces of paper attached to the cotton stitching at the seam. A page had been removed from the ledger to correspond with each side of the stitching.

Somebody had removed the record of the marriage. He wondered why, for somebody must have had a damned good reason to have eradicated it. But if anyone had thought to search they would have easily discovered the anomaly, as he had. Shoving the licence into his waistcoat pocket he left, striding off down the hill to the ferry with a thoughtful frown creasing his forehead.

Joanna and Tilda had gone into Poole together. The pair looked quite the young ladies as they walked sedately along the pavements, accompanied by David Lind.

'When are you going to London?' Joanna asked him.

'Towards the end of May. I'm to work amongst the poor, but I don't know where, yet.'

'There's an area near Covent Garden which is renowned for the poverty of its populace and the fearsomeness of its notorious criminals. The place is teeming with disease and pickpockets. Perhaps you are being sent there. It sounds to be a perfectly horrible place to me.'

'You're very well informed, Mrs Darsham.'

Joanna shrugged. 'I read about it in a book by Charles Dickens called *Oliver Twist*. I shall be going to London myself one of these days, and I daresay I shall go to the area to see for myself.'

'A foolhardy venture.'

'Joanna is often foolhardy,' Tilda ventured with a

light laugh. 'If she hadn't been, I would now be dead, I expect.'

'Your rescue was most remarkable, Miss Rushmore, and I was not attempting to censure Mrs Darsham, you know.'

'Just as well, for Joanna doesn't take kindly to unasked for advice, and would most likely box your ears for your trouble. You'd better hide them under your hat.'

Unexpectedly, David grinned at Tilda's words. 'I doubt if Mrs Darsham would do anything quite so rash.'

'She most certainly would,' Alexander said from behind them.

Joanna turned to smile at him, trying not to blush as she remembered the outcome of their last meeting. 'I thought you'd returned to London.'

'No, I went to Portland. I met your brother there, Miss Rushmore. We travelled here together. He's applying for a job at the Stannard Paddle Steamer Company.'

'Which brother?' Tilda said, fear in her eyes as her gaze darted around at the crowd.

'Leonard.'

David offered Tilda his arm to lean on before Joanna could get to her. 'What is it, Miss Rushmore? You're trembling.'

'I felt dizzy.'

'The walk has been too much for you after your illness. We'll go in that teashop across the road where you can rest, then I'll hire a carriage and escort you back home.'

'I'm sure I'll be all right in a moment. Besides, I have some shopping to do.'

'Give me your list, Tilda. I'll do it and return for you,' Joanna offered.

'You can't carry mine as well as your own.'

Alex took command of the list and Joanna's shopping basket. 'I'll carry it for her. We'll be back in an hour.' Hand under her elbow, he guided her rapidly away before she could protest.

'That was presumptuous of you,' she said when they slowed down.

'It was obvious David wanted to talk to Tilda alone.'

'Was it? Why didn't he just say so?'

'Men don't usually state what they're about to do, they wait for an opportunity to present itself.'

She slanted him a glance and grinned, remembering how neatly he'd managed to kiss her. 'Sometimes they make the opportunity, I think. You may unhand me now, Alex. What did you go to Portland for?'

His eyes were dark, almost watchful. 'To visit Lucian's grave. By the way, I noticed that somebody has altered the wording on Honor's headstone.'

How smoothly he set about finding out what he wanted to know, though she had the feeling he already knew the answer. 'The stonemason had named the infant buried there, Ross, because it was a boy. Tobias asked him to change it to Rose. It was sad he never got to see his daughter. I hope they're reunited in heaven.'

'Most probably. Tobias grieved a long time for them.'

'He told me.'

'You haven't been back to Portland since Tobias brought you here, have you?'

'No. I doubt if I'll ever return. What did you think of Leonard Rushmore?'

'He's a difficult man to know. Taciturn, but he has integrity, I think. His family burned his fishing boat and he lost his livelihood because he helped Tobias.'

'His parents and brothers are a bad lot. Leonard has always tried to set himself above his kin without alienating them altogether. I'm glad you helped him, because it repays him for helping Tobias and myself. Did he tell you Tobias offered him a job?'

'So I was given to understand. He said he didn't want to live in London, which is why I gave him an introduction to Stannards.'

'That's kind of you, Alex. Why did you want to know if I'd been back to Portland? Has something happened I should know about?'

He laughed then. 'You have a devious mind, Joanna Rose.'

'I'm not the only one. Is it something to do with Tobias?'

'Not directly, but something is puzzling me. You could say I'm collecting clues, and when I fit them all together it will give me the answer to an enigma.'

'What if you don't like the answer?'

'The enjoyment lies in solving it, not in liking the answer.' It seemed that the subject was closed, for he took Tilda's list from his pocket and ran an eye down its length. 'Pencils, watercolours . . .' Head to one side he looked enquiringly at her.

'Tilda shows a talent for painting. I intend to add to that list, and buy her an easel, as a gift. We shall simply leave the list at the shop and tell them to deliver it in the morning. As for me, I'm not talented at anything much, so I just need a few vanity items.'

'You don't look as though you need any embellishment,' he said, which brought colour rushing to her cheeks, so he laughed. 'Ah, you're not used to receiving compliments, I see.'

'I'm not. I lived a simple life in Portland and I'm astounded by all the things women seem to know and need here. What use is playing the piano, singing, dancing and stuffing one's body into a corset so tight that you can hardly breathe?'

'Men like women who are decorative and entertaining.'

'I shouldn't imagine a corset is either.'

'You'd be surprised,' he said and gave a small smile, which made her quite annoyed because she didn't know what she'd said for him to smile about.

'Well, women are certainly expected to go to a lot of effort. Perhaps you could tell me what men do to be decorative and entertaining for women?'

He placed a finger across her lips. 'I bought you a kitten to do the entertaining on my behalf.'

'I called him Albert, after the Prince Consort. I was going to name him after you but your name is too long.'

'You're in a provocative mood, Joanna Rose.'

'I'm restless. I'm not used to sitting around the house playing the lady.'

'What would you like to do? I'm at your service.'

'Go into the hills, just be myself and walk for ever.'

'Then I'll stay an extra day and we shall. Tomorrow,

remove your corset, wear something sensible and don't forget your walking boots.'

Her face fell. 'I have a painting lesson tomorrow morning.'

'I'll be there at eight-thirty with a hired horse and carriage, and I'll carry you off from under Charlotte's nose, for I can't bear to see you suffer.'

She rewarded him with a wide smile. 'Thank you, Alex.'

'Now, Mrs Darsham. Go into the haberdashery across the road and buy your ribbons and combs. I shall find us a table in a little while and order us some refreshment in this tea shop.' He handed over her basket. 'Don't be long.'

She was back within ten minutes with her parcels. He rose to his feet as she entered, took the basket from her and held her chair whilst she seated herself. He'd secured a table at the window, and there was a small posy of fragrant flowers lying on the table in front of her.

'Did you buy these for me?'

'I did.'

Her eyes came up to his and her breath caught in her throat. 'Thank you, they're lovely.'

'The pleasure is all mine.' The words were so intimately uttered that everything inside Joanna came alive. Suddenly, she couldn't wait for tomorrow to come so she could spend the whole day alone with him.

When they rejoined the other two, they could see there was an awkwardness between them, and Tilda looked downcast.

'What has happened?' Joanna asked her later in the privacy of her small sitting room.

'David Lind has asked me to marry him.'

She gave her friend a hug. 'Oh, that's wonderful, Tilda. Anyone can see he's very fond of you. We must tell Charlotte and Richard. They'll be delighted, I know.'

'I've turned him down.'

'But why? You like him, don't you?'

'Of course I do. It's just . . . I can't marry him, Joanna, because of what my brothers did to me.'

'But that wasn't your fault.'

'I know. But I don't feel right about it. Men like David Lind expect their wives to be . . . innocent. What would he do if he found out?'

'Then tell him what happened. Why should you have to pay for something that isn't your fault? If he loves you, he'll support you. If he doesn't, he's not worth having for a husband.'

'I can't. I'm too ashamed. You don't know what it was like, Joanna.'

'Then tell me, my dearest friend.'

Vehemently, she shook her head. 'I can't speak about it, so don't press me. And you must promise me you won't say a word about it to David. I couldn't bear to see the pity in his eyes.'

'Oh, Tilda.'

'You must promise me, Joanna. Folks think differently about such matters on the mainland.'

Joanna promised, but her heart ached for her friend.

*

The following morning Joanna dressed in a summery gown of white muslin spotted with blue. Dark blue ribbons streamed from her waist, matching those of the net holding her hair to the nape of her neck.

Tilda and Richard Lind were still asleep when she went down for an early breakfast.

She'd envisaged opposition from Charlotte, and she got it. 'You intend to wear that gown to painting lessons?'

'No, Charlotte. I'm not going to the lesson today. Mr Morcant is picking me up soon. He's taking me to walk in the hills.'

Charlotte's lips pursed. 'Why did you not think to tell me of this yesterday?'

Calmly Joanna spread a piece of toast with butter. 'I'm a grown woman. I didn't see the need to.'

'You're a guest in my house. Common courtesy requires it of you, Joanna.'

Joanna slid her a glance. She was sorry for upsetting her, but she had to have some freedom. 'I apologize for not telling you. In future, I'll advise you of my movements.'

Charlotte said nothing, but disapproval hung heavy in the atmosphere throughout breakfast.

'Tobias wouldn't like it,' Charlotte said at the end of the meal when Joanna lifted the table napkin to her mouth.

'I doubt if he would have objected. From what I heard of his will, he practically ordered Alex to marry me.'

'Something Alex will no doubt consider in his own good time, since his future comfort depends on it.'

'So does mine,' Joanna reminded her. 'But I won't marry for the sake of the business, whatever Tobias wanted. He cannot rule me from the grave.'

'Even so, Alex will judge your behaviour. He's a very attractive man, one who is not only mature, but hot blooded. He will take advantage of everything you offer him. You're a young girl who has not yet learned how to behave with men. It would not be wise to allow him to turn your head, less he misconstrue the situation.'

'What is it you imagine I will be offering him, Charlotte?' Joanna gave a light laugh. 'Alex is taking me for a walk in the hills, that's all.' She crossed to where Charlotte stood, her face troubled, because the woman had been good to her and she didn't want to hurt her. 'I know you mean well, and I appreciate what you're doing for me. You're suffocating me though. You must stop acting as though you're my grandmother. Tobias was my husband, not my father. I must be allowed to make my own decisions.'

Charlotte stared at her, her face draining of colour. 'My dear, I'm not trying to suffocate you, just trying to advise you and prepare you to face the future.'

Hearing the carriage pull to a halt outside, Joanna went upstairs to fetch her shawl, gloves and reticule before returning just in time to see Alex being admitted by Charlotte.

He stood tall and straight, a strong elegant figure in black. She smiled at him, saying straight away, 'Charlotte doesn't approve of our outing. Will you reassure her that you'll behave in a gentlemanly manner.'

There was a small tincture of hurt in his voice as he turned to Charlotte. 'Is it true that you don't trust me with her?'

Embarrassment filled Charlotte's eyes. 'I admit, I was a little perturbed. Of course I trust you, Alex. After all, Tobias thought he could.'

'Yes he did, didn't he? It was quite a responsibility he handed me. I'll try to live up to your expectations, and Joanna's, of course.' There was a moment of speculation in his eyes, then they cleared. 'I've taken an extra day from my schedule especially to take her walking, and have come complete with picnic basket. But if you don't feel easy about it, we'll cancel the arrangement. Or perhaps you'd like to come with us, Charlotte. I was going to take Joanna on the trail through the woods to the sea, since she expressed a wish to walk for ever, and that's a taxing walk for anyone.'

How clever he was at manipulating people, Joanna thought, when Charlotte capitulated to his easy charm with a flustered, 'That would be much too far for me to walk, at my age. Just look after her, Alex, there might be some rain on the way and I don't want her to catch cold.'

At the door, Joanna turned and, noting the worried look in Charlotte's eyes, she rushed back to hug her tight. 'Don't worry, Charlotte,' she whispered. 'I know how to take care of myself.'

But when Alex turned his dark eyes her way and smiled, Joanna felt as though she was falling into a pit of dark honey.

*

Alexander had no qualms about attempting to seduce Joanna. The girl was a means to an end, he told himself. Through her, he'd have what he'd always wanted, complete control of the Darsham and Morcant Shipping Company.

When they were wed he'd persuade her to sell Tobias's house, or perhaps they would live in it, then he could mortgage his own to raise enough money from the bank to buy Oliver out. He felt a niggle of conscience for being so cold-blooded about the matter as she smiled happily at him.

The day promised to be fair, despite Charlotte's prediction of rain and a smudge of smoke-coloured cloud colouring the horizon.

Joanna's appearance pleased him. Her figure in the muslin gown was superbly feminine and fresh. There was a swift thrust of lust into his groin at the thought of finding out what lay underneath her petticoats, and his palms itched to cup those provocatively thrusting breasts so he could kiss the dark nubs.

They left the horse and carriage at the inn. He carried a picnic basket and rug along a rough track for a mile, before leaving them in a storage barn at the edge of the wood. Taking her hand in his, he indicated the heavily wooded hill before them. 'The sea is about a mile on the other side of the woods.'

He tried not to walk too fast for her, but she kept up with him easily, using long strides that carried her rapidly over the ground. For a while they watched the sea from the cliff. The Isle of Portland thrust up out of the water in the distance, looking slightly sinister, for it wore a cloak of grey cloud to shroud it in secrecy. Between the island and themselves, the water was a ripple of white-crested pewter that drew curtains of clouds down into it.

'It's raining on Portland,' she said.

'And will soon be raining here, so we'd best get back to the barn.'

They'd been inside the woods for almost an hour when she pulled him to a halt, her eyes shining. 'I've never been inside so many trees. Can we stop for a moment? I want to catch my breath and listen.'

He pulled her down beside him on a fallen log and she leaned against his shoulder, took in a slow, deep breath and whispered, 'It smells wonderful, like nuts, mushrooms, moss and hobgoblins spying on us from boggy patches. Close your eyes, Alex.'

He saw no harm in humouring her childish fancies, though he'd rather have looked at the sweet curve of her mouth and the rise and fall of her bodice. The side of her breast pressed softly against his arm and a strand of her hair, loosened by the freshening wind, brushed against his cheek.

'Up in the canopy of the trees the wind is sighing. It sounds sad, like a sailor stranded on the shore, looking for his lost love.'

He smiled at that.

'There's a speckled thrush singing to cheer him up.'

'And where is the sailor's love?' he murmured.

'She's in her grave, waiting for him to join her. You can hear her gown rustling as she dances to entice him.'

He chuckled. 'I wouldn't have thought a coffin had

264

much room to dance in. It sounds more like leaves on trees to me.'

'You have no romance in your soul. Tell me what you hear?'

He opened his eyes and gazed at her, running a finger across her lips. There was a faint sheen of perspiration on her forehead, for the day was warm and humid. 'I hear your heart beating faster when I touch your face, and the intake of your breath. And I can hear your stomach rattling with hunger.' He smiled when she giggled. 'When I open my eyes I can see your lashes quivering against your skin, which shines like the bloom on a pearl. Behind those lashes I can see the glitter of your eyes, and I know you're looking at me and wishing I'd kiss that delicious mouth of yours.'

Her eyes shot open and she glared at him. 'You're extremely arrogant, Alexander Morcant. I most certainly was not!'

'Then we'd best get on.'

As he stood and took her hands in his to pull her to her feet, there was a splatter of rain above them in the canopy.

'You may kiss me if you wish,' she murmured, being so obviously offhand about it that he chuckled.

The sound of rain amongst the trees became heavier as he gazed at her. Thunder grumbled in the distance. She was too trusting, and her innocence filled him with guilt. 'There's going to be a storm. Let's get back to the barn before we're soaked through.'

As they broke from the trees he took her hand and they ran pell-mell across the open ground, jumping from one tussock to the other like children, the rain chasing them. Half soaked, they threw themselves into the hay, laughing and out of breath. Alex had never enjoyed a day so much.

Propping himself on one elbow he gazed down at her, wondering if he had the will power to prevent himself from taking advantage of her when her hair, freed by the chase from its constricting net, tumbled and curled damply all about her.

'Are you hungry, my Joanna Rose?' he murmured.

Her smile faded. Her eyes drew him to her and her mouth became a moist, trembling pout. 'Yes, Alex . . . oh yes. I'm hungry.' She caressed the curve of his mouth and her own lips trembled into a smile. 'Kiss me. It will be all the sweeter for the wait.'

As his mouth brushed against hers, her arms slid around his neck and she gave a tiny murmur of satisfaction.

He set his guilt aside as, above them, the heavens opened.

14

Nothing could be as wonderful as being in love, Joanna thought, wondering when Alexander would return to Poole. Her body felt wonderfully alive, for it seemed as though every second she could recall the caress of his fingers, the touch of his tongue and the power of the hard, driven muscles that kept her rising to meet him as he took his pleasure, and pleasured her in return.

He had drenched her in loving on that wet afternoon, taking her innocence gently, then, afterwards, with a sensuous and demanding strength, so she knew both the power and the weakness of him and was made aware of the passion of her own response.

It was a wonder to her that Charlotte hadn't noticed anything different about her, for her emotions had filled her with happiness, like a shining beacon of light. She had arrived home dishevelled, her mouth feeling bruised and swollen, her breasts tingling and the moist folds between her thighs tender and throbbing from the thrust of him, yet yearning for more.

He'd said, smiling tenderly as they sat in the carriage at the front door with the hood up against the driving rain, 'Tidy your hair a little in case Charlotte notices.'

'I don't care if Charlotte notices,' she'd told him.

'I do. She trusted me to look after you.'

'And you did, most beautifully. I feel wonderful.' She kissed the side of his mouth. 'When will I see you again?'

He'd been matter of fact. 'I don't know. I have a company to run. Can you keep this afternoon a secret? Charlotte wouldn't understand.'

'I want to shout it to the world.'

'So do I. But it's the wrong time. To all intents and purposes you're still married to Tobias.'

'But his body has been found.'

'For the sake of decency there must be a memorial service and a mourning period. To declare ourselves now would bring censure down on our heads and your reputation would be in shreds.

Rebellion had roiled inside her for a moment, for she didn't give a fig for her reputation. She was being driven by love and found it to be a powerfully potent force.

'It's natural to lie with the man you love in Portland.'

His eyes met hers, the turmoil of passion she'd evoked in them earlier now quite spent as he'd told her flatly, 'You don't live in Portland now, self-control is expected here,' which hurt slightly, because it had been her own self-control he referred to, not his own. He'd given her a lingering kiss then, but she'd sensed his withdrawal from her in spirit.

Charlotte had opened the door just as a gust of wind dishevelled Joanna's newly smoothed hair, which her hands immediately abandoned in favour of anchoring her lifting skirt. Charlotte had laughed. 'You'd better come in before you fly off into the air. I was beginning to worry that you'd got yourself lost. Are you coming in, Alex?'

Avoiding Charlotte's eyes he fiddled with the reins. 'No, I'm afraid I must be off, I need to get the horse and carriage back to the livery stable.'

'Thank you for a lovely day,' Joanna called out to him as he turned the carriage around.

Considering the intimacy of their time together his reply had been almost offhand.

'My pleasure, Joanna. We must do it again sometime.'

A month had passed since then and Joanna hadn't set eyes on Alex, but it didn't stop her dreaming about him or remembering every moment between them. She turned when Charlotte came in from the garden to interrupt her reverie. Her mother-in-law had some inportant news.

'I've just received a letter from James Stark. Tobias has now been officially declared dead. James has enclosed a copy of the cost of the funeral, twenty-two pounds, four shillings and sixpence. What an odd thing to do. There will be a service in London on board the company's newest ship, *Joanna Rose*, when she returns from Australia.'

'*Joanna Rose*? But that's my name.'

Charlotte sent her a fond smile.'Yes . . . Tobias named the ship after you. He was going to surprise you with it.'

'He has. It was nice of him.' Her eyes lit up. 'Will Alex be there, at the service?'

A slight frown creased Charlotte's brow. 'Of course. He's asked if he can read the eulogy. Alex and Tobias were very close. His elder brother Oliver will be in port at the same time. Plus, Oliver and Alex's mother will be on board the *Clara Jane* when she docks. Clara Nash will be coming across from America with her twin daughters, Irene and Lydia. They'd be about fifteen years old now.'

'Is anything the matter? There was a disapproving note in your voice when you mentioned Clara Nash.'

'I must tell you that I have never seen eye to eye with Clara. Tobias disliked her, too, and he was a good judge of character.' There was a long drawn out sigh from her. 'Oh dear, I cannot believe I'll never see Tobias again. I keep expecting him to turn up on my doorstep any day now.'

Feeling sorry for Charlotte, Joanna crossed to where she stood and took her hands. 'The service might help finalize it for you, and perhaps that's why James Stark sent you the receipt, as proof, to convince you that your son is dead.'

'Yes, of course. He might think I need convincing, but I don't think I gave him the impression I believed otherwise,' she said rather distractedly. 'We will be on show at the memorial service, so we must wear something sober, though I do so hate black. And we must go to London the week before, in case anyone wishes to call on us beforehand. James has sent the memorial cards out already, he tells me.'

Richard had assured them he was content to be left behind in the company of the servants, along with the two dogs and Albert, the handsome and arrogant kitten, who was now the leader of the pack. 'I'm sure the maids will look after me and feed me from time to time.'

So they ordered gowns and bonnets to match, and, halfway through a gloriously warm May, the three women made the long and tedious journey to London in the care of David Lind, like three parcels wrapped in black silk.

Finally they arrived at the home that had once belonged to Tobias, a comfortably sized place in Southwark with grounds that swept down to the river.

The place had an air of neglect and smelled of dust. But even that couldn't disguise the stench in the air outside, which had forced them to hold handkerchiefs sprinkled with Charlotte's lavender water against their noses.

'Where are the servants?' Charlotte whispered in dismay, looking around the dusty hall.

Just then a woman came hurrying through from the back of the house. 'Mr Stark didn't tell me you were coming, Mrs Darsham.'

'Obviously not,' said Charlotte.

'Sorry, ma'am. There's only myself and my husband left. Mr Stark let the others go.' Her eyes flickered from one woman to the other, as if trying to decide which was her former master's widow. They settled on Joanna when she smiled encouragingly at her. 'I'll send my husband to tell him you're here, shall I, ma'am? Mr Stark's office is only a ten-minute walk. Shall I open the window for some air?'

'Certainly not. The air is foul. What's causing that disgusting odour?'

'The river, ma'am. It's been a bad year for smells.'

'Sewerage, I suppose,' Joanna said. 'I expect it drains straight into the river.'

'Joanna!' Charlotte remonstrated. 'I've already advised you that it's hardly a subject one should comment on.'

'Why not, especially since the stench can't be avoided? If it's not commented upon how will it ever get fixed? I shall write to the Prime Minister to complain about it, at once. What's his name?'

'You know very well that Lord Palmerston holds office. This is not a matter for levity.'

'Indeed not,' the housekeeper said. 'The late Mr Darsham told me there were plans afoot to build a proper sanitary system for the whole city, because of the cholera outbreaks. And he had plans to get gas lighting installed in the house.'

Joanna nodded knowledgeably while Charlotte tutted. Even though she didn't know what gas lighting was, she intended to find out. 'Yes, my husband was a very forward-thinking man. As for sending your husband to inform Mr Stark, by all means do. After that, prepare Mrs Darsham senior's room, for she needs to rest. I'll find a room for myself and for my guest, Miss Rushmore.'

'But, ma'am . . .'

'Don't worry, we shall explore and find everything, and we can shift for ourselves. What's your name?'

'Bates, ma'am. You might like to try the two rooms on the left, at the back. They're a nice size and have a view of the river. Plenty goes on with barges and the like going past. Mr Darsham always liked lookin' out over the river. He said he liked being in the thick of things, poor gentleman.' She wiped a tear from her eye with the corner of her apron. 'He used the rooms on the right, though. Kept a telescope up there so he could keep an eye on what was going on.'

David took their luggage up, making several trips up and down the staircases lugging their bags, porter fashion, before finishing his task and excusing himself.

'We're indebted to you, David. You've been most kind and patient. I do hope you'll call on us again while we're in London,' Charlotte said.

He blushed when Joanna kissed his cheek and added, 'Thank you, dear friend. I don't know what we would have done without you.'

Tilda had a miserable look on her face as she held out her hand to him. 'I hope you won't forget us, Reverend Lind.'

'Indeed no. *Never!*' he insisted with some force, then kissed her cheek and cast a hopeful look at her. 'I hope to see you at the service for Mr Darsham. You will be there?'

'Of course.' Tilda seemed to brighten up at the thought of seeing David again, so Joanna thought there might be hope for a marriage between them, yet.

It didn't take long to settle themselves. Joanna and Tilda pitched in with a will, dusting their respective bedrooms, making beds, unpacking, then boiling kettles of water in the kitchen to fill the jugs so the dust of the journey could be washed from their bodies.

Mrs Bates trotted off to a nearby shop that opened late, to purchase something for dinner. She came back smiling, carrying a jug of milk in one hand, cheese, eggs and a package containing thick slices of smoked bacon in a wicker basket held on her other arm. Soon they had a substantial meal with the addition of vegetables dug up from the garden.

Later that evening, when everyone was settled, for they were tired after their journey, Joanna took up a lamp and walked around the quiet house she'd suddenly become mistress of. The light was fading as she entered the drawing room, where a lamp already burned low.

It was a man's room, despite the velvet curtains. The couches were leather, the walls wood-panelled, the lamps without embellishment except for a sailing ship etched into the glass. A faint smell of stale tobacco hung in the air and there was a ship's decanter on the table, half filled with liquid, a glass next to it, empty, but left unwashed.

Like Tobias's generous heart, the clock had stopped. Moving the clock hands around the dial she wound it up with a brass key inserted in a hole in the dial and set it ticking. Hanging on the wall over the fireplace was a painting of a ship proud with sail upon a lively sea. A little brass plaque stated: *Joanna Rose*. Darsham and Morcant Shipping Company. 1856.

So this was the clipper Tobias had named after her? She was a beautiful ship, and Joanna was looking forward to going on board her.

She felt like a voyeur, for the house built up a more rounded picture of Tobias's character than his presence ever had. She wished she'd known him for longer.

There was a slightly lonely atmosphere to the house that made Joanna feel as if something good had gone from her life – something she'd caught a glimpse of, but which hid tantalizingly out of sight.

Crossing to the decanter she poured a little of the liquid into the glass and, placing her lips where his would have been, she took a sip from it. Fumes assailed her nostrils, prompting her to jerk her head back and wrinkle her nose as her tongue registered a fiery warmth. Gasping a little, she decided that spirituous liquors were unfit for a woman to drink, after all.

Why did Tobias wed her? Why did he leave everything to a girl he hardly knew, when there were people like Alex, who knew and loved him better?

'Alex,' she murmured and, dreamy-eyed, she allowed her fingers to drift over the black silk covering her breasts. She couldn't wait to see him again, and hoped it wouldn't be long before he came to visit, as the memory her body retained of his love-making came gloriously alive.

Alexander was shocked when Oliver told him, 'Mother wants to buy my half of the company and the Morcant house, and I'm thinking of accepting her offer.'

'I'd rather you didn't sell it to her, Oliver. I'm trying to raise the money myself. What does our mother want with a shipping company?'

'Damned if I know. I think she just wants to keep it in the family. She feels guilty about letting the truth about your parentage out of the bag and will probably leave the company to you in her will, anyway.'

The smile Alexander gave had an ironic edge. 'I

doubt if her conscience troubles her to that extent. Where is she now?'

'Gone ashore with Irene and Lydia. They'll be staying at the Morcant house, where our mother can entertain both friends and acquaintances in style. Somebody might as well use it and she'll enjoy being the lady of the house. She'll be getting in practice for when it's hers.'

'Why don't you just sell her the house?'

'She wants the whole package, Alex, and she won't accept less. I think she has plans of marrying the girls into the aristocracy. She shouldn't have any trouble, since they're heiresses to a fortune.'

'And a shipping company would enhance that.' Even though he didn't know them well, the thought of his young sisters exchanging fortune for title and the dubious honour of breeding aristocrats made Alexander slightly uncomfortable. There was something mercenary about it.

Even if Darsham and Morcant never became part of his sisters' dowries, Alexander doubted if he'd be able to run the company comfortably with his mother as part-owner, since her nature was too manipulative.

'Can't you wait a little longer?'

'I can, but not for *too* much longer. Have you proposed to the Darsham widow yet?'

'Hardly, but I'm working towards it.' A grin spread across his face. 'It's not bad work at that. Wait until you see her. Joanna Rose is definitely responsive to my overtures and, although she was as mad as a nest of stirred ants when she heard what Tobias had arranged, she's warming to me, and in more ways than one.'

'You should keep your fingers out of the treasury. Isn't

there a saying that you shouldn't mix business with pleasure?'

It occurred to Alexander that Joanna was in much the same position as his sisters. He didn't waste time feeling sorry for her, though, but convinced himself it was a sensible calculation. Without him, the company would go under, and Joanna would end up with what she'd started out with. The trouble was, if he allowed that to happen he'd end up with nothing, too!

'It's not just my fingers. A taste of pleasure has definitely sweetened the deal in this case. The widow was still intact, but she came easy.'

Oliver grinned, but said nothing.

'Once we're wed, I'll have Tobias's house to sell, his investments to draw down on, and I can mortgage my own house, if need be. I've got it all worked out.'

'You might have, but I haven't. Susannah's father needs to know when I can take up his offer of a partnership. I can give you another couple of months, Alex, but after that I sell to mother. It will keep the company in the family. She's made a good offer and you'll still have the controlling share when you wed. What have you got to lose?'

My independence, Alex thought. He said, 'Can you imagine what will happen if the brokers and customers thought the company was going to be owned by two women? Let's get the memorial service over with first. Then I'll propose to the widow and suggest we elope. She's the type who would enjoy the adventure of it. I'll keep James informed and work out the details. I hope the *Joanna Rose* is on schedule.'

'Isn't she always. Today I saw her topsail on the horizon. There's no mistaking Thaddeus Scott's mastery of a ship, he makes it look easy. She'll be tied up by this evening.'

'Good. I want to get this business over and done with. And I don't like giving the entire staff two hours off for a memorial service. It's a waste of money.'

'But not *your* money,' Oliver said, reminding Alex forcefully of their mother. 'And Tobias deserves a send-off.'

'I'm only too aware that it's *your* company I'm working for now, Oliver, not *ours*. I'm surprised you saw fit to mention it. If you'd shown a greater interest in how the company operates, and how easily it could be brought down, you might realize how hard that money is earned. Chasing after Joanna Darsham's skirt is the last thing on my mind at the moment, and the least of my worries. We have to present a united front at this memorial service.'

Shame crossed his brother's face. 'I'm sorry, Alex. That was uncalled for.'

Alexander let the telling little remark go, though anger soured the blood in his veins like vinegar. Oliver didn't know the half of it. Alexander had been juggling a nightmare to keep the company intact. If it wasn't for his constant efforts, there would be nothing left to take a profit out of. He sighed. 'Let me spell it out for you, Oliver. If you sell now it will bring down the company. If you wait until things pick up, it will be worth much more to you.'

He'd secured enough cargo and passengers for the

clippers, but the *Nightingale* would be sailing at a loss, unless something appeared at the last minute. He was of half a mind to put the ageing ship on the market, but to do so would invite rumour. He didn't want to lose her captain, either, for he'd made up his mind to give Edward Staines command of the *Clara Jane* when Oliver was ready to hand over the helm.

Personally, he had nothing to lose at the moment except his position, and he could easily find another one. He shrugged. Only his love for Tobias bound him to the company. But in death, Tobias was making him work harder than he'd ever worked to achieve what he wanted. Alexander was beginning to wonder if it was worth it.

When he'd be able to investigate the purchase of a steamship was not even a matter for conjecture at the moment.

Being mistress of her own house was wonderful for Joanna, for although Charlotte still corrected her she was careful not to do so in front of the housekeeper.

Using Mrs Bates as a guide and escort, within three days Joanna had investigated her immediate sur-roundings. She knew which shops sold what, and where, and how to get to the local markets, where she made sure she got the freshest produce at the cheapest price.

Although she couldn't do much about the smell in the air, except get used to it, she bought a large amount of pot-pourri to place all around the house, and wore a filmy scarf sprinkled with rose or lavender water when she went out.

She seemed to function in a cloud of expectation, but Alexander didn't call. In fact, she didn't see him again until the day of the service.

There was a sense of reluctance about Charlotte that day, so she was disinclined to hurry, even though James Stark came to escort them. As a result, they were late getting to the ship.

There was a soft breeze blowing as they stepped on board. The crowd fell silent and Joanna was aware of curious glances upon her as a path opened to let them through.

Alexander stood next to an upright, grey-haired man who was stern of feature until he set eyes on Charlotte, then he gave her a broad smile. She thought he might be the captain. He gave her a thorough scrutiny, which she bore, but colour seeped into her cheeks. Alexander met her eyes and nodded, but his attitude gave no acknowledgement of what they'd shared. He was very in control of himself, whereas her heart was beating very fast and she could hardly take a breath with the joy of seeing him again.

The service started almost straight away, with a prayer and a hymn. Then Alexander stepped forward and said, 'Tobias Darsham was the finest man I've ever known . . .'

When a mumble of assent came from the crowd Joanna was proud that she'd been married to a man who attracted such goodwill. Overcome by the moment, tears began to course down her cheeks.

Alexander took possession of her arm afterwards. As they took refreshment in the salon below, he stood next to her while she and Charlotte accepted condolences. She could feel the warmth from his body, standing tall beside her, and she wanted to reach out and touch him. Alexander's mother, his brother and two sisters were introduced. Clara Nash, however, was distant in manner and didn't encourage any warmth.

Someone called Henry Wetherall from the shipping office bowed over her hand. Then there were several businessmen, whose names she forgot as soon as they left. The crowd thinned out. The man Alexander had been with on deck came to stand at his shoulder. His glance had been on her all evening. Up close he was even more imposing and she'd noticed that the crew obeyed with alacrity even the most softest spoken of his command. His eyes were bottle brown, and as sharp as cut glass.

'I'm Thaddeus Scott. This is my ship.'

She nodded. 'Charlotte has spoken about you often. According to her, you're the senior captain of the company, you sail to Australia and back and smoke a foul-smelling tobacco that would kill cockroaches.'

He chuckled. 'Aye, I do all of that. What do you think of the *Joanna Rose*?'

'I haven't really seen her yet, apart from a painting hanging on my wall at home.'

'A painting that should be hanging in my salon.'

He sent a ferocious frown to Alex, who promptly grinned and said, 'Can I help it if Tobias took a fancy to it.'

Despite his stern exterior, Joanna decided she liked Thaddeus. 'Will you introduce me to her, Captain Scott?'

'You haven't got time,' Alexander said, when Thaddeus offered her his arm. 'I've promised Charlotte I'd escort you all home. Then I have to go and see James in his office. Joanna, he wants to see you, too . . . to discuss certain aspects of Tobias's will.'

Joanna knew which aspects he referred to, and since Alex had practically ignored her over the past few weeks she now felt miffed with him. 'I shall do as I please, Alex. I want to see the *Joanna Rose*. You may escort the others home. I shall stay here and will meet you at James Stark's office later. I know how to get there.'

'But, Joanna . . .'

Thaddeus slanted her a conspiratorial look. 'I'll bring Mrs Darsham to the office, since Charlotte has invited me up to the house for dinner later.'

Alexander hesitated, and Joanna thought he looked as if he were about to argue. Then he shrugged. 'As you wish.' He turned to Thaddeus. 'I'll leave her in your good hands then. Have her there by three p.m. please, Captain Scott.'

Thaddeus commented as Alexander strode away, 'The lad's got himself in a bit of a frazzle, I reckon, for he's as twitchy as a flea.'

'Alex has a lot to deal with and he takes life too seriously sometimes.' As she gazed at Thaddeus she gave him her best smile. For a moment he looked startled, then a slow smile inched across his face and he said quietly, 'I'll be damned. Now there's something I never thought I'd see.'

'What's that, Captain?'

'A smile like that on a woman. Now where shall we start? At the very bottom of the ship or the top? Could you climb the mast, d'you think?'

'If I had to, for there would be a fine view from the top. But not in this skirt, for I'd fly away in the wind like a parasol in a storm.'

'And a very pretty sight that would be.'

She laughed and said, 'It most certainly would not, for I'd display my drawers and shock the London folk.'

His guffaw of laughter drew the disapproving glances of three bewhiskered gentlemen wearing black coats.

'Black is an ugly colour, don't you think? Charlotte said we needn't wear it when we get back to Poole.'

'And when will that be?'

'Soon, for the smell of the river upsets her. I might stay longer if I can, for I'd like to learn about the company and the ships, perhaps even make a journey by sea. Perhaps I'll sail away with you to Australia.'

'And perhaps you won't,' he said gruffly, 'for the outward journey takes over two months and is too dangerous and too taxing to undertake for mere pleasure. Charlotte wouldn't allow it for a start. If she did, Alex wouldn't. Besides, you would need my permission and I wouldn't give it.'

'Would you not, Captain Scott?' Her eyes narrowed. 'Since I've been in London I'm beginning to learn just how much I'm worth. And part of that worth includes this ship. Are we about to have our first argument?'

He chuckled. 'Not unless you want to go over my knee and get your backside walloped. Tobias never gave a cuss about what people owned as a measure of their worth, but only what they were. Wealth is a responsibility. If it's not handled sensibly it will evaporate as quickly as it was acquired.'

She felt suitably crushed. 'Tobias was right. I'm sorry. Everyone is trying to make me do what they want me to do, and I'd like to please myself instead of others all the time.'

'You're a free spirit. Tobias told me you were.'

'He spoke to you about me?'

'Aye, he said you had a bright and independent manner about you that reminded him of . . . a diamond in the rough.'

'His first wife, Honor, you meant to say,' she said, her eyes bright with laughter.

'There was that about you, too, I believe.' He pushed her gently towards a staircase. 'Let's start your education, girl. We'll begin with the passenger quarters, I think.'

By the end of the tour her head was in a whirl, with terms such as bulkheads, jib-booms, poop decks, garboards, windlasses, capstans and keelsons. When they emerged into the daylight she grinned at him. 'How can you remember all the pieces that go into her?'

'I grew up with ships and have been sailing in them since I was a lad.'

'My pa was a quarryman and stonemason. His father was a fisherman, so my pa knew about the sea. He told me lots of stories. Do you believe seagulls have souls?'

'Of course, lass.' He offered her a smile. 'Tobias told me your pa's tale about coming ashore with a seagull navigating your cradle though the storm. Tobias thought it was the soul of Lucian Morcant, who died that day.'

'My pa was always making up stories like that. Some people think the tale is a silly fairy story. Some think it a true tale, though.'

'It's a powerful story, so perhaps it is true.' His eyes met hers and they contained curiosity. 'Would you mind if it were true?'

'I don't know. It would mean that my pa found me and kept me when I belonged to somebody else.'

'Aye.'

'Something like that could eat at you inside. If you got too curious and didn't find what you were looking for, you might remain for ever dissatisfied. Seeking the truth could destroy contentment of what you already have and it might give you nothing back to fill the void.'

'There's that.'

The truth of her birth had been troubling Joanna more and more of late. Joseph and Anna Rushmore had been simple, honest folk, who'd worked hard. She loved them deep in her heart and that was something nobody could take away from her. She didn't want to think ill of them.

She shrugged as she gazed at the captain. 'You remind me of my pa. He was gruff in his manner, but his heart was as soft as butter. I was young when he died, but I recall the way he had about him. I truly loved him.'

Thaddeus cleared his throat as he squeezed her hand. 'There's contentment in being loved. It's something you should hold on to.'

The sound of a squawk made her glance up to where

a seagull was perched on the tallest of the three masts. Clouds sailed past behind it, making her feel slightly dizzy, as if the world was turning too fast.

'That might be the soul of Tobias, come for his memorial service,' she said.

'Then he's late.' Thaddeus took out his pocket watch and his eyes crinkled into a network of lines when he smiled. 'So are we.'

15

Thaddeus Scott escorted Joanna to James Stark's office door. A man was just leaving. He nodded and held the door open for her to enter.

'Mrs Darsham? I'm Joel Potter. Mr Stark's clerk. He and Mr Morcant are waiting for you in the back office. You won't mind if I don't take you through, will you? I have to get these papers delivered right away.' With that he was gone, his large nose pointed towards the pavement, striding along like a stork on the edge of a lake.

Joanna exchanged a smile with Thaddeus at the sight. 'Thank you for bringing me.'

'Tobias would have expected no less, my dear,' he said comfortably. 'I'll see you at the house. Don't allow those two to pull the wool over your eyes.'

'I certainly won't,' she said, but she was looking forward with some eagerness to seeing Alex again, face to face in a more intimate setting than the ship.

As the door to the street closed behind her she stopped for a moment to allow her eyes to adjust to the dim interior of the front office, which was wood-panelled and contained a desk and chair, presumably from where his clerk reigned over his small domain. There were chairs for clients to use while they waited and files lined several shelves behind the desk.

The rumble of voices came from the end of a corridor, where light spilled from a door left ajar. As she began to walk towards it, there came a chink of glass against glass and James Stark said, 'Where has Thaddeus got to with the girl?'

'You know how Thaddeus is about the *Joanna Rose*. He's probably got the crew demonstrating the sailor's hornpipe on her behalf. But I thought I heard the door close a moment ago.'

'That was Potter going out. He has some papers to deliver and they're urgent.'

'It wouldn't take him long with those long legs of his.'

Giving a smile as the two men chuckled, Joanna knuckled her fingers to rap at the door panel when Alexander said, 'Joanna is probably late on purpose. She's a contrary madam at times.'

'No doubt you'll take her in hand when you're wed.'

'Aye. I'll probably buy a place in Poole where she can live with that cousin of hers, and be company for Charlotte. A couple of children will keep her busy, so she won't get it into her head to interfere with my life.'

Joanna's smile faded. How detached from such a union he sounded.

'I had the feeling you were going to walk away from the whole thing.'

'I was, at first. With my mother waiting to buy Oliver's half of the company I'm left with three choices.

The first is to resign and watch everything Tobias and I worked for most of our lives go under. The second is to not marry Joanna and work on her behalf with my mother, who will interfere.' He chuckled. 'My mother's business strength lies in marrying rich men. It seems as though I'm about to carry on the tradition.'

'Will Oliver sell his share to Mrs Nash, d'you think?'

'He intends to sell his share, then enter a partnership with his future father-in-law. He says he'd rather keep his share in the family. So he's giving me two months to raise the money. For the sake of the company, I think Tobias came to the right conclusion. He did intend to pass the company on to me before that girl came along, didn't he?'

'There's no denying it, Alexander. You were his sole heir before his marriage.'

'And there's no way of contesting the will?'

'Not unless you're kin, which you're not.'

'I've come to believe that two women owning a shipping company, even with me in control, will spell disaster for it. So I'm going to marry Joanna, and with the money I can raise from various investments she's inherited I'll buy Oliver's share. That way, the company will no longer be in jeopardy and I will have respected Tobias's wishes.'

'Tobias wouldn't have known that Oliver wanted to sell, so yes, I think you've reached the wisest decision. For looks, you couldn't do much better than marry the fair Joanna Rose, but she's a clever young woman with a mind of her own, and I don't think she'll let you have things all your own way.'

'Good, it will add spice to the union then.' Joanna could almost hear the laughter in his voice. 'I'll propose to her tonight, just as soon as I get her alone.'

Will you now? Joanna edged back along the corridor with her face burning and her body trembling as if she had a fever. She took a few moments to compose herself, then took a deep breath and opened the door to the street. Loudly, she said, 'Thank you, Captain Scott,' then closed it again with a bit of a thud.

Alex came hurrying out from the back, a smile on his face, scolding. 'You're late, Joanna.'

How could he look at her like that, as if he loved her, with his eyes so soft and melting and his mouth in a soft, delicious curve so she wanted to kiss him straight away? She steeled herself, trying to ignore the attraction of him, to disregard the strength of the muscular body she'd grown to know so intimately the last time they'd been together. How she would love to move into his arms, move against him, tell him she adored him. The awareness of him sent the blood tumbling though her body, so she came alive just at the sight of him, and the smile she returned was spontaneous and natural because of it.

But she could allow herself to adore him no more, not now she'd discovered how shallow he was. *Hypocrite. I despise you now!* her mind raged, but she didn't know whether she referred to him or to herself when he stooped to kiss her cheek and she turned slightly so her lips clung to his Judas mouth for a mind-numbing few moments before she pulled away from the embrace.

She managed a teasing smile for him. 'I know I'm late, Alex. Captain Scott made me climb the mast.'

'And you didn't fall?'

'Oh yes, I fell, but Portland girls grow up to be as tough as the island. I stood up again, bruised and bloodied, but still functioning.'

She gazed into his eyes for a few moments. Best to let him think he'd fooled her until she'd decided what she was going to do. Whatever that was, she knew that neither of them would like it. 'Forgive me Alex,' she murmured, but thought, *Damn you!* You've broken my heart and I'm going to weep an ocean of tears for what could have been between us.

His chuckle was as warm as the devil's breath against her ear. 'I'd forgive you anything for another kiss like that, Joanna Rose.'

She was tempted, but since her kisses meant nothing to Alexander Morcant except a means to an end, she declined. 'I think I've kept Mr Stark waiting long enough.'

James Stark stood when she entered the office, then gave her the professional smile he reserved for his clients. Alex entered with her. When she was seated he went to lean against the cupboard and smiled damnably at her.

There were many papers to sign, making her part owner of the Darsham and Morcant Shipping Company. An hour later, Joanna left the office a wealthy woman. Now she understood what Alex stood to lose, and what she stood to lose herself if she turned Alex's proposal down and he simply walked away from it.

This wasn't something she'd sought. Wealth was one thing, comfort another, and this wealth was balanced like a pack of cards and would collapse swiftly if it wasn't managed properly. She didn't want the reponsibility of it resting on her shoulders, trapping her. Why hadn't Tobias simply left everything to Alexander Morcant in the first place?'

Later that evening, she found it hard to carry on normally, when everything inside her vibrated with stretched nerves. She managed not to be alone with Alex, but she could feel his dark eyes upon her for most of the evening.

It was he who climbed on a chair to remove the painting of *Joanna Rose* from the wall when she presented it to Thaddeus Scott.

'What will you put there in its stead?' he asked.

'I'll have a look around the house in the morning, I'm sure something suitable will turn up.'

'Perhaps we could take a look around now. Then I could hang it for you.'

'There's no need, Alex. Mr Bates can do it. Besides, it's time for dinner.'

Joanna had changed into a dark blue silk gown, quite plain except for some lace trim that matched the collar. Pinned at her throat was the rose brooch her mother had given her. She saw Alex's eyes go to it, watched him give a slight frown.

She declined to sit at the head of the table, allowing Charlotte, who'd donned a lighter blue gown, the chair of honour. Tilda was demure in dove grey, while the men were resplendent in their dinner suits.

She took the seat next to Thaddeus Scott. 'A pretty brooch,' he said.

'Thank you. It was a gift from my mother.'

Alexander cleared his throat and leaned forward to take a better look at it. Joanna couldn't miss the spark of recognition in his eyes, and his expression was unbelieving as he caught her gaze. 'Nice. Those are rubies, I believe.'

'Are they? To me the brooch is precious because it's something to remember my mother by.'

Into the moment of silence that arose between them, Tilda said quietly, 'Remember when you tried to sell it so you could bury her? David, your uncle gave Joanna a loan and looked after the brooch in case it was stolen from her by my family.'

'A convenient arrangement,' Alex said, his glance going from one girl to the other, so she was left with the impression that he didn't believe the tale, though she couldn't understand why.

Joanna smiled at Tilda across the table. She was seated between David and Alexander. Who would have thought back then that they'd end up like this, seated at a table gleaming with candles and set with polished silver? There was a separate glass for every wine, which would have bewildered Joanna and Tilda a few months ago, and the dinner, which was served by Mrs Bates from dishes on the sideboard, would have fed the same company twice over. She had a moment of nostalgia for a homely mutton stew with dumplings floating on top.

After they'd eaten, Alex got to his feet and chinked on his glass with a spoon. His eyes steady on Joanna, he said, 'I'd like to propose a toast to Joanna Rose Darsham on this sad occasion, and wish her every happiness in the years to come.'

There was a mumble of assent.

Joanna didn't know whether she was supposed to respond or not until Charlotte gave her a barely discernible nod. 'Thank you, Alex,' she said. 'Tobias would have wanted my future to be happy. But I'd give away everything he left me just to see him walk through that door. I feel his presence strongly in this house, almost as if he were still alive.'

Thaddeus Scott's hand jerked and a splotch of red wine fell on his napkin.

Joanna smiled at Charlotte. 'I'd prefer that the toast be drunk to the memory of Tobias and in celebration of his life. Perhaps you'd like to do that, Captain Scott.'

'I most certainly would.' The captain raised his glass. 'To Tobias, loving son to Charlotte, devoted husband when he got the chance to prove it, mentor to young Alexander there, whether he always appreciated it or not, a generous friend to us all and a damned good man, wherever he walks.'

James Stark nearly choked on his wine.

After spending the previous evening avoiding Alex, Joanna woke early. Clear headed, she did a quick search of the house.

She first went to the rooms Tobias had used as his own. His clothes were hung in wardrobes, or neatly folded into the drawers, polished shoes were lined up on the rack. He'd had large feet. She slipped her own feet inside a pair of man-sized slippers as she examined the dressing-table. There were cufflinks on a china tray, and the gold ring he'd usually worn on his little finger. It must have been a present from Honor, for it had her name etched inside it, and his initials were on the shield. She slipped it on to her middle finger, where it fitted comfortably.

The view through the telescope was of *Joanna Rose*. Several sailors were working on the rigging and boxes and sacks were being carried aboard. She moved the viewer down to the deck and saw Thaddeus Scott. He was talking to Alex. Then the younger man strode rapidly away. She followed his progress through the viewer until he stopped at a flower stall. Then he turned a corner and disappeared from her sight.

A vase of flowers, that was it. She needed something larger and more feminine for the drawing room than the pictures presently gracing the walls of the rest of the house, which were of ships, hunting dogs, maps and a landscape of a misty Scottish mountain with a rushing stream and a man fishing from the bank with his dog by his side.

Leaving the slippers behind, her journey took her to the attics, where she was confronted with a higgledy-piggledy tumble of boxes, furniture, books, travelling cases and an army of daddy-longlegged spiders. A skylight let adequate light through as she sifted through the accumulated treasure.

She came across a picture of a near-naked women with a spaniel on her lap and a lewd look in her eyes, and giggled. Then, after a fruitless search, in the far corner of the attic she spied the gleam of a gold frame behind some boxes. It took a while, but she finally unearthed the picture and dragged it into the light.

It was a woman, blue eyed with an abundance of dark hair. Under the layers of smoke on the portrait, Joanna connected with her immediately. It must be Honor Darsham, who'd been buried in Chiswell cemetery with her drowned infant. Only it wasn't Honor's infant that was buried, for her baby had been a girl, not a boy.

She tied a sheet around the portrait and began to carry it downstairs, stopping every now and then to rest. After she'd deposited her burden in the drawing room she fetched a bowl of water, some soap and a cloth.

The grimy smoke layers came off easily, but it wasn't until the final rinse with clean water that the woman was clearly revealed. Joanna moved the portrait to where the morning light came streaming through the window, gazing at it through bemused eyes. Honor Darsham was wearing a blue gown with a low cut shawl collar trimmed in lace over short, puffed sleeves. The rose brooch nestled where the collar met.

No wonder Alex had stared; he'd recognized it, and thought she and Tilda had lied about where she'd got it from. How cynical he was. How determined to think the worst of her.

Joanna gazed at the familiar face of Honor Darsham for a long time without knowing whether to rejoice or to weep, because she felt like doing both.

'Yes . . .' she finally murmured, deciding on neither. 'Everything is beginning to make sense to me now.'

She bided her time, taking breakfast with Tilda, who was expecting David Lind to collect her.

'He's taking me to see the mission where he works with the poor and needful,' she said. 'I've volunteered to help serve soup.'

'Just be careful not to cuddle any babies. You might catch something nasty, like body lice,' Charlotte said gaily. 'The poor are none too fussy about cleanliness.'

'If you'd ever been poor and couldn't afford a bar of soap, you'd know that they probably can't afford to be fussy,' Joanna said, unintentionally sharp.

Charlotte gave her a sideways glance and beamed her a smile. 'Yes, Miss Prim and Proper, I do know. I meant no insult and I'm not going to let anything spoil my day, not even a well-deserved reprimand from you, Joanna my dearest. Have you quarrelled with Alex by any chance? I noticed you were avoiding him yesterday.'

'Why should I avoid him?'

'I have no idea, except perhaps to entice him to pursue you with more intent.'

'Entice him? Hah! That man is a serpent with a forked tongue . . . a vulture who eats stinking carrion. In fact, Alexander Morcant is lower than Thames river mud. He's a devil's brew.'

Charlotte shuddered. 'What a dreadful turn of phrase you have acquired in London, though it all sounds very biblical.' Surprisingly, she laughed.

Puzzled, Joanna gazed at Charlotte. Now the memorial service was over she seemed to have taken on a new lease of life. Her eyes sparkled and her smile was a mile wide.

'I probably will,' said Tilda loudly.

They both gazed at her, said together. 'Probably will, what?'

'Cuddle poor babies who have lice, to answer Charlotte's question. You both seem to be absent-minded today. I hope that's not something I'll catch, else I'll be serving soup to horses.'

Joanna chuckled and added her own advice for Tilda's excursion. 'Watch out for pickpockets, then.'

Tilda laughed. 'Pish! All they'll find in my pocket is fluff. They're welcome to that.'

When Tilda had gone, Joanna said to Charlotte, 'There's something I want you to take a look at in the drawing room.'

'What is it, dear? I must hurry. Thaddeus Scott is taking me out visiting. The *Joanna Rose* sails the day after tomorrow for Australia, so this is our last chance for an excursion. We shall probably go to Kew Gardens. Come with us, it's such a lovely day.'

'You'll not mind if I stay home, will you, Charlotte? I'd like to be alone with my thoughts, in fact. I might go and clear the weeds from the garden.'

'Wear gloves then, else your hands will be a disgrace.' Charlotte pulled her close. 'I do love you, Joanna.'

Which reminded Joanna of Tobias telling her that he loved her just before he left – but in his own way, he'd said. Now she thought she knew what that way was. She just needed Charlotte to confirm it.

Taking Charlotte by the arm, she led her to the portrait. 'Is that Honor Darsham?'

Charlotte's hand flew to her mouth. 'Oh, my dear. Where did you find it?'

'Does it matter? You know what I'm asking you, Charlotte.'

Charlotte gazed at her, tears glistening in her eyes as she whispered, 'If you're Rose Darsham, you mean? Then yes, *if you are*, and I do think so, then that is your mother.'

'I *have* to be Rose Darsham. I've had that rose brooch since I was a child. Then there is the tale my pa told me about the princess coming ashore in the floating cradle.'

'The one Tobias carved with his own hands.'

Joanna stared at Charlotte, another piece to the puzzle now in place. Lord, what a shock Tobias must have had when he'd seen it. No wonder he'd quizzed her over it. She turned back to the portrait. 'Our looks are so similar I couldn't possibly be anyone else's daughter, could I? That's why you fainted when we first met. You saw the likeness to this portrait straight away.'

'Yes . . . I suspected who you were, and told Tobias before it was too late.'

'So Tobias is my father, and you are my grand-mother?'

'Yes, I truly believe you are. You can imagine what would have happened if anyone had found out that you'd wed. It would have ruined everything, his reputation, yours, the company.'

Joanna held out her hand, tears stinging her eyes. 'I found this ring on his dresser. I had noticed Tobias wearing it before, but he didn't have it on his finger that last night I saw him. He left it behind deliberately. He committed suicide, because if anyone had discovered that he'd married his own daughter there would have been a terrible scandal.'

'Oh no! Joanna, never think he'd do such a dreadful thing as take his own life. Tobias has simply changed his name. He's gone far away where he'll never be found. He sent me a letter with Thaddeus, that's why I'm so happy. I never for a moment really believed he was dead, not even when they found that body. I'm so relieved to have heard from him.' Charlotte took a piece of paper from her pocket. 'Listen.'

Charlotte, my dear,

It grieves me deeply that I left without saying goodbye, and without informing you of my destination. It was not my intention to cause worry to those I love, and for that I proffer my profound apologies.

Beside yourself, there are two others whom I love dearly. You'll know who they are. I've done my best for them in the only way I know how. Both are capable people with good sense and intellect, and I can now only pray that they will draw on the core of strength that lies within them.

Remain assured, even though I'm now far away from everyone who matters most to me, those closest to my heart will be always remembered with fondness and love.

I hope to find you in good health, as am I.

I remain, yours affectionately,

Gabriel Tremayne

The will suddenly made sense. Tobias had been trying to be fair to both her and Alex, a man whom he'd always loved like a son. He'd been trying to protect her reputation and that of the company, as well.

She went into Charlotte's arms with tears streaming down her face. 'Oh, Charlotte, you must be so proud of him. I'm so glad you're my grandmother, and I'm so pleased he's alive.'

'Hush, dearest. We must rejoice for his survival, not cry. And we must keep this to ourselves, because only two other people know, James and Thaddeus.'

So Joanna sniffed back her tears and they hugged each other tight, content with the shared knowledge. The prolonged hug ended when there came a knock and Mrs Bates poked her head around the door.

'Captain Scott is here, ma'am.'

'Goodness, then go and fetch my shawl and bonnet. Tell him I'll be out directly. Are you sure you won't come with us, dear?'

'No. I need some time to myself. I have to decide what's a fair thing to do for Alex.'

'Why, you'll wed him, won't you? That's what Tobias wanted.'

'Tobias had no right to make that condition. It's not fair to either Alex or myself.'

'Well, I'm sure you'll do what's right, my dear.'

And Joanna did know what was right. As soon as Charlotte had left with Thaddeus, she fetched her shawl and made her way to James Stark's office.

'If all my private assets were liquidated, would there be enough to buy Oliver Morcant's share of the company.'

'Easily, but it would take time.'

Her shoulders slumped. 'I've got to buy him out now. Can you arrange a loan?'

'I could draw in some favours.'

'Then do it.'

His eyes widened. 'Do you know what you're saying?'

'Of course I do.'

'And if I refuse?'

Her eyes narrowed as she flatly informed him, 'I know about Tobias.'

'Ah, I see.' He traced a paperknife across a sheet of paper on the desk, then gazed at her through eyes that were bland. 'What exactly do you know about Tobias?'

'That he's still alive, living in Australia under a different name, and that I'm his daughter. I want you to buy Oliver Morcant's share of the company and transfer that and mine into Alex's name.'

A smile inched across James's face. 'So, you've decided to marry Alex then, Joanna. What a wonderful wedding gift for him. This is a very good move, since it will stop the rumours and put the company back on a solid footing. He'll be relieved when I tell him.'

'You must promise not to tell him until it's all arranged. If you don't, I'll cancel the arrangement.'

'He's going to Southampton on business later in the day anyway. No doubt he'll make an appointment to see you as soon as he gets back.'

'An appointment?'

Shrewd eyes met hers. 'Badly phrased, I know.'

Perfectly phrased.

'Despite the union being a convenient arrangement, Alex does care for you, Joanna.'

That she had yet to be convinced of. 'I need some immediate cash.' Her forehead wrinkled in worry. 'Can

I afford to have a thousand guineas for myself from the estate, do you think? I'll never ask for a penny more.'

'Easily. In fact, I can give you that now.' He took from his safe a bundle of notes and counted out the required amount. 'I'll put it in a satchel for you, but conceal it under your shawl and hold it tightly. You can give me a receipt, and I'll need your instructions in writing.' He leaned forward, concern in his eyes. 'Have you thought this through?'

'I know exactly what I'm doing.'

'Will you trust me with your plans then? What do you need this large amount of money in such a hurry for?'

'I'd rather not say. Could you just do as I ask without all these questions, since I'm sure that what I'm doing is well within the law . . . especially the law as you seem to interpret it.'

He shrugged. 'If I hadn't helped out my friend, both you and Tobias might now be in a prison cell.'

'But neither of us knew at the time of the marriage that we were closely related.'

'Be that as it may. The law doesn't take ignorance into account.'

'And the body you identified?'

'It was unrecognizable and could have been anyone. Bodies often wash up on shore; that one floated along at a convenient time.'

She gave a slight shudder. 'I'm so glad it wasn't . . .' A grin suddenly twisted her mouth as she experienced a moment of delight, '*my father.*'

'You're like him in your ways, and you have his smile, you know.'

'Have I? I'm glad.' Although Joanna would have liked to talk with James Stark about her father, she didn't have time. 'Any papers that need to be signed must be ready by tomorrow. Will that be possible?'

'Ah, you're going to surprise Alexander! Then I'll draw them up myself.'

She smiled at that innocent little assumption. 'Yes, I rather think I might, Mr Stark.'

Joanna arrived back home to find Alexander waiting for her in the morning room, a pot of coffee at his elbow. A posy of flowers lay on the table. She placed the satchel containing her money next to it.

'I've been waiting for hours,' he said with a touch of impatience. 'Your servants have gone to the market, but they let me inside to wait.'

'Why have you come?'

'Why do you think, Joanna? I wanted to see you.'

Trying to harden her heart she glanced at the flowers. 'Alex, are you about to propose marriage to me?'

He leaned forward and, seeing the weariness in his eyes, she was forced to resist the urge to reach out and caress his face with her fingertip.

'That's what Tobias wanted, isn't it?'

'But it's not what you want. I was in the office the other day when you were talking to James Stark. I overheard every word you said.' She lowered her voice a fraction. 'I was disturbed that you would betray what should have remained a confidential matter between us.'

His glossy eyes lost their brightness. 'I'm sorry, that

304

was inexcusable. It was just men talk and you mean more than that to me. I'm just tired out after months of trying to hold this company together, of chasing cargoes and digging enough money out of James Stark to pay the bills. I have to go down to Southampton today to try and secure the *Nightingale* a cargo, and haven't really got time to play the role of a lovesick swain.'

'Does the company mean that much to you, Alex?'

'I was brought up with it and owe it my loyalty. It paid for my food, my education, the clothes on my back. It's my life.'

'It seems to me that the company is a hard task-master.'

He shrugged. 'You're a woman who was brought up on an island. What can you know about business?'

'I've learned enough to observe the greed it generates.'

His face hardened. 'You seem to think I sit on my arse in an office all day and things happen around me. The company provides a service and it's taken many years of hard work by many people for it to become successful. Darsham and Morcant earns a good profit when it's run well. From that profit several hundred people gain a wage, and are able to feed their families and keep a roof over their heads. *Joanna Rose* alone is crewed by eighty men. Then there's the *Charlotte May*, the *Clara Jane* and the *Nightingale,* which, unless I can secure her that cargo, is running at a loss at the moment, I might add. She's the slowest and oldest of the company ships. And did I mention the offices and the staff employed in them? That's what I'm trying to keep going, Joanna.'

She felt ashamed. 'And you're willing to wed me, an ignorant island girl, to keep it.'

'Not so ignorant as I first thought, I admit. If we don't wed we'll both end up with nothing, for the wolves are gathering at the company gates.' He gave a faint smile and shrugged. 'At least I've discovered you'd make a willing bed partner for a man.' When he tipped up her chin and kissed her she felt her body respond in no uncertain manner. 'You have a lot to offer, Joanna, and no doubt we'd have a infant or two to celebrate our union.'

And he'd just made it perfectly clear why he'd visited her. Her fingers curled into her hands so tightly the nails dug into her flesh. 'You led me to believe you cared for me as much as I cared for you, that's what hurts me most.'

His smile had a tender edge to it. 'I do care for you, Joanna Rose. Didn't you realize that when we were caught in the barn in a storm?'

She shouldn't be listening to his lies, shouldn't allow him to play on the physical side of their relationship. But as his head bent to hers, his mouth possessed her, she experienced the awakening inside her. Her arms slipped up around his neck. A few moments later he gazed into her eyes, and she clearly saw the passion waking in them, and that was genuine enough.

'Are we likely to be disturbed?' he said huskily, and when she shook her head he simply lifted her into his arms and carried her upstairs.

They ended up in Tobias's room. Sitting on the edge of the bed he peeled the layers of her petticoats away until he reached her corset with its front fastening, which was worn over calico drawers trimmed with lace ruffles.

One dark eyebrow rose as Alex gazed down at her. 'Who would have thought the widow would wear a red corset? How provocative and wicked a woman you are under that gown, Joanna.'

She would have pushed him away then, except he kissed the rise of her breasts so tenderly that her knees lost their strength and she couldn't have stood if she'd wanted to. Besides, her hands would insist on cupping his dark head to keep him there. She gave a little groan as his tongue found a way under the material and slid around the dark nub beneath.

She began to undo the buttons of his waistcoat, eager for his flesh to yield and respond to her fingertips.

They spent two hours pleasuring each other in several different ways, each moment quivering with exquisitely executed loving that reduced her quickly to ecstasy, so she wondered if there was any part of her body that hadn't submitted to his thrust, or the delicate probing of his tongue.

He gazed at her afterwards, flushed and tumbled, to trace her face with his finger. How gentle the stallion now his urges were spent. It was wonderful to be conquered in such a way.

'Will you wed me then, Joanna Rose? We deal well together.'

She closed her eyes to hide the scorn in them. Was that how he thought of what had just taken place? Had the act of loving been a bribe for her, or a reward for himself? To wait until this moment when she was vulnerable to him was calculating in the extreme.

'Can you wait until the end of the week for an answer, Alex? I'd like to talk to Charlotte first. I think I'll have a favourable answer for you then.'

'When I come back from Southampton, then.'

She could feel the confidence emanating from him now, and watched him as he quickly dressed, his face assuming a distracted expression as company business replaced the personal.

He leaned forward to kiss her goodbye, a caress that was almost perfunctory. It would have been nice if he'd lied – if he'd said he loved her. She would have believed him, for, oh . . . needing to was such a persuasive force inside her.

When the front door closed she rose and went to the telescope. It was hard watching Alex walk out of her life.

16

Tilda had been quiet since she'd come back from the mission.

Joanna, who was seated in her nightgown on the edge of Tilda's bed and wielding the hairbrush, said, 'What's happened to upset you?'

'How did you know?'

'I've known you since I was a baby, Tilda. I know when you're sad.'

'A woman brought Mary into the mission today.'

'Your sister! I thought she was in Poole.'

'She must have shifted to the capital some time ago. It was horrible. Mary is suffering some dreadful disease. She's starving, and she has a child, a little girl of about three years old. Mary didn't even recognize me. David took them to the workhouse infirmary. The doctor said that my sister will be dead in a day or two. The little girl was so thin, and she was dressed in rags. Her name is Grace, or so the woman who brought her in said.'

'What a pretty name. Oh, Tilda. How awful for Mary and her daughter. What are you going to do about them?'

Stilling the strokes of the brush with her hand, Tilda said in a low voice, 'I don't know what to do. The girl is my niece. I could have found work, offered her a home. Instead, I kept quiet and turned my back on her.'

'You silly goose. Why didn't you tell David who they were?'

'I couldn't. I was too ashamed to admit that Mary was my sister. Oh, Joanna. I feel so guilty. If you hadn't taken me in I would have died, but I didn't have the charity in my heart to do anything for my own kin. What shall I do? David Lind is so good to people. I daren't accept his love, and although he has asked me again to marry him I've refused, for he deserves someone much better than me.'

'Can't you understand that there's nobody better than you for him, since he loves you dearly. So do I my lovely, loyal friend. Tomorrow you must tell him everything, Tilda, and as soon as he arrives. If you don't, I will.'

Fear clouded Tilda's eyes. 'What if he casts me aside?'

'Then you'll have lost nothing worth having, and will have gained some knowledge of human nature. If a man declares his love for a woman he should overlook her background and marry her for herself alone, not reject her because society says she's not good enough. Nor should he be mercenary and wed her for position or wealth, or use her without respect.' A bitter taste came into her mouth when she thought of Alex. 'Collect little Grace anyway. Bring her here. If David Lind doesn't want to care for the pair of you, at least it will have demonstrated that he has no worth as a husband, so you will no longer need to pine for him.'

'There's that,' Tilda said morosely.

Joanna placed her hand over Tilda's. 'Don't worry, my love, it won't happen. But if it does I'll buy a little house in Poole and you can look after Grace there. I'm sure you'll be able to support her through your artistic endeavours, once you find markets.'

Tilda gave a huge smile at that. 'David showed some of my pictures to a greeting card manufacturer and he's interested in ordering several designs. He said his uncle would probably be interested in writing a poem for each one. Imagine the honour of having Richard Lind's poetry on them.'

'An honour for him, I'd say. Oh, Tilda, how wonderful. See, you can afford to rescue your niece, after all.'

Tilda's smile faded. 'What if Charlotte objects?'

'Stop being a mouse, Tilda. I happen to own this house, not Charlotte. It's for me to say who comes here and who doesn't.' *At the moment* arrived as an uncomfortable afterthought.

Joanna's advice to her close friend proved to be correct. The next morning, Tilda emerged from her private meeting in the drawing room with David, looking dewy eyed and beautifully bemused. David was smiling expansively, and his usually kind face was radiant with love as he gazed at Tilda. They were perfect for each other, David with his kind nature and Tilda who needed love and protection, Joanna thought.

'We're going to collect Grace,' Tilda said. 'And I have accepted David's marriage proposal.'

Joanna and Charlotte exchanged a glance, for Joanna had seen fit to inform Charlotte of the situation regarding the child, Grace. Charlotte was not entirely comfortable with the situation of having a lightskirt's child staying at her house in Poole, yet she surged forward to offer congratulations.

'I shall hold a dinner party for the occasion when we get back to Poole, for we cannot celebrate the engagement without your uncle being present.' She sighed. 'I'm so looking forward to going home, where the air is clean and I can live in peaceful surroundings.'

Joanna and Tilda looked at each other, but said nothing.

'I'm sure this smell from the river is getting worse by the hour,' Charlotte said in her own defence, 'and if you dare mention what you're thinking, Joanna, I shall stamp my foot. It's a wonder to me that we haven't all gone down with something dreadful, like cholera.'

'I've told Mrs Bates she must boil all the water we drink, for I've heard that the process kills the germs that cause the disease.'

Charlotte scoffed. 'Who told you that?'

'Tobias, I believe. Yes, we were discussing an article he read in an engineering magazine about—'

'Then I'm sure the information was correct,' Charlotte said smoothly, but there was a glint in her eye.

David intervened with an offer. 'I'll be able to escort you back to Poole next month, Mrs Darsham, if that will be convenient. Tilda appreciates what you've done for her, but has no intention of taking advantage of your kind nature by expecting you to support her niece as well. We intend to have the banns called on Sunday. We'll be married by my bishop in a quiet ceremony as soon as they've all been called. Tilda and Grace will then move in with me. My rooms are small, but they will suffice for the moment.'

Charlotte gazed round at them with an air of satisfaction. 'I'm glad someone has told me of their plans. There is a lot going on that I don't know about. I can feel it in the air.'

Avoiding her grandmother's probing glance, Joanna wondered if Charlotte would kick up a fuss when she told her of her own plan. To divert Charlotte's mind, she said to Tilda,

'What are you and David waiting for, Tilda? Do go and collect that poor child from the workhouse. I'm dying to see her.'

Charlotte only just managed not to grimace. 'I will ask the doctor to look her over to make sure she has no parasites. Then we shall go to a children's outfitter and buy her some clothing. It will be my gift to her. I'm sorry about your sister, my dear. Unfortunately, that's what happens to women who are loose in their morals.'

'Sometimes it's not their fault, but a matter of circumstance,' David said, when Tilda bit her lip and gazed at the floor.

'Of course it is, but women have to be strong, because they were born with the sin of Eve, according to the Bible. Utter nonsense, of course, since the good book was written by men, who are the more sinful by nature, but conveniently ignore the fact. However, we won't argue about it,' Charlotte said, having just won the argument with herself to her own satisfaction. When David looked as though he was about to speak, she turned away. 'Come, Joanna Rose, we need to talk, I think.'

Joanna tried not to smile since, as her body inconveniently chose to remind her at that time, she'd enjoyed every moment of her descent into sin with Alex, and she rather thought he had enjoyed leading her into it. She wondered why he'd taken her to Tobias's room, though. Had Alex needed to prove himself? Was he finding it hard to live in his mentor's shadow, even though he thought the man was dead?

She kept Charlotte waiting long enough to give both David and Tilda a long and loving hug, for she sensed that her friend was already drawing away from her as Tilda planned a future with David, something she'd once thought she'd never have.

Joanna was going to miss her. 'Congratulations, dearest friends. I'm so happy for you,' she said before they left. It suddenly occurred to her that she'd no longer have to worry about Tilda's welfare, which was a great relief.

'My dear,' Charlotte said when she joined her, 'you cannot have that portrait of Honor hung on the wall, you know. You should destroy it.'

Joanna's chin lifted. 'It's the only likeness I have of my real mother, but I shan't hang it on the wall. I intend to remove it from the frame and take it with me.'

'To Poole. That's a good idea.'

'What I'm about to say to you is in complete confidence, Grandmother Darsham.'

The smile Charlotte gave was a trifle smug at being addressed as such. Joanna knew she'd soon wipe it off. 'I'm not going back to Poole with you. I intend to set sail for Australia on the *Joanna Rose*, where I will seek out my father.'

Hand flying against her heart, Charlotte gasped, 'But you cannot. What about your marriage to Alex and the company?'

'I'm not going to marry Alex. Knowing he wed me only to keep the company intact would rankle for ever with both of us, and we'd end up hating each other. I've instructed James Stark to liquidate all Tobias's assets, then buy Oliver Morcant's share of the company and transfer the whole lot into Alexander's name. That should solve the problem.'

Sinking on to a cushion Charlotte gazed helplessly at her. 'But Tobias . . .'

'Tobias would rather have his daughter to love than the damned shipping company, as he's already demonstrated.' She gently ran her fingertips over the signet ring and her eyes dampened with tears. 'Before he left, Tobias told me he loved me, but in his own way. Now I know what that way is. He sacrificed everything that was dear to him for me. I have to tell him his sacrifice wasn't in vain. I want to spend time with him, get to know him better, learn to love and respect him as he deserves to be loved and respected – as my father.'

Charlotte smiled at that. 'Alex won't accept such a compromise.'

'Alex will have no choice. It will be done and I'll be gone before he gets back from Southampton. Tobias wanted him to have the company. You know that, and so do I. I'm not going to be blackmailed into a loveless marriage for the sake of some company I'd never heard of until a few months ago. The Darsham and Morcant Shipping Company means nothing to me.'

Charlotte gently caressed her on the cheek. 'But you care for Alex, my dear. I can see it in your eyes. Will you not wait to see if something further develops between you?'

Joanna shrugged, knowing that was one of the reasons she must leave, for what had developed between them meant that Alex would never respect her now. 'I care for him too much to agree to such a cold-hearted liaison. If he cannot bring himself to accept me without reservation, then I don't want him.'

Charlotte nodded. 'That's how it should be between a man and woman. But I'll miss you, my dear. It seems that I have only just found you. We have so little time left together that it hardly seems fair.'

'What I'm doing is fair for everybody. Tobias should never have tried to enforce his will on Alex, or me, in such a way. You know that deep in your heart. We'll write to one another,' she said with a smile. 'Now, Grandmother, will you do something for me? Don't tell anyone, including Captain Scott, that I'll be on board the *Joanna Rose*. I shall leave Tilda a letter and you'll give it to her after I've departed. I'm going to ask James Stark to purchase my ticket under a different name, and to arrange medical clearance. Thaddeus Scott might not allow me to sail with him, you see.'

Charlotte's eyes widened, but she nodded reluctantly.

'Such skulduggery is going on around me. Thaddeus is bound to find out, you know. Remember, he is not as stern as he looks, but is a steadfast and reliable man with a heart of pure gold. Don't let him frighten you.'

Judging from her tone of voice Joanna guessed that Charlotte had some feelings for the captain. She grinned. 'Is he your sweetheart, Charlotte?'

Charlotte looked as though she was about to deny it, then she shrugged and colour rose to her cheeks. 'Thaddeus and I have always been friends . . . I suppose I do regard him with some affection. But you will not tell him that, will you?'

'Of course not,' Joanna lied. 'And his bluff manner doesn't scare me. When he finds out I'm on board, the ship will be well on her way, so he won't be able to turn back.' She looked up when a knock came at the door. 'That might be James Stark. He promised to make all speed with my affairs.'

But it wasn't James who was announced by Mrs Bates, it was Alexander's mother. Clara Nash was accompanied by two pretty girls who were the very image of each other. Elaborately and richly gowned in frills, ruffles and lace, the trio seated themselves at Charlotte's request and gazed haughtily around them.

'We were not properly introduced when you accepted my condolences,' Clara said, her voice as chilly as her pale blue eyes. 'An oversight, I expect, since you arrived at the memorial service late and kept us waiting. I am Clara Nash, the mother of Oliver and Alexander Morcant. These are my two daughters, Lydia and Irene.'

Joanna's hackles went on alert at the woman's tone of voice. 'Oh, I think we were introduced, but briefly. No doubt you recall that I am Joanna Darsham, since you are here in my home. I'm sorry you were kept waiting at the memorial for my husband. We were unavoidably detained.'

'One is expected to pay one's respects on time, Mrs Darsham, even if one is the widow. It's not polite to keep mourners waiting. But I can't blame you, since you're unaccustomed to mingling in civilized company. I'm surprised at *your* behaviour, though, Charlotte.'

'Actually, it was my fault we were detained, Clara. And may I remind you that it's not *polite* to rebuke Joanna in her own home, either.'

When the two girls sniggered, Clara quelled them with a look.

'Since I'm expected to be civilized, can I offer you some refreshment, Mrs Nash,' Joanna offered into the silence. *Essence of hemlock, perhaps?*

'No thank you, Mrs Darsham. I have some business I wish to discuss with you.'

Joanna hoped the woman would get it over with, since she was expecting James any moment. 'Which is?'

'I want to buy your share of the Darsham and Morcant Shipping Company.'

'May I know the reason why?' Joanna asked.

'It's obvious why. That dreadful will Tobias left, of course. May I speak frankly?'

'I'd prefer it, Mrs Nash.'

Clara gave a thin smile that was pure malice. 'All his life, Alexander was led to believe that the Darsham share of the company would be his. I will not allow him to marry a girl who is little more than a peasant – someone who isn't fit to clean his boots.'

Charlotte gasped.

If this woman thought Joanna could be hectored into doing what she wanted, she could think again. Joanna rose to her feet, prepared to do battle. 'Under no circumstances will I sell my share of the company to you, and I daresay Alexander will do as he pleases. Goodbye, Mrs Nash. Thank you for coming. Your girls are delightful, I expect they take after their father.'

Charlotte gasped even louder.

'Don't think I'm going to back off from this, girl. Oliver isn't due to sail until this afternoon, but I'm staying on in London. I shall go from here directly to his ship and I'll persuade him to sell me his half of the company. Then I shall spend every minute of my time making life miserable for you. You'll never be accepted in London society. Eventually, I'll ruin the company and you'll be bankrupt.'

'A stupid thing to do, since your son would then stand to lose his living, and you your investment.'

'The investment means nothing to me, since I can afford to lose it several times over. I'll compensate Alexander. I'd prefer to do that than have him be forced to marry you and regret it every day of his life. Although I've never liked the Darsham family, I feel sorry for Tobias. He must have been insane to be taken in by a slut with her eyes on the main chance. You shall not have Alexander. I have another in mind for him.'

'One as *civilized* as you, perhaps?' Flags of colour steamed in Joanna's cheeks, and she put a comforting hand on Charlotte's arm when the woman gave a distressed cry. Her eyes narrowed in on Clara Nash and she said quietly, for she didn't want to shout it out like a fishwife and make Charlotte feel ashamed of her, 'As you had another man in mind to father him?'

'Who told you such a lie?'

'Alex himself. Now, who was it you were calling a slut?'

In the ensuing silence, Joanna heard a commotion in the hall and the rumble of James Stark's voice. The door to the morning room opened and shut. Thank God Mrs Bates hadn't shown James into the drawing room.

She let out a slow, jagged breath as she crossed to the door, knowing that if Clara Nash said another word she'd punch her, and to hell with behaving with dignity! The less Mrs Bates saw the better it would be, so she sent the servant packing from the hall, saying, 'Prepare some refreshment please, Mrs Bates,' while Clara gathered together her reticule and gloves.

Clara swept off, with her daughters following after and Joanna and Charlotte bringing up the rear. The two girls were red faced with the excitement of the encounter and exchanged nervous grins. Joanna suddenly felt sorry for them.

Clara dragged the front door open and ushered the girls out, then turned. 'You'll rue the day you decided to oppose me, you disgusting little leech.'

'Why don't you go and float in the Thames with the rest of the . . . *stench*.' Picking up the nearest object, which happened to be James Stark's round hat, Joanna set it spinning at Clara.

'Hussy,' Charlotte said loudly, as the woman pulled the door shut just before the hat thudded into the door panel.

James, who'd just opened the morning-room door to see what all the fuss was about, picked up his dented hat to gaze at it ruefully. Then his eyes came up to Joanna's and he gave a throaty laugh. 'What an extraordinary creature you are. And Charlotte, I'm surprised at you.'

Behind her, Charlotte gave a series of nervous giggles.

'You sound like a horse with a hayseed lodged in its nostril,' Joanna observed drily. 'Really, Charlotte, can't you control yourself.'

Charlotte exploded with laughter and sank on to the nearest chair, holding her stomach. 'Oh, Joanna. I've been dying to say something like that to Clara for years, but I've never had the courage before.'

'No wonder, she's a gutter fighter.' Joanna grinned at James. 'I'm sorry about your hat. But it was wounded in a good cause.'

He indicated a vase of flowers on the hall table. 'Well, I suppose it was better than hurling that at her.'

'But less effective; I almost wish I'd seen that first.' She gazed with some anxiety at him, for it was now imperative that her plan go through. 'What did Oliver Morcant say?'

'He agreed to sell. Despite my misgivings about this, and my advice to the contrary, it's a done deal.' He lowered his voice. 'God knows what Tobias will have to say about it, though. He likes things done *his* way.'

She failed to hide her grin. 'A pity he chose death over dishonour then, for he effectively silenced himself.'

'So he did,' James said with a chuckle, 'and that will rankle with him no end.'

Joanna's grin turned into a gleeful smile. 'That crocodile Clara Nash will gnash her teeth when she finds out what we've done.'

'So will Alex, I suspect,' James said reflectively. 'He has his pride.'

'Then it will be interesting to see exactly where that pride leads him, won't it?'

'Very interesting indeed,' James agreed. 'Now, I have a huge amount of paperwork for you to sign, so shall we make a start . . .?'

It wasn't until afterwards that Joanna took him into her confidence regarding her plans to sail on the *Joanna Rose.*

'You fool, Oliver. I would have paid you much more. You've played right into that woman's hands.'

Oliver secretly admitted to a feeling of satisfaction at his mother's chagrin. The money didn't matter to him as much as doing what was right, since he thought Alexander deserved more than life had thrown at him. Firmly he told her, 'You knew I wanted my share of the company to go to Alex; now it has. I'm happy with the price she offered. It was a fair one and there's nothing more to be said.'

'That sly little puss. She thinks she's purchased Alexander with the share she's bought from you, and she now owns the whole company. Oh, I know her type,' Clara said bitterly. 'She'll have him jumping through hoops for it. Alexander will *have* to dance to her tune when they're wed.'

'Alex doesn't dance to anybody's tune but his own. He never has. Why don't you leave well alone, Mother? Joanna Darsham seems a nice enough young woman and Alexander is old enough to manage his own affairs. It's too late to suddenly become a mother to him, and he won't thank you for interfering. That company has been his life since I can remember. He spent most of his holidays in the office with Tobias.'

'Not that it did him any good in the long run. I would never have thought Tobias was the type to fall for the scheming of somebody so young, and from the island of Portland, of all places.' She shuddered.

'Don't be such a snob, Mother. The islanders are perfectly good people who work hard for their living. Look around you while you're in London. Most of the churches built by Christopher Wren are built of Portland stone, including St Paul's Cathedral. Joanna Darsham's father was a stonemason, I believe.'

'The woman is a vile-tempered vixen. The upstart ordered me to leave, and she threw a hat at me. She's no lady, and never will be.'

'A lady wouldn't suit Alex anyway. He needs someone who will challenge him.' Oliver tried not to let his grin show, for usually nothing was allowed to ruffle his mother's calm and dignified demeanour and he knew she'd finally met her match in Joanna Darsham. He thought Alex might have met his match, too.

'Joanna Darsham has good looks, and also a good mind on her, I understand. Alex has been unsettled since Tobias died. A wife of her mettle could be the making of him. She'll probably give him children and a purpose in life besides that damned shipping company. He's been a slave to it for far too long.'

Later that day, Tilda brought her niece to the house. The thin and dirty little urchin clung to Tilda's neck and gazed at everyone through large and fearful brown eyes. Her hair was a lustreless tangle of brown, her skin pale except where it was bruised, and she was covered with the infected bites of bed bugs.

'This is my niece, Grace Rushmore,' Tilda said. 'She was orphaned this morning.'

'Oh God, I'm so sorry,' Charlotte said, almost bursting into tears at the sight of the child. 'The poor little mite, what a terrible environment she must have lived in. How can you bear to work amongst the needy, Tilda? We must clean her up and give her something to eat.'

Tilda tightened her hold on the girl, as if she was frightened Charlotte would take Grace from her. 'I'll do it. I want her to get used to me.'

The love in Tilda's eyes for this pathetic scrap of humanity made Joanna remember the woman she'd always thought to be her ma. Joseph Rushmore had found her by chance and had saved her life. Anna had taken her in and given her a mother's love. Anna would have given her own life in exchange for Joanna's had she been threatened. Although the Rushmores had been wrong in keeping her, they'd been motivated only by the need to love and be loved.

Everyone should be loved, she thought. Tobias knew how to love. He'd loved her mother and grieved for her and his lost infant all his life, according to Alex – poor, poor Alex, who needed to be loved so badly. And just when Tobias had found something in her that he'd been missing, he'd had to sacrifice everything for her. That was a love worth having. She hoped Alex would come to that conclusion one day, too.

Her eyes filling with tears, she kissed Tilda's cheek, then Grace's. 'I'll go with Charlotte to purchase her some clothes.'

She didn't tell Tilda she wouldn't be there to celebrate her wedding to David.

Joanna Rose slipped from her mooring just after dawn. Passengers crowded the rails, waving goodbye to friends and family.

Only James had come to see Joanna off. She'd said a tearful goodbye the night before to Charlotte, written her letters and left an amount of money for Tilda as a wedding gift, for she thought she and David might need it.

She left early, before the others had risen, her luggage having been taken aboard the night before. James had come to escort her, entrusting her with a letter for Tobias. She had a letter from Charlotte for him, too.

'I wish you a good journey,' James had said, and, surprisingly, he'd kissed her on the forehead. 'I almost wish I was going with you.'

'Tell Alex I wish him well, and I hope he'll be happy in the future.'

A wry smile flitted over James's face. 'He'll probably

strangle me with his bare hands for allowing you to do this to him. You should have left him a letter.'

'He's got what he wanted now. It's not your place, or his, to forbid me to do anything.' She took Tobias's ring from her finger and dropped it into James's palm. 'Give Alex this. I found it in Tobias's room and thought he'd like it as a keepsake.'

Joanna, wrapped in a grey cloak with a hood over her hair, had then joined a crowd of other people going aboard at the last minute, slipping into the middle of them to hand over her ticket and cross the gangplank.

There was no sign of Thaddeus Scott, and, pulling her hood over her head, she'd hurried on board, leaving James standing on the corner.

Now the boat was making her way smoothly down river and her stomach was churning with the excitement of the unknown. She watched the mist rising from the river, which was brown and turgid like soup. Flotsam of all kinds floated on the surface and swirled in the currents. No wonder it smelled so.

Gradually the water thinned to be almost clear, then the rhythm of the river changed, becoming choppy with little golden ripples that sparkled as the sun crept over the horizon. The land slid past quickly until it ran out and there was none left to see. There came the sound of orders shouted, of ropes being run up the mast, the eager tugging of the ship as the sails were hoisted. Then the ship surged swiftly forward, the water hissing as she cut through it.

Excitement filled her like the wind fattening the sails. They were at sea! Familiar with the layout of the ship from Thaddeus Scott's tour, she went down to her cabin, a quiver of apprehension replacing the excitement. The adventure she was on suddenly seemed too frightening, the ocean seemed too vast and the love she felt for Alex too strong to abandon. But she couldn't hold Alex to a condition set by another, one they would come to regret for the remainder of their lives.

Then she thought of her father, alone in his new land. It gave her strength. 'Lord,' she prayed, 'look after those whom I love and left behind, and guide me in the new life ahead so I may prove myself a worthy daughter.'

She didn't want to reveal herself to Thaddeus Scott yet, so she lay on her bed, listening to the unaccustomed sounds going on about her.

Her tiny cabin had a comfortable bunk and a small wash-basin in a cupboard. Halfway down was a shelf with a metal chamber pot fitted with a tight lid. A hinged door at the front tipped outwards and down when the shelf was slid out.

'For making pee-pee,' the Chinese crew member who had brought her here had said, and she understood he would be looking after her for the journey.

She smiled, for there had been a seagull flying alongside the ship as they'd made their way down-river. Its golden eyes had looked into hers and its beak had opened in a farewell squawk before it had glided upwards into the sky. A good omen? She hoped so.

The water rocked her so gently that her eyes drifted shut. She wondered if it had felt like this in her cradle all those years ago, with the soul of Lucian Morcant in the seagull guiding her ashore.

She dreamed she was a child in Portland, riding on

her pa's shoulders as he climbed the stone hills. Far below them was the sea, stretching like a stipple of silver into a mist. A lone boat floated on the water. It was the *Linnet*. There was a man on board, searching the water. She could feel his incredible sadness, so the tears filled her eyes. She had an urge to fly across the water to him and give him comfort. But her pa kept a tight hold of her ankles and the boat spread its sail and was borne away by the currents into the mist.

A hard rap at the door woke her. Disorientated, she sat up, her face wet with tears. She scrambled to her feet, thinking it was the Chinese crew member.

Pulling open the door she was confronted by the glowering countenance of Thaddeus Scott. His body filled the doorway.

He followed her in as she backed away, her heart beating erratically. Closing the door behind him he leaned against it and said, 'Did you really think you had me fooled, Joanna Rose? Why are you crying?'

'I was dreaming about Tobias, but I was too small to get to him and he sailed away in *Linnet*. He was lonely, and it made me sad.'

His expression softened. He handed over his handkerchief and said gruffly, 'You'll get to him this time, girl, I'll make damned sure of it.'

'You're not going to make me walk the plank, then?'

His glower was replaced with a grin. 'Aye, I might, if you misbehave. Tell Chin Lee if you need anything or if you begin to feel unwell. He's my personal servant and I've instructed him to look after you. I've told him you're my niece.'

'Niece?'

'Well, if you come aboard under the name of Rose Tremayne, what can you expect? Gabriel Tremayne was my half-brother. And you're his daughter.'

'Can I give you a hug then, Uncle Thaddeus,' she sniffed.

A deep chuckle came from him. 'I can't say I'm a man with hugging instincts, but aye, I reckon you can, seeing as you're family.'

Held close against his chest, she didn't feel sad any more.

17

'Joanna's gone! Gone where?'

'To the Australian continent. She sailed on the *Joanna Rose* with Captain Scott.'

Alexander felt a rush of dismay mixed with anger. Then he just felt hollow and miserable. 'Thaddeus should have known better than to have encouraged her in such foolishness, and so should you, James. God knows, the company's in a big enough mess without the owner going off on some pleasure jaunt.'

'To be fair to Thaddeus, he didn't know anything about it, since the ticket was purchased under an assumed name. I booked the passage myself.' James poured a brandy and slid it across the table.

He frowned. 'It's too early in the afternoon for me, James.'

'Take it, you'll need it after what I'm about to tell you.'

Alexander stared into the golden depths of the liquor, thinking, What next? It had been one thing after another of late, and although he'd secured a cargo for the *Nightingale* he'd had to accept lower rates, which would pay the ship's expenses but make the company no profit at all. Unable to stand the suspense, he gazed up at James. 'Let's hear the worst then.'

A smile twisted at James's mouth. 'Oliver has sold his half of the company.'

Alarm filled him as he stared at James. *Damn! damn! damn!* Oliver said he'd fob my mother off for the time being.'

'He sold his share to Joanna Rose Darsham.'

'*What!*' Subsiding on to the nearest chair he took a gulp of the brandy. What had started out to be a passable day was now in ruins. 'I'll have to wed her now, whether I want to or not.'

'Not at all, Alex, she's removed the hook from your mouth.' Leaning back in his chair James gave a quiet chuckle. 'Joanna has liquidated the assets Tobias left her, except for the house, which I'm instructed to sell to cover the loan I raised on her behalf. She said she'd come to the conclusion that you were entitled to have the company without conditions attached, so she's signed it over to you. Although I made some token resistance, I didn't put up much of a fight.' He slid a small object across the desk. 'She asked me to give you this as a keepsake. It's the ring Honor Darsham gave to Tobias. You're rid of her, Alex.'

Alexander knew he should have felt relief, but he didn't. All he could do was stare dumbly at James while the information attempted to filter through the fog that was his brain. Joanna had walked away from the wealth and everything it could buy her. Was she insane? She must be to set sail on a long journey like that. It would be at least five months before she returned.

His face darkened. What sort of sadistic creature was she? He was going to suffer until the *Joanna Rose* returned. Then she'd come tripping ashore with that damnable smile on her face, acting as if nothing had happened between them. And not only would he feel like the recipient of her charity, he'd be forever obligated to her. If he accepted the company as his she'd own him as surely as if she'd put a ball and chain around his ankle. The scheming little wretch!

A scowl crossed his face as his palm closed around the ring. 'The moment that woman places a foot ashore I'm going to haul her into this office by the scruff of her neck and make her eat every paper she signed. In the meantime, I'd be obliged if you'd draw up an agreement whereby I can pay her the company's worth in instalments. And don't you dare sell her house. I'll sell mine. In the meantime, I'll live in hers and pay rent, so it will provide her with an income.' He grinned as something dawned on him. 'Although she doesn't know it she's done me a favour by having it put in my name. At least this will put paid to the speculation, though it will take me a few months to set the company straight.'

'What makes you think she doesn't know it, Alex?'

He chose to ignore that. What would an island girl know about running a business? Opening his hand he gazed at the ring. 'I never saw Tobias without this on his finger. He must have put it aside when he married Joanna. Is Charlotte still at the house?'

She intends to remain there until David Lind escorts

her back to Poole next month. He and the Rushmore cousin are about to be wed.'

'Joanna has gone all that way alone? She must have a brain the size of a pea.' He felt a worm of worry eat at his guts. 'What if something happens to her?'

'Thaddeus will look after her, no doubt.'

'Yes, there's that. But he might throw her overboard when he finds out she went on board under an assumed name. I wouldn't put it past him.'

When Potter knocked at the door to tell the lawyer his next appointment had arrived, James stood and held out his hand. 'If you think everything over carefully I'm sure you'll reach the conclusion that what Joanna did was for the best. Lunch with me at the club next Wednesday so we can discuss your plans for the future.'

Alexander went straight from James's office to see Charlotte, who immediately told Mrs Bates to bring refreshment for them. Charlotte was in the drawing room and, for once, had nothing to occupy her hands. The room was stuffy because the windows were shut against the foul smell rising from the river and the glass gathered the sun into the room to heat the air. Dust motes performed a demented dance in a beam of sunlight, disturbed by his entrance.

She said, when he was announced, 'An empty house is a sad thing, Alex. I can hear the floorboards creak, the clocks ticking the time away and there is nobody to laugh with me. Joanna gave me a purpose in life, you know. Now she's gone and I feel quite alone.' She gazed around the room, her eyes filled with sadness. 'John

Darsham brought me here as a bride when I had just turned eighteen. The house had just been built then. It's hard to believe I was ever that age now.'

Alexander took her hand and kissed it, smiling, because she was still a beautiful woman, and many men must have courted her after she was widowed. 'You're ageless, Charlotte. You should have married again.'

'I thought that nobody could have ever matched John Darsham in my eyes. I turned down a perfectly good man once, and that was the biggest mistake I could have made. Perhaps he will ask me again one day, or perhaps I will ask him.' She smiled at the notion and indicated the chair beside her. 'You look troubled, my dear.'

'You know why, I suspect.'

'Of course I do. Joanna has put you in an impossible position, hasn't she?'

'I can't believe anybody would be foolish enough to give all that wealth away.'

'Joanna has been raised differently to you and I, my dear. Her . . . uh, *parents* were honest, hard-working folk by all accounts and she grew up secure in their love. So her values are a little different to yours. I believe Joanna came to the conclusion that you'd earned the company; and she was right – you *have* earned it.'

'The girl ran off to sea before I could argue the point with her,' he grumbled. 'I would have wed her, you know, Charlotte. I would have done what Tobias expected of me.'

'Of course you would have, Alex, for you're a man of honour. But didn't you ever consider that Joanna might not have wanted to marry you?'

'There was no indication of that on the occasions I courted her.' A smile touched his mouth as he thought of Joanna in her flaunting red corset, her head thrown back so her throat formed a creamy pathway his lips followed to the curve of her breasts. How sweet their loving had been, how satisfying the little intakes of her breath and the soft moans of pleasure whispering from her mouth.

'I do hope you didn't take advantage of Joanna's naivety.'

When he realized that Charlotte's gaze had narrowed in on him, he avoided her eyes, shrugged and said again, but lamely, for he was no longer the conquering hero in his mind, but clearly the predator. 'I would have wed her, she knew that. I will, of course, propose to her again when she returns home on the *Joanna Rose*.'

About to blurt out that Joanna wouldn't be returning, Charlotte bit down on her lip. Though she longed to tell Alex the truth, she didn't dare. He'd been worried sick about the company over the past few months. Now it would surge ahead, for Joanna had made it possible for Alex to be answerable to nobody but himself. It would serve no purpose to worry him further.

She had no intention of distracting him from the task in hand, which was to get the company back into a strong trading position. It would be five months before the *Joanna Rose* was back in port, and that would give him the time he needed. She would tell him the truth then. 'At least Joanna gave you the freedom to act on your own now.'

'On that she displayed a modicum of good sense.'

Mrs Bates came in with a tray of refreshment. As Charlotte poured the coffee she brought Alex up to date about the impending marriage of Tilda to David Lind. 'They're going to start married life with a child to look after, for Tilda's sister has died and her daughter has come to live with us. She's a dear little girl. Her name is Grace.'

'I had forgotten about Tilda Rushmore. I knew she had brothers, but not a sister.'

'The woman was from her father's first marriage and worked in London,' Charlotte said vaguely. 'As for Tilda, she's so quiet that she's often overlooked. But she has a lovely nature and is very kind and loyal. I'm sorry she'll not be coming back to Poole with me, though I do wish them every happiness. They're a couple who are well suited.'

Alexander asked, 'Is there anything you'd like me to do?'

'Yes, I'd be very grateful if you would go through this house before it's sold and remove everything that's personal to Tobias. Keep anything you'd like to have, send the rest to me at Poole and I'll store it in the attic. And if you can find time, would you escort me back to my house at Poole after the wedding. David Lind has offered, but I would prefer you to take me since I want to go as soon as they're married.'

'I'll make time.' Alexander rubbed the ball of his thumb over the signature ring. 'I've decided not to sell this house to cover the loan Joanna took up. I'm selling my own to pay her back, then I'll move into this one on a rental basis. I shall sort out Tobias's effects gradually.'

'You can start moving in as soon as you wish, Alex, for there's plenty of room and I'd enjoy your company. It will save you having to do it all at once, and will mean you can put your own house on the market straight away. I know you well enough to realize what you're about and how impatient you'll be to make a start.'

'Thank you, Charlotte.' Placing his cup in the saucer he stood. 'I must go now. I have a lot to do.'

'I'll see you to the door.' She linked her arm though his. 'You have no idea how sorry I am that Tobias has put you through this.'

'You talk as if he's still alive.'

She tried to keep the alarm she felt from showing in her eyes. She must try to be more careful. 'I suppose James Stark told you about your mother coming here to see Joanna?'

Alexander shook his head. 'Should he have?'

For the sake of her granddaughter, and wishing to get her side of the story in before Clara could, Charlotte quickly related what had taken place, finishing with, 'Your mother was at her most objectionable and Joanna routed her from the house.'

'Joanna did? How exactly?'

Charlotte tried not to laugh as she remembered the scene. 'First of all they had words, and *such* words! Joanna was fierce, she threw James's hat at Clara, very naughty of her.'

Alex's chuckle came from deep within his stomach, but he sobered quickly and began to look thoughtful. 'So . . . my mother was after buying all of the company. Did she say why?'

'It was for you, I understand.'

The expression of scepticism in his eyes was as marked as hers as he said drily, 'Very generous of her.'

When they reached the door Alex took her face between his hands and kissed her forehead. 'When I was growing up I always wished that *you* were my mother.'

'Oh, Alex,' and she gave him a hug, 'I always regarded you as my second son, and I always will. And I have to say that, although you might not like what Joanna has arranged, she did it for a good reason, so don't be too hard on her. The arrangement will solve your immediate problems. Joanna knew it and so do you, for already you're looking less careworn.'

'Aye, and I feel it, but her running away won't stop me from taking her to task the next time I see her.'

'And what if she doesn't come back?'

He gazed into her eyes for a moment, an uncertain frown forking between his brow. 'Why wouldn't she? Joanna has no reason to stay away, since the only people she knows and loves are here. But if she doesn't come back, I shall just have to go after her and bring her back.'

'You'd do that?'

An odd, slightly bemused expression gathered on Alexander's face, as though he'd just realized something but couldn't quite bring himself to admit it. Softly, he said, 'Yes, I rather think I would . . . for Tobias, of course. After all, he did entrust Joanna's future welfare to me.'

'So he did.' Charlotte smiled to herself.

*

The following month Alexander took Charlotte back to Poole and renewed his acquaintance with Richard Lind. He delivered a letter from David containing an account of his marriage to Tilda and the acquisition of a ward, the orphan girl Grace.

Since the bed was already made up, Alexander had been given Joanna's room for the night. There were reminders of her all about him. Ribbons on the dressing-table, a bottle of rosewater, and a handkerchief fragrant with her perfume, which he slid into his waistcoat pocket. Clothes hanging in the wardrobe retained her shape. In the corner stood something very familiar to him. The cradle Tobias had carved for his infant daughter.

His heart seemed to falter for several beats before it settled down again. He sat on the bed and stared hard at it. The last time he'd seen the cradle it was being taken aboard the *Cormorant* by his father, Lucian Morcant. But first he'd watched Tobias carve it, week after week, with love in his eyes and a wide smile on his face at the thought of seeing the infant who would be occupying it. What was it doing here?'

He moved closer to set it rocking with his foot, then he ran his fingers over the rose carved inside. That rose had been hastily added when Tobias had learned he had a daughter who would be called by that name. She'd been named after the brooch Tobias had given Honor – the brooch Alexander had seen Joanna Rose wear.

'Rose,' he murmured, shaking his head and feeling slightly bemused, for he couldn't fail to notice the coincidence staring him in the face.

Charlotte, tired from her journey, had already retired. Outside the summer evening was assuming a dusky hue. The air smelled fresh after London. He wouldn't mind living here in Poole, where plenty was going on. He could sell the company, pay Joanna back and become a shipping agent or a chandler. He was a shore man and the challenge for him had always been found in the business side, not the lure of the ocean or the beauty of a ship under canvas.

He gently rubbed the ring on his finger. He'd never seen Tobias without it, for it had been precious to him. It was odd that Tobias hadn't been wearing it when he drowned. And just as soon as he thought that, something else hit him with the speed of lightning squarely in the midriff.

'How the hell was Tobias able to give Joanna Honor's jewellery?' he muttered. 'Honor would have had it with her, and it would have gone down on the *Cormorant*.'

Other things came flooding in. The missing marriage records, Joanna's innocence – for he'd have sworn she was intact, though she certainly wasn't now. His conquerer's grin was followed by a slight frown. But what about the body they'd identified? It had been the right size and hair colouring. But the corpse could have been anyone, he realized. It had just been convenient for James Stark's purpose, for it had freed up the estate and made life easier for all of them.

He heard Richard Lind clear his throat. Knocking on the adjoining door, he went through to the sitting room. Richard looked up, an enquiry in his eyes. He smiled.

'Alexander, do come in. I was just about to have a nightcap, would you care to join me?'

A bottle of malt whisky and two glasses were produced from the bureau and the pair nursed their drinks in companionable silence.

'About Joanna,' Alexander eventually said.

'Ah . . .' Richard offered him a smile. 'I wondered when you'd get around to asking me about her.'

'I couldn't find an entry in the marriage registry in Portland. It had been removed, I think, for I only found the licence.'

'Had it? I find it strange that you were even looking for one.'

Alexander shrugged. 'I sense a mystery. Too many things about the marriage don't add up.'

'I can't help you, Alexander. You'll understand when I say that any confidences I'm privy to must remain just that . . . the rest would be conjecture, and conjecture could be unhealthy if it became rumour. Sometimes, it really is best to just let things lie. Now, did you go to my nephew's wedding by any chance? Tell me about it.'

'I thought David had written you a letter.'

'Yes, but he's tediously long-winded.'

'It was a very quiet affair with just myself, Charlotte and little Grace in attendance. Tilda was wearing a blue gown and bonnet. She and David looked very happy. They obviously care for each other and I believe they are a good match. However, your brother was put out of countenance and decided not to attend the ceremony, I believe.'

'He cannot fail to come round in time, for Tilda is

341

such a sweet-natured girl. I'm pleased they've found a place in their hearts for her sister's little girl. Like most of Tilda's family, Mary Rushmore had a bad reputation, but the females in that family were badly abused.'

Alarm filled him. 'Joanna as well?'

'Not Joanna Rose . . . at least, not until her mother died. When things became intolerable she fled the house and came to me for protection. Joanna was precious to Anna and Joseph Rushmore, for they'd never been blessed with a living child until—'

'The night the *Cormorant* was lost.'

There was a moment when silence stretched, then Richard nodded and said vaguely, 'There were many ships wrecked off Portland during that storm.'

'Do you know about the cradle in Joanna's room? How did she get it? And did her mother give her the rose brooch?'

'So I believe. She certainly owned it long before she met Tobias, if that's what you're asking.' Richard smiled and rose to his feet. 'I really am very tired, and when I'm tired I'm prone to seizures The next time you see Joanna you should ask her to tell you the story her father used to tell her about the cradle. Goodnight, Alex.'

Alexander watched him go, then returned to his room and undressed for bed. He slid between the sheets naked, aware he lay where Joanna's body had slept.

He imagined the clipper *Joanna Rose* in a wide ocean, tossed by the waves, her sails full of wind. The unflappable Thaddeus Scott was with Joanna, his arm around her for support as her skirt was flattened against her body and her hair unravelled to the elements.

Clearly enjoying herself, she waved and smiled hugely at him.

The image of Joanna's smile bothered him as he tossed and turned all night. Finally, he fell into a shallow sleep. Woken by the scream of seagulls, Alexander sat up in bed, wide awake, the answer he'd been seeking astoundingly obvious to him.

'The crafty old fox,' he said, full of laughter, and couldn't wait to get back to London.

When he did, he went straight up to the attic and searched for Honor Darsham's portrait. All he found was the empty frame – something which served only to strengthen his suspicions.

No wonder Joanna had suddenly bought herself a passage to Australia, he thought, and a sense of elation filled him.

It was the second week of August. The weather had been fair for sailing, according to Thaddeus, though sometimes the waves seemed to contain large rocks and potholes to bump through. Joanna was used to the motion of the ship now; in fact, she hadn't suffered at all from the malady of seasickness. So when she rose one morning to experience nausea, it surprised her.

The feeling soon passed, only to recur the next morning, and the one after that. She grinned as she realized what was causing the sickness. No wonder she'd missed her menses. She was in what the ladies of polite society would describe as a delicate condition, if they could bring themselves to describe it at all.

Only she didn't feel delicate. She felt as vibrant as

April daffodils, as energetic as a rushing stream and as dewy and unfolding as a rosebud coming into bloom. How lovely to have an infant in her arms, one who would have Alex's beautiful dark eyes.

'What are you smiling at?' Thaddeus said when she went up on deck, for she'd learned which was his favourite place on the hatch cover, where he stopped to have his smoke undisturbed. Thaddeus had such an insular presence about him that it was only rarely a passenger would intrude on him to pass the time of day. They kept their socializing for mealtimes.

'It's such a lovely day.'

He gave a bark of laughter. 'Take a look at the sky, Joanna.'

Indeed, her hair was nearly being torn from her head by the wind, which was such an icy torrent of air she had to turn her back to it to breathe out comfortably.

Above them strands of ragged grey clouds hurtled over the masts at breakneck speed and the horizon was massed in an ominous bank of roiling purple. The waves were higher, too, rearing glassily in all directions, the wind blowing spindrift from each crest.

'It's magnificent, isn't it?' she said. 'I've so enjoyed being at sea. Every day is different. The *Joanna Rose* just loves the sea, too. She has a heart, you know, and you can feel it beating. When you allowed me to hold on to the wheel I could feel her quivering through my hands, going where I wanted her to go.'

When she saw Thaddeus try to hide a grin, she giggled. 'Oh, I know it was really you, plus the crew doing all the work, but I felt the ship respond anyway.

You can go all manly and pretend you don't feel anything romantic about it if you want, but I know you do. Sometimes I see you gazing into the sky or at the sea, and your eyes are all distant and dreamy and I know you're feeling it too.'

'Perhaps I'm dreaming of the woman I left behind.'

'Do you have a sweetheart then, Thaddeus?'

He smiled. 'Girl, you're right about that. I asked her to wed me once but she reckoned I wasn't ready to settle down. Now I am, so if she'll still have me I'm still willing. Fact is, she looks a bit like you, Joanna Darsham, but she surely isn't so independently natured.'

'I think you'll find that she is. Did I tell you that Charlotte has a sweetheart, too? I couldn't get her to reveal his name, though she said she loves him true. Do you know who he is?'

Thaddeus grinned. 'Could be I do.'

'Could it be you then, Captain Scott?'

He gave her that hard stare of his, making her giggle. 'Now don't you go sidestepping me, missy. We were talking about you. Tobias went through a lot to provide you with an acceptable future; he's not going to appreciate you going against him.'

With some asperity, she said, 'May I remind you that I didn't ask him to provide me with anything. I would much rather have been consulted about the matter and been told about our relationship at the beginning, so I could have been involved in the decision making. Besides, he made it clear he wanted Alex to have the company, one way or another. But Tobias Darsham's way is not *my* way. Now Alex has what he's always wanted and my father will have his daughter back. But he has to realize that I'm not the infant he lost. I come fully grown with a mind of my own, and my future will be what I make of it. Damn the company, Captain Scott. I can earn my own living and I don't mind getting a bit of dirt under my fingernails to prove it.'

'Now there's a mouthful of wind you've blown, enough to fill the sails and take us halfway round the world. I reckon you swallowed the storm that carried your cradle ashore. What's more, you're getting too big for your drawers now you know you're a Darsham.' Thaddeus chuckled when she opened her mouth to protest. 'It's a waste of breath arguing with you, since once you get a notion in your head there's nothing short of a miracle to change it . . . 'cepting a good clout around the ear might have an effect, if I was of a mind.'

Her eyes widened. 'You wouldn't do that, would you?'

'No . . . but only because you're a female, and a right contrary one you are, at that.' He stood when the ship canted, taking her by the elbow to steady her. 'Go below and have breakfast while you can, then stay in your cabin until the squall blows itself out. Stow everything loose away. It might be a day or two before the weather blows over. If the ship rolls too heavily, pull the mattress off the bunk and lie on it, that way you won't be thrown around so much. I'll send Chin Lee down to check on you now and again.

'Bosun,' he bellowed, making her jump. 'I want all available crew up on deck and the lifelines rigged. Lower the skysails and royals, and send a man to inform

346

the passengers they're not allowed on deck under any circumstances until further notice, and I'd prefer it if they stayed in their cabins.'

'Aye, aye, Cap'n.'

His glance turned her way, and she'd never seen brown eyes so ruthless. 'We have half an hour before the weather hits, girl. Why are you still here? Get below, *now*!'

'Aye, aye, Cap'n,' she said with a grin, but obeyed with alacrity because she was finding it hard to keep her feet. She didn't notice the tiny smile that followed her departing figure.

The two days that followed were the worst of her life. The ship bucked and juddered. She'd never heard such a cacophony of sound, shrieks, creaks, groans and shouts. At odd intervals, running footsteps echoed overhead. Joanna clung for dear life to her mattress on the confined deck space her cabin provided her with. She tried not to give into the sickness the storm had brought with it, and prayed for her life to be spared, as well as that of the crew. She couldn't imagine what they were going through on deck.

The darkness pressed in on her with only an occasional visit from Chin Lee to tell her they were still above the water. Her cabin remained snug, though condensation trickled down the walls. As the storm progressed she became frightened by the power of the sea, but exhilarated by it, too, as she wondered if the hull would crack open to flood her small domain and drown her in her bed.

She slept little, but on the third morning she woke to

347

find that the movement of the ship had changed to a long rolling motion. Cautiously, she opened the cabin door to gaze palely outside. Chin Lee was coming towards her carrying a jug, a big smile on his face.

'Is it over?'

'Yes, missie. The master wants you to take breakfast with him. I've brought you some warm water to wash in.'

She gazed down at her creased clothes, for she hadn't bothered with nightgowns in case they had to abandon the ship. 'Thank you, I need it. And I need to change.'

He nodded and spread his fingers. 'The master don't like to be kept waiting. I'll come back in ten minutes.'

'No need, Chin Lee. I know my way to his quarters.' She changed quickly into a dark blue gown and pulled a shawl about her shoulders, wishing it was the warm Portland shawl she'd given to Tilda instead of the fancy fringed silk wrap that matched the gown. Brushing the tangles from her hair she quickly braided it, then made her way aft to starboard, to the cabin that belonged to the captain.

Thaddeus looked tired, but when he gazed at her pale face with some concern, she felt a rush of warmth for him as she said with heartfelt emotion, 'I was sick a few times, but it wasn't much. I stand in total awe of your skills, Captain Scott. The ocean is such a large and powerful force, and the ship is so small to pit against it, yet somehow I never doubted you'd get us through the storm.'

He looked slightly embarrassed by the praise. 'I've been through worse weather, but not with *Joanna Rose*.'

'Did she enjoy it?'

'Aye, she did, though it stripped some of her fancy paintwork off. Even so, she's the finest ship I've ever commanded. Eat your breakfast, you must be hungry.'

He served her himself, from dishes brought in by Chin Lee. Smoked bacon, and fresh eggs, to which she raised an eyebrow. 'This is better than the usual provisions.'

Thaddeus grinned at her. 'The crew must be fed well, since they do all the work. We have livestock below for fresh meat, and a hen coop. We usually celebrate the evening meal before our arrival with a chicken stew, a good meal for the passengers to remember us fondly by.'

The bread was freshly baked, crusty, still warm in the middle. He poured her coffee, sweetening it with a spoonful of honey. 'Eat hearty now, Joanna Rose, for I've got something to show you afterwards.'

That something was a low smudge of land on the horizon. She experienced a tingle of excitement at the thought of seeing her father again.

There was chicken stew and herb dumplings for dinner that evening.

18

Tobias had watched the *Joanna Rose* come over the horizon with a surge of pride. Now she was anchored off Williamstown at Point Gellibrand, her sails furled, the Darsham and Morcant flag proudly fluttering from her mainmast. Her passengers were being ferried by lighters to the commercial pier. In a little while they'd be unloading mail and cargo.

Thaddeus would come ashore later, bringing with him news of home.

Changing his identity had been harder than Tobias had thought it would be, especially getting used to answering to a different name. He preferred his own name to Gabriel, but the die had been cast the moment he'd thrown himself into the cold arms of the English Channel.

There were so many things he missed about his comfortable life in England. His club, where he could catch up on industry gossip, his home and friends, family. And the fact that he no longer had access to almost unlimited funds.

He hadn't given in to homesickness, though.

Melbourne was shaping up to be a fine place, and had a sense of permanence about it. He had a life and future to build here, and he had the feeling it wouldn't take him long to do it.

In the previous few months he'd established a store selling general household goods. The Tremayne Hardware and Ironmongery Store employed two male assistants. One was an older man who could clerk as well as serve the customers. Samuel Stitch had burned down his own business after the bank had foreclosed on a mortgage he knew nothing about, for his stepson had forged his signature on a loan and taken off with the proceeds.

The second was a strapping young lad of about fifteen years of age called Bert. He'd been kicked out of home by his stepfather. A bit backward intellectually, Bert was amiable and had a fine set of muscles suitable for the heavy lifting. Both of them slept in the back room of the shop.

But being a shopkeeper wasn't entirely to Tobias's liking, even though it was profitable *when* he could keep up the supply of goods. To that end he'd set up an account with one of the other shipping companies that plied the Australian route, so a constant supply of saleable goods would be maintained in the future.

Before his money from Lucian's gold had run out, Tobias had purchased a timber cottage set in five acres of land overlooking the Yarra river. It was registered in his assumed name of Gabriel Tremayne. The cottage was snug, consisting of two bedrooms, a kitchen of sorts and a living room. There was an outhouse built of iron sheeting, which served as a wash-house. A small grove of established grapevines had been planted by the previous owner, and come summer he was going to try his hand at making wine.

It was primitive compared to what he'd had in England, but he intended to extend the house when he'd built up sufficient funds. He'd also met a woman he liked enormously and was attracted to. Jane Haver was a widow of about thirty years of age, (modest in manner), who had lost her husband and only child and now taught school for a living. Drawn together by loneliness, he'd found Jane to be affectionate in other ways, too. A comforting sort of love had grown between them and there was an understanding that they would wed.

His horse fidgeted between the shafts of the cart. 'Steady girl, Thaddeus will be ashore before too long,' he said, drawing his coat collar up over his ears, for August was winter in this southern region of the world, and there was a cold wind blowing off the water.

Even as he said it he saw a lighter detach itself from the ship. There was no mistaking Thaddeus's upright figure, though he had his back towards him. A grin spread across Tobias's face, for there was a woman with him, a cloak drawn tightly around her body to shield her from the cold.

The woman came ashore first, clutching a satchel close under her arm. A seaman in the lighter began to toss the luggage ashore. It looked as if she'd come to stay, for she'd brought a staggering amount with her. First a trunk, then another, then several large bags. She gave a little squeak as she sidestepped and overbalanced, nearly dropping her satchel in the process.

Clutching it tighter, she laughed when Thaddeus put a steadying arm under her elbow. 'You didn't tell me I'd have to find my land legs again, Thaddeus. How are we to carry all my luggage between us?'

Thaddeus! She was on first names with him? Had the captain taken a woman, given up on winning the hand of Tobias's mother after all this time? Curiouser and curiouser.

'I'm sure we'll find a way.' Thaddeus gave a broad smile when he spotted him, and touched his finger to his cap. 'I wondered if you'd be waiting, Mr Tremayne. Come and help me with this young lady's luggage, would you?'

Tobias's heart thumped as the woman turned towards him and a pair of dark blue eyes gazed into his, then widened. His mouth formed her name, but the sound wouldn't come out.

She covered the ground between them with tears filling her eyes.

'You shouldn't have come,' he whispered, his glance hungrily going over her face. *His daughter, his own lovely, beloved daughter. How like Honor she was.*

She didn't bother with any niceties, just stated accusingly, 'Did you think I'd stay away once I knew? It was easy to piece things together. You should have told me yourself, for I have the right to know you, my father.'

Taken aback, he mumbled, 'Why didn't you leave me be? Thaddeus shouldn't have allowed you on board. Oh

'. . . stop spouting those female tears, you're making me feel guilty.'

She gave a watery sniff. There was a sense of withdrawing, a wounded look in her eyes. 'Have I been wrong about the kind of man you are, then? Have I presumed too much on our blood tie? You're not going to turn me away, are you?'

About to deny the existence of either notion, he appreciated that she'd come all this way because there was a need in her for them to know each other. He recognized the same need in himself. He'd convinced himself he would rather she had stayed in England and left him dead and buried, for that would have been easier for both of them. But now she was here his thinking had turned, and a weight seemed to have lifted from his shoulders. She would complicate his life no end and be an added responsibility, he thought, but what the hell? He'd lost her once, and now that she'd come back into his life he wanted her so very much to stay.

'Turn you away? How could I when I loved your mother so much and you're the very image of her. Oh, my dear. Come here.' When he held out his arms she came into them and they hugged each other close.

There would be time later to catch up with what was going on in England.

In Poole, Richard Lind's life was coming to an end.

Woken from a sound sleep by the thud of a falling book just before dawn, Charlotte hurried to his bed-chamber. Taking one look at him and recognizing that the seizure was much more severe than those Richard usually suffered, she roused the maid and sent her scurrying for the doctor.

'Don't worry, Richard dear,' she said when he came round. 'I'll look after you. Is there anything I can do to help relieve your condition?'

He squeezed her hand, but his eyes were faraway and she wasn't sure he'd heard her. A little while later another fit overtook him, and she stood helplessly by as his teeth chattered and the bed jerked and juddered with the violence of it.

'I'm afraid his brain is greatly affected by irritation, and he won't last much longer, Mrs Darsham,' the doctor said, wiping the bloodied froth from Richard's chin, for he'd bitten his tongue. 'I can give him a dose of laudanum, which might help settle him down. Shall I have him removed to the infirmary?'

'Certainly not, for my cousin's home is here. He might appreciate some laudanum, if it will help him. Perhaps I should send for his brother, though.'

'No,' Richard gasped out with great effort. 'My personal journal, Charlotte, don't let my brother take it. Destroy it.'

'Don't worry, Richard. I'll do exactly as you say.'

'*Promise?*'

'I promise. Now take the laudanum and try and relax, my dear, for I want you to get better. I'm going to see you through this.'

'Thank you . . . Charlotte, for making my life . . . ' His back suddenly arched and another seizure was upon him.

When it was finished she moved aside while the

doctor administered a dose of the drug. She was disturbed by the amount of the laudanum dribbled into his mouth. But Richard wasn't going to get better, the doctor had made that quite clear, and perhaps this was a way of making his patient's end more peaceful.

Richard's seizures came at half-hourly intervals, each one less violent, without rousing him from sleep. At eleven o'clock the seizures ceased altogether and he became comatose, his breathing more laboured.

The doctor felt for his pulse and shook his head. 'There's nothing more I can do to make him comfortable. It's just a question of time, now. I have another patient to see but will be back in a little while.'

Charlotte talked soothingly to Richard, even though he wasn't responding. 'It's been lovely having you living with me, Richard, and I'm so sorry you're leaving. You, Joanna and Tilda have taught me the value of having good friends. I didn't tell you about Thaddeus Scott, did I? He has loved me for a long time. I've decided that when he returns to England I shall accept the proposal he made to me all those years ago, after John Darsham died. I just hope he will have me now I am old.'

A soft noise came from her cousin's throat. It sounded like a chuckle, but she knew it wasn't. His breath started to come with a harsh rattle.

Richard's dog came waddling in from the sitting room, turned his face up to hers and gave a doleful sigh, as if he sensed what was going on. 'Hello, Walter dear, I don't think you'll get your walk today.' When she picked him up he licked her hand and settled comfortably on her lap. Fondling his ear she turned her attention back to Richard, who had quieted. 'I shall look after your little dog, Richard. Walter will want for nothing, including love, and he and Judy will be fine companions in their declining years.'

It struck her that the rattle had stopped. Richard's face looked very relaxed and peaceful. The rise and fall of his chest had ceased. Tears trickled slowly down her cheeks as she bent to kiss him. 'Goodbye, dear cousin, suffer no more,' she said, saddened by his loss, but glad his passing had been made as easy as possible.

Then Charlotte remembered his journal and went through to the sitting room. A paper dropped on to the table as she picked the book up and flipped it open. Unfolding it, she gazed at the writing. It was the entry of marriage between Tobias and Joanna. Richard must have torn it from the register when he'd gone back to Portland to collect his books.

His journal was penned exquisitely. *My life began when my cousin offered me the hand of friendship,* he'd written on the first page. *For that alone, I will love her always.*

The journal had not been meant for anybody's eyes but Richard's. 'Thank you for that, Richard dear,' she whispered. 'May your soul rest in peace. I won't read on.'

She smiled and went down to the kitchen. One of the maids was pegging out the washing. Sending Stevens to fetch David Lind's brother, she gently caressed the signatures of the two people she loved with the ball of her thumb, then dropped the marriage entry and journal into the fiery heart of the stove and watched them curl into ashes.

*

357

Alexander walked with a new spring in his step. He might not have liked what Joanna had arranged in his absence, but it had worked. The company ships were booked out for some time to come, money was rolling in and he was thinking he might have to purchase another ship.

Compared to other shipping companies, Darsham and Morcant was fairly small, but they had a good record of safety and reliability.

He'd discarded the idea of steam for the time being, since the ships had to make landfall to refuel, which was difficult when the route from one point to another was directly across a vast expanse of ocean. The company couldn't afford it if the ships were to take a longer route, but when the time was right he'd pursue a partnership with steam prospects.

In the meantime he intended to put *Charlotte May* on the lucrative Australia run, alternating with *Joanna Rose*. The ageing *Nightingale* had undergone a refit and was being used for carrying cargo and steerage passengers to and from America. She was slower than *Clara Jane*, but the cheaper tariff ensured she sailed fully laden.

Alexander didn't see much of his mother these days. She'd bought the Morcant family home from Oliver, and she entertained constantly. He had always been dubious about the people she mixed with, and still was, for she was attracting a reputation. He stayed away as much as possible.

Recently Clara had returned from America where she'd attended Oliver's wedding. She'd sent a message that she wished to see him.

He called Henry Wetherall into the office that morning to present a notion to him that he'd had in mind for some time.

'You've been with the company a long time, Henry, and you know the business inside out. How would you feel about being promoted to general manager? It would free me up for other business, and you could promote whoever you wanted into the head clerk's job.'

Henry looked as pleased as a dog with nine tails to wag. 'I'd consider it a great honour, sir. A great honour.'

'Your salary would increase considerably, of course.'

'Thank you, sir.'

'Right, that's settled then. You can have the office Tobias Darsham used to use. It probably needs a bit of a clear out, though.'

'Then I'll get on with it, sir.'

He smiled. 'No, Henry, you will not. You'll tell the office boy to get on with it.'

Later in the day, Alexander duly presented himself at his mother's house. He gave his two half-sisters a hug on his way through the hall. They were pretty girls, well mannered and vivacious. He received a kiss on both cheeks at the same time.

'We are invited to Lady Sanderson's ball at the weekend,' Lydia chatted. 'You must come and see our gowns before you leave. I wanted a pink one and Irene wanted blue, but mother said we must wear white. Do you think you can change her mind?'

Virgins to the slaughter, he thought morosely, promising to try.

Irene looked despondent. 'Viscount Durrington has

expressed an interest in me. Lydia thinks he's too old, but he dances very well. Mother said they are negotiating.'

How sad that his two sisters were to be married off in this way, and sadder still that they'd been trained to accept the process as normal. 'Just say no if you don't want to wed him, Irene, and mean it. Mother can't make you marry him, you know. If she tries, you must let me know.'

The pair gazed at each other, wide-eyed. 'She'll be angry if we oppose her. She said she'll send us to live with our grandmother in America if we misbehave.'

'That's better than being married off to old men whom you don't care for. Just don't let her bully you, that's all.'

Which was easier to say than do when you were that young.

When he entered the drawing room his mother nodded towards a chair. She didn't waste time. 'I've been negotiating a match with Viscount Durrington for one of your sisters. He's keen on boating and is interested in having a share of the Darsham and Morcant Shipping Company as part of her dowry.'

'The company is not yours to negotiate with.'

Clara sighed. 'Don't be so tedious, Alex. That island girl bought it from Oliver cheap. It was worth much more and she cheated him.'

'It wasn't at the time of sale. As far as I can see he was paid a good price, since the company was almost on its knees. I'd have offered him less.' Joanna had displayed a surprisingly good head for business at the time of the transaction, he thought, and Oliver, who'd had no idea of the worth of his share, had deserted what he'd thought to be a sinking ship.

'I'll pay you twenty per cent more than she bought it for, and will leave you the controlling share.'

'Darsham and Morcant is not for sale, besides which, what used to be Oliver's share is worth a damned lot more now. As far as I'm concerned, until I've paid off the debt the company belongs to Joanna Darsham.'

'How very noble of you, Alex,' she sneered. 'You're a fool to even contemplate giving back something that Tobias had promised you in the first place. You owe nothing to the Darshams. What did they ever do for you? Both Lucian and Oliver sailed the ships while Tobias Darsham directed things from the office. Your father lost his life for the company.'

Alexander raised an ironic eyebrow. 'Did he? I thought my father was a French diplomat.'

'You know perfectly well I'm referring to Lucian, Alex. And if you want to know why I sought love outside my marriage, it's because Lucian was less than a man. Did you never wonder why he was so thick with Tobias Darsham?'

Alexander managed to keep a lid on his anger at her slanderous tongue, but it ate away inside him so he was forced to say, 'Mother, that statement is totally untrue. If I ever hear you repeat it, not only will I make it known that you were unfaithful to your husband, I shall name my father.'

'Anything you say would only be conjecture on your part.' Her nostrils pinched as she inhaled and she placed a hand on his arm. 'I wouldn't repeat it, of course, because I know you idolized Lucian and Tobias. But you only saw Tobias through eyes that worshipped. Think on. Now the company is in your name you won't have to marry that dreadful island girl. She was extremely rude towards me. How she fooled Tobias into marriage is a mystery.'

Alexander hoped it would remain a mystery for ever to Clara. But he smiled inside at the mention of Joanna's name, for however much his mother slighted her, his own heart now sang at the very thought of her. A few more weeks and he would see her again, and he could hardly wait, even though he knew those weeks would be a lifetime.

'Who are you to advise me when you're willing to sell my sisters for a title? Stop interfering in what no longer concerns you,' he said.

She shrugged. 'Viscount Durrington is keen to build a steamship.'

Alexander's dark eyes rested on her for a moment, interested despite his senses telling him not to be. 'What's stopping him?'

'He needs to be in partnership with someone who knows the shipping business. Meet him,' she said.

'I'll think about it.' Not because of the steamship, but because his mother sounded a little too desperate, and he wanted to see for himself what type of man his mother was prepared to barter one of her daughters for.

Her smile slid across her face like an eel on ice, and it was slightly malicious. 'Charles is waiting in the morning room. I said he could meet you, and it would be rude for you not to. You might learn something from him.'

He frowned. What the hell was she up to? He soon found out. It was obvious to Alexander that Viscount Durrington was too familiar with his mother. And it was obvious from the way she fawned over him that she was in love with him. He felt pity for her.

The man was in his late fifties and had a dissolute look to him. What came as a shock, too, was the resemblance between himself and the Viscount. Alexander suddenly realized he was not the son of a French diplomat, as he'd first thought. He was this man's son.

'You seem to have known my mother a long time,' Alexander said, shooting her a look that contained all the disdain he felt for her. 'I'm surprised we haven't been introduced sooner.'

'It wasn't in your best interests,' Clara said with a smug smile.

'Nor yours, mother, it seems. Your desperation is showing if you're prepared to marry off your daughter to your former lover. You are my father, I take it?'

The man acknowledged their relationship with a nod. 'I met you twice when you were young, Alexander, but I was married and I lived abroad for most of my life. My legitimate son died and now I need another heir. Either of your sisters would suit my purpose, for they're young enough to breed.' His eyes hooded over and the tip of his tongue moistened his lips.

As they gazed at each other, something flickered between them . . . On Alexander's part it was total dislike. He turned to his mother. 'It's out of the question, of course. If you think that knowing this man fathered me will give you leverage, you have no idea of my character. It will make no difference to my decision.'

'But, Alex, you said you'd think about it.'

He was more brutal than he'd intended, and his mother flinched when he said, 'I have thought. If my sister's marriage to this man hinges on me selling the shipping company, then there's nothing more to be said. You'll have to find some other way of buying his favours, for once he gets his hands on younger flesh, he's not going to want yours. To my mind such a marriage has the whiff of incest, and I shouldn't be at all surprised if the law disallowed it.'

'But who will know, Alex, since you were born with another man's name?'

It became obvious that his mother was utterly without morals. He thought then of Joanna and Tobias, and understood why Tobias had decided to disappear.

'I will,' he said. 'And believe me, that should bother you a great deal, Mother. So be very careful.' He turned to the peer. 'Touch either of my sisters and I'll have you taken out to sea and dropped overboard in the middle of the Atlantic Ocean.'

He strode away from them, then picked up his hat from the hallstand and went outside to draw in a deep breath of the October air. The smell coming from the river was better than the stench of corruption inside the house of his mother.

He remembered that he'd promised to inspect his sister's ball gowns. To compensate them, Alexander stopped at a dressmaker's establishment and chose two gowns, one of pale pink, the other of blue. He left instructions for the gowns to be delivered to his sisters, and prayed for their safety.

November, and the fog crept up from the river to choke the streets and alleyways of London.

The *Joanna Rose* was overdue. He hoped nothing had happened to her. Alexander swung the telescope towards the Darsham and Morcant berth, trying to pierce the curtain of gloom without success. The fog was so thick that it condensed on the window glass and ran, leaving grimy streaks behind. His ears strained for the clop of a horse, the toll of a church bell or the whistled tune of street vendors as they passed. But not a sound from outside penetrated through its thickness.

Behind him the clock ticked and tocked, but the hands didn't seem to move fast enough.

Mrs Bates brought in a tray of tea, then attacked the fire with a brass-handled poker. Sparks cracked from the coal and spat up the chimney with the vigour of her attack. Fire stirred to her satisfaction, she placed the poker in the coal scuttle. 'Shall I draw the curtains, sir. It's right miserable outside.'

'No, leave it. I'll see to it. Is Mrs Joanna Darsham's room ready for occupancy?' he asked, as he had the last time she'd entered the room. 'She'll be staying for a night or two before she goes to Poole to stay with Mrs Darsham senior.'

'Yes, sir. The fire is lit so the room will be nice and aired when she comes home. Fancy going away to sea for all that time. The mistress must have been overcome by the adventure of it, to go off so sudden. Though I can't see much adventure in sailing in this weather.'

Joanna's incentive had been much stronger than adventure, Alex thought with a grin, and he hoped she didn't throw him out when she came home, for his own house had been sold, and he didn't fancy sleeping in his office.

'Now, you come away from that window and have your tea while it's hot, sir. There's some nice buttered muffins, and some gooseberry conserve to put on them.'

'Thank you, Mrs Bates.'

He gazed at the clock again and his thoughts turned to Joanna. He'd have loved to have seen Tobias's face when she turned up on his doorstep. He wondered, What was Joanna doing now?

Joanna, her skirt tucked into her waist, was weeding along a row of spring vegetables. Her hands went to her back as she straightened, and she arched her shoulders and sighed.

Tobias gazed at her swelling stomach and grinned. 'I can't believe I didn't see the state you were in until last month. I just thought you were gaining weight. Do you feel all right?'

She laughed, placing her hands against the result of her union with Alex. 'Of course. Stop worrying.'

'I'd feel better if you were wed to the baby's father. I can't believe Alex took advantage of you. He should have known better.'

'He's just a man, and you must know what men are like, since you're one yourself. Besides, he didn't force me.' Her palms smoothed gently down over her stomach. 'I can feel the baby moving inside me. Sometimes he kicks so strongly that he wakes me at night.'

'It's a boy, then.'

'Could be, but it doesn't matter.' She gave him a sly look. 'Isn't it about time you stopped meddling in my affairs and proposed to that woman of yours?'

'The devil, you say. How did you learn about Jane?'

'I see you with her in the shop on occasion. Anyone with half an eye could see that you adore each other.'

'I never thought I'd love another woman after your mother, Joanna.'

'But you married me.'

A shamed look came to his grey eyes. 'Aye, don't remind me of it. I had the strangest feeling we belonged together, and we did, but not in the way I expected.' He smoothed a strand of hair back from her face. 'This time we're spending together is precious to me. Jane understands that, because I've told her everything. That's why she's keeping her distance.'

'Then you'd better bring her up for dinner, so we can meet each other, because I don't know how long I'll stay here in Australia. It might be for the rest of my life and it might not, for although I like it fine here, and Melbourne town is grand with its wide streets and fine buildings, I feel homesick. I miss Charlotte and Tilda and . . . everyone.'

'Alex, you mean.'

She nodded. 'And him, I suppose, though it's hard to admit to it, because he's so proud, and he never listens to reason unless you shake him or shock him. He's . . . *infuriating.*'

Tobias raised an eyebrow at the accuracy of her statement. 'I imagine he might have that effect on a woman, at times.'

'You do see, I couldn't possibly marry him for the sake of the company, even though he was willing to do what you asked of him. It wasn't fair of you to demand that of him, or of me, come to that. I'm not company stock he needs to take on, and neither will I be bartered as such.'

'But you must tell him about his child, Joanna, for he has some responsibility towards it. Whatever you think of Alex, he will never evade his responsibilities, and he goes after what he wants with singular purpose.'

She gently patted her stomach and glowered. 'There's no denying that. I will think about it, I promise. But it might be better for Alex to remain in ignorance. His child and I can make a good life for ourselves together.'

'Then you'll be doing exactly what I did: making Alex's decisions for him, and also for his son or daughter.' He took her face between his hands and, looking into her eyes, said softly, 'Joanna, I should so much have liked to have known you were alive and watched you grow up. I'm pleased you had a happy and secure childhood, though. It's something Alexander never had, for he spent his life in boarding school, then learned that the man he thought was his father was no relation to him.'

'I know.' She smiled at him, perfectly at ease. 'But Alex had you, and that's something I missed out on. And you have Jane now, and will have other children to raise in time and a life to make for them here. We have only the here and now in which to know each other, and that will form our present and our past. I want you to make room in that to know how very much I love you for doing what you did. It was a sacrifice I didn't deserve, since I married you as a means to an end.'

Taking his hands she placed them over her stomach. 'Feel how it kicks, this grandchild of yours. If it's a boy I shall name him Tobias Alexander.'

A smile lit his face as the child surged under his hands. 'I feel honoured,' he said gruffly.

Gently, she kissed his cheek. 'I promise I'll let Alex know in due course, if him not knowing worries you. He doesn't deserve it, though, and he probably won't care, or else he'll think I'm trying to trap him into marriage, for he has a rare conceit on him.'

Tobias tried to hide his smile. If Joanna thought Alex would ignore something as important as this, she would soon learn differently. Indeed, she would.

When Alexander woke, it was to find that the fog had dispersed and the *Joanna Rose* was being nudged up to her berth by the small steamer that had brought her up river.

Still naked, he swung the telescope round. Seamen were swarming up the masts and the ship was a hive of activity. He saw Thaddeus Scott stride from his quarters and bellow something to someone up the mast. A moment later a seaman came shimmying down the rigging. He patted his pockets, said something to Thaddeus, then shrugged and shook his head.

369

Alexander grinned when Thaddeus threw his cap on the ground. He must have run out of his favourite tobacco.

The passengers would not be ready to disembark until the formalities had been observed and the luggage brought ashore. Alexander dressed carefully, ate a hearty breakfast and, whistling to himself, set out for the berth, stopping at the tobacconist shop on the way.

Thaddeus beamed him a relieved smile when he handed over the tobacco. They ducked through the staterooms into his cabin, where Thaddeus immediately took his pipe from his pocket and filled it. His head disappeared into a cloud of blue smoke while he went through the ritual of lighting it.

'I haven't had a pipe for six days,' he grumbled when the smoke cleared. 'How did you know?'

Hiding his grin, Alex shrugged. 'Instinct. How was the voyage?'

'Fair sailing most of the way. She weathered a bit of a squall on the outward leg, lost a bit of varnish and shredded a couple of sheets. The only casualty was a passenger who broke a bone in his arm. We had a sawbones travelling with us, who took care of him.'

'Cargo?'

'Stuffed to the gills with wool, and 60,000 ounces of gold on board for the royal mint. The mail is being taken ashore now.'

'And Tobias . . . how's he?'

Thaddeus stared hard at him, but eventually his eyes slid away under Alexander's confident and constant scrutiny.

Alexander grinned. 'Don't pretend you don't know

what I'm talking about. Once I figured out who Joanna reminded me of, the whys and wherefores came easy. Where is she?'

Thaddeus exhaled slowly. 'Can't rightly say.'

'Stop playing games, Thaddeus. You know which cabin she occupies. Don't worry, I'll be gentle with her.'

'Last time I looked, you had no claim to Joanna Darsham, mister,' Thaddeus said gruffly.

'Like hell I haven't. I intend to marry her.'

'Not under the terms of Tobias Darsham's will, you're not. The girl had something to say about that the last time I saw her, and she wasn't too keen on the idea.'

Alexander's face heated at the thought. She just needed a little persuading. 'That I'll hear from her own mouth. Which cabin, Thaddeus?'

'Joanna Darsham is not travelling aboard my ship.'

Disappointment flooded through Alexander's body and he muttered, 'The hell she isn't. Which ship is she on, then?'

'As far as I know she's still in Australia, where she's visiting *a relative.*'

'When does she intend to return?'

'I don't know that she does, since she purchased a one-way passage.' Thaddeus stuffed his spent pipe in his pocket and stood. 'You'll have to excuse me, Alex. I want to leave for Poole as soon as possible and there should be a wherrie going along the coast in an hour or so. And I might as well tell you now, I intend to retire after the next voyage.'

The bottom seemed to fall out of Alexander's world, but not at the thought of Thaddeus's impending retirement, for he knew he'd earned it. 'Then I shall have to go and fetch her back. Keep a cabin empty for me.'

There was an unbelieving guffaw of laughter from Thaddeus. 'For a man who will never step aboard a ship lest it be tied safely up to its berth fore and aft, that's quite a statement. Don't be daft, lad. You're petrified of the ocean, you always have been. Ten guineas says you won't make it on board.'

'Fifty guineas says you're on.' Alexander grinned. 'You said I just needed the incentive to go to sea, and now I've found it. You see, I just happen to be in love with Joanna Rose Darsham, and I intend to tell her that to her face.'

What better incentive could a man in love have than that? Thaddeus thought.

19

It was the eighth day of January 1858 and the sun beat down from a flawless blue sky.

Joanna felt fatter than a greased hog and as listless as the willows dipping their branches into the Yarra river, which flowed sedately past the end of the garden. Even the baby was asleep. So low was the infant inside her now that her stomach rested comfortably on her lap, and she doubted that it would ever flatten back into shape again. Sweat trickled between her breasts and the pressure was such that she seemed to need to pee every five minutes of the day and night.

She smiled as Jane came from the kitchen on to the veranda carrying a jug of lemonade. Joanna placed the tiny garment she was hemming to one side. How odd that a human being could be born so small and grow into someone so large, she thought. She had made many such garments from the material from one of her chemises, each one stitched with love. Although her infant felt as big as a donkey inside her, Joanna already loved it with a passion, and she couldn't wait to hold it in her arms.

Each day was a torture to her now. She waddled like a duck, and when she lay on her back she was as helpless as a turned turtle.

'Will this baby ever arrive?' she complained, and tears came into her eyes as she suddenly remembered Anna, and wished her ma was with her to help her through the birth. Portland seemed such a long way in the past. Had it only been three years since Anna had gone from her life?

'It can't stay in there for ever, my dear.' Jane's smile lit her brown eyes as she kissed Joanna gently on the forehead. Jane was a woman who was beautiful in a quiet, calm way. She and Joanna's father were married now, in a quiet ceremony that had been conducted a month earlier. The ceremony had been a Christmas present to one another. Theirs was a contented but slightly cramped household, the bond between them all one of love and trust.

Joanna drank the lemonade, which was sharp and refreshing. It trickled coldly down inside her. There was a sudden pressure on her bladder and she felt it trickle out of the other end of her and soak through her skirt. The liquid dripped on to the wooden slats of the veranda then rolled onwards toward the edge, where it fell over the side to water the border of flamboyantly red tomatoes Joanna had planted.

Waste not, want not, she thought inconsequently, then gazed at the liquid with some perplexity. She was ashamed by her lack of control. Although she was trying to squeeze it back it wouldn't cooperate, for it just kept trickling.

'I didn't think there was that much lemonade in the glass,' she said, glancing at Jane with an apology in her eyes.

Jane gave a quiet chuckle. 'No, my dear, there isn't. The water sac your baby is growing in has just ruptured, and soon your infant will be born. We must prepare.' Jane went back inside the house and Joanna heard her say, 'Will you go to fetch the midwife, Gabe, my love. Your grandchild is about to put in an appearance.'

Her father's deeper voice came, laced with panic. 'Look after her while I'm gone.'

Joanna grimaced when a pain appeared in the small of her back, gathered force and squeezed fiery ripples across her stomach. More water came, but now it spurted. Another pain drove strongly through her.

'I think you'd better hurry, Pa,' she shouted. 'Everything's happening too fast, I think.'

He had hardly galloped off when the pressure increased and Joanna felt herself stretching.

Jane took a quick look between Joanna's thighs and said, 'You haven't got time to reach the bed, the baby's head is coming out.'

Jane quickly placed a padded sheet beneath Joanna as she went on to her hands and knees on the veranda floor. Now, it was one pain after the other. 'Damn Alex Morcant,' Joanna said as she grunted, strained and pushed for several more minutes. There was a prolonged moment when she yelled out loud, then something warm and wet slithered from between her thighs and a baby began to squall. She felt like giggling at the relief it gave her.

'Just a moment,' Jane said when she turned her head to try and see what she'd produced, 'the afterbirth is coming.' Another small contraction and she was no longer attached to her child. Jane wrapped a towel loosely round the infant and Joanna rolled over on her back, exhausted. A pillow was placed under her head.

The pair smiled at each other as Jane placed the noisy parcel in her arms. 'What is it?' Joanna asked over the noise it was making, with some anticipation.

'See for yourself.'

Opening the wrapping, Joanna saw a boy who looked to be the very image of Alex, with dark liquid eyes and a twist of dark hair on his head. Gently she caressed his face. 'Hush now, my darling son,' she said tenderly, almost overawed by the beauty and perfection of him. 'It's all over now.'

He quieted at the sound of her voice and she unfurled his tiny fingers and placed a kiss in his palm. His wrinkled, skinny legs stretched towards the sun, so they quivered with the effort, but his mouth turned towards her breast and he made helpless mewing noises that were totally beguiling. When his tiny fists began to knead at her breast, the bounty of them became an aching anticipation.

Ah yes . . . she thought, smiling as she opened her bodice, the male instinctively knows how to get what he needs from a woman. She allowed her nipple to slide wetly into his mouth and his lips adjusted around it and he began to suck. Tears ran down her cheeks with the poignancy of the moment and when Jane held them both close she began to sob and she wished that Anna

Rushmore, the woman she'd always regarded as her ma, was here with her.

But her joy soon overtook her sadness. 'Look, Jane, see how helpless and sweet he is, and how handsome.' She kissed the top of his head. 'Welcome into the world, my precious Tobias Alexander.'

But her son had fallen asleep, and Joanna couldn't stop admiring this miracle she'd just produced, as every mother before her had done with their sons.

Six weeks later, Tobias gazed down at his namesake and grinned at Jane. 'He does nothing but sleep. What's Joanna feeding him on?'

Jane gazed out through the window to where Joanna was hanging the washing on the line and laughed. 'I don't know, but he's thriving on it and so is she.' Sliding her arms around his waist she hugged him close and gazed into his eyes. 'I was going to wait until I was sure, but I think we are to become parents in the latter part of the year, too.'

Tobias smiled at the thought, for having his grandson around had shown him what he'd missed all these years. 'Dearest Jane, I'm overjoyed for myself, and so pleased for you. A child of our own will help you to grieve less for the little one you lost. I'll have to start planning the extensions to the house so we can all fit in. The shop is beginning to make a profit, now so the bank might give me a loan.'

'Let's not get into debt, Gabe. We can manage, I'm sure. I can work for a while longer, and Joanna has helped by establishing a good vegetable garden, and planting fruit trees, which will cater for the years ahead. With that, the chickens and sheep, we can eat well enough. And Joanna has brought more clothes with her than we can wear in years to come, and has been generous with them. She said she doesn't need so many and it's share and share alike.'

Joanna, who must have overheard Jane's end of the conversation as she came inside, said in her usual forthright manner, 'Are we short of money then?'

The enquiring look Tobias offered Jane was met with a slight nod. He curled a smile at Joanna. 'We were discussing whether we could afford to extend the house, since I'm to become a father again.'

Joanna's initial grin turned into a smile. She hugged him, then Jane. 'Congratulations. I'm so pleased. And the house extensions?'

'We've decided to wait a little longer. It's not quite right, financially.'

She gave little smile. 'Wait there.' Going into the tiny bedroom she used, Joanna came back with a leather satchel, undid the buckles and tipped the contents in a heap on the table. She gazed at them in triumph. 'There!'

Tobias stared at the small mountain of money in silence.

Jane spoke first, her voice sounding slightly strangled. 'Joanna? You haven't robbed the bank, have you?'

'I brought it with me.'

Tobias remembered watching her clutch tightly to the satchel when she first came ashore. 'Where did you get it from?' he asked.

'From James Stark. When I arranged for the company to be put in Alexander's name I asked him for a thousand guineas.'

'And he gave it to you?'

'Straight away. He knew what I was doing would stop the shipping company from disaster, and I promised I wouldn't ask for more. He probably thought that, long term, it would be cheaper to pay me off than put me off, especially when I gently mentioned your name to remind him he'd broken the law.'

Tobias grinned at that, protesting, 'But I can't take your money.'

'It's not my money, it's yours. After all, it was your company.'

'But—'

She placed a finger over his mouth. 'Have you any plans for the extension? I'm sure Jane would be interested in seeing them.'

When her infant stirred she turned towards the basket that served as a cradle for her son. He smelled of milk, he smelled . . . her nose wrinkled . . . rather like the Thames river in summer. 'You smelly little wretch,' she scolded, 'what have you done?'

'What was that you said about him doing nothing but sleep?' Jane whispered against Tobias's ear.

The most demanding member of the household gazed at his mother, broke wind from both ends and offered her his first smile, an unashamed and very gummy grin.

*

379

Alexander wondered how he'd managed to survive the voyage as land hove into view.

He'd thought he'd left his stomach behind in the English Channel, but no, there had been worse to come as they progressed.

He'd finally found his sea legs four weeks after they'd set sail, and now he hoped they'd stay seaworthy long enough for the return voyage. Apart from his initial sickness, he'd learned a lot from his time at sea. It had given him an insight into the working of the company ships, and of the camaraderie of the men who commanded them and the crew who sailed them. He would never regard the ships purely in terms of profit again, but he knew he'd never want to make such a long sea voyage again, either.

He gazed around him. The sea was a dark blue, reminding him of Joanna's eyes, and a warm breeze blew through his hair. Seagulls wheeled and screamed overhead.

Thaddeus came up behind him. 'Will you be returning with us when we sail?'

'If Joanna will come with me.' His confidence fled. 'If not, I don't know what I'll do.'

'Just turn on the charm, lad. Joanna Rose gave up the company because she knew what it meant to you and didn't want you to feel trapped. She didn't give a damn about the shipping company, only about you. If you ask me, she got the result she wanted.'

'Did she say she wanted me to chase after her?'

'No, I just know it. Women aren't logical like men. They have a sneaky way of going about things. They work on a man's conscience, and when he's at his weakest they grab him by the balls as well. It's a winning combination, believe me, lad. Before we know it we're being led to the altar like a prize bull into a show ring. What's more, they manage to make us believe that's what we wanted in the first place.'

Alexander grinned as he turned to Thaddeus. 'Is that what Charlotte Darsham did to you?'

Thaddeus shrugged. 'I went down there like I had a storm up my tail, because I thought that fancy poet fellow was after her. But he had upped and died on her. When I told her straight of my thoughts in that direction, her smile went all smug, like a cat who'd licked the cream off a spoon.

'"Of course I loved Richard, he was my cousin," she said, her voice like syrup. "Thaddeus Scott, you're a bloody fool. I would have wed you years ago, but you kept running off to sea and never demanded an answer to your proposal."'

'"Well, I'm demanding one now", says I, all manly like, to which she smiles and gives an affirmative nod before I could turn round and run away again, as if it was all planned that way.'

Thaddeus tapped his forehead. 'I reckon that granddaughter of hers is the same. She's got some fox-brain cunning in here, and you're her prey.' He punched Alexander on the shoulder and began to laugh. 'Come hell or high water, the little lady's going to get you, too.'

He was probably right, Alexander thought a little later, when the lighter had pushed off from the ship and he spied Tobias waiting there for Thaddeus. A lump rose in his throat as he stepped ashore with a group of passengers, for his former mentor's eyes were turned towards the ship and there was a nostalgic look in them. Dammit, Alex had missed him, but he understood why Tobias had chosen to disappear and appreciated how hard it must have been to cut himself off from friends and family.

Alexander slipped from the crowd and walked right up to the horse and cart without being noticed. 'Gabe Tremayne?' he said. 'The master of the *Joanna Rose* sends his regards and said he'll catch up with you at the hotel later on.'

Cautious grey eyes turned his way, then widened. A smile sped across Tobias's face, disappeared, then reappeared again, twice as wide. 'Alex, I'll be damned to all hell and back,' he said. 'How did Thaddeus get you on board?'

'With great difficulty.'

'What are you doing here?'

Alexander threw his bag on the cart and clambered up beside him. 'I expect you know exactly why I've come here. To talk some sense into your daughter, Joanna Rose. She *is* staying with you, isn't she? Is she all right?'

'She's as healthy as a horse.' Tobias grinned. 'Speaking as a father, Alex, what are your intentions towards my daughter?'

'You might as well know that my instincts are to throw her over my knee and beat some sense into her,' he growled. 'Joanna has led me on no end of a dance.'

'I asked what your intentions are, mister.' Alex found

himself a recipient of a hard stare. 'You would have extended every respect to her in your dealings, I imagine, hmm . . .?'

Alexander's glance slid away and he thought, Joanna is Tobias's daughter so his reaction to certain matters relating to her are predictable. For her sake, it wouldn't do to tell him of those matters private to them both, as she'd once made clear to him. Nevertheless, he felt guilty when he said, 'Joanna has always had my respect. In fact, I'm here to propose marriage.'

'Are you now?'

'Yes. And I'd prefer to have your blessing.' He felt suddenly anxious. 'Does she mention me, at all?'

'Sometimes, when she's reminded of you. I don't want to dash your hopes, but it's rarely complimentary.' The smile Tobias gave him was full of amusement, but his eyes were bland. 'You have my blessing, though, and good luck to you. I'll drop you off at the gate and catch up with you later. There's plenty we need to talk about.'

'And not least the fact that the company will need a representative here in Melbourne, for I'm putting the *Charlotte May* on the Australian run, as well. You're tailor-made for the job, Gabriel Tremayne.'

'Aye, I am at that. And I've got an office above my shop that can be used for the purpose and an assistant to run such a venture. By God, it will be good to be involved again in some small way. I now have a wife to keep and a baby on the way. I'll introduce you to Jane later.'

Tobias's house was small and made of wood, including the shingle roof. It stood on several acres of land, which sloped gently downwards to a river lined with willows. How odd that Tobias would live in such a small house, Alexander thought. Then he realized the proximity of it to the city and, remembering the house at Southwark, he quickly calculated what the value would be of the land this house stood on in the years to come.

Mouth dry, Alex rapped on the door.

A curtain was pulled aside. Joanna gazed out at him and her eyes widened. He wanted to laugh at the shock in her face. If she'd been expecting him, as Thaddeus had indicated, she had a funny way of showing it.

'Let me in, Joanna Rose.'

The window was opened a chink. 'No . . . wait there. I'm not fit to receive visitors.'

'This isn't England and I'm not a visitor who needs entertaining. There's unfinished business between us, and I'm here to sort it out.'

Her hands went to her hair. 'I look a mess.'

'I don't care.' He grinned at her, said softly, 'I've seen you in a worse mess, remember.'

'You're no gentleman, Alex Morcant.'

'And you're no lady.'

'So you've indicated to me several times.' Her face heated but her smile was all sorts of mocking. 'How is the Darsham and Morcant Shipping Company? I'm surprised you can tear yourself away from it. Actually, I expected a letter.' She gave a wide and gleeful grin. 'Lordy me, Alex, I didn't expect the owner of the company to present himself to me in all his glory. I'm honoured. What did you want to see this lowly island girl for?'

'Damn the damned company, and . . . *damn you*! If you don't let me in this minute I'll kick the bloody door in and tan your hide for you.'

She began to laugh. 'Why are you being so aggressive, Alex? The door is unlocked. All you have to do is turn the knob and push.'

He felt all sorts of fools when he stepped into the dim interior and she was still laughing. As his eyes adjusted he feasted them on her. She was wearing a blue taffeta bodice, unbuttoned at the top so the proud column of her neck was revealed. Her skirt was a darker blue. Her hair tumbled in a dark, damp cloud about her shoulders. She smelled of soap, as though she'd not long stepped out of a tub. Her breasts thrust ripely against her bodice, her smile told him all he wanted to know, and he was warmed by the knowledge.

'I'm going to wipe that smile off your face, Joanna Rose.'

She took a step back, her smile fading somewhat. 'There's something I need to tell you, Alex.'

'Later, because this won't wait.' He closed the gap between them, tipped up her face and kissed her senseless.

Weak at the knees, Joanna hoped this hungry kiss of his would last for ever. But baby Tobias decided differently. It was time for his lunch and he let his mother know it in no uncertain terms.

Alex released her and brushed a thumb gently over her bottom lip. 'I think the cat needs to be let out.'

'It isn't a cat. It's Tobias.'

He smiled down at her, his eyes intent on hers. 'Tobias

has a better singing voice than that, besides which, he won't be back until later.'

She drew in a breath, smiling because she couldn't help it. 'It's Tobias Alexander. He hasn't learned to sing yet, but he certainly knows how to complain.'

Alex became very still, his eyes as deep as pools. 'Can this be the something you had to tell me about?'

Sucking in a deep breath, Tobias displayed the full, awesome power of his lungs.

She nodded. 'He has no patience.' She raised her voice above the hungry clamour coming from her bedroom. 'He's like you, Alex, not only in looks but in that he knows what he wants and goes after it. But let me feed him before you meet. It will put him in a good mood. Help yourself to coffee. It's heating on the stove.'

She fed the boy, experiencing contentment as his mouth tugged hungrily against her breasts. Then she made him comfortable and took him through to the living room to meet his father, who managed to kiss her as she placed his son in his arms.

The father gazed down at the son, and the son gazed back, their eyes identical as they took the measure of each other. Eventually, little Tobias stretched out his arm and opened his palm. It closed tightly around the finger Alex offered him.

'I'll be damned,' he said. 'Look at him.' And there was all the pride in the world in his voice.

Her eyes filled with tears when the pair smiled at each other, as the bond was forged between them. Alex glanced at her, every emotion he experienced shining clearly on his face.

'This is the best gift I've ever received, Joanna Rose. I love him and I love you. I didn't realize what I'd lost until you left. Come back to England with me.'

'Is that a proposal, Alex?'

His eyes pulled her into their darkness. 'Aye, it is. I love you.'

She crossed to where he sat and kissed him. 'Yes, my love. I will, for not only do I love you, I want Tobias to grow up knowing his father, as every child should.'

Their eyes clung for a moment, then she leaned forward and her lips touched against his.

Oblivious to what was going on around him, Tobias belched in satisfaction.

POCKET
BOOKS

Beyond the Plough

Janet Woods

Now a wealthy young widow, former peasant girl
Siana Forbes has overcome her humble beginnings to
become mistress of Cheverton Manor, the handsome
estate which her infant son, Ashley, will one day
inherit. When the man she has always loved, country
doctor Francis Matheson, asks for her hand in
marriage, it seems her happiness is complete.

But trouble lies ahead. An unexpected tragedy
means Francis must leave for Australia – a land where
danger and hardship await. Left behind to raise a
growing family, Siana too has problems when a sinister
figure from her past emerges, determined to cause
havoc. And a terrible ordeal suffered by her
stepdaughter on the night of the harvest supper leaves
Siana with a heartbreaking choice. Will she be able to
overcome the odds stacked against her and keep her
family together? And will she ever be reunited with her
beloved Francis?

ISBN 0 7434 6800 7

PRICE £6.99

**POCKET
BOOKS**

A Handful of Ashes

Janet Woods

After an unhappy period apart, Francis and Siana
Matheson have settled into a loving marital
relationship in their comfortable Dorset home. Siana's
only sorrow is that so far she has been unable to bear
her husband another child. Francis however is content
to be a father to his grown-up daughters and his young
son, Bryn, born while he was overseas.

But Siana is hiding a secret. Although she hates keeping
something from her husband, the need to protect all
concerned has left her with no choice. She must keep
quiet and live with the guilt of her deceit.

No one can keep the truth hidden forever – and when
Siana's shocking secret bursts into the open, there will
be tragic and far-reaching consequences for the close-
knit Matheson family.

ISBN 0 7434 8401 0

PRICE £6.99